A MINDHUNTERS NOVEL

ACCEPTABLE
RISK

AWARD-WINNING ROMANTIC SUSPENSE

ANNE MARIE
BECKER

ALSO BY ANNE MARIE BECKER

The Mindhunters Series
Only Fear

Avenging Angel

Deadly Bonds

Dark Deeds

Acceptable Risk

End Game

The Mindhunters Novellas
Christmas Stalking

Until Death

Wicked Night

Deadly Holidays (A Collection of Mindhunters Holiday Novellas)

A "Nico & Eve" Short Story
Deceit in the Desert

The Redemption Club Series
Stacking the Deck

Sleight of Hand

Raising the Stakes

The Redemption Club Collection (Books 1-3)

ACCEPTABLE RISK

THE MINDHUNTERS, BOOK 5

ANNE MARIE BECKER

For Danny, awesome brother and everyday hero.

And, for Crista. I'm blessed to call you sister. You are beautiful in every way.

CHAPTER 1

A sea of bluebonnets along Interstate 35 reminded Catherine she was close to her final destination and eased some of the tension in her neck and shoulders. April in Texas was beautiful, and held the promise of the new start she was looking for—back where her life had gone off course years ago.

A few country love songs later, she was stiff again, her body and mind on full alert as she drove through a sketchy neighborhood on the west side of San Antonio. She pulled her Jeep Cherokee, along with the small trailer it towed, behind a strip mall that housed a clinic, an insurance office, a florist and a check-cashing and quickie loan establishment. Catherine had mapped out the location of Pecan Grove Community Health Clinic the moment she'd heard the news about Rachel's new job, wanting to picture what her sister's life was like so far away from Chicago, where they'd lived for the past few years while Rachel attended medical school.

The dust-and-grass scent of fresh spring rain hung thick in the air as she picked her way across a cracked and puddle-strewn parking lot. A quick storm must have moved through earlier.

Inside, the receptionist greeted her from behind a tall counter. "May I help you?"

"I'm here to see Rachel. Dr. Montgomery. I'm her sister."

Her smile bloomed. "Catherine? I'm Teresa." She reached across the counter to shake Catherine's hand. "Dr. Montgomery is expecting you. And you've got great timing," the woman continued, dropping her voice. "The police just left."

Catherine glanced around the waiting room, which held seats for about a dozen patients but was nearly empty now. An elderly couple sat in the corner reading magazines. "Police?"

"We had a threat. Someone called and demanded drugs. Prescription pill abuse is such a problem lately. The guy threatened to show up with a gun if we didn't have them ready when he stopped by." Teresa scoffed. "As if we did to-go orders."

"Tough neighborhood?" The graffiti, barred windows and plethora of potholes had certainly given her that impression.

"It has its moments, but usually the worst holds off until after dark. We try not to be here past six."

"Try?" Catherine struggled to absorb a chill that radiated from the nape of her neck. It was nearly six now.

"Go on back. She's taking a couple minutes before her last appointment to fill out charts. I've been trying to get her to take a break, but she likes to keep on top of everything." They'd learned a lot about diligence, adaptation and sacrifice in their upbringing. *Do or die.* "Maybe you'll have better luck. Exam room one."

Four exam rooms jutted off the short hallway just past the reception area. She found her sister hunched over a chart, her blond curls twisted into an efficient tangle at the back of her head, her hand moving at a furious pace.

"Handwriting legible yet?" Catherine asked from the doorway.

Rachel looked up and the furrow between her brows smoothed out as she grinned. "Only to me, probably." She kicked the stool out of the way so she could embrace Catherine. "I'm so glad you're home."

Home. Catherine's chest squeezed.

"I'm sorry I couldn't get away earlier to meet you at my place. Looks like you found me okay, though." Rachel pulled away. "Now tell me everything. What's wrong? Why the sudden move from Chicago?"

Catherine had prepared herself for the questions, but now wasn't the time to delve into that twisted tale. She hadn't told Rachel what had happened six weeks ago and she hoped she never had to share the experience. "Isn't it enough that I want to be near my little sister again?"

Rachel examined her further, a doctor looking for a diagnosis. Would she notice the dark smudges beneath Catherine's eyes? She'd taken extra time that morning to cover them, not wanting to worry her sister. "I wish that's all it was, but I thought you loved your job at SSAM."

SSAM was the acronym for a private organization known as the Society for the Study of the Aberrant Mind, and pronounced *Sam* in honor of the founder's daughter. For the past few years, as Rachel attended the University of Illinois at Chicago's medical school, Catherine had worked as SSAM's receptionist. It had been more than a job, however. She'd prided herself on being a support system for the incredible agents who apprehended the worst monsters society had to offer—serial killers and violent repeat offenders who'd evaded the justice system. Even operating from home base, she'd felt a part of something bigger than herself.

It had all been a lie. Even her name was a lie. She'd changed her last name from Montgomery to Montague before leaving for Chicago. It had been one more layer of insulation against someone discovering her past.

She looked away from Rachel's penetrating gaze. Though their features were similar—narrow nose, high cheekbones, elegant eyebrows and a bow-shaped mouth, Rachel's eyes were a mossy green while Catherine's contained more blue. Rachel's hair was a pure blond, while Catherine's was touched with hints of red.

But inside lay the real differences. Where Rachel was filled with a burning desire to help people, Catherine was numb and empty. She'd had difficult choices to make, ones she couldn't afford to regret, but she was tired of the lies. If only she could change what happened ten years ago…. Still, looking at a tired but glowing Rachel, every punch of acid rain that had eaten at Catherine's conscience was worth it. The payoff had been worth the sacrifice. She had to constantly remind herself of that.

"I do love SSAM, but it was time for a change." Before they discovered she was a fraud and a liar.

The sound of raised voices from the lobby was followed by a crash and a stern command from Teresa, ordering someone to leave before she called the police. Catherine's entire body trembled with a fear born of her recent trauma, even after weeks of therapy, but seeing her sister moving toward the door to confront the intruder brought out her protective instincts.

Catherine grabbed Rachel's arm. "Stay here."

"I can't. This is my clinic. I'm responsible."

"Let me check this out. You call the police." Catherine gestured to the phone in the corner. "I'll be careful. Besides, I'm trained to deal with unruly customers."

Another, louder crash sounded through the thin wall. Rachel headed for the phone as Catherine closed the door behind her and tiptoed to the end of the hallway, where she could peek around the corner. Teresa stood like a sentinel behind the chest-high counter. The man across from her had dark, wiry hair going in every direction, as if it were trying to escape his scalp. Lines carved his face like a craggy rock, indicating a hard, unyielding life. In contrast, his eyes were wild, his pupils dilated.

"I just need something to get me through until my next appointment." His voice was part plea, part I'll-do-anything desperation.

An empty pencil cup rolled to a stop in the waiting room and various pens and pencils were strewn across the linoleum. That had to be the source of one of the crashes. Still in their seats, the elderly couple huddled together, warily eyeing the man. What had once been a vase of flowers now lay shattered behind Teresa's desk —the other crash. Water dripped down the cabinets. A thin smear of red on Teresa's arm suggested a rebounding shard of glass must have nicked her, illustrating the threat of violence behind this man's demands.

Catherine's hand rose to her neck, but there was no noose there this time. She forced herself to breathe. Adrenaline trumped anxiety. *This isn't like before. He's just a strung-out man looking for a fix, not a serial killer intent on murder.*

"I can leave a message for Dr. Montgomery, and if you're due for a refill, she'll contact you, Lee." Teresa's voice was shaky. Her fingers slipped beneath the edge of her desk. Was there an alarm button there? Either way, Rachel should have connected with the police by now. Survival was just a matter of distracting Lee until help could arrive.

Lee's chin jutted out. "I saw the doctor's car in the parking lot. I'll wait. I'm not leaving until I get what I need." He thumped the counter so hard with his fist that Catherine jumped. So did Teresa. Her hand popped back out, and she held both of them up as if he'd aimed a gun at her. Guilt was all over her face.

"Can I help?" Catherine stepped forward, ignoring the fissures of fear shooting through her. The fight-or-flight response was meant to protect the body. Her body definitely wanted to flee, but her mind was on her sister and these other innocent people.

Lee turned to her. "Who are you?"

"I'm Dr. Montgomery's sister."

"You a doctor, too?"

"No, but I can see you need help." Lee had the pinched, pale appearance of someone whose entire body was wincing, contracting in an attempt to smother the pain. "What hurts?"

She stepped closer until she was only a couple feet away. Teresa's eyes were wide with silent warning, but Catherine had faced down the worst evil she could imagine and survived. Lee was only a temporary nuisance—with the potential to be more, she realized as she rounded the edge of the tall counter and saw the gun tucked into the front of his waistband.

"My back, my joints, my everything." Lee slapped a palm against his thigh as if punishing his body for its betrayal. "Your sister prescribed me something. It worked for a while. Now it's gone."

"Did you follow the directions on the label?" Rachel came out of the hall, looking a little short of breath, but her expression was calm and controlled, even compassionate. "If they're gone, Lee, you took too many, too fast."

"I had to. The pain…" His face crumpled.

As her sister stepped forward, Catherine shifted to stop her, placing herself between the pair. Rachel came to an abrupt halt, looking at Catherine in confusion. Catherine gave a slight shake of her head.

Lee's eyes narrowed on her, as if he realized Catherine was an obstacle keeping him from what he wanted, from what he *needed*. His hand moved toward the gun.

Pounding fear and memories she'd thought she'd left behind in Chicago—the throbbing in her neck that felt like a noose tightening, the flush of heat in her cheeks, the sharp intake of breath—rose up. She ignored the riot of emotions and focused, as her therapist had taught her, on the subject at hand. She was at a violent man's mercy once again, but this time, she had more than survival instincts in her toolbox.

She held her palms out as she took slow steps toward him. "Sounds like you've been through a lot. I can help. I'm good at getting people what they need."

"I've told you what I need." His words built to a shout, and he tried to look around Catherine to Rachel. "You'd better have those pills out here in thirty seconds or—" As he reached for the gun at his waist, Catherine shot forward.

She grabbed his hand before it could connect with the gun and quickly shifted behind him, twisting his arm behind his back. His joints cracked in protest, his bones brittle in her grip. But he was a danger and had to be dealt with, so she held on tight. "Down on the floor." To encourage compliance, she nudged the back of his knee sharply with hers. She needed him horizontal before he formed a coherent thought and went to grab his gun with his other hand. At the moment, he was focused on the pain she was inducing. With a moan, he knelt.

"He's hurt!" Rachel rushed over now that Lee was subdued. "Stop!"

"Get his weapon." The calm in her own voice surprised her, but it buoyed the confidence that had been sagging for the past six weeks.

Rachel froze. "I didn't see the gun." She looked at Lee with shock and crouched to pull the weapon from his waistband.

Through the front window, she saw a couple of police cruisers screech to a halt. A moment later, two SAPD officers entered cautiously through the front door and quickly assessed the situation. Rachel held the gun out, letting it dangle from her fingers to appear nonthreatening. One cop rushed forward to take it as another took control of Lee. Catherine released her hold, rose to her feet and pressed a hand to her lurching stomach.

Rachel wrapped an arm around her. "Where'd you learn to do that?"

"Comes with the territory when you work for an agency like SSAM." And when you'd been through a situation you shouldn't have survived and didn't care to repeat. She watched one of the officers escort a handcuffed Lee from the premises as the other removed a notepad and began questioning Teresa.

Rachel's gaze turned thoughtful. "I think we have a lot to talk about."

More than you'll ever hear from me.

MAX COULD SEE ONLY A SMALL SLICE OF TEXAS FROM THE BACK OF the prisoner transport van. The high, narrow windows framed a rectangle of the sky, where the setting sun slanted rays through the clouds, creating an orange-pink haze. It would have been more beautiful if he weren't spending his Friday night in the company of a potentially violent prisoner on the outskirts of San Antonio, Texas, but he had a duty to see Tony Moreno safely transferred to his new prison cell. Despite Max's reservations about returning to his place of origin, he felt a pang of homesickness.

Nothing the company of a beautiful woman wouldn't cure. Especially if they were sipping margaritas on the Riverwalk at his favorite Tex-Mex restaurant.

Catherine Montague was rumored to be visiting Texas during her personal leave from SSAM. Maybe he should get in touch with her for a bit of fun before he returned to Chicago. Of course, he wasn't supposed to be thinking about his coworker as a potential date, no matter how close they'd become over the years. Sure, there'd been that one kiss, that one lapse in judgment, but it wouldn't—*couldn't*—happen again. *You're just friends,* his conscience reminded him. Really good friends, and he'd be an asshole to ruin that because of some testosterone-driven fantasies. But damn, those fantasies had been good.

His brow creased as they hit another pothole in the ravaged dirt road. "You sure this is the way?" Max had to speak through the bolted metal screen that kept the rear cabin separate and secure in order for the driver to hear him. There was no sign of their destination, a prison west of San Antonio.

"Just following the directions HQ gave me," the driver said over his shoulder.

A second transport agent was seated beside Max, flipping through a magazine. Across from them, Tony was secured at the wrists, waist and ankles. The agent's name was Steve-something. After a red-eye flight from Chicago to Dallas, a delay at the airport as some confusion with the transport company was straightened out and a long drive to San Antonio, Max was too exhausted to remember names.

Steve looked up. "Heavy rains flooded one of the roads, so we're taking a detour."

Would have been nice to know.

With the hills and valleys, the recent spring downpours could easily have made a low-lying road impassable. Still, something felt off.

Max tried to relax. Beside him on the bench, Steve resumed his reading, clearly unworried. There should be no reason for the prickles of unease that crept across Max's scalp, but he'd been in the field—six years with SSAM, and several years with the SEALs before that—long enough to know not to ignore his innate warning system.

Max cast a suspicious glance at the prisoner they escorted. Beneath his brown skin, Tony looked decidedly yellow. His usually cocky attitude was gone, which made Max even more nervous. If a serial rapist and murderer like Tony was overcome with fear, something was definitely wrong. Or maybe it was the rough road and occasional skidding of the tires in mud that caused his pallor.

"What's up?" Max asked. He wished he could pull his pistol from the lockbox beneath the bench and lay it across his thigh. Tony would respect the hardware more than Max's attempts to engage him in conversation.

"Don't know what you mean." Tony's chains jangled as he shifted his feet, clad in prison-issue shoes.

Max's instincts were yelling at him. He and Tony had gotten to know each other over the past several weeks while Max's latest assignment with SSAM put him undercover as a prisoner in Chicago's Metropolitan Correctional Center. Playing bodyguard to an unrepentant convict had been Max's least favorite assign-

ment to date, but an organized crime organization known as the
Circle would have killed Tony to keep him quiet. Meanwhile,
Tony's knowledge of the Circle's operations in Chicago was something Max's boss Damian Manchester had desperately wanted to
tap into. Tony had earned a prison transfer in exchange for valuable information.

Like a steady diet of greasy food, sticking close to Tony while
awaiting this transfer had soured Max's stomach and hardened his
insides. He'd be glad when this operation was over, but he'd do it
again in a heartbeat to help Damian, who had a personal stake in
the knowledge locked away in Tony's ugly head. The convict had
worked for the Circle's organized crime group and had admitted
to kidnapping Damian's daughter Samantha decades ago, though
he denied murdering her.

Thankfully, Max would be free once Tony was installed in his
new home at nineteen hundred hours. Max would fly back to
Chicago tomorrow and move on with his life, infinitely less
queasy. By next Friday, he'd be back to his usual routine, probably
looking forward to a hot date and some no-strings sexual release.

Despite his seatbelt, a jolt of the van nearly threw him out of
his seat as the rear wheel hit a pothole. Was the prison really off of
an unpaved road?

Max checked his cell phone. No bars. The prickles on his scalp
multiplied. "Is your radio working?" he asked the driver.

The driver glanced down. "Not at the moment."

"Turn around. Go back to the main road and let's check in with
your office."

He'd spent many rainy spring days in his youth tracking toads
and chasing fireflies by the creek that ran through his parents'
ranch, and he recognized the scent of incoming rain. It wasn't just
twilight darkening the clouds to purple-gray—they were in for
another storm. He'd enjoy the lightning display from his hotel
room once they dropped Tony off. Then he'd catch the first flight
back tomorrow before his parents realized he was within state

lines and hunted him down to try to force him into accepting the life that he'd inherited but never wanted—a prison of a different sort.

"Can't," the driver replied. "I have my orders." The private company was in charge of this transfer. Max was merely a nuisance they tolerated because Damian had pulled some strings to allow Max to travel with them.

Beside him, Steve flipped a page, but Max sensed he was alert and listening.

Max turned back to Tony. "Piss anyone off lately?"

Tony couldn't hold Max's hard stare and looked away. "Other than the Circle? What I've done for your boss is enough to get my throat slit a hundred times over." Which is why Tony was counting on this transfer. He'd already caught the attention of his previous employers. His narcissism had led him to sign lucrative contracts for a tell-all book and movie deal. Not that the Son of Sam law would probably allow him to touch any money made off his victims, but he'd found a way to funnel it elsewhere. "I've done everything Manchester asked."

"Everything but lead us to the man in charge of the Circle."

Tony scoffed. "If I knew anything that could do that, I'd be dead for sure." The head of the crime ring, the man who'd paid Tony to kidnap Sam all those years ago, was known to them only as *the Boss*. Despite weeks of interviews, Tony hadn't been able to provide any details that would lead them to the mystery monster.

"Aw, but think of the hero you'll be when we take down the Circle because of your cooperation." Not that he'd done it without the expectation of profit. Fame and a change of venue were Tony's goals. "It'd make a great ending for your book."

The van hit a bump that, had he not been wearing his seatbelt, would have dumped Max on his ass on the floor. Across from him, Tony squirmed in his restraints, but he remained locked securely in place. Sweat beaded on the man's forehead. With this detour and his increasing unease, Max's temper, usually hidden behind a

Texas good-ole-boy laid-back façade, was dangerously close to the surface.

But before he could press Tony harder, a sudden *pop pop pop* was followed by a boom that rang in Max's ears. The vehicle shook, and then suddenly listed and swerved.

Max's vision narrowed as though he'd been given a shot of adrenaline to the heart. His muscles bunched in response to the attack, his fingers closing as if they gripped his pistol.

Across from him, Tony had turned greenish-white and his eyes were wide with alarm. If someone was coming for him, he hadn't expected it. Or, if he'd expected it, it wasn't a welcome rescue. Which meant the attack was most likely the Circle's doing. Nobody else cared enough or had the resources to follow them a thousand miles across the country to take out a hardened criminal who'd been in and out of the prison system since he was eighteen, had been permanently locked away for a year now and would never take another breath as a free man. Tony had already spilled the beans in every way that mattered to SSAM. Either the Circle was cleaning house, acting on revenge, or Tony had more to reveal.

"Got some sins to confess before they run us off the road and kill us all?" Max yelled over the sound of gunfire. He looked to Steve. "Keys for the lockbox?" He wanted his weapon. Now.

The van shot to the right, nearly tipping as the wheels sought purchase.

"Hang on," the driver shouted from the front. "Shooter twenty yards to the northwest, in the bushes. Shit! Incoming!"

Through the barred opening, Max saw the driver's tight jaw, his white knuckles on the wheel as he tried to correct the vehicle's trajectory. The sound of another explosion came a second later. The van lunged and flipped onto its side. Held in midair above Tony by his seatbelt, Max gasped for the air that had been squeezed from his lungs. Below him, Tony moaned. His skull had cracked against the side of the van that was now the floor. Blood drizzled down the side of the man's face from a wound at his temple.

Tony's eyes shot open, then glazed with fear. "Don't let them get me."

"I won't." Max may have failed himself, but he hadn't failed a mission yet. And he'd never left a man behind, no matter how evil that man might be. He was responsible for getting Tony to the prison. His SEAL training kicked in and his focus sharpened.

"You loaded?" His question was for Steve, who, like Max, hung from what was now the ceiling. He looked a bit green too.

The agent nodded. "In the lockbox, but my seatbelt's jammed. Can't get loose." His fingers fumbled with the buckle.

Max was already bracing his feet on Tony's bench. He reached for Steve's belt. The stuttered, pulsing, bullet-meets-metal sound of submachine gunfire echoed as he grabbed the key and retrieved their weapons, including his rebar knife. He holstered his pistol at his shoulder and cut Steve free before handing him a pistol and a spare radio from the lockbox. He hadn't heard a word from the driver since the crash, but the flickering orange light and dark shadows that stretched across the van walls indicated something in front was on fire. There'd be no way to get to the man from the separate, secure back compartment, anyway. They'd have to get out through the back doors, which were now horizontal, and go around the side to pry open the cabin's door—all while evading their attackers.

Smoke seeped in from the front cabin and began to fill the compartment. Using the bottom edge of his shirt, Max wiped the sweat from his brow and placed the moistened cloth over his mouth.

"I'm stuck!" Tony's panic brought Max crouching at his side. Blood now flowed freely from the wound on Tony's head.

"We're not unlocking him." Steve eyed Tony warily as he used the radio to call for help with one hand, aiming his pistol at their prisoner with the other.

"Just the leg shackles so he can get out," Max said. "We'll leave his hands cuffed."

Another explosion rocked the van, tossing Max against the side like a sack of rice. Unfortunately, he wasn't nearly as malleable, and his right shoulder met resistance in the form of the bench where Tony was secured. Max groaned as the familiar pop and pain of tendons stretching in unnatural ways signaled he'd dislocated his shoulder. *Fuck.* It wasn't the first time he'd had to function in a crisis while injured, but he hadn't been prepared for this.

You're slipping in your old age, Gypsy. He could hear his SEAL team commander's voice in his head, using the nickname Max had earned in the military, and it got him moving again. Besides, he was only thirty and deserved to see thirty-one. He damn sure wasn't going to die because someone wanted Tony Moreno out of the picture.

Max's ears still rang from the explosion and he gritted his teeth against a wave of nausea. His dominant arm hung, useless, at his side. His position, farthest from the doors, made him even more ineffective. "The doors," he shouted to Steve. "Get out fast, but be alert. They'll be waiting."

Not that the outside risks mattered. If his calculations were correct, the entire van could blow sky-high any second now. Fresh air and freedom first, and then Max could focus on the Circle thugs waiting to kill them. The Circle wouldn't leave behind any witnesses.

Steve unlatched the handle, but the doors refused to give. He threw his weight against the seam of the doors, rocking the van. Fighting to clear his watery vision, Max finished unlocking Tony's shackles and pulled him upright. Joining Steve, he used his uninjured shoulder to add his weight against the middle. They were all coughing steadily now. If they couldn't open the jammed door soon, they'd die.

As if reading his thoughts, Tony moaned again. "I can't die."

"Grow a pair, Tony. Better yet, help out." The words cost Max precious oxygen and he coughed again. But Tony's whining also pissed him off, working him into an angry frenzy he could channel toward something productive. And Tony was a decent-sized guy who worked out in the prison gym. He maneuvered so the three of them were squeezed close by the door. Max took hold of the handle. "On three, we all throw our weight against it. One, two, three."

Max threw his good shoulder into the door. The bottom half crashed open and he went rolling over it, grunting as his injured shoulder hit the ground. The storm had begun, releasing cold raindrops that had already soaked the dirt road. Mud sucked at him as he continued to roll, ignoring the pain while instinctively making himself a moving target and hoping to get to the side of the road where there might be cover.

From the back of the van, Steve rushed out with his pistol drawn. The smoke, finding release, billowed upward and got lost in the long shadows of nightfall. More gunfire from their unseen enemy pushed Max to lean on his left arm in an attempt to push himself to a standing position. He had to get to the van to help Tony and the driver. But before Max could stand, Tony stumbled out of the van and scurried around the edge, using the vehicle as a shield as he headed toward a ditch along the side of the road. His hands were still cuffed, but his feet were free.

Blinking through the mixture of smoke and rain that stung his eyes, Max tracked the fugitive and crawled toward the ditch. The smell, the noise, the chaos were similar to so many missions before, but this was Texas, and he'd be damned if he'd survived Afghanistan to die twenty miles from the ranch where he grew up.

Then a third explosion knocked him flat against the dirt. Wanting a piece of the action, Mother Nature released a crack of thunder and a torrent of Texas-sized raindrops. Max rolled the rest of the way into the three-foot-deep ravine, which already held several inches of water, and tried to focus past the brain-numbing pain shooting from his shoulder. *His shooting arm. Dislocated.* And with no way to knock it back into place.

"Tony?" In Max's bid for safety, he'd lost sight of their prisoner. Despite the rain, flames now engulfed the van, casting the now-dark road in a golden light. At least the gunfire had stopped, but he could no longer see Steve, Tony or their ambushers, and there was no sign of the driver, either. Fuck him if he'd be a sitting duck, though.

With his good hand, he aimed his pistol. Pressing his body flat against the slope of the ditch, he was able to peer over the edge. He'd trained extensively for shooting weak-handed, but there was always the possibility of a stovepipe jam, leaving him defenseless in a shootout. He also had the low ground in this battle. In fact, the ditch was rapidly collecting runoff and had become a foot-deep roaring creek as the clouds continued to dump on him.

He blinked water from his eyelashes and made out the form of a body splayed on the dirt road. *Steve.* A breath of relief whooshed forth as the man shifted, his hand moving to grip his thigh.

Visually sweeping the area, Max didn't make out any other bodies—living or dead—and the shooting had stopped. The quiet was unnerving, giving away nothing as to his enemy's location.

"Where's Tony?" he shouted.

Steve pointed to the northeast, past the ditch, toward a thick stand of oaks several yards away, illuminated by the fire from the van. There was only darkness beyond. Night had fallen quickly.

Steve's face contorted with pain. "Two guys took off after him. Didn't get a clear look at their faces, but they were carrying some major hardware."

Max left the cover of the ditch and performed a one-armed crawl to get to Steve's side. "How bad is it?"

"Bad." Blood soaked Steve's thigh and ran into the mud beneath him.

Max tore a strip from his cargo pants to make a tourniquet, and then ran at a crouch to check on the driver. The cab was still engulfed in flames. He couldn't get close.

Max returned to Steve's side. "Where's the radio?"

Steve pointed toward the rear of the van, where the radio had been dropped in the mud. Max ran for the device, praying it would work though it had been soaked. Returning to Steve, he shoved the radio into the man's hands. As Steve reported their situation, Max took off running toward the stand of oaks and the hills beyond, biting back a wince as every step on the uneven terrain or slip in the mud jostled his gimpy shoulder or torqued his knee, aggravating another old injury. He could fight through the pain, but with total darkness encroaching, the odds were stacked against him.

Tony Moreno—rapist, killer, ex-Circle minion and all around bad guy—was now a fugitive.

CHAPTER 2

The air in Lucky Dick's Gentlemen's Club actually had a taste. Old sweat, happy hour half-price nachos and baby oil. The scent clung to the tongue like a shag carpet—if one were possessed to lick a shag carpet. Still, it was familiar to Johnny Walker, his home away from home—and with a name like Johnny Walker, it should be. There was nothing like a cold beer and hot tits on a Friday night to loosen up the muscles and tighten the pants. The fact that he got paid to be here was the cherry on the sundae.

The woman on the T-shaped stage was draped in a silk kimono-style robe, though no part of her was remotely Asian. As she maneuvered to the music, she came close enough to touch. Johnny didn't touch, preferring to make his women work for his attention. Besides, the club didn't allow touching. But he kept one hand in his lap, casually brushing it against his erection, and the other on his beer.

Knowing his habits, his favorite cocktail waitress brought him another cold bottle the moment he drained one. Darla set it at his elbow, her low-cut shirt dipping to give him an instant view of the swells of her average-sized but nicely shaped breasts, but the action barely registered in his peripheral vision. His focus was on the woman on stage releasing her sash, opening her robe to reveal the double D's he was certain no self-respecting geisha, or whatever the hell she was supposed to be, would flaunt. It was spectacular, however, when she pulled two chopsticks from the back of her head, releasing a dark curtain of hair that tumbled across her shoulders. He'd enjoy sinking his fists into that hair and holding on while she writhed and bucked beneath him. Despite her coy act, her secret smile promised she'd be a wild ride.

She aimed her smile at him and they locked gazes. *She wants me.*

A snort beside him indicated he'd spoken the thought aloud.

"She wants everyone—or pretends to." Darla dropped a bowl of pretzels beside his drink. "They're paid to tease." Darla was one of the stick-arounds. She made enough on tips to be hooked on this kind of crap job, but she could never compare with the quality of flesh on stage, or was too chicken to try.

"Aren't you kind of young to be cynical?" She had to be in her early twenties, a few years younger than him. Despite her attitude, Darla had some things going for her—physical things, anyway. She was young, taut and attractive enough in her short skirt and tight shirt. And there'd been that one time, when he'd given her a ride home... Yeah, she had some good qualities, for sure.

Darla planted a hand on her cocked hip. "By the way, have you seen Bea lately? She was supposed to be on shift ten minutes ago. Dick's shitting bricks." Her gaze flicked to the two-way mirror behind the bar, behind which the manager's office was located.

"Not since a couple of days ago." But if Dick was upset, Johnny would steer clear of him. The man oozed charm, but he had a temper and was higher up on the Circle food chain. Johnny didn't want to rock the sweet boat he was in.

As a bagman for the Circle, Johnny's route across Texas sometimes only allowed him to be here once a week, which was a bitch and a half. He was at the beck and call of the managers at the various strip clubs across Texas that served as home bases. His job was to sit tight until he was given instructions. In the meantime, he could enjoy the view. It was a hard life, but somebody had to do it.

At least he hadn't been one of the guys paid to blow up the van tonight. What a fuckup. If the rumors he'd just heard were true, Tony Moreno was running free instead of dead and the Boss was not happy. The *big* boss, not Dick. Although that might be part of why Dick was in such a shitty mood.

"She's never missed a set." Darla chewed the lipstick off her bottom lip. "What do you think happened?"

"No clue." And he didn't really care. He and the stripper known as Busty Bea had gone out after her shift a couple times, but just because he enjoyed the hot sex didn't mean he was dating the woman, or any of the other women with whom he enjoyed a similar arrangement. Paying for sex meant there were no strings, so hell, no, he didn't know where Bea had gone, but there were a dozen more like her who could fill in just fine.

Speaking of which... "Who's the new girl?"

Darla followed his gaze to the stage. "Hong Kong Kim. Started a couple days ago."

"Hong Kong? She's not even Asian."

Darla shrugged. "Does anybody here really care?"

Johnny watched the voluptuous woman shimmy and smiled. *Nope.* Didn't make a whit of difference. Kim sashayed to the opposite side of the stage, her curvy ass swaying like a hypnotist's watch, mesmerizing the men in the crowd. She looked over her shoulder at him. Oh yeah, she wanted him. He was a badass with a large bank account—one place where size definitely mattered.

She gyrated in front of some newcomers, young businessmen looking for a happy hour or two. As they tucked twenties into her G-string, she gave them a hell of a show, ignoring the rest of the crowd. Ignoring *him. Tease.*

He was the one with connections in the neighborhood. She was dancing in the Circle's turf, and he was a key player. In fact, he could have her gone, sold on the sex slave market, within hours. She should get on her fucking knees and worship him.

Instead, she let another man's fingers stroke her thigh until the bouncer moved to intervene. Was she trying to make him jealous? Johnny's pulse pounded harder against his temple.

Bitch.

He'd show her what she was missing and who deserved her attention. They always came around. She'd be moaning his name by night's end.

CATHERINE GRABBED HER SUITCASE FROM THE BACK OF HER JEEP AND followed Rachel along a cobblestone path toward a charming one-story cottage. Like a fairytale house, it was tiny, only meant to serve as a guesthouse to the larger estate that sat a hundred yards away. Still, it was a far cry from the postage-stamp apartment they'd shared in northwest San Antonio while Catherine had worked to put Rachel through college. Or the broken-down trailer they'd spent their childhood in.

Rachel looked back over her shoulder as she unlocked the door. "It's not much, but it's not too far from the clinic and the rent is cheap." And it was in a decent neighborhood, judging by the size of the houses and their neat exteriors and groomed lawns. "It's quiet, too, which I love after a long day."

"Especially after a day like today." Catherine's initial fight-or-flight response, triggered by Lee and his gun, had given way to shaky muscles and a sense of fatigue. "I hope that doesn't happen often."

"Of course not. In the months I've worked there, we've had a break-in and some graffiti on the exterior walls, but nothing violent. The clinic *is* in a high-crime neighborhood, but for the most part, we're left alone. It's not normally dangerous."

"And yet a man with a gun walked right in." Her blood ran cold thinking about what could have happened to Rachel. *I'd have no family.*

Rachel gestured to the living area, which held a small couch and a television on one side and a small kitchen on the other. There was a door off to the left. "It's only one bedroom and one bathroom, but the couch isn't bad. You can have the bedroom."

"No, I'll take the couch." Catherine was a bit taller than average, but she'd make do. "You need the sleep so you can go out and be super doctor."

"I can look for a bigger place for us as soon as you give me the go-ahead."

"Us?" Catherine set her suitcase down.

"I'd like you to move in with me. You know, live together again. I got the idea when you mentioned you were thinking of leaving Chicago for good. Until now, I've been too busy getting the new clinic up and running, but you could convince me to make the housing search a priority. Or maybe you'd like to do the looking?"

"I'm not sure I'm staying." At the age of eighteen, Catherine had taken her sixteen-year-old sister under her wing and they'd clung together in the face of tragedy. She'd worked to support them both, and when Rachel had gone to Chicago for med school, Catherine had followed, still providing financial support. But Rachel's career was poised to take flight. She was ready to achieve great things while Catherine was…broken. Still, this was the first time Catherine had been free to make her own choices—at least, she *would* be free, once she cut her final ties to the past.

"But you towed your things all the way across the country." The Jeep and rented trailer were currently parked on Rachel's portion of the long driveway.

"Actually, that's mostly stuff you left behind after graduating and moving back. I got rid of a lot of my belongings." She'd felt weighed down, but uncluttering her life hadn't helped. Her conscience was still burdened. There was only one way to make it right and feel whole again, which was why she had returned to

Texas. "It's time to move on, but I don't know where I'm headed yet. It depends on how some...*things*...go."

Rachel spun toward the kitchen. "Fill me in on the details while we cook. I'm starving."

As they pulled together a dinner of pasta and tossed salad, Catherine turned the conversation to Rachel by asking a steady stream of questions. Though she seemed her normal, energetic self, Catherine doubted Rachel had really faced the fact that a patient, someone she'd tried to help, had put her life in danger tonight.

"Are you happy at the clinic?" Catherine knew from previous conversations that the place was Rachel's entire life.

"I enjoy the research I'm doing at the Medical Center, too, one day a week. But the clinic"—passion lit her sister's eyes—"...that's where I'm needed. I can do so much good."

"It doesn't seem safe."

"Lee is a small minority. One man's desperation won't scare me away. I fought to open this clinic. It offers treatment to an under-served population. Many of them don't have the transportation or funds to go elsewhere. It's me or nothing." So similar to the way they'd grown up, poor and isolated.

"You can't relocate?"

Rachel laid out a couple of placemats and napkins on the coffee table, as the cottage had no eating area. "That would involve some expenses that aren't within the budget. Besides, the clinic has to be near the patients who need it most."

Catherine didn't push. Medicine was more than a job to Rachel. Caring for people had always been a calling. Ever since their mother had died of breast cancer and their father, in his grief, had spiraled out of control, Rachel's passion had resided with preventing others from suffering similar fates.

A twinge of jealousy hit Catherine at her core. Her sister had a purpose—one that helped people. Rachel had earned the trust and respect of her community while Catherine had not. Sure, her coworkers at SSAM liked and respected her—but that would change soon, when they found out the truth. "There's got to be a safer way to serve those needs. Maybe hire a security guard?"

Rachel opened the small refrigerator and reached for a bottle of Pinot Grigio chilling inside. "No money for it."

"There are no other options?"

She looked thoughtful. "There is an empty building I looked at a mile or so to the north that would be perfect. Right on the bus route. It's a safer neighborhood, just down the street from the police department."

"Sounds perfect."

Rachel shrugged. "We wouldn't be able to afford the rent, which is why I nixed the idea. Besides, what happened with Lee was an aberration. I can't let one event scare me away. Some of these people have become like family."

Family. Like Catherine's coworkers at SSAM had become to her. For two sisters who hadn't had much in the way of familial or community support growing up, they'd each found ways to make those kinds of connections.

Catherine's thoughts shifted to Max Sawyer and the casual working relationship that had morphed into a friendship over the years—and could possibly become more, if she pursued it. And there was Becca, the security specialist who'd become Catherine's best friend and was currently on an extended honeymoon with her new husband Diego. Becca hadn't been happy when Catherine had told her she was relocating. And she wasn't the only one to care about Catherine. Damian had become like a surrogate father, someone she felt safe asking for advice. What had initially been a receptionist job had become so much more. But her love for these people was also the main reason she needed to leave.

Catherine plated their food and they sat side-by-side on the couch.

"Do you think Lee will go to jail?" A worry line creased Rachel's brow.

"I don't know, but you can't save everyone. All you can do is be there for them."

"And let them be there for you." Rachel shot her a look. *Yeah.* Catherine had always struggled with leaning on other people. In her experience, those people she came to depend on either let her down or left. It was much better to count only on oneself. Then you knew what to expect.

They ate in silence for a few minutes. The garlic and citrus of the shrimp primavera made Catherine's taste buds sing and she released a blissful sigh. The candy bar she'd grabbed earlier at a gas station outside of New Braunfels hadn't satisfied her for long. Then again, she hadn't made a meal for herself or eaten regularly in weeks. She simply hadn't felt like it.

Rachel seemed to read her thoughts and she examined Catherine more closely. "You've lost weight—weight you couldn't afford to lose."

Catherine lifted a pasta-filled fork. "Been too busy to think about it."

"Why?"

"Why what?"

"Why have you been too busy? I thought you quit SSAM weeks ago. Which brings me to my biggest concern. Why'd you quit your job?"

"So many questions..."

"Which you continue to deflect."

"Actually, I'm on a personal leave of absence." Technically, she hadn't quit her receptionist position at SSAM. *Yet.* It had been a matter of needing time to heal and get her priorities back on track. But once she'd told everyone the truth, they wouldn't want her back, so she'd have to figure out where she was headed next. "I'm supposed to return to work in six weeks."

"Could have fooled me." Her gaze moved to the front wall of the cottage. No doubt, she was picturing the packed trailer dominating the driveway beyond.

"I told you, most of the stuff in there is yours."

"Still, something happened. I can tell."

Yeah, *something*. Something in the form of a serial killer who'd made her beg for her life, forced her to lay out the pros and cons of letting her live—and brought her to the realization that her current life might not be worth begging for. Not in its current state.

Over the past several years, she'd lost herself. Become a fraud. She wanted to like herself again.

Catherine evaded her sister's probing questions. "I don't want to talk about it. Not yet, anyway."

"A man?" Rachel's frown was sympathetic.

"No." Catherine's immediate reply was sharp. The image of Max filled her mind, but he could never be hers. Not as more than a friend, and not even that for much longer.

Rachel sputtered out a laugh. "Okay, then. A male had *something* to do with it. But you never do anything without thinking things through."

"We have that in common."

Rachel raised her wineglass toward Catherine in salute. "We do. So what happened to tip the scales? I thought you vowed never to return to Texas."

"I didn't say that. Dad's here, after all." In a prison cell twenty minutes west of town.

She had obligations to fulfill. Debts she owed. She would set about severing those ties soon and then reclaim her life. The Caulfields had to be wondering why she hadn't given her monthly status report in a while, and they'd be shocked when she showed up in person to resign from the covert operation they'd sent her on.

Rachel picked at her salad. "Have you talked to him?"

It took Catherine a second to organize her thoughts and realize Rachel was referring to their father. "Not recently. Called him on his birthday last month. I still write him every few weeks."

Rachel nodded. "I attended his parole hearing a few months back, though he didn't want me there."

This was the first Catherine had heard of it. "I take it that didn't go well?"

Rachel shook her head.

"It's been ten years," Catherine said. Their father was still alive, but gone. One impetuous act had left them basically orphans.

Catherine's cell phone rang. At SSAM, agents often kept irregular hours, and as their main source of information and support, she'd developed the habit of always having her phone nearby. Now, it rested on the table, beside her plate, though there would be no reason for anyone to call her. Everything that mattered in her new life sat within a hundred-foot radius.

"You going to answer that?" Rachel asked around a bite of noodles.

The number on the screen was familiar and churned a tumbler of emotions inside her. Past pain and prior allegiances—her old life. There were two people on the planet whose calls she couldn't ignore, and one of them was beside her. The other was on the phone.

CHAPTER 3

It was nearly ten o'clock in Chicago when Damian made the call. It was late and a long shot, but Catherine was his only hope. He never left an injured team member to face things alone, and he'd been unable to make contact with Max since the man had called him an hour ago, groggy and barely making sense, from a San Antonio hospital emergency room. The members of his SSAM team deserved the very best treatment, and as their employer, he was responsible for making sure they got it, even from his office a thousand miles away.

"Damian?" Worry rippled through Catherine's voice.

"I'm sorry to bother you while you're on a leave of absence." He wanted to ask how she was doing and whether she was recovering from the traumatic events that had unfolded in February. A killer SSAM had been tracking had made Catherine a target. Though she'd been SSAM's receptionist for the past five years, Catherine hadn't been trained for the frontlines. Still, she'd done an admirable job holding up under the pressure. But halfway into her three months of personal leave, she hadn't mentioned returning to her position. He was starting to worry. She was part of his team—

hell, she'd become as invaluable as his right hand—and he wanted her back. But he also wanted to respect her privacy.

"It must be important." Catherine's tone lacked her usual vibrancy.

Damian understood how one day, one incident, could change everything. "It is. A team member was hurt during a mission."

"Oh, no. Unfortunately, I don't think I can help. I'm in Texas."

"I know."

"You do?" Her laugh held only a trace of humor. "Of course you do. You know all."

"About my team, yes. I even keep tabs on the ones who are on vacation, but only because I care."

When she spoke, her voice was thick with emotion. "I know."

"You used to help keep track of everyone and make sure we all had what we needed. What we need is *you*. Back here, as soon as possible. We all miss you."

There was a long pause before a sigh filled the other end. "I miss SSAM too, but…"

"I can help arrange for counseling, if you want it. After going through what you did, you might find it helpful." He'd offered before, but she'd insisted she'd find her own help. Had she?

"I appreciate that, but no."

He sensed there was more behind her refusal, just as he sensed pushing her would backfire. "The offer will remain on the table indefinitely."

"Thank you. You said I could help from Texas. Who was hurt?"

"Max."

"What? How?" The emotionless tone was long gone, replaced by one filled with alarm.

"He was assisting in the transfer of Tony Moreno to a prison west of San Antonio." Guilt stabbed at him. This mission had been personal for Damian, and Max had been injured because of it. But solving Sam's murder meant everything. It always had. It was the sole reason the SSAM agency had been created years ago, though the mission had quickly evolved to help others in situations similar to his own and to serve the community in general. "Their van was attacked."

"Oh, my God. Is Max okay?"

"I'm not sure. He called from University Hospital, but that's about all I could understand. He was pretty out of it and when I call the hospital directly, I can't get anyone to talk to me because I'm not family. I haven't been able to reach the people we were coordinating with at the prisoner transport service." It was damn frustrating. "The hospital's not too far from where you are, I believe. I'll be there by morning, but I'd appreciate if someone I trust could make sure he's getting the appropriate attention and treatment until I get there."

"Of course. I'll go right away."

Some of the tightness in his chest eased. "Thank you. I'll call if I receive any more information."

TWENTY MINUTES LATER, CATHERINE'S HEART WAS STILL POUNDING when she entered the University Hospital emergency room. She'd left Rachel with a hasty explanation and insisted her sister stay home and relax rather than accompany her. While Damian's call had been out of the blue and reluctantly pulled her back into SSAM business, her primary concern was Max—but she'd do the same for any of her friends from SSAM.

Yeah, right. Keep telling yourself that.

Her feelings for Max went far deeper than for her other coworkers. Or any man, woman or child other than her sister and father. How had he slipped past her defenses?

More southern charm than a man had a right to, and a body built for sin.

Not that anybody knew the effect he had on her. For the most part, she'd kept a tight rein on her feelings. For five long years. Her one slip-up could be attributed to a night of slight inebriation and an atmosphere of celebration. Max certainly hadn't thought twice about the kiss they'd shared last New Year's Eve. With a quick apology for his unprofessional behavior and a plea to return to their just-friends status, they'd gone right back to being congenial coworkers by morning. Though she valued Max's teasing remarks and casual conversations at work, now that she had a taste of more, she wasn't sure her appetite for him would ever be satisfied.

Damian hadn't had any specifics on Max's condition in his first call, but he contacted her again on her way to the hospital. The prison transport company had confirmed Max and one of their agents had been airlifted from a deserted road where the van had been engulfed in flames. The U.S. Marshals and Texas Rangers, as well as the SAPD, had been notified that Tony Moreno, the convict SSAM had been interviewing for nearly two months, had escaped on foot. That last part was probably going to hurt Max the most. Despite his laid-back, roll-with-the-punches attitude, he hated to fail. She could just imagine what it would do to him to be cooped up in a hospital bed while a serial rapist and killer was on the loose. But—*dear God*—airlifted? Had Max been burned? Or shot? Was he even still alive?

Her hands were trembling by the time she reached the nurse's station. "I'm here to see Max Sawyer." Catherine's voice quavered as she faced a nurse in raspberry-pink scrubs and a neat ponytail that bobbed with every efficient movement.

The woman's face was pinched with fatigue. "Unfortunately, I can't let you in unless you're immediate family."

She had to see Max and verify with her own eyes that he was okay. And if he wasn't, well, she'd make sure he became okay as soon as possible.

"I'm...I'm his wife." Mentally, Catherine crossed her fingers behind her back and prayed for forgiveness. Not that God would listen anymore. Out of necessity, lying had become second nature. Corrosion of her soul had become an acceptable risk to achieve the greater good.

The tired lines on the woman's face evened out as she smiled. "Lucky woman. He's in bay three, third curtain on the left." She gestured toward a hallway just beyond the nurse's station.

"Is he...will he be okay?"

"He's sedated, waiting for surgery. Unfortunately, the man who came in with him was in more critical condition and we had a multiple vehicle accident come in at about the same time, so your husband's been in a holding pattern."

"Surgery?" Her hand migrated to her throat before she clenched it into a fist and dropped it back at her side. Images of skin grafts and bullet removals danced in her head. Why were they making him wait so long? She'd fight tooth and nail to make sure he received the help he needed immediately.

The woman must have sensed Catherine's fear. "Fortunately, the only injury was to his shoulder when it was dislocated. Didn't stop him from running after the escaped prisoner, though." The woman's expression softened with admiration. Catherine understood the feeling well. "The shoulder reduction is more of a *procedure*, really, than a surgery."

Catherine was breathing a little easier by the time she located bay three, divided from two and four by curtains for privacy. She stood outside for a moment, willing her nerves to calm. It had been hard enough leaving him—leaving *SSAM*, rather—the first time, when she hadn't even said goodbye. How could she face him again?

Damian needs you. Max needs you. You owe them both.

Squaring her shoulders, she pushed the curtain aside. Monitors beeped softly and the lighting had been dimmed so he could rest. But her surroundings barely registered as every sense Catherine possessed focused on the man lying prone in the bed. His muscular six-foot-five frame filled it.

Max Sawyer, unmoving. She'd never seen him this way and it chilled her to the bone.

His right arm was bandaged, his chest bare beneath the thin

blue blanket. His brown hair was dark against a starchy white pillow. She should have thought to bring him more comfortable items from home.

Home. She didn't have a home with a stash of soft, warm blankets.

His right arm was tucked into a sling. Her gaze traveled south to where his left hand, strong and highlighted with sun-dusted brown hairs, rested on his abdomen. It rose and fell in a regular, reassuring rhythm. No burns, no bloody wounds. Max was in one piece. The tightness in her chest uncoiled and she suddenly felt weak in the knees, as if stress and worry had been the only things holding her together.

"Miss me, darlin'?" The southern drawl was standard issue with Max Sawyer, but it came and went with his moods. This time, it was exaggerated by sleepiness. It was still sexy as sin.

Her eyes shot to his face. His grin was lopsided, his eyes heavy-lidded. Was he even fully conscious? The nurse had said he was sedated.

She crossed the last few feet to his bedside and stood there, resisting the urge to reach for him. How many times had she had to tamp down the desires that threatened to overpower her when he was near? She'd been right to leave Chicago and the fruitless temptations there—except the temptations had followed her.

"How are you feeling?" She cursed the husky rasp in her voice.

"Been better." He grinned. "Been worse, too." It was the wink he added that told her how much pain he was in. That extra effort to reassure her meant he was truly hurting.

When he turned toward the table to his left, Catherine jumped to pour him some water, and then held the cup with one hand as she used the other to aim a straw at his dry lips. Even parched, they looked like they offered an oasis of pleasure. She'd had a taste of him just over three months ago and her body had thirsted for him ever since. Kissing him ranked among the best experiences— and biggest mistakes—of her life.

He wrapped his mouth around the end of the straw and sucked. The action sent a shiver of awareness along her skin. She jerked and her knuckle brushed the stubble of his day-old beard. He sank back against the pillows and squeezed his eyes shut.

She set the cup back on the table. "You're in pain."

"Sweet Cat." *Cat.* His nickname for her. Her skin warmed as if she'd been stroked from head to foot. But the sweat beading on his brow told her the real story. He tried to summon a smile, but failed. "Nothing you need to worry about."

"I'll get the nurse." She turned to go.

His uninjured arm snaked around her waist with surprising speed and accuracy. "Stay."

"You need some pain meds. They've kept you waiting so long, the other dose wore off."

"Stay," he repeated, but his eyelids slid closed.

"I'll be right back." Reluctantly, she unwound herself from his arm and slipped out.

The same woman looked up as Catherine approached the nurse's station. "How's he doing?"

"He's hurting." Seeing him like this twisted her stomach. "There's got to be something we can do."

"I'll check with the doctor. They should be ready to do his procedure soon, and then some X-rays, and you can take him home after that as long as he isn't driving. If the doctor approves, I'll be right in with more sedative." The nurse hustled down the hall.

Catherine was about to return to Max when a familiar, deep baritone boomed from the sliding doors that led from the ER to the waiting area. "He's my son, Lillian. I won't stay away. I don't care what he wants."

A flood of anxiety turned Catherine's skin clammy and cold. She had hoped Max's parents wouldn't have learned of his hospital-ization, at least not yet. Once again, she'd underestimated the reach of the Caulfield influence. Max wouldn't have called them, which meant someone on the hospital staff had recognized him and earned a big favor, or big bucks, by notifying Hayworth and Lillian.

Catherine shifted behind a column so she was hidden from view as Mr. and Mrs. Caulfield passed by, heading down the hall. Hayworth's tall frame could barely contain his large ego. Like a vacuum, he seemed to suck the air from the corridor as he barreled forward, clearly on a mission. Lillian's heels clicked crisply along the polished floor. Her white-blond hair bobbed against her shoulders as she hustled to keep up, her lips pursed in disapproval. Catherine had been on the other end of that look many times.

Once they were out of sight, Catherine backed toward the main doors, trying not to feel like a coward. She'd fulfilled her obligation to Damian. Max would soon be busy with his procedure and then sleeping off his sedative. It was self-protective instinct that had her hurrying for the door. She didn't feel strong enough to stand up to the Caulfields tonight, or to explain to Max why the hell she'd *need* to stand up to them. He didn't need that chaos during his recovery, anyway.

Better to retreat. She'd have to come clean with all of them some time. Max *would* end up hating her, but not tonight. She'd enjoy the reprieve just a little longer.

"OH, MAXWELL!" MAX'S MOTHER RUSHED INTO THE SMALL SPACE that held his hospital bed, several monitors and a single chair.

He winced as his whole body contracted, bracing for impact. Not physical impact, since that wasn't the Caulfield way. Emotional, mental or any other kind of manipulation, however, was fair game. So he was surprised when, instead of halting at his bedside, she leaned down to brush a quick kiss against his forehead, then feathered a hand over his hair.

"You've let it grow long." Her mouth tightened in disapproval, but the gaze that assessed his features brimmed with concern.

"Why didn't you tell us you were in town?" From behind his mother, his father's scolding voice boomed, increasing the tempo of the throbbing in Max's shoulder and echoing the new pain starting in his temples.

"I was supposed to be gone in a few hours." Max thought of the itinerary in his jacket pocket—the jacket that was still in the van, probably destroyed. He should be landing in Chicago by early afternoon tomorrow, after taking a morning flight. He still could, if they released him soon. If it weren't for Tony Moreno and the Circle, he'd leave on time, with or without a banged-up shoulder. While his head was clearing, he needed to check in with the Marshals office, which had undoubtedly taken over by now, and get an update on the manhunt, as well as Steve's condition. He struggled to remember the last few minutes before they'd been rescued. As darkness fell and it became clear Max wasn't going to be able to track Tony or their attackers, he'd returned to an unconscious Steve and waited for help. Once the helicopter had airlifted them to the hospital, they'd been rushed off in different directions. And had they found the driver of the van? Was he dead?

Damian would be expecting a complete report ASAP so they could plan SSAM's next move. Catherine usually helped coordinate with other agencies. Maybe they could lure her back to help with the manhunt.

Catherine. His still-fuzzy brain grasped at something. She'd been here. *Hadn't she?* His bare shoulder tingled, remembering the brush of her long hair as she'd bent over him, offering water. She'd been so close to his lips, and yet so far.

"*Gone?* You weren't even going to say hello?" His mother's horrified questions slammed him back to reality. "We haven't seen you in two years. We barely get a five-minute phone call on birthdays and holidays."

There was good reason for that. He couldn't stand the thought of being roped back into their world like some wayward calf. Still, the look in her eyes stirred the guilt he normally tamped down. The physical pain must be lowering his defenses.

"You'll recuperate at the ranch, of course." Hayworth Caulfield was the master of making completely unreasonable demands sound logical.

Max was too exhausted for this discussion. "I have work to do. There'll be a massive search for a convict who escaped." He couldn't just leave Texas, no matter how much he wanted to. Tony had escaped on *his* watch, and it was Max's responsibility to find him.

Where had Catherine gone? He wouldn't mind a little friendly support and encouragement. She was so good at that. Wasn't that her job, anyway?

The call button was out of reach. Talk about being trapped. The night had gone FUBAR in so many ways.

"*Work's* what landed you here." His mother frowned. "From what the doctor told Hayworth, you'll be out of commission for at least a few days, probably a couple weeks, while you heal."

Max bristled. He hadn't even had a coherent talk with the doctor yet, and his parents had all the pertinent details? His dad was probably a golfing buddy of the doc's.

"I know a good physical therapist in Chicago." Max left out how he'd met the guy six years ago, while rehabbing a knee injury from his last mission in Afghanistan. With hard work and Damian's support, as well as the lure of a job at SSAM when he healed, Max had recovered over a period of several months. He could only hope his shoulder healed more quickly.

"We'll have the best specialists on call night and day," his father assured him.

The best money can buy. It sounded like a genuine offer from a concerned parent. In reality, he knew it was a ploy to get him home again, for good this time, and in a position where he would owe them.

Money could buy anything—except Maxwell Sawyer Caulfield's soul.

The nurse walked in and scowled at his parents. "You shouldn't be here. Visiting hours are over and Mr. Sawyer needs his rest."

"Mr. Sawyer?" His father's eyes bulged.

"My name," Max said calmly. "I had it legally changed a few years back." It had been one more layer of defense against his past.

His mother gaped.

The nurse turned to him. "I have the sedative your wife requested. She's making sure we take very good care of you."

Wife? Max was careful to hide his reaction but nearly choked on the water he'd just taken a sip of. Confusion cleared as he realized that if his own parents weren't tolerated here, the only person who might be at this hour was a spouse. So Catherine had lied her way to his bedside and then abandoned him? Where was his better half in his time of need? What happened to *for better or worse?* He nearly grinned.

"You're *married?*" His mother had gone white. She pressed a hand to her chest. "What's her name?" No doubt, she was mentally running through the shrinking list of eligible Texas debutantes and realizing he'd selected someone outside of her chosen pool for the coveted role of daughter-in-law. After all, pedigree was paramount when a son was to follow in his father's footsteps—and beyond—by taking on the family business *and* entering the political realm. Max couldn't give a damn about pedigree, especially since he wasn't going to do either of those things.

Though the urge to protect Catherine from their probing was strong, he realized they would use other resources to dig for a name if he didn't provide it. "Catherine Montague. Sawyer," he added, and the first genuine smile of the day touched his lips.

The nurse busied herself checking monitors in the corner, listening to every word.

His mother shot his father a look, exchanging some silent

communication Max couldn't decipher. "Well, we expect to meet her right away, of course."

"You can't control the whole world, Mom." Suddenly exhausted, Max sank against the pillow.

Sensing the tension in the room, or maybe reading his elevated blood pressure and accelerated pulse rate on the monitor, the nurse once again made her presence known. "I think it would be best if you came back in the morning," she said to his parents.

Or not at all. He smothered the guilt that rose at his mother's hurt expression. This was his life and he'd live it how he damn well pleased, not according to her blueprints. Joining the Navy at the age of eighteen was the best decision he'd ever made. He'd learned the true meaning of loyalty and family as part of a SEAL team. And then he'd found the SSAM agency through a fellow SEAL known as Einstein, and had the good fortune to join a new kind of family. Being trapped in Texas again, injured, was a cruel twist of fate.

"It shouldn't be much longer before the doctor is available to do the reduction procedure," the nurse said. She took the cup of water from Max and refilled it from a small pitcher before handing it back. He remembered how Catherine had gingerly supported the straw as he sipped. His mother only continued to glare, not thinking to offer him water or comfort of any kind. And he'd be damned if he'd ask them for anything.

CHAPTER 4

Tony's stomach rumbled. Someone in the middle-class neighborhood was torturing him with the scents of frying bacon and brewing coffee. *Safety first, then food.*

As an SAPD patrol car cruised slowly down the street, he crouched lower behind the clump of bushes where he'd been camped since daybreak. After the storm had petered out a few hours ago, Tony had rolled in mud near the creek, muting the bright orange color of his jumpsuit. He could do little about the cuffs that chafed his wrists, but he hoped to rectify that soon.

Following the creek had been genius, hiding his tracks, helping him evade the two Circle idiots as well as Max Sawyer and whoever else might be following him, and also leading him straight to this neighborhood. On a Saturday, most of the people in these tidy little houses might not be leaving for work, but he'd survived this long. Some solution would present itself.

Across the street, a garage door creaked and groaned as it rose. A woman clutched a giant travel mug as she ushered her son around the back of a car. She wore skin-tight jeans and a baseball-style jersey and her long dark hair was pulled back into a ponytail that dangled between her shoulder blades. Tony wanted to wrap his fist in that hair and ride her like a bucking bronco.

Too bad her voice was shrill with the orders she shouted at her sleepy-eyed son. "Grab your cleats. Don't forget your hat. Honestly, you'd forget your head if it wasn't screwed on…"

The kid looked to be about nine. Shit, at that age Tony would have been plunked in front of the TV watching cartoons on a Saturday morning.

"What about Dad?" the kid whined. He probably wanted a go-between to shield him from her demands.

"He'll be right behind us." She loaded an athletic bag and slammed the trunk shut. Her son climbed into the back seat and she moved around the opposite side of the car. A moment later, she pulled out onto the street and sped away, leaving the garage open, presumably for her husband.

Tony would have preferred to take on the woman—she would have been a heck of a lot of fun to subdue—but when opportunity knocked, he answered.

He looked up and down the empty street, then back at the open garage and the sedan that remained. He grinned and hoped Mrs. Bossy's husband was about his size. He'd need new clothes for the next part of his escape. Thank God for Little League and people who believed the world was a safe place. Fortune was shining on him again.

WHEN MAX LOOKED UP FROM HIS ATTEMPTS TO SPOON A LIMP CUBE of pear from the fruit cup using only his left hand, he found Damian, Lorena and Einstein in his hospital room doorway. The morning suddenly seemed brighter. His SSAM family had arrived.

He grinned. "You're late to the party."

"Some party." Einstein, SSAM's communication and technology expert, eyed Max's bandaged shoulder and gave him a look that spoke volumes. The pair had served on the same SEAL team and been discharged after the same fucked-up incident. They were familiar with injuries, recoveries and everything in between. "We can stop having these kind of parties any time, bro."

"Yeah, I hear you."

"Good to see you in one piece, though." Einstein smothered a yawn. They must have taken the redeye from Chicago to get here so fast.

Lorena, one of the mindhunters who worked with SSAM to profile the monsters they hunted, stepped forward and smiled. She was fifty-something and her straight, coffee-black hair, dark eyes and olive skin gave her an exotic kind of beauty. "You look better already."

"It was just a shoulder reduction. Didn't need surgery." *Thank God.* "I would have been out of here last night if it hadn't taken so long for the doctor to get to me." And if he'd been willing to accept his parents' offer and be in their debt. He hadn't been that desperate, though. "You didn't have to come all this way. Didn't Catherine fill you in?" He looked behind Damian, toward the door, half-expecting to see Catherine there. She was part of this team, too.

He'd worried he'd screwed up royally when he'd given in to impulse and kissed her on New Year's Eve. Lord knows the urges shooting through his body at that moment had nearly done him in. But even after his momentary lapse in judgment, they'd been able to get back to the friendship he valued, or at least, he thought they had. Was that why she'd taken this leave of absence, because he'd crossed the line? She reminded Max of what was gentle and good —and why he fought every day for justice. Her smile and calm, steady presence was what got most of the SSAM agents through the long days in a gritty, shitty world. She *had* to return to manning the front desk at SSAM.

"Catherine called me." Damian pulled a chair closer to the bed and gestured for Lorena to sit. He pulled another up beside her and took a seat while Einstein propped up the wall. "Told me you'd pull through."

Max looked away. "I failed. Did she tell you that, too?"

"You were ambushed. Someone—I'm guessing they worked for the Circle—altered the plans given to the transport service."

That they'd been specifically targeted didn't make Max feel any better. Tony was still free. "The Circle either rescued or pursued Tony. Either way, he escaped. Do you know anything about the driver?"

"They found his remains in the van," Einstein said. "But the transport company he worked for is saying he's the one who changed the plans. I did some cyber-digging and found a hefty deposit in his bank account."

The man had lost his life because of his greed. "And Steve?"

"Steve?"

"He was the other agent, the one who was shot."

"He's still unconscious. Had surgery to repair his leg."

Guilt tasted bitter on Max's tongue. He should have forced the driver, by whatever means necessary, to turn around the moment his instincts told him to. "We've got to stop the Circle. They're everywhere."

"We will." Damian's gaze moved to Max's right shoulder. "Are you going to be okay?"

"I'd like to kill someone with my bare hands, but I'll heal. I've been told to avoid exercise for a couple days, come in for a follow-up, and then they'll likely prescribe a workout regimen to strengthen the muscles and joint. I know the drill. I'll survive."

"And you'll take the time you need to heal properly."

Max's jaw clenched. He wasn't one to sit on the sidelines while others made up for his mistakes. "I want in on the manhunt."

"Don't we all," Einstein said. "But we've been shut out."

"What?" Max struggled to sit up, but winced as he forgot about the shoulder ensconced in a sling.

Damian's frown deepened, carving creases that bracketed his mouth and eyes. "The SAPD, the U.S. Marshals, the Rangers—

they're circling the wagons, cutting us out. At least Tony's picture is plastered all over the media."

"Yeah, I saw that." Max's gaze flicked up to the muted television in the corner of his room. He'd watched the news all morning, trying to pick up on what was going on.

"The Marshals' office, which is coordinating the manhunt, said they have search dogs and dozens of men on the case, but that's all they'll say."

"Do you think Tony's dead? Maybe the Circle caught up to him."

"I'd say his odds of escaping were better last night than any other day," Einstein said. "With the storm, there was a strong runoff, so any tracks were wiped away. There was a creek not far from the place of attack. We plan to check areas downstream, particularly a neighborhood a few miles south. We'll look for reports of stolen cars, of course. The SAPD and Rangers are already canvassing the area and alerting residents."

Damian turned an incredulous look on Einstein. "You know all of this how?"

He shrugged, but a smile tugged at one corner of his mouth. "It's my job. I had a little time at the airport while we waited for the bags and did some research on the computer. But for the rest of the details, you'll need some cooperation."

"Have the authorities given you a reason they're shutting you out?" Max asked.

Damian frowned. "No, which is unusual in itself. Granted, San Antonio is a long way from Chicago and we don't have the inroads with local authorities we've made back home, but I usually at least get an explanation. Especially since we're trying to offer our resources and experience to find Tony Moreno. I can't even get someone to return my calls. Apparently, someone had the pull to block us."

Max's gut tightened. His father wouldn't interfere in this... would he? His thoughts went back to what he'd said the night before, when his parents had shown up without notice. A fuzzy memory of Catherine's sympathetic expression emerged, replaced by his parents' disapproving glares. Had he mentioned why he was in town? Probably.

The only local person with enough power and motive to blatantly shut SSAM out of the investigation was Hayworth Caulfield. And Max would bet the man was sitting back, waiting for his son to call and plead for a reprieve. The only question was, what did the old man want in return?

THE PHONE ON THE COFFEE TABLE VIBRATED WITH ANOTHER message. Catherine pulled the pillow over her head and burrowed under the blanket. Maybe if she disregarded the sunlight slanting across the couch in Rachel's living room and went back to sleep, she could restart her morning in an hour or two. So far, she had missed—*ignored*—several calls from Max, one from Damian letting her know he, Lorena and Einstein were in town, and one from an irate Hayworth Caulfield, demanding to know when, where, how and why she'd married his son.

None of them truly needed her. She'd already phoned the nurse's station early that morning to check on Max's condition. Hearing he was on the road to recovery, Catherine had decided she could avoid talking to him. He was probably just curious what stroke of fate had placed her in his neck of the woods, and she had no explanation that wouldn't lead to more questions. Better to maintain radio silence. Besides, now that Damian was in town, Max's every need would be met.

And Hayworth...well, she planned to see him soon enough. None of her answers would satisfy him, either. It was a confrontation she wasn't looking forward to, but it was a necessary step in reclaiming herself and putting her life back on track. But taking that step would disappoint everyone else in her life.

She had just pressed the pillow into her face when Rachel

emerged from the bedroom and tried to cross quietly to the kitchen. But the soft slap of her feet against the kitchen tile had Catherine tossing the covers off. "You're up early for a Saturday."

Startled, Rachel spun from the counter. "Sorry. I didn't mean to wake you. Want some breakfast?" She turned back to the counter to stick a couple slices of bread into the toaster and depressed the lever. She kept her back to Catherine, her shoulders hunched as she stared down at the counter.

"What's wrong? I didn't snore that loudly, did I?"

Rachel looked over her shoulder with a small smile. "No. No snoring. Was the couch okay?"

"It was fine." Catherine's back was achy, and her muscles a bit tight from the drive and the limited sleeping space, but beggars couldn't be choosers. "No dodging my questions."

Rachel sighed and turned to face her. "I got a call from the police this morning. Someone threw a brick through the clinic's front window. I have to go take care of it and I have patients to see later this morning."

"I'll come with you."

"No, you're my guest. Besides, I want you to go job hunting. Find something that'll keep you here." The mischievous twinkle was back in Rachel's eyes.

Job hunting. The concept held no appeal. What if nothing could top working at SSAM? "Let's tackle today first. I'll help you clean up, get the clinic open for your Saturday hours, and then I'll make myself scarce."

"You really don't have anything else to do today?"

Nothing but ignore persistent males, she thought as her phone vibrated again with another incoming call.

"You've had my son long enough. It's time for him to come home." Hayworth Caulfield entered the hospital room with the momentum of a gale-force hurricane and stared down the nurse.

Damian had never met the man, had never even heard Max speak of his father, but he knew him on sight. After all, Damian fully investigated all of his potential hires, and Max Sawyer, born Maxwell Sawyer Caulfield, was no different.

Hayworth stopped short when he spied Damian sitting in the corner. Einstein and Lorena had gone to the cafeteria in search of breakfast. The man's gaze shifted to Max, surveying his condition with a flick of his eyes, pausing a moment on the sling. "How are you this morning, Son?"

"Ready to leave." Max turned a charming grin on the nurse. "Right?"

"I'll see if I can track down the doctor and get that discharge paperwork going." Her expression softened in the face of Max's southern charm. She smiled before bustling away. Damian knew about Max's playboy reputation in Chicago. The man didn't want to settle down with one woman. Or he hadn't found the *right* woman. Observing the crisp, humorless father and the equally brusque woman—presumably Max's mother Lillian Caulfield— who'd entered right behind Hayworth, Damian couldn't blame him.

Lillian tucked a phone into her purse. "I've had Claudia make up your room. It'll be ready within the hour."

Max's good humor dissipated in a flash. "You didn't have to waste her time. I told you, I won't be recuperating at the ranch."

"Surely you see the benefits," Lillian persisted, ignoring Max's now clouded expression.

"I'll be renting a house in the area for my team," Damian said. "Max can stay there, where he can help us with the manhunt."

Hayworth smirked. "Oh, yes, the Tony Moreno manhunt. How's that going?"

Max stiffened. "We wouldn't know yet, but as soon as I get out of here, I'll make sure I find out."

"I don't think that'll be happening," Hayworth said. Tension swelled in the room as father and son faced off.

"So you *did* interfere." Max's words were sharp as razorblades. "You took advantage of my drugged state and things I shouldn't have mentioned. I don't know why I'm surprised."

Lillian laughed curtly. "I'm sure we wouldn't have found out about your *wife* otherwise."

Rarely was Damian shocked. He prided himself on being informed and prepared in an effort to avoid potential disasters. But this took the cake. "Wife?"

A smile tugged at Max's mouth as he turned to Damian. Einstein and Lorena stood in the doorway, coffee cups in hand, quietly assessing the scene they'd just walked in on. "Catherine told the nurse she was my wife to get in to see me after visiting hours."

"So you're not married?" Lillian put a hand to her chest as if she'd just survived a heart attack.

"No, but you can keep that debutante list locked away. I don't intend on settling."

"Settling down, you mean." Lillian looked confident she could change his mind.

"No. *Settling.* For a woman who only wants what the *Caulfields* have to offer." Max's tone was thick with disdain. That explained the name change, but Damian had already suspected the discord in the family based on what his investigator had unearthed years ago.

"Forget the marriage talk." Hayworth sent his wife a silent message to back down. "Healing should be first on the agenda."

Max snorted. "*Agenda.* Sounds like business already. I'm not returning to the family fold, especially not when you're manipulating my life again already."

"We're just talking about a few weeks while you heal," Lillian insisted.

But the look on Hayworth's face told the real story. Desperation and fear had forged a stone-like stubbornness. Damian had seen the same expression in the mirror many times over the past couple decades—he wanted his daughter back with a ferocious, burning ache that kept him awake nights, kept him chasing monsters, kept him seeking justice for her murder.

Hayworth wanted his son back. And he'd do anything to make that happen.

MAX SPOKE OVER THE ROAR OF BLOOD IN HIS EARS. "CAN I HAVE A moment with my parents, please?" He addressed Damian, Lorena and Einstein, but his eyes were on his father, who was looking smug.

Behind Damian and Lorena, Einstein paused at the door, giving him a look that meant he had his back. All Max had to do was give him the signal. *Yeah. Appreciate that.* Einstein was the only person he'd confided in about his past and how it had shaped who he was today.

Max nodded, and with a soft snick of the door closing, was left alone with his parents. If he'd fallen in line with their wishes last night and gone home with them rather than insist they leave before his procedure, no doubt he'd be in five-star accommodations right now, likely in his boyhood room at the ranch with a beautiful nurse tending to his every need.

And they'd make sure he came to need them like he needed his next breath, take over his life again. Make him a man he couldn't be proud of.

Not worth it.

Except his father wouldn't have taken steps to keep SSAM out of the manhunt if Max had simply agreed to go to the ranch for a few days.

"I know Tony Moreno, probably better than anybody else," Max said. "Certainly better than anybody out there looking for him." He'd spent the past six weeks in prison, undercover as the guy's bodyguard. He knew how Tony thought and just how dangerous he was.

His father shrugged. "That may be true, but you're injured."

"I can still help from the sidelines. And my injury isn't that severe. I'll be healthy again in no time."

"And that time would go even faster at the ranch."

Max doubted that. "What's it going to take for you to open up the investigation to people who truly can help?"

"You make it sound like blackmail," his mother whispered. Her gaze darted to the door to see who might have heard. Family secrets were never discussed outside of the ranch. In fact, they were hardly discussed at all.

Max snorted. "It *is* blackmail."

"It doesn't have to be. If you would just come visit once in a while…"

"Move back in while you recuperate," his father ordered.

Max looked toward the window. Sunlight tickled the tops of the trees. A new day was beginning, and he had the sick feeling his freedom was about to end.

He swallowed, choking down his pride. "Is that the price?"

After a long moment, his father released a heavy sigh. "I suppose it is. You're too stubborn to do this any other way." *Pot, meet kettle.*

"Give me the terms, in detail. I want to know exactly what I'm agreeing to."

"Live at the ranch for six weeks. You may work with SSAM on the manhunt, but you spend equal hours at Caulfield Industries, learning the business."

Max had to resist the urge to pull the collar of his hospital gown away from his neck as he felt the noose tighten. He knew little about the gargantuan oil company his father owned, or the other businesses he'd brought under the CI umbrella over the years. "The manhunt could be over in hours."

"Six weeks. Take it or leave it."

"And after six weeks?"

His father shrugged as if it didn't matter. "You have a place at CI, but it'll be up to you. If you want to leave, you can leave. Just stay through Mother's Day." His mother gaped, but she didn't have a say in the matter. His father and Max held all the cards and she knew it.

Could he survive with his identity intact? He wondered if that amount of time was beyond the limit of his endurance.

"Well?" His father asked. "You've heard my demands."

"And if I say no, you'd rather stick to your guns and leave a known felon, a man who preys on women, running loose in your community rather than loosen the reins?"

His mother gasped. "Of course not."

His father shot her a look to silence her. "We'll do what we have to in order to get our family back on track. It's time you learned your place in the world—and it's a damn good place. I've worked hard to ensure your inheritance. But if you refuse to even try to meet us halfway..." He shrugged. "The Marshals can find Moreno without you."

But maybe not in time. "I can help find him. I *need* to help."

"Then accept the terms." His father wasn't going to back down. For whatever reason, this was important to him. His expression was chiseled in granite.

And the pros outweighed the cons. Hayworth Caulfield had the necessary relationships with local officials to make things happen. Having served in local politics and donated chunks of money to community programs, he held a place of honor and respect around these parts. If it meant opening the doors to SSAM so they could catch Tony sooner, Max would do whatever he had to do. But that didn't mean he had to do it alone. He could have his *wife* along for the ride. Having an outsider around would encourage them all to behave civilly. Catherine had an innate sense for dealing with people, a gift for knowing what a person needed most and how to smooth things over in a crisis. No doubt things would be infinitely easier with her at the ranch.

"I'd like to bring a friend," he said.

"Who?" his mother asked.

"Catherine."

She pursed her lips in thought and then nodded. "It might be good to have a friend there. She can have the guesthouse. I'll have Claudia stock the fridge with your favorite things. You'll heal more quickly at home." She glanced at his shoulder and frowned. Was she thinking about his brother? But her expression cleared before he could assess it further. "We'll get you released from here immediately."

"No." As much as he wanted to leave the hospital, he wasn't getting sucked into his parents' world before he was guaranteed his side of the deal. "I need today to make some arrangements. And the investigation?" He directed the question to his father.

His dad took out his phone and scrolled through his contacts. "I'll make a call right now. But we'll expect to see you and Catherine at the ranch by dinnertime." Or he'd be reversing that call. *Yeah, Dad, I get it. You're in control, just how you like it.*

Max had to find Damian and the others, and then Catherine. He could only hope she'd agree to help him with this devil's bargain.

CHAPTER 5

hatever Max wants, say yes.

W Catherine dumped the bits of glass she'd collected into the trashcan with such force, they nearly bounced back in her face. The text she'd just received from Hayworth still had her blood boiling. How had this happened? She'd returned to Texas to break ties with the Caulfields and get away from Max. Instead, the universe was conspiring against her.

"Careful." Rachel swept, again filling up the dustpan Catherine held against the waiting room floor.

"Sorry." Catherine had to work harder to hide her feelings. In the last few weeks away from SSAM, she'd given herself permission to let down her guard, to be herself. She'd forgotten what it was like to be cautious.

"Are you okay?"

Catherine rolled her eyes. "I believe that's my line."

After disposing of the last of the window's shards, Rachel straightened and tucked the broom back into the utility closet. Her fingers trailed over the brick lying on the counter and her lips pressed together. "I'll be fine. Even better when the window people get here and things get back to normal. I've got patients to see in about an hour." The clinic had limited hours on weekends.

"Is anything missing?"

Rachel's eyes darkened. "Some drugs. Painkillers, mostly."

"Do you think it was Lee?" They'd found out this morning that the man who'd brought a gun to the clinic yesterday had been released on bail last night.

"Not sure. Could be kids looking to get high, for all I know. Luckily, I don't keep many prescription drugs on hand, but they were determined. Broke into a locked cabinet."

"No surveillance cameras?"

"No money for that, which reminds me... I need to make another call to the insurance company. Can you man the front desk for a few?"

"Sure." Catherine brushed her palms on her jeans and glanced toward the gaping hole where *Pecan Grove Clinic* had once been carefully stenciled. She spotted two familiar men crossing the parking lot and her heart thumped harder as they drew closer. She drank in the sight of Max, his right arm supported by a sling, but walking steadily on his own two feet. Those feet carried him over the clinic's threshold. His hazel eyes zeroed in on her and his lips curved. It was the charming smile he usually reserved for his woman *du jour*. Her BS meter kicked on.

Whatever Max wants... Hayworth's text demanded she accommodate Max's needs. Something was up.

Max's smile faded as he caught sight of the garbage can and the glint of broken glass. His eyes narrowed on the hole in the wall. Beside him, Einstein mirrored Max's stance.

"What happened?" Max asked.

"Good to see you, too." She pulled the bin out of the waiting room and tucked it back behind the reception counter. "Hey, Einstein," she added.

"Hey. It's been a while." Einstein was distracted as he examined the empty frame where the window had once been.

Max's face turned stormy when she deflected his question. "Are you hurt?"

"Just a broken window. Don't worry about it. We've got it covered." The last thing she needed was Max in her corner, a concerned friend, sucking her back into the world she wanted very much to be a part of but very much needed to leave. Catherine stayed behind the counter, a wussy barrier, but better than nothing. It held her back from rushing to Max and running her hands over him to feel if everything was okay. "How are you feeling?"

"I'll heal. Thanks for stopping by last night."

So he did remember. "How'd you track me here?" Had they dug into her past and if so, how deep?

Einstein—the guilty culprit—flushed bright red. "He insisted the only way he was leaving the hospital was if I brought him to you." His gaze landed on her cell phone, which lay on the counter next to the brick.

"You traced my phone?" Catherine would have admired his skills had it been anyone else he was tracking.

Max's gaze narrowed on the brick. "This wasn't an accident. What happened here?"

"Brick. Glass. The brick won."

Max's jaw tightened with annoyance. "If you'd talk, maybe we can help."

"It'll be fine. I don't need rescuing."

Einstein gazed at the apartment complex across the street. Spray-painted gang signs tagged dumpsters and sides of buildings. "Tough neighborhood."

Yeah. One more thing she couldn't control. Like Max being in her life again, after she'd done everything possible to stay away from him.

"Do you work here?" Max asked.

She shook her head, seeing no hope of hiding. "My sister does."

"Why'd you disappear?"

"From the hospital?"

"The hospital. Chicago. SSAM." His voice turned soft. "You had a rough time, but I would think being around friends would help." He frowned. "I didn't know you had family here."

She hadn't talked about her family or background with anyone, always steering conversation toward other people. She had her reasons for holding back and they were no different today than they'd been the past five years.

"Guess we had more in common than I thought," he mused.

You have no idea.

"You left so quickly last night. Left me to handle my parents alone." A dimple formed beneath the stubble of his unshaved cheek as he teased her. "Not exactly an angel of mercy."

"You seemed like you were in good hands. You don't get along with your parents?" She pretended she had no clue. *Fraud.*

His smile slipped, but he maintained his casual attitude. He was definitely trying to charm her, but why? "Not really. And they were shocked to learn I had a wife."

Catherine stiffened. Einstein was surveying the window and the neighborhood beyond while listening to every word they exchanged. "Sorry about the lie, but Damian wanted immediate reassurance you were okay. Saying we were married was the only way I could see for myself."

"Relax." He chuckled. "I'm glad you came, even if you had to use that as a cover story. But you've opened a can of worms, darlin'."

"What do you mean?"

"My parents want to meet the woman I chose to marry."

Heat pooled low in her belly and slowly spread to her limbs. She ruthlessly ignored the pleasurable sensations. "You didn't straighten them out?"

"Where's the fun in that?" Max the playboy was all about fun. She'd do well to remember that. She would have to give her libido a stern talking-to.

Einstein snorted. "Let her off the hook, man. She's obviously had one hell of a morning. You're making her uncomfortable." He went back to examining the damage, but mumbled something that sounded like, "…and *he's* the ladies' man."

Max sobered. "Sorry. I guess being around my parents has me strung tight."

"So they know we're not married and there's no way in hell we're even considering it?"

"Ouch." Max rubbed his chest as if she'd wounded him. She knew better. She didn't come anywhere close to the caliber of women he preferred. And yet *she* was supposed to give him whatever he wanted.

Einstein coughed to cover a laugh. "I see a glass repair truck circling. I think I'll go wave them down."

As Einstein left them alone, she sighed. "Why are you here, Max? What do you want?"

With his good arm, he reached across the counter and took her hand. His fingers entwined with hers and her breath caught. Though they'd been friends, it was unusual for him to reach out to her like this—physically or emotionally. Theirs had been a casual friendship, formed from working together and strengthened by dealing with danger and stress on a daily basis.

"I wouldn't turn down a bit of help," he said.

She sucked in a breath at the intensity in his eyes. He hadn't looked at her like that before, except in her dreams. This couldn't be real, but she couldn't pinch herself with her fingers caught up in his strong, tanned ones. "What kind of help?"

"The kind that comes from a friend."

He'd come to the wrong place for that. She was a backstabbing, two-faced liar. But she'd also tried to rectify that, to walk away from him, from the forces that threatened to pull her apart.

She attempted to tug her fingers free, but his grip tightened. What was it with him and touching her lately? She'd worked with him for years and he'd always been hands-off, except that one time. A flash of memory of his lips on hers, the taste of champagne as the clock counted down to midnight and a much-too-brief embrace brought a flush to her cheeks.

He brushed a thumb over her knuckles. "Whatever's got you running away from Chicago, from the people who care about you, I can help. But I need your help, too."

Rachel stepped out of the hall that led to the exam rooms. She eyed their joined hands and followed the bigger hand up a muscular arm, to Max's face. Her lips curved. "You must be Max Sawyer."

He answered her smile with one of his own, finally releasing Catherine so he could shake Rachel's hand with his left one. "In the flesh. And you must be Catherine's sister."

"Dr. Rachel Montgomery."

"Montgomery?" Noticing the slight difference in the sisters' last names, Max looked at Catherine, his eyebrows raised. "Is one of you married?"

"No. I changed it several years ago," Catherine hurried to explain. She'd changed her surname from Montgomery to Montague to keep anyone, especially Damian or Max, from finding out her family history—or why she might have ulterior motives for working at SSAM.

"Why?"

"I had my reasons."

Rachel eyed his sling and jumped in to save her. "How's your arm? When Catherine rushed out last night, she was so worried—" She stopped talking when she caught Catherine's expression. Catherine didn't want Max to know how panicked she'd been. She was supposed to be walking away from him, damn it.

Max grinned. "Dislocated, but I'm all patched up now. I'll be good as new in a couple weeks."

Was that true? Catherine exhaled a breath of relief that he'd be back to his normal life, in Chicago, in no time.

Einstein entered the clinic with two men in tow, who immediately went to work assessing the damaged area. Catherine introduced her other SSAM coworker to Rachel.

Einstein jerked a thumb toward the broken window. "Strange way to treat a neighbor."

Rachel's smile evaporated. "Probably teens looking for drugs. Unfortunately, it goes with the territory. Though I do wonder where they found the unusual brick."

"Unusual?" Max asked, glancing at the brick on the counter. It was tan in color, and looked a little rough around the edges.

"It doesn't match any building or wall nearby. In fact, I think it's homemade. But there's more..." Rachel turned the brick over.

Catherine gasped. "Why didn't you show me this before?"

She shrugged. "You took charge the moment we walked in, just grabbed a broom and went to work. Why? Do you recognize the symbol?"

"What?" Einstein looked over Max's shoulder to see what they were looking at. "Oh, shit."

Rachel's gaze scanned their faces. "Would somebody clue me in?"

Max pointed to the stamped image of a circle with flames coming off it. "That's the sign of an organized crime syndicate called the Circle. The group's into some seriously bad shit. Could you place that in a plastic bag, please? I'm sure Damian will want someone at SSAM to get a very close look at it after the police are done."

"I'll find something. Be right back." Rachel scurried away.

"I'll help." Einstein followed her to the back. The pair of window repairmen had left to get their equipment from their truck, leaving Max and Catherine alone again.

"You okay?" Max's gaze, both gentle and considering, moved across Catherine's face.

Memories of her time in the hands of a man who'd used Circle facilities to hold her prisoner were tumbling through her mind, but she focused on Max, shutting out the noise of her recent past. "I'll be fine."

"We need to show this to Damian. He'll want to get SSAM agents working on it right away. We didn't even know the Circle had an active cell in San Antonio, though it explains why they were so well prepared to attack the transport van in a remote area last night."

"Or maybe this was Tony's work?" The man had been a Circle thug for his entire adult life. "But why would he target Rachel's clinic?"

"We don't know it was Tony."

"We don't know it wasn't, either. What if he was able to find my sister because of me and my connection to SSAM?" The thought that she'd led such a vicious group to Rachel's doorstep sent shivers across her skin. "After all, you were able to find us."

"We didn't trace you to your sister, only to your phone. If Einstein didn't make the family connection, I seriously doubt Tony did. Besides, he's running from the Circle. I'd bet he's lying low. Throwing a brick through a window like this is a message."

"But what are they trying to say?" Catherine looked around as if she expected to find an explanation, maybe another symbol they could decode.

"Can you come with us to meet with Damian and Lorena? I need to talk to you anyway."

Ah, yes. The real reason he'd stopped by. *Whatever Max wants, say yes.*

"I can't leave my sister." Especially when she might be on the Circle's radar.

Rachel and Einstein returned from the back with a biohazard bag and latex gloves in time to overhear her comment.

"Teresa will be in soon if you need to go," Rachel assured her. "Something tells me you've just found a task to occupy your day. Besides, I'll be busy with appointments, insurance quotes and the window people. If you can figure out who threw this brick and why, it would be a load off my mind."

"I can stay here until the police come back," Einstein offered. "I'm going to call them and have them look at this brick. It'll give me a chance to ask them about Circle activity in the area. You two go talk to Damian and Lorena."

Rachel grinned. "Looks like your calendar just opened up."

"You're sure?" Catherine felt trapped. Rachel was in good hands, but she didn't want to go with Max, or get any deeper into SSAM business. How could she explain why without revealing the horrible ways she'd betrayed him?

"Go."

"Be careful." Catherine hugged Rachel before grabbing her phone and purse and walking out. Without looking back, she crossed the parking lot to her Jeep. She'd unhooked the trailer and left it at Rachel's place.

Max dogged her. "You can drive?"

At her rear bumper, her doubts stopped her again. She whirled to face him. "Maybe I should just lend you my car—" She glanced at his sling, having forgotten his injury. "Oh."

"Yeah. *Oh.*" He took a step forward, bending slightly to look into her eyes. "So, you'll give me a ride? I promise I won't bite."

"And then what? What do you really want?"

"It's nothing bad. In fact, it's important both to finding Tony and to my recovery, and it won't cost you a thing. It might actually save you some money."

"What is it?"

"I want you to move in with me at my parents' ranch."

She stiffened. *Whatever Max wants, say yes.* Oh, God, how she wanted to say yes. But then all hope of reclaiming her soul would be lost.

"I'd like to help—" Catherine began.

Max felt a moment of triumph. She was going to say yes. He could see it in her eyes. He nearly swept her up in a hug. Her cooperation was vital to the success of two missions: finding Tony and helping Max survive six weeks with his parents.

"—but I can't." Her expression became shuttered.

"Let me clarify. We wouldn't actually be living *together*. Please —" He stopped, realizing he was dangerously close to begging. "Let's talk about it on the way."

"The way?"

"To the house Damian is renting during the manhunt. It's just a few minutes from here. I'll explain, and if you still don't agree…"

"Whatever it is, I can't do it." Misery was etched on her face, as if she wanted to say yes but was holding back.

"Why not? You haven't heard the details."

"One of the reasons I took this leave was to figure out what I need to do next. And I need to leave SSAM."

"But SSAM might be able to help your sister. And I'm willing to help, too, in any way I can. Look, just give me a couple hours to convince you."

"To *move in* with you?" She made it sound horrific.

"Sort of. My parents are insisting I recuperate at the ranch." He sighed, realizing he'd have to let her in a bit if he expected her help. "My folks and I don't exactly get along. It would be easier if I had a friend there. A kind of…buffer."

"Gee, Mr. Sawyer, such sweet words. Flattery will get you nowhere."

Well, this was new. Usually he only had to ask a woman once. Sometimes he didn't even have to ask. "Okay, then, tell me what *will* get me somewhere."

His biceps flexed as he planted his good hand on his hip, causing his polo shirt to stretch across his pecs. She'd placed her palms right there, one on each amazing side of his chest, when they'd kissed.

"What do you want?" Max asked. Catherine bit her lip against a moan of sexual frustration. Hadn't a dozen or more dreams begun with Max asking her that very question? "Seriously, name your price. I need your help and I'm willing to repay the favor."

She admitted defeat. She wanted to help Max because she cared about him, and she was still bound by duty to the Caulfields to obey their command and say yes to whatever Max wanted.

She looked toward the clinic. "A little help here, maybe? I'd like to see some security for Rachel and her patients, at least until I can get her moved to a building a few blocks away."

A frown creased Max's brow as he leaned beside her against the rear of the Jeep. "What does a few blocks matter?"

"There's a police station up that way." She'd scouted the area herself on the way here this morning and scribbled down the address. "I figure there'd be less chance of crime there."

When she didn't continue, he gave a short laugh, gazing at her in disbelief. "You're not going to ask for anything for yourself?"

"What do you mean?"

"I asked what you want in return for doing me a favor and you ask for something for your sister." He shook his head, confused by her. "I'll see about increasing police patrols here and providing security after dark."

"You got some money stashed away or something?" His trust fund was locked up tight until he met his father's requirements, but Max didn't know she knew that, or that she was proud of him for resisting the allure of the money.

His expression tightened at her jest. "I have connections around here. If you help me, I can make things happen for you, Cat."

Disappointment sank in her stomach like a rock. Maybe Max was more like his father than he cared to admit.

CHAPTER 6

J ust looking over at Catherine in the driver's seat soothed Max's nerves and steeled his backbone. Her hair caught the sunlight, the hidden strands of red turning fiery among the spun gold. He had to resist the urge to reach out and touch its silkiness.

"You're free to say no," he said.

She arched an eyebrow, but didn't look away from the road. "I know."

"I wouldn't ask if this weren't important. My parents and I..." Damn. Where to begin? "We don't get along. Haven't since I was in high school. That's when my brother died, killed by a drunk driver." All the pressures that had been heaped upon the firstborn had transferred to their only other child.

Her grip on the wheel tightened. "I'm sorry."

"He was no angel, but his death changed everything for me. I'd watched Mike struggle with the future laid out before him, seen him turn to alcohol and drugs and make increasingly bad decisions. And then he made the worst decision of his life when he let some drunk guy give him a ride home. I enlisted in the Navy after graduation, just to get off the ranch. I was trying to find myself."

"Is that where you got the nickname Gypsy?"

He laughed. She must have overheard Einstein call him that. "Yeah. I wouldn't talk about my past and liked to go wherever the wind took me, as long as it was far away from home. Einstein and I served together, got hurt together"—he was definitely glossing over *that* story—"and were discharged together. When I had nowhere to go, he recommended SSAM. He's from Chicago and had heard of the great things SSAM did. He applied for a job there and encouraged me to do the same. It seemed only natural to see where the wind was taking me this time."

"To the windy city." Her soft lips curved.

"Exactly."

"And did you? Find yourself, I mean?" She sounded wistful. She'd worked at SSAM for five years, about a year less than him, but he didn't know much about her personal life. She'd always symbolized home base at SSAM, but he'd kept himself distant in many ways. Now, he realized he wanted to understand her. What hurdles had she overcome to land at SSAM? And what was she still running from?

"I don't know, but I was doing a damn good job being satisfied with life until yesterday."

"You really don't like your parents, do you?"

"They're controlling. They've done things…" More stories he would avoid. She didn't need to know the nasty details. "They have definite plans for me and that starts with me staying at their ranch for the next several weeks while I recuperate."

"If you don't want to be there, why not just say no?"

"They're powerful in this area." He stopped, thinking about how his life would have been different if he'd allowed their influence to open channels for him that would have been closed to everyone else.

Catherine gasped. "They're the reason the manhunt was off limits to SSAM."

"Excellent guess. If I accept their terms, they'll grease the wheels for Damian. I want to make that happen more than anything, but I'm afraid if I'm around them for long, I'll lose it and make things worse. The past is bound to bubble up to the surface while I'm here."

"That's why you need a buffer."

He met her gaze. "That's why I need *you*. You have a way of diffusing tension. I feel calmer just being around you."

She glanced at him, thoughtful, then looked back at the road. Her knuckles had turned white on the steering wheel. "If I say yes, what would the sleeping arrangements be?"

He wished she'd look at him so he could read her expression. Was she afraid of being at the ranch with him, or was she excited at the possibilities? He couldn't help the surge of anticipation that shot through him at the thought of having Catherine so close by, and practically all to himself.

Only to convince her to remain at SSAM, his conscience reminded him.

He couldn't have her in his bed, no matter how much he wanted her there. Sex would change everything. Besides, he'd already told her he wanted a just-friends relationship. His gaze went to her lips and his gut tightened. He was a fool to reject an attractive, intelligent, caring woman, but he had his reasons, a credo he lived by that had served him well. Near the top of the list was to never get involved with a SSAM coworker because the relationship wouldn't last, leaving only awkwardness. Still, he couldn't imagine things being awkward with Catherine. She was as dependable as the moon and tides.

He shoved his primal urges aside. "I'll be in the main house. You'd be in the detached guesthouse." Would it be far enough away for him to keep his desires in check?

She nodded, but still didn't respond. He wanted to see those baby blues, wanted to know her thoughts. Was she disappointed or relieved?

"This must be it." She pulled the Jeep up to the curb in front of a modest suburban three-bedroom home and unlatched her seatbelt.

Max reached out to touch her arm, halting her. "Come to dinner tonight at the ranch. You don't have to make any decisions about moving in right now." She didn't answer. "Just think about it."

At the door, Damian answered and grinned at Catherine. "What a nice surprise. Glad to have you back. Thank you for helping us out last night."

Catherine looked uncomfortable. "Happy to do what I can."

"Einstein will be along shortly," Max said. He'd share their news about the clinic and the brick once they were all settled.

As they moved deeper into the house, Lorena looked up from the sprawl of books and files she'd been studying at the dining room table opposite the kitchen. "There's fresh coffee in the pot. Help yourself."

Max filled a mug for each of them and handed one to Catherine. She looked like she could use a pick-me-up.

"The local authorities are meeting tomorrow," Damian said as they all claimed seats around the table. "We've been invited, but they haven't requested any assistance."

"At least the door is open again." Max was relieved his father had worked so quickly to contact them. Every second Tony was on the run was an opportunity for the convict to hurt someone.

"The prison transport service has confirmed that the driver of the van had been disgruntled after recently being passed over for a raise," Damian said. "It's possible he accepted a bribe from the Circle to take the van on that detour, not realizing it was a suicide mission."

"Any thoughts on where Tony would go?" Lorena asked Max.

Max had thought of little else. "I'd say wherever there's a female population to select from. But he was wounded, and it's still cold at night. Food, shelter, clothing and safety would be his first priorities."

Lorena nodded. "Sexual needs would come later, but not much later. Tony craves that feeling of domination like an addict and he's been behind bars for over a year. That craving has only intensified. Besides, established patterns of behavior aren't easily altered, especially when there's only external motivation to change."

Catherine hugged her arms around her waist. "We have to find him before he hurts someone."

"And we have to find the people after him," Damian reminded them. "The people who hurt Max."

Max nodded. "They're even more dangerous." While in prison, Max had foiled a couple attempts by the Circle to harm or kill Tony. Inmates had been paid well and supplied a weapon. "There has to be something Tony didn't tell us. Otherwise, why would the Circle go to such lengths to kill him? Could it be about Samantha's murder?"

"The thought crossed my mind." Damian suddenly looked exhausted. The sixty-three-year-old was physically fit, but he'd been up all night because of this screw-up.

Frustration and guilt gnawed at Max. "Is the CPD or FBI re-opening their investigation?" Though two decades old, Samantha's case had been high profile due to Damian's position among Chicago's elite and his international business connections. The Chicago Police Department had to be taking note of the recent developments.

"Yes, especially after what happened." Damian's gaze shifted to Catherine and he watched her with concern. After what had happened to her a few weeks ago, it was clear the Circle still had ties to Chicago. Occupied with looking at the files splayed out in front of Lorena, Catherine wasn't paying attention to their conversation. "With Tony's confession, we've got new information about Sam's disappearance and a definite connection to organized crime and human trafficking, so multiple government agencies are getting involved. We're so close to finding the man—the *Boss*—who paid Tony to kidnap Samantha I can nearly taste justice." Damian's jaw tightened. "The attack on Tony only makes me more certain we were on the right track."

"I'll go to dinner." Catherine's sudden statement surprised everyone. Judging by her wide eyes, she'd surprised herself.

Max's body went taut. "You're sure?"

Damian's gaze moved between them. "What's this?"

"My father made a deal. He'll help SSAM get involved with the manhunt," Max explained.

"And in exchange?"

"I move onto the ranch for a few weeks. I'm trying to entice Cat to be my backup." He grinned at her, but she didn't relax.

"You don't have to do that," Damian said. "I could find another way."

But that would cost precious days and Tony could be well away from here or have done serious harm by then. "This is quicker. And it's a small sacrifice if SSAM gets more information on Samantha's murder *and* takes down the Circle. My father already made some calls and that's why you've been able to make contact with the authorities."

Damian studied him a long moment, then nodded. "As long as you're okay with it."

The front door opened and closed. A moment later, Einstein stepped into the kitchen and glanced over at the table where they'd gathered.

Catherine looked up. "How's Rachel?"

"I made sure she's in good hands." Einstein snatched an energy drink from the refrigerator and leaned against the counter as he popped the tab. "The police agreed to have someone patrol the area almost constantly, especially when they saw the symbol on the brick."

"What symbol?" Lorena asked. "What brick? And who's Rachel?"

"I was working up to what we found this morning," Max said. "A homemade brick was thrown through the window of the clinic where Catherine's sister Rachel is a doctor. There was a symbol stamped on it—a ring of fire."

Lorena's jaw dropped. "The Circle's symbol."

"Not only did they send people after Tony, but they must have an active contingent here in San Antonio and they're targeting that clinic for some reason."

"We wondered if the brick was from the guy who came in with a gun," Catherine said.

Max swung to her. "What guy with a gun?"

"Yesterday, a guy came into the clinic and demanded painkillers."

"Why am I just now hearing about this?"

"The Circle was involved in drugs in Chicago and New York, so maybe they are here, too. Maybe the painkillers weren't for him, though he did seem to be suffering. When I took him to the ground—"

Max scrubbed a hand down his face, attempting to cling to his patience. "*You* took him to the ground? Why didn't you run? Call the police?"

Her smooth forehead wrinkled. "He was only a few feet away and I wasn't about to leave my sister and the others who were there at his mercy, especially when I saw the gun at his waist. I've been taking self-defense classes, so..."

So that made her an expert in dealing with a drug addict with a weapon? *Jesus.* His heart was tapping out a staccato rhythm against his ribcage at the image of Catherine lying prone, shot and bleeding out on the waiting room linoleum.

She must have sensed his distress, because she put a hand on his arm. "I was scared, but we're all okay. Rachel called the police and the man—Lee—was taken away." But Max got the impression she was leaving something out. She seemed so cool, so emotion-less, as if the incident hadn't bothered her. But deep down, it had to have made an impact. She was good at hiding her feelings, and once again Max had the thought that he couldn't get a read on her.

Damian looked to Einstein. "Find out where Lee is now. We should at least see if there's a connection to the vandalism or the Circle."

Tony rubbed his sore, but unrestrained, wrists. The cuffs *had* come in handy as a weapon against the husband. A lethal one, he thought, grinning as he recalled the man crumpling to the floor after Tony had strangled him. And then he'd found a way to pick the lock and free his hands. He still wished it had been Mrs. Bossy who'd been home alone. Then again, he'd have taken more time to enjoy her...and that would have been dangerous.

He touched his temple. Thankfully, the blood from the wound there was still dry and his dark hair mostly hid the two-inch gash. A new set of clothes, courtesy of the dead husband, covered the rest of Tony's body. He could blend in again.

An SAPD cruiser drove by the end of the alley. Tony hunched further against the brick wall where he'd been camped for over an hour, concealed beside a dumpster and underneath a shabby blanket he'd found.

Remembering the Circle had eyes everywhere, but particularly in this area, he glanced around nervously. It was the middle of the day, but the alley was cast in shadow and empty. There was no safer place than hiding right under the noses of his enemies. And he'd be even safer once he made a deal with the Boss.

He wasn't going back to prison and he wasn't going to let the Circle take him down without a fight. He was counting on his former employer having a presence at Lucky Dick's, the gentle-men's club within these walls. That was how the Circle operated, using strip clubs, restaurants and loan facilities as fronts for its illicit activities. Sometimes they even used the clubs as farming grounds for their international sex trafficking operation known as the Cattle Call.

Tony had found Lucky Dick's in the phonebook at Mrs. Bossy's place and helped himself to Mr. Bossy's car. The dead guy wouldn't need it any more. But Tony had ditched it at least a mile away, not wanting to lead the police to this place.

During his long night on the run, Tony had given his future a lot of thought. His best shot at survival might be to get a message to the Boss and offer up a deal. The Circle would never back down. Not until he was dead. He'd been safer in prison, but he'd rather die than go back there.

He was counting on his lucky charm to buy his freedom. He'd withheld an important piece of information from his interviews with Damian Manchester, something that could lead the authorities to the Boss, something the Boss would pay dearly to make disappear.

A large Saturday night crowd at Lucky Dick's would serve as his disguise. Judging by the roars of approval he heard through the metal door several feet to his right, there was a good number of men to hide among. He'd see if he could scrounge up something to eat and watch for his man.

If the Circle followed its normal operating procedures, there would be a low-rung guy camped out at a strip club, awaiting instructions on a new drop or pickup or staking out the merchandise, looking to find a candidate for their human trafficking ring. The identification of quality flesh had been Tony's favorite part of the job. The Circle might be difficult to penetrate, but once you were in, you worked your way up from the bottom. Tony had been there twenty-five years ago and had gone to prison while he'd been damn close to the top. He'd been stupid and lazy and got caught by SSAM. Then he'd been cocky and greedy and let Damian Manchester encourage him to talk. Now he was on someone's hit list.

But this time he was going to be smart.

The back door swung open and a man in a grease-smeared apron ducked out back, using a crate to prop the door open. He didn't notice Tony as he fumbled in his pocket, all of his focus on getting to his smoke. He stabbed a cigarette between his lips, lit it and pulled out his cell phone. He moved down the alley to get better reception and watch the street traffic.

Tony ducked inside the open door. He could have used the front door, now that his cuffs and orange jumpsuit were gone, but he didn't know the bouncer and the guy might be on the lookout for Tony, depending on how far the Circle had infiltrated this club. Tony's two gold teeth were a sure giveaway to his identity. The management could be bribed, possibly, but Tony didn't have any money. Unfortunately, Mr. Bossy hadn't stashed any extra cash around the house for wayward travelers.

Inside the club, the pumping music and gyrating female body on stage instantly lifted his mood. He shifted along the outer edge of the room, covertly scanning the occupants at the tables, but the dancer distracted him. It had been too long since he'd enjoyed a woman. He stifled a groan as the woman bent to touch her toes, meeting his gaze from between her legs. The old urges flared.

Play it smart. You have a second chance at freedom. Don't get caught.

He *was* smarter now. He wouldn't get caught again. Not by the police, SSAM or the Circle. He would play all the sides against each other and come out the winner, and there would be plenty of women in his future.

"The job was done." Johnny's eyes followed Kim on stage while he talked on the phone. He tried to restrain his excitement, but this could be big for him.

"And the symbol?" the Boss asked.

"I stamped it into the brick myself before I gave it to Lee and he did what I told him to do." Lee would have done anything for

Johnny after he'd given him a few happy pills as payment. "And he was more than willing to show the doctor bitch that she's not in control of the neighborhood." The best part was, Lee would keep his mouth shut and take the fall if he got caught, knowing he'd get more pills from the Circle as a reward once he got back out on the street. It helped to have addicts depending on you for their next fix.

The Boss chuckled. "Oh, this is much bigger than a neighborhood. SSAM will learn they can't mess with the Circle, and none of them are safe."

"I can help. Just tell me what to do."

"You've done enough." The Boss abruptly ended the call.

Johnny ignored his frustration that he might be left out of the next stage of this operation and tried to focus on the good vibes. He pocketed his phone and flagged down Darla. "Another beer."

"You look happy."

"Scored major points at work." He was on his way up the not-so-corporate ladder and it felt amazing. Maybe the Boss would just remember him next time he had a big assignment. Johnny would find a way to stay in the man's good graces.

Darla left to fetch him the beer. A man pulled out a chair at Johnny's table and sat.

Johnny shot him a dark look. "What the hell, man? This table's occupied."

The man shrugged. Two gold teeth flashed as he spoke. "You share with me, I share with you."

"I never did like sharing."

The man glanced at Johnny's hand. "Bet you don't like being low man on the totem pole, either."

Johnny shifted his hand under the table, hiding the tiny tattoo at the base of his thumb—the Circle's symbol. "Don't know what you're talking about."

The man's laugh was like a rock tumbler. "Sure you do, kid."

"I'm no kid." He was twenty-seven, damn it. And he'd more than earned his stripes.

"I guarantee you're just a baby, especially when it comes to dealing with the Circle. And if you get me something to eat and drink, I'll tell you everything you need to grow up and be a man."

Johnny flexed his fingers but resisted the urge to plow his fist into the man's face.

Darla brought his beer and eyed the man with suspicion. "You look familiar."

Come to think of it, he did. "Shit, you're Tony Moreno." The man who had dodged the Circle, evaded the police and been the talk of the town had walked into the club and sat across from Johnny as if he owned the place. Holy fuck, if Johnny could turn this guy over to the Boss, he could name his price. Maybe even get a top-level position. "I should turn you in right now."

"And miss out on the best opportunity of your life?" Tony's grin told Johnny he had a damn good bargaining chip up his sleeve. Nobody was that cocky unless they had an advantage. Tony's head swiveled as he surveyed the room, but the men nearby were too busy ogling the meat onstage to pay them any attention. "I'll tell you more if you get me something to eat."

"How about you eat shit?" Johnny wasn't going to let some freeloader take advantage, especially on Circle territory. Then again, if this man was who he seemed to be and the Circle was after him, he could know things. Secrets that would move Johnny even farther up the ladder. And if Tony didn't have anything good, Johnny could always turn him over to the Circle. It was a win-win. He jerked his head toward Darla. "Bring him the special and a beer and put it on my tab."

"And don't contact the cops, sweetheart," Tony added. "It wouldn't work out well."

"I mind my own business," she said, and then looked at Johnny. "Unless you tell me otherwise." She left to fill the order.

"So, what do you have to say, old man?" Johnny asked, impatient to get to the good stuff.

"I'll talk when I get the beer."

Son of a bitch. Johnny reeled in his anger, showing nothing on the outside. Thankfully, Darla was quick and returned a moment later.

Tony took a sip of beer and let it sit on his tongue a moment before swallowing. "Give me a moment. This is my first taste of freedom in over a year."

"I doubt you'll taste freedom for long."

"Don't even think it, kid." Tony took another long sip of his beer, his eyes moving to the stage. "What I have to tell you is infinitely more valuable than my hide."

"I doubt it."

"I know the ins and outs. Drug dealing, shakedowns, human trafficking… I bet they have you doing the dirty work for all of the above."

Johnny shrugged. "I'm a man of many talents."

"And I'd bet once those talents are no longer of use to them and someone more talented comes along, or you end up in jail, they'll cut their ties."

Is that what had happened to Tony? "No, man. That's not how it is. They're grooming me to someday take over this area." His gaze flicked to the office door, where Dick had the next job he coveted. Running this club would be a nice promotion. Or maybe Johnny could skip right over that to the next level.

Tony's cackle made Johnny's insides itch. "You keep believing that."

Darla returned with a plate of sliders and fries, sent Johnny a questioning look and hurried away again when he nodded. Tony laid into the plate like it was his last meal. *It might be, at that.* Johnny grinned.

"I know what you're thinking," Tony said around a mouthful of hamburger. His gold teeth winked briefly. "You can be the one to turn me in if you choose, but give me a few days to show you how it really is. I know stuff, things that could accelerate your career in amazing ways. Otherwise, why would the Circle try to kill me? I'm already in prison for life." He grinned. "Or I was supposed to be."

He had a point. "What do you want from me?"

"I need a place to hide out for a couple days and I want to get a message to the Boss."

"What message?"

"That if he wants to work with me again, I'm open to the idea. But if he fucks with me, his real identity will be known to all the world, including Damian Manchester."

CHAPTER 7

"Why would Tony kill the homeowner?" Catherine's fatigue compounded at the thought of the senseless violence. It had been a hell of a long day, starting with the brick through Rachel's window, which was somehow connected to the Circle, and followed by the meeting at the SSAM house and hours spent scouring the neighborhood closest to where Tony had escaped—where Tony had, in fact, hid out until he'd killed a homeowner and ditched his prison clothes. And the day wasn't even over yet. She'd agreed to dinner at the ranch. "This murder only adds to his list of crimes."

"One more wouldn't matter to Tony. He's in prison for several life sentences already." Max sat down hard on the couch in the living room of the SSAM rental and rubbed at his temples. He'd taken the news of Tony's latest victim hard, blaming himself. She was tempted to wrap her arms around him, but resisted. Getting close to him would only lead to heartache. They were alone, but the rest of the team, driving a separate car, would arrive after they'd grabbed some dinner.

Instead of taking the seat next to him, Catherine noted the

tired lines on his face and kept walking, going to the kitchen and pulling a couple water bottles from the fridge before returning to the living room and handing him one.

"Thanks." He slugged back half the bottle.

She sat on the far end of the couch, toed off her shoes and drank from her own bottle. "You still plan to go to dinner at your parents'?" It was already early evening.

Max looked toward the hallway that led to the bedrooms. "Thought I might grab a shower first, but yeah, I'm still going, especially after today. We may need Dad's help. I had hoped to catch Tony before he hurt anyone, but..." He stopped and took another swallow of water.

The memory of the victim's wife and young son being questioned outside the home, their faces a portrait of shock and grief, twisted Catherine's insides as well. "You are not responsible for that man's death."

He looked up sharply. "You sound so certain about that."

"I am." She injected as much ferocious faith as she could into her statement. "You're a good person. Tony isn't. He's the one who did this."

Max digested this a moment, but didn't respond. Instead, he finished the rest of his water and stood. "I'm going to take a shower."

"I'll go change, too, and come back in about an hour to pick you up. Unless..." She eyed his sling. "Do you have everything you need?"

His lips twitched. "You offering to scrub my back?" He paused a moment as if it were a genuine invitation. "No, I'll be fine. My bag's in Einstein's room. The others should be back soon if I need anything. I'm glad you were there today. It helped."

Along with Einstein, Lorena, Damian and the SAPD officers, they'd been able to check out the rest of the homes in the neighborhood. It seemed Tony had done his damage and left the area. He'd been on the run now for twenty-two hours, and there was no sign of him. And now he had a vehicle. He could be anywhere.

She shook her head. "I'm not sure I was useful, but it felt good to try."

"Are you kidding? You convinced those SAPD officers to let us ride along with them. And then you held off the press, giving them just the right amount and type of information to sate their appetites but protect the investigation."

"The liaison from the Marshals office had something to do with that."

"No, he gave the bullet points. You repackaged them in a way that made the press think they were getting a deal."

She'd learned how to use tact, confidence and charm as effective tools during her time as an assistant at SSAM, working with victims' families and the press, but she was uncomfortable with Max's praise. It wouldn't be too much longer before he came to see those qualities as tools of manipulation. For now, she would do what she could to ease the heaviness she sensed in his heart and soul. And she'd help him with his parents, for as long as she was welcome to. Maybe she'd found her purpose after all.

"THAT'S THE TREE WHERE I FIRST DISLOCATED MY SHOULDER." As they got closer to his parents' ranch house, Max pointed out Catherine's window to the ancient oak he'd climbed many times during his youth. The waning rays of the sun had turned the trunk and branches a pinkish orange.

His statement seemed to break through Catherine's distraction. "You've dislocated it before?"

"A couple times. But I'd always been able to pop it back in place." Either against a sturdy post or wall or with the aid of his SEAL buddies. "The last time, I used a boulder."

She was fully focused on him now. "In Afghanistan?"

He nodded. "Our final mission. We'd been hiking through

rocky terrain when an explosion threw us to the ground." The impact had popped his shoulder out of place. And he'd injured his knee. He'd had to ignore the pain while carrying an unconscious team member back to the extraction point. Two of their team had died that day, and he and Einstein had come stateside with a haunted look in their eyes that lasted long after the physical wounds had been rehabbed. But catching killers with SSAM had gone a long way toward healing the nonphysical damage.

"Does it hurt much now?" Concern crinkled her forehead and nose. Still, she looked beautiful.

She's off limits. It was torture to look at her and not be able to touch. "Only a little."

Blue eyes narrowed on him. "Which means it *does* hurt. You don't have to be Superman. Why won't you take a pill to manage the pain, at least for a day or two?"

"I thought your sister was the doctor." His shoulder was throbbing like a son of a bitch but he'd thought he was hiding it well. However, he wasn't above using her concern to get what he needed. "I could use a nurse to help keep me on track for the next few weeks. You up for the job?"

She looked away, treating him to her profile again. The curve of her cheek was soft, the extension of her neck long and smooth. She projected the same quiet grace with which she seemed to handle everything at SSAM, and probably everything in life. Still, beneath her calm exterior, he sensed something had her running scared—all the way to Texas.

He struggled to keep his distance. A SEAL, even a former one, was nothing without his beliefs, and Max believed was that he was meant to be a perennial bachelor, unattached to anybody who could either use his name or money or be hurt by those same things. While Catherine wasn't the type to use people, she could end up as collateral damage in the crossfire of his relationship with his parents. Yet here he was, letting her drive into a bad situation, wanting her to stay there with him. He should tell her to drop him off and leave, but he was just selfish enough to keep her by his side as long as she'd let him.

She leaned forward to peer through the windshield as the ranch came into view. "It's breathtaking."

He tried to see the place through her eyes. A sprawling single-story ranch house hugged a flat portion of the property, but in the distance, gentle hills bubbled up from the land, dotted with scrub bushes and pecan, oak, crabapple and ash trees and sprinkled with wildflowers. Half a mile away, a lake provided water for the cattle and a cooling off area for the cowboys. "The house needs a paint job, though. Dad's probably too busy."

"Well, he does have a large business to run. He's probably not here much."

"How'd you know that?"

She shot him a look, but quickly refocused on pulling into the circular drive and parking. "Growing up around here, I must have heard about Caulfield Industries somewhere."

Reluctant to leave the comfort of the Jeep and Catherine's company, he turned to look at her. "It's nice to have someone with me who has my back, you know?"

"Any of those girlfriends you tossed aside would have been happy to look out for you if you'd given them more than a few hours of your time."

So she'd noticed his dating habits. He found that interesting... and disturbing. He didn't want to think of her along with those come-and-go women. "Those women were just looking out for themselves."

"Maybe you don't give the female gender enough credit."

He paused to acknowledge the truth in that statement and then scanned her face for signs of judgment. He didn't see it there. "Maybe I don't give *some* members of your gender enough credit, but that's due to experience. Be on your guard with my parents." They'd tear her apart if they sensed weakness.

"I'm sure I've dealt with worse."

Catherine got out of the car and walked to the door, chin up, ready to face anything because he'd asked her to. She was a true friend. Warmth hit him square in the chest and radiated outward, dangerously close to thawing his heart and making him forget why he'd kept it frozen all this time.

At the front door, Catherine halted and resisted the urge to wipe her sweaty palms on her jeans. She'd known she'd have to face the Caulfields again, but hadn't expected it to be under these circumstances. She'd have preferred to deal with Hayworth and Lillian at Caulfield Industries, on more neutral territory, and certainly not with Max within hearing distance.

Then again, he'd need to know the truth at some point. Would his parents unmask her? Would Max then tell her to get the hell out of his life? How much time did she have left with him—days, minutes, seconds?

She forced herself to take a deep breath. Hayworth and Lillian wouldn't want their son to know the truth unless it was somehow to their advantage. They weren't likely to tell Max they'd helped Catherine get a job at SSAM years ago so she could report back on his every move, or that they'd been desperate for the opportunity to lure him back into the family fold.

She waited for Max to open the door and was surprised when he stopped beside her and rang the doorbell. Seeing her arched eyebrows, he shrugged. "Haven't been home in a while. And it's not really my home anymore. I haven't had a home in…years."

"That must be difficult." This whole situation was a challenge for both of them, but they'd each done what they had to do to survive. She'd made choices to spare her father further pain and make a good life for Rachel. For that, she couldn't be sorry.

Catherine squared her shoulders like a soldier preparing for battle. The front door opened.

"I'm so glad you came." Lillian smiled at her son. The smile slipped as her gaze landed on Catherine, but she quickly shored it up again. It appeared they were continuing with the charade for now. "Hello."

"This is Catherine Montague." Max pulled Catherine in front of him. The thought of a big, tough warrior using her as a shield nearly dragged a laugh from her.

"It's nice to meet you." Catherine held out her hand, keeping up with the pretense.

Lillian took it with her cool smooth one. "Likewise. Anyone who can bring our son back to us is welcome in our home."

Catherine hid her shock at the sincere, if lukewarm, welcome. She'd half expected the door to slam in her face.

Max leaned down to speak in Catherine's ear as his mother turned away. "Don't be fooled. They can be accommodating when it suits them."

Catherine tried not to stare as she followed Lillian to a sitting room just off the foyer. Twenty-foot vaulted ceilings with rough-hewn wooden beams gave the house a warm, rustic feel that was unexpected. Somehow, Catherine had envisioned a cold, marble mausoleum. In all her years working for the Caulfields, even before her move to Chicago to watch over Max, she'd never been to the ranch. Log cabin style furnishings, copper statues of cowboys in the saddle, roping stray calves, old horseshoes, Indian blankets in warm colors and a bull's whitewashed skull decorated the walls and tables.

"I'll have some iced tea brought in. Unless you'd prefer something else?" Lillian's uncertainty tugged at something inside Catherine. It must be tough for a mother to be unsure of her son's love, or even his beverage of choice.

Max waved his mother off. "Tea would be fine." He sat on the couch and patted the cushion next to his uninjured side. Catherine obediently sat.

"Your father will be along shortly. He was on a conference call. I reminded him it's a weekend, but—"

"It's okay. How are you, Mom?"

Her face softened at the endearment, and moisture shimmered in her eyes. Catherine had never seen the woman cry. Lillian was tough as a rangy Texas longhorn.

"I'm okay. I'd be better if I'd been invited to my son's wedding." Lillian sniffed and shot a look at Catherine, whose hands grew suddenly clammy as her skin flushed.

"We're not—" Catherine's admission was interrupted as Max put a hand over hers.

"She knows we're not technically married," he said. "Yet." He met Catherine's shocked gaze. What was this new game? He squeezed her hand as if willing her to submit.

Lillian's ruthlessly assessing gaze moved between the two of them, then narrowed on Catherine's left hand, noting the absence of a ring. Lillian looked up and smiled. "There's still time."

"Time for what?" Max's words were spoken with the same ominous undercurrent he used when stalking a threat, but usually that threat took the form of a serial killer. He interlaced his fingers with Catherine's and gently squeezed. Heat shot to her core. He was using her as a barrier to keep his mother's machinations at bay, and perhaps she should feel affronted, but at the moment, she couldn't care less.

Time to get rid of her? Time to talk some sense into their son? The Caulfields knew how to use their money and influence to make things happen, the outcome always in their favor.

"It's understandable your mother is concerned." Catherine adopted a tone one might use to soothe an angry beast. Outwardly, Max looked calm and composed, but she sensed he was in combat mode, expecting an attack.

"Dear, could you help me in the kitchen with the tea?" Lillian was looking at Catherine.

Max put his mouth by her ear to whisper, "Don't let her wear you down."

In the back corner of the house, the pristine chef's kitchen held the heavenly scent of fresh-baked bread. An older, honey-skinned woman bustled about, loading a tray with a pitcher of iced tea and all of the accompaniments. She looked up with a start as they entered. "I was just about to bring it in, ma'am."

Lillian waved a hand. "Excuse us for a moment, Claudia. And could you please send Mr. Caulfield in here right away?" With a nod, the woman left. Lillian waited until the door closed before turning on Catherine. "What do you think you're doing, trying to entrap my son? Is this why you haven't sent a report in weeks? You've been too busy manipulating Max into a relationship?"

Catherine felt her cheeks flush with guilt, and knew it weakened her attempt at a confident exterior. Should she tell them she wasn't engaged to Max, wasn't planning on it—that she was, in fact, the furthest thing from his ideal woman? Or should she let Max continue to use her as a shield and absorb the blows for him? She'd rarely given detailed reports to the Caulfields, glossing over the particulars of Max's life to give him some privacy. They'd constantly asked for more information, and she'd had to hold them off. She'd agreed to be Max's buffer here tonight and that's what she was going to do. "I did what I had to do."

"Which tells me very little, as usual." Lillian's lips pursed as if she'd sucked one of the bright yellow lemon wedges lying in a small bowl on the tray. "You're not the first woman with greedy claws I've had to pry off my son, but I thought you knew better than to cross us, after all we've done for you and your family. You'd do well to remember to whom you owe your debt."

Hayworth entered the kitchen. "What's this powwow about?" His gaze narrowed on Catherine. "You didn't return my calls or texts."

"Max brought her," Lillian said. "He's implying they might get engaged."

Hayworth's gaze turned calculating and businesslike. "You did get him back here, I suppose."

Lillian whirled on him. "We can't let *her* marry our son."

"Well, of course not, but she had to get close to him to make him fall in line."

Catherine stiffened against the storm of emotions their exchange had stirred up. She was from the other side of the tracks and had a convict for a father to prove it. These were the reasons she worked for the Caulfields, who were tied to her family, to her history, in a horribly mangled way.

But some blessings had also come of their terrible past. Catherine's job with the Caulfields had helped her give Rachel a good life and a bright future, and kept the media from attacking her father and dredging up his mistakes over and over again. But no matter what she'd done for the Caulfields or their son, she was, and always would be, the hired help.

And the daughter of the man who'd killed their oldest son.

She should remember her place—and her debt. She'd walked away because her heart had gone too soft to deceive Max anymore. She'd come to care too much for him. And where had that landed her? Even deeper in the manure the Caulfields were shoveling.

"She should continue the ruse for now." Hayworth arched a brow at her. "I assume this *is* a ruse. I mean, how will Max feel when he learns your family is responsible for our family's pain?" They all knew the answer to that, so Catherine didn't bother to reply. "When you didn't report back last month, I assumed you'd gone AWOL."

"I kind of did." She'd been dutiful and punctual in sending her monthly report until she'd taken a personal leave from SSAM and everything else in her life to reassess her goals.

"I beg your pardon?"

"I kind of did go AWOL. I was preparing to hand in my resignation."

Lillian's cheeks flamed. "You can't quit now. Our son needs you."

"But you just said…" Catherine shook her head as if to clear the confusion.

"Well, of course I don't want you to marry him, but you're our only source of information at the moment. He does seem to lean on you and he'll need someone to help him with adjusting back to his life in Texas, the life he had before he went astray. I figure it'll take a few weeks to get back in the rhythm, and then you can disappear."

They actually expected her to make Max love her and then break things off. What they didn't seem to understand was that one couldn't *make* Max do anything he didn't want to do.

Hayworth cleared his throat. "What'll it take to have you stick by his side for a few more weeks, just until he's recovered? We want him to stay here at the ranch and learn the business by working at CI. Once he sees the possibilities, I'm sure he'll make the right choice for his future and stick around."

Catherine nearly laughed out loud. "He'll never agree to that." Max, at Caulfield Industries, working nine-to-five in a suit and tie? They really didn't know their son at all. But was that their fault? Despite working for the Caulfields for years, she didn't know the full story. She'd come to work for them shortly after Max had joined the military. He'd turned his back on them. Was the wedge between them because of the car accident that had claimed his brother's life?

The guilt swamped her, and reminded her of her obligations to her own family. When Hayworth had approached her months after her father had gone to prison, offering her a job, it had seemed like a godsend. Despite Hayworth's loss, he'd pitied her family's plight. He'd eased the sting by giving Catherine a steady job at CI when she'd needed one, paying Rachel's way through college and medical school and ensuring their father no longer had to deal with the media's spin on what had happened that night. But at what cost? Her soul. Her sense of obligation had made her do things she wouldn't normally do. She'd paid her dues and then some.

Except Max still needed her. SSAM needed her. She could run

interference and make sure the Caulfields didn't disrupt the investigation to suit their own purposes.

Hayworth sensed her concerns. "We'll let Max choose for himself—once he's given CI a try. He can't make an educated decision unless he gives it a chance. If you support the idea of Max staying at the ranch and working at CI while he gets a bit of therapy for his shoulder, we'll do the rest."

"And in return?" Catherine hated how callous she sounded, but greed and business were two things Hayworth understood and respected.

"We'll pay you for the added time. And we'll continue with our usual arrangement as well." Meaning they wouldn't make things worse for her dad.

An idea formed in her mind. She'd never taken money for herself that she hadn't earned as a regular wage at CI or SSAM. She hadn't been able to stomach accepting payment for spying on Max. Besides, Damian paid her a comfortable salary. Every extra penny had gone toward Rachel's education and her father's defense attorney. Her sister had graduated, but still needed help. Even if Max came through on his promise to find security for Rachel's clinic in the evenings, it wasn't a long-term solution. "There is something I need."

Hayworth smirked, sensing triumph. "Everyone has their price. Name yours."

"I want you to rent the vacant building on Elm Street for my sister and relocate the Pecan Grove Clinic. If you leak to the public that you're helping fund a service that's such a benefit to the area, it will only help your image."

Lillian looked thoughtful. "And Max's image when he runs for office someday."

"Done," Hayworth said.

That had been too easy. As she followed Hayworth and Lillian back to the sitting room, Catherine couldn't help thinking she'd just allowed the Caulfields to get the better end of the deal and buy her like a ten-dollar whore. Again.

MAX WAS JUST GETTING OFF THE PHONE WHEN CATHERINE WALKED in with his parents. She appeared unscathed, but refused to meet his gaze. He had the distinct impression something significant had happened, but he couldn't read her expression. It was irritating not knowing what went on in her head. He'd never wanted to understand a woman as much as he wanted to understand her.

He observed his parents, who were looking smug and satisfied. What had he missed? He would have gone looking for Catherine several minutes ago if he hadn't received an important call from Damian.

"We brought refreshments." His mother set the tray, which held a pitcher of iced tea and four glasses, on the coffee table. "Dinner will be ready in twenty minutes."

His father stopped in the middle of the room and examined Max. "Looking good, Son."

Max was surprised at the wave of emotion that hit him as he assessed his father right back. Frustration, anger and…pity. He hadn't noticed earlier, while he'd been sedated or intent on figuring out a deal with his father, but now he saw what time had done to Hayworth Caulfield. The crags defining his features had deepened. Shadows skirted eyes that had lost some of their brightness. Was he sick?

Max shot a questioning look at his mother, and was surprised to notice there were more wrinkles on her face, too, though she looked fresh and crisp in a flower-patterned blouse and pressed slacks, her hair carefully styled by her hairdresser.

Of course, time apart accentuated these differences. Between tours in Afghanistan and then working in Chicago, Max had only returned for a couple quick, obligatory holiday visits over the past twelve years. His parents hadn't ventured out of Texas to visit him.

"Glad you could get out here," his father said. "And it's nice to meet your friend and future...*wife?*"

"We haven't worked out all of the details," Max winked at Catherine, hoping it would reassure her. She gave him a small smile in return.

His father cleared his throat. "Right. Maybe you'd prefer something stronger than tea? We can celebrate your homecoming."

"He's on pain pills," Catherine said. "Or he should be." Her protectiveness touched him. When had he ever had someone in his life who put his needs first, without expectation of gain?

"How well do you two know each other?" Lillian asked the question as she poured out the tea and stepped forward with glasses for each of them.

Max put an arm around her waist, wanting to ask her what had put the shadows in her eyes. What had his parents said to her? She stood stiffly next to him and he skimmed his hand up her back and beneath the soft waterfall of her hair to lightly knead her neck. "She's been a good friend for years."

"She works with you?"

"She's the glue that holds SSAM together." And she'd glued him back together a few times, after the frustration and disappointment of failed missions had nearly torn him apart. Seeing the death and destruction that hardened killers created could weigh on a person's heart, but Catherine always had a warm smile and an encouraging word—and often, home baked goods—waiting to lift the troops up again when they returned to home base.

"It's easy when we work for a great boss." Catherine turned to him. "Is that who was on the phone right now?"

"Yes. The SAPD found a body at a truck stop on the edge of town, just twenty minutes from here."

"Another victim?"

"The SAPD isn't sure yet if it's connected to Tony, although the female appears to have been sexually assaulted before her murder. We're waiting for the coroner's report."

"I can help expedite that," his father said.

Max frowned. "For a price, I'm sure."

Just like that, his father's warmth was gone. Back was the sharp, steely gaze of an astute CEO. "Maybe we should talk in the other room, Son."

Son. "Whatever you have to say can be said in front of Catherine." She stiffened under his hand and he resumed the gentle pressure against her neck.

"We have a business proposal on the table."

"And dangling the cooperation of the local authorities as a carrot is your way of ensuring you get what you want."

"We'll both get what we want, at minimal cost."

Max released a humorless chuckle. "It's always business with you, even with your children." Mike had turned to alcohol and drugs. Max had run away from home. And still, their father pushed his agenda. When Mike had chosen a dark path, Max hadn't been able to save him. He'd been making up for that waste of life ever since, determined to create an existence he could be proud of.

Then again, Mike hadn't had anybody in his life to turn to. Nobody with a warm, understanding smile waiting at the end of the day—nobody like Catherine.

"Let's drop this argument," his mother said. "We have a guest."

Catherine's neck muscles bunched beneath his hand again, and no amount of massaging would loosen them. Who was his mother fooling? She never talked about Mike, guests or not, and if others brought up his name, she shut them down fast.

"You can settle into your room after dinner," his mother said. "And you'll show Catherine to the guesthouse."

"I'm staying with my sister in town," Catherine said.

Disappointment flooded Max. He'd told her she could choose her course of action and she was choosing to keep her distance. He couldn't blame her.

"We insist." His mother nailed Catherine with an over-bright smile. "You'll have more privacy and I'm sure you'll see your sister often. Max will need a driver to take him to CI every day, anyway." She turned her megawatts on Max. "We'll have a therapist come by as soon as you're cleared to start working on your shoulder. Your dad's planning to install a state-of-the-art gym in the old barn he converted into a garage."

Max felt a noose squeezing off his airway. "Let's be clear. I'm not planning to stay in Texas. I'm not a businessman." He'd tried like hell to never become one. To become like his father—rigid, eye on the bottom line, unsatisfied with what he had—unsatisfied with the son he had. Always wanting more. "I don't think I can give you what you need."

His father scowled. "With one word, I can use my influence to get the coroner to move fast on identifying that dead body. The Caulfield name opens doors, Son. To you, to Catherine, to SSAM and your precious mentor."

Was that jealousy...of *Damian*? The idea was ridiculous, yet once it took root, Max was surprised to find it fit. Hayworth Caulfield wouldn't tolerate yielding to the competition in any aspect of his life, even fatherhood. And he was right. Max would do anything for Damian Manchester, who was a father figure—steadfast, loyal, dedicated, understanding—and mentor to his employees. If finding resolution for Damian by locating Tony meant Max had to be a model son to his father for a few weeks, Max would comply. But he didn't think he could do this without his other half.

Max turned Catherine to face him, looking into her fathomless eyes. "What do you say, Cat? Will you help?"

Her smile seemed sad. "If it'll help you...and SSAM."

His chest squeezed. She'd put him—his needs—first, and without any expectation of reward. When had anyone done that before? The answer was immediate. *Never.*

CHAPTER 8

Monday

Max groaned as he slid into the passenger seat. He yanked at the tie around his neck, loosening the knot. "The suits are going to strangle me. They're even worse than this sling."

No matter what he wore, Catherine thought he looked sexy as hell. How was she supposed to serve as his chauffeur day in and day out and still resist him? As it was, his musky scent and natural heat filled her Jeep. "It was only your first day."

"I can't wait to have my equal time at SSAM." As part of the deal with his father, Max could spend equal time on the manhunt, but Hayworth had demanded all of his son's time for his first day at the office. Besides, Max had spent yesterday with Damian and the others, coordinating with the authorities and scouring neighborhoods. There'd been no new leads on Tony's location, but there'd also been no new murders. Catherine had spent the day at

Rachel's place, unloading the trailer and then returning it to the rental place before moving into the ranch's guesthouse. She hadn't told Rachel exactly who she was going to be staying with, just that Catherine would be with a friend, and only for a few days—she hoped. Telling Rachel about moving onto the Caulfield ranch would only generate an onslaught of difficult questions.

"First, we focus on getting you healthy. Damian's orders." Catherine pulled into the hospital parking lot and walked Max inside. She was tall enough that normally her long strides could match his, but he seemed in a hurry. "Looks like you can't wait to get out of that sling."

Inside the lobby, he caught her hand and tugged her to a stop. His thumb brushed over her wrist, making her pulse jump. "Thank you. And not just for being my driver. You're a good friend. I couldn't ask for better." He scanned her face as if he wanted to say more but thought it might not be welcome.

Uncomfortable with his gratitude, she simply nodded and sat in the waiting area off the lobby while he went into his appointment. She tried to phone Rachel at the clinic, but Teresa informed her that, an hour ago, her sister had run out suddenly without explanation.

Max came down the hall twenty minutes later, his eyebrows arching as he scanned her face. "What's wrong?"

"I can't reach Rachel. She left the clinic suddenly, and she's not answering her cell."

"Let's go." He took her arm, and that's when Catherine realized he wasn't wearing his sling.

"You're healed?" She pulled him to a stop and couldn't resist running her hands over his now free arm. "That's fantastic."

"Not totally healed. It'll take time to get back to full function." Max held up the sling and a sheaf of papers in his other hand. "Doc recommended exercises to regain the strength in my shoulder. But I only have to wear the sling part of the time. I decided I'd give it a break for the evening."

"That's wonderful." She bit her lip against a wave of relief.

His gaze fell to her mouth. His nostrils flared as he sucked in a breath and seemed to focus again. "Let's go look for your sister."

"No, that's okay. You wanted to work with Lorena on Tony's profile tonight." Hayworth had encouraged the Marshals to let Lorena present the profile tomorrow to the group hunting for Tony. Understanding the escaped convict's personality and habits might help them find the man. "She's expecting you."

"It can wait."

"No, it can't. Tony's killed at least one person, and could be targeting more innocent people. The coroner was supposed to get the report on that female victim back to the team today, too, right?" Even with Hayworth's connections, identifying the victim had taken a couple days. The unknown woman's features had been sliced, and she'd been stabbed multiple times. Catherine suppressed a shudder. "I'll drop you off at the SSAM house and then go to Rachel's. I'm sure she just wasn't feeling well or something."

He scanned her face, hesitant. But duty to his employer and a need to find Tony won out. "Call me as soon as you find her."

THE INTERIOR OF RACHEL'S TINY BUNGALOW WAS COMPLETELY DARK when Catherine arrived an hour later. Catherine called out softly, wondering if her sister might be asleep. "Rachel?"

"In here." Her sister's voice was weak.

Catherine followed it to the bedroom and found Rachel lying down, her body dimly lit by the sliver of daylight coming in through the closed curtains. "Bedtime already?" she teased, but Rachel was still fully dressed, curled up on top of the covers and facing the window. A hiccup indicated she'd been crying. Catherine sat on the bed and ran a hand down Rachel's back. "What's wrong?"

Rachel swiped at her cheeks and rolled over to look at the ceiling. "It's stupid, really." But her face crumpled. "I lost a patient."

"Someone died?" Catherine looked around as if she expected to see the body lying there. "How? Where?"

"She was murdered. Some savage hacked her up so badly they couldn't identify her right away." A chill of foreboding rippled through Catherine. "Worse, the police came by the hospital today to show me pictures and ask me some questions."

Catherine continued rubbing Rachel's back. "That must have been awful."

"Her name was Bea." Rachel gave a watery laugh. "She was known as Busty Bea at the club where she worked."

"She was an exotic dancer?"

"Yeah, at a place called Lucky Dick's. I guess she had my business card lying around in her apartment. She had an appointment last Friday, but missed it. She missed her shift at the club, too."

"Friday?" Tony hadn't escaped until Friday night. "What happened to her? Where did they find her?"

"A ravine behind a truck stop a few miles from here. She'd been stabbed repeatedly."

So it *was* the same victim. Did the SSAM team know an identification had been made? Had they received the coroner's report?

Suddenly, Rachel shot to her feet. "I can't just sit here, I have to do something." She stumbled and Catherine reached out to steady her.

"Have you eaten today?"

"I may have had a granola bar for breakfast." Rachel's red-rimmed, unfocused gaze turned toward the window.

"Hon, you've had a difficult few days. Sit." Catherine pulled her sister back down onto the bed and wrapped an arm around her shoulders. A patient had threatened her and then nearly pulled a gun on her, a brick had been thrown through her window and another patient had been viciously murdered. It was a lot for anyone to take. "I'm going to run to the supermarket on the corner and get you something to eat. You'd better be sitting here when I get back."

Rachel nodded. "Food would be good."

She nudged Rachel to lie down, then pulled a fuzzy throw blanket from the end of the bed to tuck around her. "I'll take your key and lock your door behind me. I have some good news to share when I get back." She'd wanted to wait for confirmation from Hayworth, but Rachel looked as if she could use a boost, and Hayworth's text this morning had said he was working with the Elm Street building's owner on converting the location into something appropriate for a clinic. It was progress, but it meant Catherine needed to stay at the ranch and make sure he followed through.

Catherine couldn't stand the lost look in Rachel's eyes. "We'll find the person who killed Bea. I have resources, even if the police don't."

Rachel gripped Catherine's hand and urgency filled her voice. "That's right. You work for people who can find this bastard."

She did, though they had their hands full tracking down Tony. And Max would be busy jumping through hoops for his parents. Unless it *was* Tony who'd killed Bea. Catherine would talk to the SSAM group when she returned to the house to pick up Max.

"Let's get some food in you and we'll talk," Catherine said. "I can even stay the night if you want." Einstein could give Max a ride back to the ranch.

"No, I'll be fine. I already feel better knowing we'll be taking action." She was looking better, her eyes now lit with purpose.

"*Me.*"

"What?"

"Me, not we. *I'll* take action. *You* focus on your clinic. You're going to be moving it to that building we talked about."

"What?"

"You'll be relocating." Catherine felt better about her decision to help the Caulfields than she had all weekend. If it would get her sister farther away from the neighborhood where Bea had been killed and closer to the police station, Catherine would do anything to make that happen.

"RACHEL'S OKAY?" MAX ASKED AS HE STOOD ASIDE TO LET Catherine enter the SSAM house.

She steeled herself against the desire to step into his arms as she walked past. She'd never needed anyone before, and she wouldn't succumb to weakness now. Instead, she continued into the living room. "Yes, but she's shaken up." Catherine had texted Max that Rachel was safe while she'd been out picking up food for her sister, but hadn't given him the details. "I need to talk to the team."

"They're outside, on the back porch."

"How are you?" Damian asked as she stepped out to join him, Lorena and Einstein. Max followed, sliding the screen door closed behind him.

"Hanging in there," she said. "Did the coroner send his report?"

"We were just discussing it." Max pulled out a chair and invited her to sit. "Guess my father's prodding helped."

"It was a woman named Beatrice Downing." Einstein pushed the coroner's report toward her.

Catherine didn't need to see the details. "She's also known as Busty Bea. She was an exotic dancer."

Lorena leaned forward. "How do you know that?"

"My sister was Bea's doctor. She was questioned by the police today. Guess they got the coroner's report, too. Rachel couldn't tell them much, other than where Bea had worked and that she thought Bea had started selling sex on the side since she'd asked a lot of questions about STDs and the risks of having multiple partners."

Lorena tapped a finger against the wicker armrest. "So there *could* be a tie to Tony Moreno, if he is lurking around strip clubs as we thought."

"Except Bea went missing early on Friday, when Tony was still being transported. And when he escaped that night, he was on foot. Could he have gotten to the club, picked up Bea and killed her within such a short time? And then ended up back in the neighborhood, several miles from where Bea's body was found, in time to kill that homeowner Saturday morning?"

Max grunted. "Not likely, since his prison jumpsuit and hand-cuffs were found at the scene of the homeowner's murder, which meant he would probably have been wearing them until mid-morning on Saturday."

Lorena gestured to Einstein, who seemed to know what she wanted. He disappeared inside the house and reappeared with a large roll of paper, then laid it out in front of Catherine. It as a map, with four or five stickers scattered within a ten-mile radius around the immediate area. "What are the gold stars?" she asked.

"Based on what we know of Tony's past habits, crimes and personality, we highlighted the areas where he might feel most comfortable, including the local strip clubs." Lorena pointed at one of the stars.

Catherine's hair slid over her shoulder as she leaned in to read the fine print. "Lucky Dick's."

"Based on Tony's history," Lorena said, "he'd likely feel most comfortable in a gentlemen's club or casino. Those were the kinds of places that had become home to him during his time with the Circle. Not to mention he often preyed on women in lower-class neighborhoods who were less likely to say no to his power and money. Of course, those were usually the neighborhoods where the Circle found their candidates for human trafficking, too, so he spent a lot of time there."

"He sounds like a real charmer," Einstein said.

"Actually, he is," Max said. "I got to know him pretty well while I guarded him in prison. His survival depended on him being someone of value and the prisoners saw him as the person who could get them what they wanted. And he was always good for a story or a joke. He could talk his way out of, or into, anything."

"Lucky Dick's..." Damian repeated the name and frowned. "Don't suppose it's related to Lady Luck, do you?" He seemed to aim the question at the entire group.

"What's Lady Luck?" Catherine asked.

"A gentlemen's club in Chicago," Max said. "It served as a front for the Circle's drug and sex trafficking operations several years ago. There could be a link between the two."

"I'll do some searching in the business records," Einstein offered. "And I'll touch base with Nico."

Catherine looked up sharply. "Are you still in contact with him?" Nico been part of the team that had rescued her months ago. He was an undercover DEA agent working within the Circle in Chicago to bring the organization down.

"I know how to find him."

"Maybe if Rachel knows any of the other dancers, I could get them to talk—"

Max's jaw tightened. "I think you should stay out of this, Cat."

"Why?" she asked.

"You're not even sure you're coming back to SSAM, right? That you want to be part of the team?" His eyes held a challenge from which she should walk away.

She shifted in her seat as several pairs of eyes focused on her. "I can still help."

"Max is right," Damian said. "There's no need to put you in danger again. We can take it from here."

Of course they could handle things perfectly well on their own, but she wanted to be a part of this, and she'd promised Rachel she'd try to find Bea's killer. "It might help to have someone on the inside."

Max shook his head. "Tony would recognize half of us."

"You're gimpy, anyway," Einstein added.

Max shot him a glare. "Not for much longer."

But he had put his sling on again. Catherine couldn't let Max put himself at risk, certainly not with an injury. "What about me?"

"What?" Max's face tightened.

Maybe what she was thinking wasn't such a good idea. Maybe she should have kept her ideas to herself. But she was a business-woman at heart, and knew she could find a use for herself at the club. And if they didn't need an assistant or bookkeeper, then it was possible they'd be looking for a dancer to replace Bea. She swallowed hard, realizing just how exposed that would make her.

"We don't need to go to those lengths," Damian said. "We can't focus our limited manpower on one place on the off chance Tony might show up there. Besides, if he's smart he'll stay far away from anything to do with the Circle. They want him dead."

Catherine could be the necessary manpower, just to keep an eye on things at Lucky Dick's. "Still, it's worth a—"

"No, it isn't." Max gave her a fierce look. "It's not worth risking yourself when he won't likely be there."

"Then it isn't much of a risk."

Damian held up his hand. "Let's not worry about getting someone on the inside right now. We'll keep patrolling the neigh-borhood, keep building our relationship with the authorities. Tony's got to pop up sometime."

But Tony hadn't savagely murdered Bea. And if Tony hadn't killed her, that meant there was another threat out there— someone SSAM might not have time to find when they already had their hands full.

TIRED FROM A FORTY-EIGHT-HOUR RUN TO THE BORDER AND BACK, Johnny entered Lucky Dick's and immediately felt at home. The pounding beat of grunge metal throbbed deep in his marrow and all the way to the tip of his cock. On the stage, Hong Kong Kim wrapped herself around a pole.

As he claimed his usual table, Darla hustled over with a cold beer. The hot pink fringe that lined the edge of her short black skirt skimmed her fishnet-clad thighs.

He took the beer with a grateful sigh. "Slow night. Typical Monday, I guess."

She tucked her tray against her body. "Or it might be the murder keeping people away."

Murder? Johnny shifted in his seat, wondering what he'd missed while he'd been making a Circle delivery. "What murder?"

"One of the girls. Police found the body a couple days ago but didn't ID her until today."

"Who?"

"Bea. You went out with her, didn't you?"

"Only a couple times." He wouldn't exactly call it going out. She'd been fresh meat, new at selling herself beyond the stage, and he'd had the chance to sample the services.

They'd had a quickie in his van on Thursday. He hadn't seen her since, but some of the events of that night were a little hazy. He'd woken up groggy, with a hangover and little memory of the previous evening, but had shrugged it off. Sometimes he partied hard, but he deserved the break. He'd been celebrating a bonus after branding and delivering one of the Circle's girls to the border and successfully handing her over to the buyer. The van had many uses.

He rubbed the scruff that lined his jaw. "They found her this weekend? When, exactly?"

"Saturday evening." Darla turned her gaze on him, her brown eyes narrowing. "You talk to her since you last saw her?"

Johnny put his hand on his thigh, under the table, hiding the way it shook. "Nope. It's been several days."

"Maybe Dick gave the police more to go on. They were here asking questions earlier." Dick probably led them in the wrong direction, if he was smart. His job was to shield the club from things like police investigations. In exchange, the Circle kept the club under its protection.

"Bea had other *customers* besides me." God, he hoped so.

"You okay?" She tipped her head toward his beer. "You want something stronger? A double, maybe? You look a little shaky."

"Been working like a dog. Not much sleep. Hey, do me a favor and don't mention me to the police, okay? It would hurt my position within the Circle. Besides, I didn't hurt Bea." Not that he could remember, anyway.

"I know that, Johnny." Her gaze swept the room. "You're not like the rest of these guys. You work hard. Let me know if you need anything else. I'm not too busy tonight."

Johnny heard the invitation in her voice, but he couldn't rid himself of the picture of his father, passed out drunk on the floor of their living room. Johnny and his brother had peeked through the spindles of the banister at his mother beating his unconscious father with a broom while she cussed up a storm.

Blackouts. Alcoholism.

Johnny had known about his father's issues, but had never experienced them himself. He knew how to hold his liquor. Fuck, why couldn't he remember Bea leaving Thursday night?

Nah. It wasn't a blackout. He might have forgotten parts of last Thursday, but he had nothing to do with Bea's death. Everyone knew the kind of company she kept, and what she did for money on the side. Besides, forgetfulness didn't equal guilt.

It took a couple doubles of the hard stuff before his shaky hand evened out. By then, Hong Kong Kim and two other girls had finished their sets.

Draped in a silky robe with a Japanese-style flower print, the elegance of it in conflict with her heavy stage make-up, Kim emerged from the back and settled in his lap. Her smooth fingers ran across his shoulders in a soothing massage. "Want some company tonight? I got some nerves to work out."

He'd learned Friday exactly how she liked to unwind after a

night of dancing. Apparently, it wasn't only the guys who got off when she danced. The image of her breasts jiggling as he pounded into her from behind got him hard.

He grinned. "Count me in." He'd work out his own nerves, too. "I'm parked out back." He couldn't take her back to his apartment. For all he knew, Tony was still hiding out at Johnny's place, though Johnny hadn't been back since he'd left for his two-day run, so maybe the man had moved on. If he hadn't, well…that was another problem Johnny would have to deal with soon. It was wearing on him, thinking the Circle might discover he'd been hiding Tony, but the man had proven to be a goddamn goldmine of information that first night, telling him all kinds of stories about Circle ops. Still, the Boss hadn't seemed too keen on Tony's message when Johnny had delivered it. Maybe he'd made a mistake. Then again, Tony had promised to teach him more about the Circle business. Perhaps they'd resume their lessons tonight—after Johnny had some fun with Kim.

"Meet you in your van in ten." She gave a little finger wave before she disappeared into the back.

Nah. Johnny Walker didn't do blackouts. And he wasn't a fucking alcoholic. He held down a good-paying job, for fuck's sake. He was stronger than that, stronger than his dad, and definitely smarter.

There was no way Bea was tied to him. No way he killed her.

No way he'd ever know for sure unless his memory returned.

He shoved the rest of his drink across the table. He was damn well going to remember Kim and her dancing breasts.

CHAPTER 9

After the SSAM gathering, Catherine dropped Max off at the ranch and told him she was going back to town to check on her sister again. After all, what was one more lie?

A personal appearance at Lucky Dick's would be the most likely way to get answers, no matter what Max said. She was the only SSAM employee the Circle wouldn't recognize, and Max was injured. Plus, she'd promised her sister she'd look into Bea's murder and SSAM was too busy. Catherine would interview Bea's employer and coworkers and see if it led anywhere. Maybe they'd at least know who Bea had hung out with, or if Tony had been lurking around the club.

It sounded good, in theory, but as she pulled into the parking lot and spied the windowless building with the neon sign, her courage wavered. Blowing out a breath, she added some steel to her spine and headed for the door. *No fear.* This was the kind of thing true SSAM agents did every day.

She'd changed into office attire and hoped it would give her an edge. It certainly boosted her confidence and reminded her of her strengths. Glancing down at her pencil skirt and buttoned-up blouse, she was confident she wouldn't be mistaken for a dancer—unless leaving the top button undone was considered sexy.

Catherine nodded to the bouncer, who examined her with unconcealed interest but waved her through.

"You lost?" A woman in black stockings and what appeared to be the black-and-hot pink uniform of a cocktail waitress smirked. There were several small circular tables packed in around the stage and filled with men. Some were chatting loudly over the pumping music, some were drinking. Currently, nobody was on stage.

"I'm looking for Dick."

"You'll find plenty here."

Catherine smiled, thankful for some humor to break the tension. "*The* Dick. Is the owner around?"

The woman jerked her head toward a door in the corner, at the end of a long bar. "Yeah, but he's not in a good mood. That might change if you're here to apply for a job." Her gaze moved over Catherine, assessing her.

"Afraid not."

"Too bad." On three-inch heels, the woman moved with confidence and grace toward one of the occupied tables.

At the office door, Catherine raised her hand to knock, but hesitated as a voice shouted an obscenity. "I fucking need an extension, Ray. You know I'm good for it. A week, that's all I ask."

There was a long pause. Dick must be on the phone with Ray, which was a good thing. If the tense vibes Catherine was picking up on were any indication, Dick and Ray would have been at each other's throats if they'd been in the same room. Could Ray be someone in the Circle, or even *the Boss*?

"After all I've done, this is how you treat me?" Dick asked.

The door was open a crack, and Catherine pushed it gently, peeking inside. She spied a handsome man in his early forties wearing a well-cut suit. She wasn't sure what she'd expected, but it certainly wasn't *GQ*'s businessman of the year. Then again, maybe the Circle believed in projecting a professional image in its management positions.

The man tapped long, manicured fingers against the desk, his other hand still holding the phone. "I've lost a couple girls this week, but I'll have your money. And I'm not going to sell a story to get it, so forget it. *All* my girls would walk out if I did that. Ray? Well, shit."

Dick slammed down the phone and ran a hand through his hair, but Catherine was encouraged. Frustration was something she knew how to deal with. She'd talked more than one SSAM agent out of a funk after a tough day or listened when they needed to vent. Helping solve their problems had made her feel better about being at that receptionist's desk under false pretenses.

Feeling more confident, she pushed the door the rest of the way open. "Maybe I can help."

Dick's dark eyes narrowed on her. "Who are you? And if you say you're a reporter, you might as well turn around and walk your sweet ass out of my club. I'm not talking about Bea."

She forced herself not to fidget under his scrutiny. "I'm Catherine Montague and I'm just what you need."

He arched a brow. "How do you know what I need?"

She gestured to the phone on the desk. "I couldn't help but overhear the end of your conversation. Sounds like you need someone with business skills."

"My girlfriend was my last bookkeeper."

"Ah."

He grunted. "Yes, *ah*. Never mix business and pleasure, Miss Montague."

"I never do." Except that one time with Max, that wayward kiss, and she'd learned her lesson.

"So which are you here about—business or pleasure?"

She took that as an invitation to talk and came farther into the room, refusing to be cowed by his blatant perusal. She stopped in front of his desk. "Business. I'm a trained bookkeeper and have ten years of experience as a personal assistant. I'm new in town and looking for a job."

"And you thought working in a gentlemen's club was the perfect place for you?" He grunted. "No offense, sugar, but you don't seem the type to frequent these locations, much less understand the business."

"Business is business. I learn quickly."

He sighed. "It just so happens I need help." He gestured to the stack of papers in his inbox. "Bills haven't been paid in weeks. The accounts aren't balanced, and I think someone's been stealing from me. If I'd known what my ex had planned—" He abruptly stopped and pushed himself up from the desk, then stuck out his hand to shake hers. Surprised, she accepted it. "I'm going to take a chance on you. You're hired on a temporary basis, and we'll see if you work out. When can you start?"

She slid her hand from his. "I can start tomorrow."

"Great. I'll show you around, introduce you to the girls, and the guys at the door, and we'll see if you can work miracles with my creditors before a shitstorm falls from above." *From above?* Did that mean he worked for the Circle, or was he being dramatic?

"I'm sure I can work something out." If there was one thing she knew, it was how to handle people and juggle everyone's demands.

"If you can figure out where my money went and settle these bills without any extra fees, you're permanently hired. I can't afford to lose any more money or personnel."

Bea. "Sounds like you've been short-staffed."

His expression darkened. "You may have seen in the news that a woman was murdered. She was a dancer here. A popular one, too."

"I'm sorry. How's everyone taking it?"

His gaze shifted to the window that stretched wide across one wall. The opposite side of that window had looked like a mirror that hung behind the bar, but from this side, she could see the stage beyond. A two-way mirror. His lips pressed into a thin line.

"We had a couple girls walk out. If you're planning to scheme, betray me or lie to me, you'd better tell me now. I won't stand for any more disappointment."

It was too late to back out now, especially when her gut told her the answers to so much lay within this club's walls. Working here would satisfy her promise to her sister and be her parting gift to SSAM.

Wednesday

MAX'S JAW DROPPED AS HE EYED THE EQUIPMENT SET UP IN THE refurbished old barn. "You did all this in three days?" He'd spent much of that time away from the ranch, dividing his energy between CI and SSAM, and his parents had been busy.

His mother nodded, beaming. "I was assured it's top of the line."

His father grimaced. "It'd better be for the price I paid."

"I'm sure it is." Max ran his free hand over a gleaming stainless steel rack of hand weights. The large barn had been half-filled with an entire gym's worth of machines and free weights. It was the perfect place to take out his frustrations. The manhunt. Two murders. Catherine's quiet displeasure. He could work it all out here.

He wished Catherine had come with him to see this, but after driving him back to the ranch from the hospital—where he'd tried to see Steve, only to be told the man wasn't seeing visitors—she'd disappeared into the guesthouse. Since he'd deflected her offer to help at the SSAM meeting a couple days ago, she'd seemed angry with him. He'd only wanted to protect her, but at what cost?

Maybe she was simply tired of chauffeuring him between the CI offices, the ranch and the SSAM house. He wasn't sure what she'd been doing with her days, or with her nights, for that matter, but the guesthouse's lights were normally on late into the night. He could see them from his bedroom window. She was sleeping right across the yard, yet unreachable. Untouchable.

What had she done with her nights in Chicago? Had she dated? Certainly there was nobody she was serious about, since she'd left so easily. Unless someone had come back to Texas with her, but then, where was the guy now? The more Catherine tried to keep her distance, the more Max was determined to close the gap. He wanted to know her, to know what she did with her time—and whom she did it with.

His mother glanced at her watch. "The physical therapist should be here any minute. She's fabulous."

Max stiffened. The private smile his mother shot his father told him this therapist was part of a plan—one of the women on her marriageable material list, no doubt. "I don't need a therapist. The doctor cleared me to do certain exercises. I can handle them myself."

He still had to wear his sling for support on occasion, but the pain was gone. He remembered the relief in Catherine's eyes after his appointment on Monday, when he'd told her about the progress he'd made. She understood what it was like for a wounded agent sitting on the sidelines. She supported him. And what had he done in return? He'd shut her down when she'd offered to help with an investigation. But damn, he couldn't imagine her in a club like Lucky Dick's, dancing in front of all those men...

His mother clapped her hands together once. "I have an idea. Why don't you invite Melissa to the main house for dinner after your workout? I'm sure you'll both be hungry."

Melissa. Already on a first-name basis. She was definitely one of his mother's candidates.

Max didn't comment, just continued surveying the equipment. But if she'd seen the set of his jaw or the clenching of teeth that held him back from voicing his thoughts, she'd have known he wasn't thrilled. He'd do his best to dissuade Melissa from any ideas about a long-term relationship. Just a few months ago, he might have contemplated a brief arrangement if a woman was intriguing enough, but flings had started to lose their appeal. His gaze went toward the windows that faced the guesthouse. He wondered what Catherine was doing at this moment and whether she'd save him this time.

"Here she is now," his mother said, moving toward the barn doors, which were open to the evening breeze.

Max turned sharply, his thoughts so filled by a certain woman that he expected to see Catherine. Instead, his mother was greeting a woman with dark brown hair.

His mother brought Melissa over to Max. "This is Melissa Rogers. I met her when I ran a fundraiser for the hospital last year. She's a very talented physical therapist."

Melissa was beautiful, and no doubt had the right pedigree for a potential Caulfield mate, but Max gave her little more than a cursory glance. "Nice to meet you, but I'm afraid you came all this way for nothing."

Melissa arched an elegant brow. "Really?" She eyed his sling-encapsulated arm. He'd been wearing the sling off and on, when he felt it needed the support—or when it earned him a sympathetic glance from Catherine, who couldn't hide her concern, no matter how much she tried to stay aloof. "You look like a man who takes care of his body. I'd think you'd want to get back in shape as soon as possible."

Out of the corner of his eye, he saw his parents ducking out of the barn. "I can do this alone."

Melissa's laugh was soft, a sound most men would find charming. "I'm guessing they didn't tell you I was coming?"

"No offense, but they've got more in mind for us than therapy, and I'm not interested. I already know what I need to do. I've been down this road before."

"Wounded in combat?" Her gaze turned professional as it roved over him, cataloguing his body.

How much had his parents told her? Or was it in a medical file somewhere? He gestured to the equipment surrounding them. "As you can see, I've got the best money can buy."

"It can't buy me. I'm not really looking for anything long term, anyway. I like to have fun." She ran a finger down the center of his chest. "Something tells me you know how to have fun."

Well, shit. That sounded like a challenge the old Max couldn't resist. When the hell had he become a *new* Max?

He glanced up to see Catherine, dressed in black yoga pants and a form-fitting, pink sleeveless workout shirt, in the doorway. She seemed to have frozen in midstride and looked as if she might pivot and flee. But then their eyes met.

Stay. Don't be a coward. Stop hiding from me.

As if she'd heard his silent challenge, her chin went up, her back went straight, and she approached. "Hello."

Startled, Melissa dropped her hand from his chest. Her gaze moved between Catherine and Max.

Catherine's lips curved in that distant but warm way Max recognized as her receptionist's smile. "I'm Catherine Montague, Max's babysitter. And chauffeur. And physical therapist."

Max grinned. "And friend."

"I see." Melissa sighed. "I'm really not needed here, am I?"

"I think I have it covered." Catherine held up the handouts the therapist at the hospital had given Max after his visit Monday. Though he'd left them in Catherine's car, he'd been doing the exercises in his room with hand weights. The thought of doing them here, with Catherine, had him actually looking forward to rehab.

Melissa gave Max a look of regret. "You know where to find me if you need me."

When Melissa left, Catherine's posture lost some of its rigidity. "The playboy in you wants to go after her."

"The playboy in me is glad she left, because now I have you all to myself." Tension coursed through his body—the good kind of tension, the kind that coiled in anticipation of something wonderful. The thought of Catherine's hands on him, of watching her sleek limbs and tight torso moving through the exercises with him, had him imagining where things could lead... Maybe to the floor mats over in the corner. There was a mirror there as well. That could be interesting.

Luckily, Catherine heard none of his thoughts as she surveyed the equipment. "She's the right kind of woman for you."

He snorted. "Now you sound like my mother."

Startled, Catherine spun to face him. "Melissa's the type you used to date in Chicago. Model-beautiful. Smart. Sexy."

Like you. How had he not seen that before? He *had* seen it, but his brain had been in control, stifling any flares of desire. Lately, however, the more time he spent with Catherine, the more it seemed his brain had taken a vacation. He reached out and stroked a finger down her cheek. A pink flush bloomed there, as if his touch had stirred it.

"I'd rather spend time with you."

"As a friend." She caught his finger, which had paused at her collarbone, and pulled it away.

He dropped his hand. "A friend." That would be the sensible path. Catherine deserved better in bed, anyway. He'd worked hard to earn his bachelor image and keep the husband-hunters at bay. She deserved a man who would be there for her always. He wasn't that man. But damned if he didn't suddenly want this new Max to learn how to be that for her. Because the thought of never being able to touch her body...

Reading the heat in his gaze, she rolled her eyes. "You must be desperate, so far away from your hunting grounds."

Her self-deprecation annoyed him. "I'm not desperate. Is that the kind of man you think I am, or the only way you think I'd want you?"

She shrugged, but he could see that was exactly what she thought. And maybe she was partly right. He didn't like that she thought him so shallow, or thought herself so unworthy.

"It doesn't really matter," she said. "I'm here to help you work on that shoulder and make sure you take it slow and easy."

Slow and easy didn't sound good at all. "Have dinner with me after."

"Not a good idea." She moved to a machine.

"I'll take you someplace nice, in town."

"Let's get to work, Gypsy. You need to get back in the field before you forget who you really are."

IT DIDN'T TAKE MUCH TO HIDE OUT ON AN EXPANSIVE PROPERTY, IF one was careful. Nobody would think to look here for Tony, away from the comforts and crowds of the city.

Sending a message to the Boss hadn't worked. Or maybe he'd gone wrong when he'd decided to gamble on Johnny. Either way, the truce was a no-go. Two of the Circle's men had shown up at Johnny's apartment yesterday, ready to exterminate Tony. Fortunately, he'd been smart and planned for this eventuality. Figuring he might not be able to trust Johnny, Tony had helped himself to camping equipment, including a camping knife, that had been stashed in Johnny's closet.

And fate continued to smile on him. While lying low, he'd been watching the news and reading papers. The local buzz had been full of reports on the return of the prodigal son, otherwise known as Maxwell Sawyer Caulfield.

But that bitch fate had looked the other way when the thugs had come after him. They'd gotten off a few rounds as he'd ducked down the fire escape. Though he'd gotten away, the gash in his thigh where a bullet had winged him ached and throbbed like a jungle cat had sliced it open. He'd ignored the pain, grabbed the camping gear from where he'd hidden it off site and made his way to the only place he knew he'd be safe. Right under Max Sawyer's nose.

The lights in the distance seemed brighter as darkness fell. The barn, a hundred yards beyond the outcropping of rocks where he'd made a temporary home with his sleeping bag and limited food supply, seemed to invite him right in. The guesthouse looked even more welcoming. And it was empty at the moment.

He wasn't meant to be outdoors, enduring the elements. He wanted to be inside, especially with the hot woman he'd seen leave the guesthouse a few minutes ago. There was a time he would have lain in wait for a different reason, his heart pumping with adrenaline at the thought of being with a woman, making her his. But he couldn't risk getting caught. A return to prison would be unacceptable, not to mention he'd be a sitting duck for the Circle's hitmen. He had to plan carefully, continuing to lie low unless desperation pushed him beyond reason.

He fondled the rebar knife that lay across his good thigh. Max Sawyer and his woman had better hope it didn't come to that.

CHAPTER 10

Friday

Max was going crazy. After an entire week at the office, the scent of paper and the heat of running computers were cloying—not at all like the familiar and comforting smell of hard-won sweat and a freshly fired H&K pistol. How the hell was he supposed to last another five weeks here?

"You look like you're about to bolt." Catherine sent him a sympathetic smile as she entered the large office his father had insisted he occupy for the few hours a day he was here. He felt sorry for whomever he'd displaced, but it was a temporary arrangement.

"Ah, my savior has arrived." Max leapt to his feet. "Ready to get out of here?"

Her lips twitched with amusement. "Big plans for the weekend?"

No plans, actually, though several things sprung to mind now that Miss Montague was here. Which reminded him... "Why did you change your last name?"

She released a short, nervous laugh. "Why do you ask?"

"I'm not judging, having changed my own name, but I was running from my past." Was it the same situation for her?

She shrugged. "I was moving to Chicago and wanted a fresh start." Which implied there was something not-so-fresh about her past. "I'd rather not talk about it right now."

Curiosity chomped at the bit, but Max reined it in. Besides, he didn't want to scare her away. If it hadn't been for Catherine's presence this past week, he probably would have blown this deal with his father and bunked with Einstein at the SSAM rental. Seeing her each day was a balm that soothed the bad feelings.

She changed the subject and pulled two cans of soda out of her oversized purse. "You survived your first week. Congratulations."

"Thought about escaping a time or two." He caught the can of soda she tossed to him.

Her smile bloomed. "You caught that with your right hand."

He was pretty darn happy about that, actually. "Could be I have a fabulous workout partner who drives me..." He'd been about to say crazy, but her keep-your-distance vibes had warned him not to push his luck.

"I'm good at cracking a whip when I have to."

He swallowed hard at that image, then glanced at the can in his hand. It was his favorite brand. "You don't have to play assistant here, you know."

"Some habits die hard."

"You *are* going back to SSAM after your leave is up, right?" Tingles of apprehension tickled the base of his neck. He'd lost so many friends over the years, first by leaving Texas to start over, and then in Afghanistan, and then by relocating to Chicago. There were few people he knew he could trust. Losing Catherine, he suddenly realized, would be tough.

"I don't know." She avoided his gaze, sipping on her own can of soda and glancing out the window at a cluster of pecan trees. She didn't seem to see them, lost in her thoughts instead. Was she still traumatized by what had happened? Hell, he'd known strong, fearless men who'd never been the same after a violent experience.

Max had been out of town on assignment when she'd gotten caught in the crosshairs during that fateful investigation. He wished he'd been there to help demolish Catherine's demon. The bastard was lucky he was in jail, safe from Max's clenched fists.

"Do you have someone to talk to?" he asked. "What about Becca? You and she are good friends, right? Sorry, I know it's none of my business, I'm just worried about you."

"It's not that. I..." She stood. "Never mind."

"What? You can talk to me."

Again, curiosity ate at him. What was she thinking? And where was she going during her days in town? They drove to and from town together in her Jeep, and between the CI offices and the SSAM rental, and of course there was the daily workout together, but in between, she'd disappear. Going to see her sister, most likely. Helping her move the clinic was probably a full-time job.

"You've got enough on your plate. Besides, you can't save everyone, Max."

But he'd sure as hell try. "Just know the door is open anytime. I owe you."

She grimaced and waved him off. "You really don't. Speaking of saving people, has there been anything new about the manhunt?" She'd missed the last few days at SSAM, preferring to drop him off and go God knows where until she picked him up again a few hours later.

"It's like Tony walked off the planet." Frustration formed a knot in his stomach. "We tracked down Lee, and he admitted to vandalizing your sister's clinic, but said he was acting on his own and didn't know anything about the design on the brick."

"You must be itching to get back to the investigation."

He glanced at the stack of folders on his desk. "I should have called you. I need another hour or two. I promised someone a report by the end of the week."

"How about I come back in a couple hours? I have an errand I've been thinking of running." She looked toward the door, her mind suddenly on something, or *someone*, else. *Who, or what, has your attention, Miss Montague?*

"You're not going to babysit me?" His words pulled her attention back to him, where he wanted it. "Helping your sister again?"

"For now, Rachel's seeing her patients in the old location, but the move is almost complete."

"That's great." At least Catherine could worry less about her sister with the clinic moving to a safer area. He frowned at the papers. "I wish I could help." He'd kill for some extra physical exertion, especially outside in the spring weather.

"No need. We're handling it."

Still, he wanted to be there for her. And it had been way too long since he'd had some time to play. "Have dinner with me tonight."

"I told you, that's not a good idea. Besides, we see each other all the time."

"Just in passing or at the gym, and your mind has been elsewhere. Even when we're working out, I can see you're thinking about something, or someone else." He took a step closer. "I want you all to myself."

Her eyes grew shadowed, and he wondered what hurdles he'd have to clear to see inside this beautiful woman's thoughts. "Why?"

"Because I want to get to know you. After the SSAM meeting tonight, let's grab a bite. No pressure. Just friends."

Emotions swirled in her gaze, but he couldn't decipher them. "I can't. I've got plans with my sister."

"Bring her along, then."

Her fingertips turned white on her soda can. It was a miracle the aluminum didn't crumple. Was he causing her that much anxiety? It was just dinner. *With a notorious playboy,* his conscience reminded him. *What would a good girl like her see in you?*

She gave him an apologetic gaze. "I'm just not ready."

It's not you, it's me, babe.

How many times had he said that while giving a woman the brush-off? Turnabout was fair play. Hell, he'd even brushed Catherine off after the most amazing kiss of his life. How could he explain he'd been scared by his reaction to her? At the time, he'd chalked it up to his slight inebriation, but deep down, he recognized their chemistry had been off the charts. And damned if he wasn't curious enough to break his no-involvement rule and explore it.

He toyed with the end of a strand of her hair. She sucked in a breath. She wasn't totally immune to him—unless she was scared.

He released her hair and stepped away. "Consider it an open invitation. For when you're ready." *Be ready soon.*

"Maybe. But we'll likely be going our separate ways soon, so it's a moot point."

Frustration flared. "You don't feel this connection between us? Give it a chance. Life's too short to be constrained by *moot points.* Sometimes you have to grab life by the hand and jump."

Maybe it was the suit and tie, and the feeling he was no longer allowed to be his free, impulsive self, but he'd had enough of the straight-and-narrow Max. He grabbed the soda from her and set it on the desk, then pulled her against him. His lips captured hers before she could protest. Her hands went to his shoulders, but even in her surprise, she was gentler with his right shoulder, thinking of his needs.

With a groan, she opened her mouth and let him in. *The taste.* Good Lord, the sweet taste of Catherine was one he'd tried to forget, but his subconscious remembered and welcomed her back. His hand cupped the side of her neck, his thumb brushing the pulse that beat like a drum there. His own pulse was throbbing throughout his body, making him feel alive. Like when he'd jumped out of a plane. Or made it through Hell Week. Or come through three days of desert survival training to find a hot shower and meal waiting for him.

With a moan, her arms lifted and wrapped around his neck. He skimmed his hands down her waist to her hips and tugged her close. She slanted her mouth against his, letting her tongue dance and driving him wild with need.

His body wanted her. *Now.* His brain ran through the necessary calculations.

Desk? Cluttered, but that could be rectified in seconds with a swipe of his arm.

Floor? There was an area rug, but the wood planks underneath weren't ideal.

Straddling him in his leather chair? *Oh, God, yes.*

But that wasn't how he wanted his first time with Catherine to go down. She was gentle and sweet. She deserved to be wined and dined. Roses—lots of them. He'd give her the whole deluxe package tonight at dinner. She had to accept his invitation now, had to see how good things could be between them.

A knock at the door had Catherine jerking her lips, and her hips, away. His body ached at the loss and he groaned with frustration.

With shaky fingers, she swiped at the lingering moisture on her mouth. "We can't."

"So you said before. And yet, we just did." Guilt and confusion were all over her face. "Let's talk over dinner."

"But—"

Another knock resounded, this time more insistent. "Son? You in there?"

"Oh, God." Catherine paled.

"Caught by the parents?" Max chuckled and brushed a finger across her cheek, willing color back into it. "It's not like we're in high school. Besides, you're supposed to be my near-fiancée, remember?" He kissed her on the tip of her nose, enjoying the forgotten, fizzy feeling of anticipation pumping through his veins.

"This is your office, during a work day."

"I tried inviting you to dinner, outside of the office, at night." He shrugged his good shoulder unapologetically. "I'll take what I can get."

"That's right. You *take*. And then you toss aside."

Her words were like a knife to the chest, sliding between the ribs to catch the delicate, vulnerable tissue beneath. That her assessment was true didn't hurt any less. "This is different."

She shook her head and spun on her heel. "I'll pick you up in two hours. To go back to the ranch."

CATHERINE COULDN'T STOP SHAKING. HER BODY QUAKED AS IF IT were going through withdrawals from Max's touch.

Hayworth had given her a knowing look when she'd emerged from Max's office, which had only worsened her guilt. She sat in her Jeep for several long minutes, trying to gather her scattered wits.

Max had kissed her. While totally sober. She pressed her fingertips to her lips, which still tingled. Max wanted her? Why? Why *now*?

He had to be out of his mind. Or maybe he was vulnerable and out of his element. If they were back in Chicago, he'd never give her a second look. Besides, he didn't know the real Catherine Montague, so it couldn't be *her* he really wanted.

She tried to call Rachel, but Teresa said she was busy finishing up her last couple of appointments for the day. So Catherine drove to Lucky Dick's, feeling lighter as Caulfield Industries grew smaller in her rearview mirror.

After nearly a week of working at the club, the bouncer, the dancers and the waitstaff were familiar. She'd casually questioned most of them, and the only name that had come up consistently in connection with Bea was Johnny Walker, a regular customer.

Instead of heading into the office, she stopped at the bar and watched Johnny. Kim was giving him a private dance at a table right next to the stage and he looked to be thoroughly enjoying it, his head tipped back as he watched her. What kind of man spent days on end at a gentlemen's club? The kind who had business there. One of the dancers had said Johnny was frequently gone for a couple days at a time, but he always came back, and he often *dated* the girls. Was he involved with the Circle? From what she'd observed this week, he and Dick seemed to have a tense relationship. She'd never seen the two talking, but they'd exchanged some dark looks.

Her phone rang and she saw Rachel's number. She ducked into the office where the music wasn't so loud and answered. "Hey."

"Hi. I heard you called earlier?"

"Just thought I'd see if you wanted to grab a quick bite to eat after work." And it would give her another reason to tell Max she couldn't have dinner with him.

"Unfortunately, I have a lot of work to catch up on."

"You'll be staying late?" Catherine frowned.

"Relax. The security service your boyfriend hired follows my car home every night."

"He's not my boyfriend." But Max had really come through for her.

"Whatever you say. The new clinic's coming together, too."

A stab of guilt hit Catherine. "I'm sorry I wasn't there more this week."

"That's okay, as long as it was because of your *boyfriend*." She laughed. "Come on, I know he's the one you're shacking up with."

Catherine hadn't told Rachel she was staying at the Caulfield ranch. Just the mention of the Caulfield name would dredge up horrible memories. Thankfully, Rachel knew Max as Max Sawyer, so the conflict hadn't come up. If she knew he was a Caulfield...

Catherine also hadn't shared her new job at Lucky Dick's with Rachel. Technically, taking this job had been for Rachel's benefit— and Bea's—but she didn't want to worry her sister. "We'll catch up soon," Catherine said.

She was due to head back to CI and pick up Max, but as she hung up, she caught sight of Johnny through the two-way mirror in the office. He threw a wad of bills on his table and grabbed his jacket off the back of his chair. Catherine snatched up the paper-work she was supposed to work on over the weekend, counted to ten and followed him, keeping a safe distance but staying close enough to see what car he climbed into.

A van. And an old, dinged-up one at that. With plenty of room in back for...whatever. She didn't want to contemplate that. He could be completely innocent. But her instincts were overpow-ering her logic. Something about Johnny—his cocky attitude, his confidence or the wads of bills he dropped nightly—seemed suspicious.

She followed him a few miles to an apartment complex. She pulled into a visitor's spot in front of one of the buildings as he parked in a numbered space reserved for tenants. He got out and started to cross the lot, then suddenly veered in her direction. His long strides ate up the pavement. Her adrenaline spiked and her stomach squeezed. Had he seen her or was his apartment in the nearby building? She hit the lock button on her doors.

He walked behind the Jeep and her eyes followed him in the rearview mirror until he hit her blind spot. Her gaze shot to the side view mirror as he rounded her vehicle. A sudden sharp rap of knuckles on her window had a scream leaping to her throat, but she swallowed it when she saw his grin.

She looked left and right, but there wasn't another live body in the parking lot. She rolled down her window just a bit. "Yes?"

"It is you. I thought I recognized you from the club. Catherine, right?"

He knew her name? Maybe he was more observant than she'd given him credit for. "That's right."

"You going to sit out here all night or you want to come up?" His grin turned sly. Was he used to women following him home and throwing themselves at him?

"I just..." Oh, Lord, how to explain what she was doing here? There was no way in hell she wanted to go upstairs with him. Her gaze fell on the Lucky Dick's ledger sitting in the passenger seat and she formed a hasty plan. "I had some questions, and I thought you might be the man to answer them." That part, at least, was the truth.

The grin disappeared. "What kind of questions?"

"Well, that's just it... I think I've changed my mind."

His hand went to the door handle. "Oh, no, honey. You don't get to play games with me like that."

CHAPTER 11

Saturday

"Y ou thought you'd pulled one over on me, didn't you?" Max's low voice came from the open door of the guesthouse. Catherine had left it open to enjoy the evening breeze, but she'd lost track of time and it had grown dark.

She closed the Lucky Dick's ledger she'd been studying and tucked it beneath a magazine on the coffee table, hoping she hadn't drawn attention to it. She stood to face him. "I beg your pardon?"

"Dinner. Last night."

Last night. Her evening had taken an unexpected detour. She'd wormed her way out of a situation with Johnny—barely. The man had thought she was hot for him and she'd disabused him of the notion, but she'd had to scramble for an explanation as to why she'd followed him. And he'd actually bought it. What's more, it gave her a reason to talk with him again. Maybe she could learn more about him.

"I left a message for you," she said.

"With the *secretary*. You could have called me directly."

"Didn't want to bug you while you were finishing up your reports." She'd texted Einstein and asked him to pick Max up from the CI offices and include him in whatever investigative plans SSAM had in store last night. Einstein had then returned Max to the ranch. She'd thought it would be a happy solution to both of their problems—and a way to avoid an intimate dinner and what might follow.

He arched a brow. "And all day today?"

"Busy." Busy avoiding him.

He closed the door and came further into the living room. As elegant as the ranch house, the guesthouse had all the amenities she could need, including a small but fully equipped kitchen, a simple dining area, a comfortable living room and a separate bedroom and bath. With Max's large frame filling the room, it suddenly seemed tiny and inadequate. "We hadn't finished our...discussion."

The discussion that had devolved into a kiss. She still wasn't sure how to handle it. She ignored the hum of anticipation as he slowly stalked toward her.

His gaze went to her mouth. "Unfortunately, there's no time now. We've been summoned."

"Summoned?"

"My parents would be pleased to have us join them for dinner this evening. Apparently, there is now an addendum to the deal. We're expected to join them for dinner at least once a week. I chose Saturdays."

"This includes me, too?"

He wouldn't meet her gaze. Catherine sensed a BS statement was about to follow. "Yes. They want to get to know my near-fiancée better." *Yeah, right.* "I'd like to get to know my near-fiancée better, too. And since this seems to be the only way you'll have dinner with me, I'm starting to see the upside. They want us to start tonight, unless you've already eaten?" He glanced toward the kitchen.

Lost in balancing the mess Dick's ex-girlfriend had left the books in, she'd forgotten to take a dinner break. She'd hoped to find some connection between Dick and the Circle, too, especially since she'd told Johnny she'd thought there was something fishy about a receipt in his name—her supposed excuse for following him to his apartment complex last night. He'd demanded to see the ledger and she'd put him off, saying she'd prefer to dig up more information first.

She sighed. "I haven't eaten, but I don't think it's a good idea." She doubted the Caulfields wanted her at their table, making chitchat and avoiding the truth, any more than she wanted to be there, but she knew better than to stir things up, especially with Max looking so determined.

"But you're my buffer, remember?" He came closer and she caught the scent of musk and spice that was unique to Max.

She couldn't let him touch her again, or this would go further than was wise. "Fine. Give me a moment to freshen up." She'd have to go around him to get to the bedroom.

Instead of moving out of her way, he stepped closer, then lifted a lock of hair that had come loose from her messy ponytail. He studied it a moment before he scooped it behind her ear. "You look fine to me. More than fine." His gaze was penetrating. "Are you hiding because I kissed you?"

She had to clear her throat before she could find her voice. "No, I...I got a job, so I've been doing some studying up." Might as well confess that much. Maybe it would keep him from worrying about where she was in the coming weeks.

His brows drew together. "You already *have* a job. You love working at SSAM. Don't let one man keep you from staying where you love."

One man? It took her a moment to realize he was talking about the man who'd kidnapped her. "I need a new start. You should know what that's like."

His eyes flashed with anger and some amount of pain. "Yeah, I do. Because getting out from under my parents' shadow was an act of self-preservation. You can't tell me running away from SSAM—a supportive, caring family—is the same thing."

"Your parents care. I can see how much your parents need you in their lives. Doesn't that matter?"

"At what cost? They want me to run the company, to be a clone of my father, not a son, and certainly not my own man. There's a difference. But, once again, you're avoiding me by changing the subject." He turned on his heel and stalked toward the door. "Dinner's in twenty minutes."

Stunned by his anger, Catherine stared at the closed door. He was hurt that she hadn't supported his case. As a friend, she supposed she should have. But as his father's employee, she had other duties.

Stiffening her resolve, she went into the bedroom to change. She paired a casual sundress with a light sweater, then touched up her makeup and swiped pink gloss across her lips, hoping the ensemble would serve as battle armor against his parents. No matter what Max thought, she would be there for him. He'd asked for her help and she cared too much about him to let his parents control his life.

She took the stone path that led from the guesthouse to the back door of the estate. The cloudless, moonless sky looked like a velvet blanket encrusted with winking jewels. There appeared to be so many more stars here than in Chicago. It reminded her of the trailer park where she'd grown up, just a few miles from the ranch, off a cracked and dusty highway. Out there, you could see all of the stars, big and bright, and enough wide sky to imagine there was more to the world and that escape was possible.

At the French doors that opened from the back of the house

onto the patio, she swiped a sweaty palm against her thigh and let herself in.

"There she is." Lillian smiled and poured white wine before handing the glass to Catherine. The welcome was so unexpectedly warm, especially after she'd avoided the Caulfields for most of the week, Catherine had to keep from turning around to see if she'd come in the right door. Where were the cold, assessing looks?

Even Hayworth wore a smile. "Thought maybe there was trouble in paradise when Max returned by himself." He examined her closely. "Haven't seen you around the office much, or the ranch, for that matter." Except for when he'd caught her slinking out of Max's office yesterday. Was that what tonight's summons was about? Would Hayworth and Lillian *out* her and shatter what bond, shaky though it may be, she and Max had? "Not exactly acting like lovebirds, are you?"

Max moved closer to Catherine and smiled, but the warmth didn't reach his eyes. "She's been busy helping her sister move into the new clinic and starting a job."

Hayworth's full white brows nearly met his equally full white hairline. "A job? I didn't realize you were looking. I could find you one at CI."

Been there, done that.

Max stiffened. "She has one at SSAM—as do I."

"It's just a temporary thing to get me on my feet." Catherine sipped the wine and tried to think of a change of subject.

"Speaking of jobs..." Hayworth clasped Max's healthy shoulder. "It's been good to have my boy at the office. The whole place has a new energy and the employees like you. You're a natural leader."

Max's expression was similar to that of a trapped animal. "I'm sure they wouldn't insult me to your face."

"Is it not challenging enough?" Catherine was genuinely curious. She didn't see the spark of life he had when he worked as a SSAM agent.

"It's different," Max admitted. "Paperwork, numbers, reports… They just aren't my thing."

Lillian returned with a couple of platters of food and Catherine put her glass down to help her set them on the table. Apparently, Lillian had heard Max's comment. "What about the social aspect? You always enjoyed being with other people." She gestured for everyone to take their seats. Catherine was seated opposite Lillian, and next to Max. "That reminds me, there's a fundraiser this coming Friday. You'd be the perfect candidate."

Max paused in the middle of spearing a slice of brisket. "Candidate?"

"It's a bachelor auction and someone dropped out at the last minute, so we need a new bachelor."

"I don't think so."

Lillian's excitement barreled over any protest. "It's for a fantastic cause. The hospital and its community outreach programs." Her eyes met Catherine's. "So, in a way, it would support your sister."

More likely, it would support Lillian's cause to find a new fiancée for her son. Catherine had no right to feel hurt, but she did. She kept her mouth shut, however. This was the Caulfields' rodeo. She'd let Max decide for himself what he should do.

"I'm not really a bachelor anymore." Max reached under the table to take her hand. "I've got Catherine." Had he seen the doubt and hurt in her eyes? She offered a smile in truce and he squeezed her fingers.

"Oh, she can share you for one evening," Lillian said, shooing away their relationship as if it were nothing.

It is nothing. Her brain tried to smack her body with the truth, but the connection she and Max shared sure felt like *something.*

"Melissa will be there," Lillian added.

Max looked confused. "Who?"

"The physical therapist."

"Well, good for her. I hope she finds a date." His drawl was like syrup running thick and sweet, hiding the extent of his irritation from all but Catherine, who knew all of his defense mechanisms.

"Besides, Son," Hayworth said, "Caulfield is a respected name. You stand up for the little guys, and people notice. Supporting a charity is the perfect way to spin your return to town."

Max's mouth tightened. "And launch me into the public domain so I can one day be a council member like you were?"

"City council?" Hayworth laughed. "We're aiming higher than that, Son."

MAX REINED IN HIS TEMPER AND TOOK STRENGTH FROM CATHERINE'S warm fingers beneath his. "I don't need to make a name for myself here."

"Of course not." His mother must have detected his mounting impatience, because she was quick to soothe. "You've already got the Caulfield name—or you did."

Catherine turned her palm to join his, as if she acknowledged how the barb hurt him. He'd had his reasons for changing his name. Not the least of which was to distance himself from any political aspirations here in Texas. He needed to be himself, Max Sawyer, without any outside influences, before he could be anybody else. Hell, he didn't *want* to be anybody else.

His mother shrugged. "What could it hurt, though, to attend this one event? It's for charity. I'm certain Catherine understands that. Besides, if you two have a strong relationship, something like this can't break it apart. Everyone knows it's just a dinner date you're auctioning off, not your whole future."

Leave it to his mother to make them all feel like they were overreacting. He'd forgotten her expert skill at twisting situations to her advantage. The thing was, he didn't want to go on a dinner date with anyone but Catherine. He was surprised by how much he wanted that.

"How about I donate some money to the cause?" he asked.

"That's no fun." His mother turned her focus to Catherine. "I'm sure you understand how the excitement of going after a handsome man can raise the stakes."

Catherine's expression was guarded. "You *would* bring in a record amount of money."

"Whose side are you on?" He pulled his hand from hers.

"I feel caught in the middle here. I suppose you should do whatever you feel is right."

Max's gut tightened. He'd been wrong to bring her into this. His parents were skilled at manipulation and she'd gotten caught in their web. She wasn't going to fight for him or for their relationship, whether it was a false one or not.

His mother maintained her smile. "Well, let's table this for now. I'll talk to Phyllis on the charity's committee and see what she thinks."

"Not exactly *tabling* it then, is it?" Catherine muttered. Max snorted. There was the moxie he'd been missing.

Lillian's mouth tightened but she changed the subject. "You've been learning the ropes at the company?"

"Yes," Max dug into his twice-baked potato. "That was the deal. There's certainly a lot to learn." Unfortunately, it was time wasted, because he wasn't staying.

"You can handle it," his father said.

"Just in time to climb into the saddle," his mother added. Hayworth shot Lillian a glare with the not-so-subtle message to back off.

Max caught it. "Is something wrong with you, Dad? Are you ill?"

He waved him off. "Just thinking about retirement. I'm nearly seventy, Son. Should enjoy what good health I have left."

Was this some new manipulation, or was his father hinting he had health issues? He couldn't tell. Fuck, why did everything have to be so secretive with them? A child should be able to trust his parents.

"I don't want you to have false hope," Max said, because someone had to be reasonable. "My shoulder's nearly healed, and I'm eager to get back to what I do best." Putting bad guys behind bars. Finding justice for the victims. There was a satisfaction in that he'd never find behind a desk.

"You owe us a few more weeks, don't forget."

How could he? "You love running the company and you're good at it. I don't think you'd like the lack of excitement here at the ranch if you retire."

"Plenty of excitement here," his mother said. "In fact, just yesterday, there was a break in the fence line."

"Somebody cut it," his father clarified. "Probably after the stray cattle on the southeast acreage, but all were accounted for." Pride rang in his voice. His eyes narrowed on Catherine. "Plenty of excitement in town, too. How's your sister doing settling into her new clinic?"

Catherine set her fork down and toyed with the stem of her wineglass. "She's doing much better."

"Glad we could help her out."

"Help?" Max asked. Catherine hadn't mentioned anything about his father's involvement. His internal alarm system went on alert. Then again, when it came to beautiful women, he was always watchful, waiting for the slightest of transgressions.

This is Catherine, friend and confidant. At the moment, however, she seemed nervous.

She took a sip of wine before replying. "Your father facilitated renting the building for the new clinic. It's a perfect location, close to Rachel's patients, but not far from a police station."

Had she fallen into the trap of using the Caulfield name and money? Disappointed, he choked down his dinner, biding his time until dessert was over and he could get Catherine alone to find out more.

The moment she pushed her nearly untouched chocolate cake aside, Max excused them. "We have an early day at the gym tomorrow, and then a meeting about the manhunt." With the team, he'd spent the week presenting the profile Lorena had generated until every law enforcement officer within a hundred-mile radius possessed the latest information on Tony Moreno. Max and Einstein had also joined the patrols searching neighborhoods for signs of Tony or the Circle.

Catherine seemed as eager to escape as he was, expressed her gratitude for the meal and headed out the back door. Max followed her and shut the guesthouse door behind them.

She spun around and pinned him with a look. "Out with it."

"With what?"

"I can tell you have something on your mind. Go ahead and ask."

"Okay. Why didn't I know the details of Rachel's relocation project? Or, more specifically, why didn't I know about my father's role in it?"

"He was nice enough to offer last weekend, and you're not exactly open to hearing how helpful your dad can be, or how he gives back to the community. Besides, it was something Rachel needed."

His father wasn't *nice enough* to do anything that didn't serve some selfish purpose. Even when he'd come to career day at Max's high school, his father had passed out campaign buttons and insisted the students take them home to their parents. But maybe it was Max's own fault Catherine had been tempted to accept his father's so-called generosity. After all, he'd led her into the lion's den.

"Take my advice," Max said. "Don't accept any more gifts from Hayworth Caulfield. You'll get tangled in the strings until they choke you."

She flinched. "It was a nice thing to do for my sister. Her clinic had just been attacked—twice in twenty-four hours."

Shit. She was right. And Catherine, on the opposite side of the greed spectrum from his father, did everything for other people. "I'm sorry. It touched a hot button, that's all."

She shook her head. "I should have said no. It's just that I want the best for my family and friends."

"Then you won't mind spending some time with me now—assuming I'm still considered a friend." He brushed her hair back over her shoulder. His hand lingered for a moment before drifting down the length of her arm to her elbow, and then to her fingers. Fingers he wanted coasting across his skin. Something about Catherine made him want to break through her good-girl walls and bring out the wildcat in her—the sexy Cat he sensed whenever he touched her. Like now. "You're shaking."

"It was cool outside."

"You don't feel cold." In fact, her skin was warm, her cheeks pink, her pupils dilated. Her lips parted ever so slightly. If he didn't know any better, he'd say she was aroused.

She pulled her hand away and turned to the kitchen. "Would you like a drink?"

"Is that an invitation?"

"Just a friendly one. As much as I want you—" She stopped abruptly, turning wide eyes on him. "Forget I said that."

No freaking way. "I want you, too."

"It's ridiculous."

"Some things just don't make sense."

"We'll be going our separate ways in a few weeks." She groaned with frustration.

Join the club.

A lot of affairs worked that way. Brief. Satisfying. No strings and no future. But the thought disturbed him this time. He didn't want to make love to Catherine and then walk away. He wanted more than that. Hell, she deserved more than that. But an affair—no, a *relationship*—of that nature would require more of him. It would require trust. He wasn't sure he had any to give.

She's not just any woman. She won't break your heart. She's not after your family name or money.

The ringing of her cell phone broke the silence and she turned to retrieve it from the kitchen counter where she'd left it to charge. "It's my sister."

As she took the call, he tried to reel in his lust and organize his thoughts. Could he really make something work with Catherine? He wandered the guesthouse as she talked. His eyes drifted to the back door, which led to a small, flagstone patio with an incredible view of the low hills that rippled across the ranch. What drew his attention, he realized, was a smear of something on the doorjamb and knob.

He crouched to get a better look. Blood? Definitely out of place. The door wasn't completely closed, either. A different set of survival instincts took over.

Catherine followed him with her gaze, silently questioning as he moved through the small house, checking the bedroom and bathroom, the closet. Nothing. Nobody.

What? She mouthed the question while listening to her sister. "I'll have to call you back, Rachel. Better yet, let's meet for lunch Monday." She hung up and turned a worried gaze on him. "What's going on?"

He pointed at the back door. "Did you lock that recently?"

"Yes. I always do, and I double check ever since..."

Since she'd been abducted from her own home a couple months ago. "Yeah, well, it isn't locked now. It looks like somebody picked it."

"Somebody broke in?" Her eyes went wide.

"Yes, but there's nobody here now. You're safe." He pulled her close and ran a hand over her back, reassuring both of them. Still, she quaked against his chest. "You're moving into the main house with me."

She pulled back. "What? No. I can't."

"Sure you can. Better safe than sorry, right?"

"Who says I'd be safe?"

She had a point. Just a moment ago, he'd been developing a strategy to break down her walls. "I'll keep my hands to myself—unless you say otherwise. You can't stay here. My parents will have to get someone out here to fix the lock. Whoever did this could still be lurking about the property and it's too dark to go on a hunt right now." But he itched to do just that.

"I can move back here tomorrow?"

Stubborn woman. "Is staying near me so difficult? I'm sure there's a spare guest room made up."

"Or I could stay with Rachel in town." She glanced at her phone as if ready to call her sister back that instant. Was she that worried about being near him? He didn't know whether to be flattered or annoyed.

"It's getting late. Stay in the main house. I promise not to bite." Even if the effort to resist her killed him. She nibbled her bottom lip and he had to look away. "Was anything taken?"

"I didn't even think of that." She went to fumble inside her purse, then to check some books on the coffee table. Finally, she went through the counters, cupboards and closets until she'd picked her way through the house. "Some cans of food. About forty bucks from my wallet. I think a blanket or two from the bedroom closet, but I don't remember what was in the linen closet. Maybe your mom would know, or Claudia?" The rate of the words spilling out of her mouth and the clenching of her fists told him it was time to get her out of here.

He didn't mention her phone. She'd left it behind to charge on the kitchen counter while they'd been at dinner. Whoever had broken in hadn't taken it, but had they scrolled through her personal contacts and information? He'd talk to her about making sure she had a secure password tomorrow.

He put his hands on her shoulders, leaning down to look into her eyes. Her expression was laced with worry, but not panic. He kept a lid on the anger that simmered in his gut. Someone had threatened the sweetest, gentlest person Max had ever known. His need to protect her was strong. "Let's get you settled at the house. Maybe another glass of wine and I'll tuck you in." She raised an eyebrow and he sighed. "And then I'll go back to my own bed. Tomorrow, we'll figure this out." He would personally search every square inch of the ranch for the asshole.

"You'll check the main house, too?"

"Of course. First thing." And he'd sleep on her floor if she'd let him. In her bed would be better, but the relationship he'd been contemplating just minutes ago had been shelved. Peace of mind came first—unless she invited him between the sheets. That was a request he wouldn't be strong enough to refuse.

CHAPTER 12

Sunday

By the second night in the main house, Catherine was wound so tight she could barely lie still. Max slept two doors down, their bedrooms separated only by a bathroom they shared. The smell of his soap had hung heavy in the air this morning, encouraging her to take up residence in the bathroom and breathe him in.

To want and not be able to have, to care and know she would be out on her ass in seconds once he knew the real her—that was the definition of torture. And she'd brought all of it upon herself.

Max seemed interested in her, or in the woman he thought she was. What was it about Texas that had brought out this side of him? He'd been sending signals for days now that he'd like their friendship to become something more, but there was no way she could breach that final barrier. She'd crossed too many boundaries already, though he didn't know that.

Besides, she didn't want to join his legions of ex-girlfriends. He viewed women differently once he'd had them in his bed. She'd fielded numerous calls from admirers looking to reach him at SSAM after he'd broken things off. *She* was the one with elite status at the moment, as one of his few true female friends.

Some friend.

Restless, she called her sister. Rachel answered on the first ring. "How are things with Max?"

Catherine sighed. No part of this felt like home, and lying to her sister about where she was staying was grating on her. "They're...there." No need to worry her sister about the break-in, either.

Catherine was certain it had to be one of the ranch hands who lived in a compound of trailers a little ways down the road. Nothing had been taken besides basic necessities. Max was probably exaggerating the threat level. He'd spent all day today riding around the property, looking for signs of her intruder, and hadn't found anything. On the plus side, his father had insisted on accompanying him, saying he could lead Max to the area of the fence that had been cut earlier in the week. Maybe they'd gotten some quality time together.

On the downside, Max had taken a shower before dinner to rinse off the dirt and dust from his explorations. After he'd left the steamy bathroom again, Catherine had indulged in some deep inhalations that tied her body and mind in knots of frustration.

Rachel laughed. "Sounds dull. We're still on for lunch tomorrow?" There was a rustle of papers. Without Catherine there to bug her to get more rest, Rachel probably worked all hours of the day and night.

"Are you still at the clinic? Rachel, it's Sunday and—"

"I'm home. Just catching up on some charts."

"If you're too busy…"

"I'll make it happen."

"Okay, but please get some rest tonight." One of them should. "It's getting late."

"And you?" Rachel asked, a hint of humor in her voice. "Will you go to sleep or entertain yourself in other ways?"

"What?"

"Max is one hot, muscled hunk of man."

Catherine sputtered out a laugh. "Did you just say *hunk of man?*"

"I'm sure you've noticed he has some very fine features—something you failed to mention to me in the years we were in Chicago together, by the way."

Catherine had carefully kept her personal life separate from work. "He's a coworker. And he dates models, actresses and debutantes."

"And you're better than all of them combined."

"Thanks." Her battered ego and bruised conscience could use a boost—and a reality check, which was why she'd called Rachel in the first place. "How are you?"

"Haven't had a date in weeks, and definitely no hunks in sight."

Weeks? Try years. Catherine hadn't had the time, energy or desire to seek male companionship while in Chicago. "No, I mean, how's the clinic doing? Need help this week?"

"We're ready to start seeing patients at the new location tomorrow. Teresa can handle the transition. She's as organized as you, and even bossier," Rachel teased. "She told me to focus on treating the patients and she would figure out how to make sure they follow us to our new location." There was a pause before Rachel spoke again. "You sure you're okay?"

Had Rachel heard the anxiety in her voice? "Yeah. I will be. Just trying to figure some things out."

"Want to talk about it?"

And tell her sister she was a liar and a fraud? Or how she'd let guilt about their family's mistakes allow her to shove her conscience aside and let the Caulfields dictate the type of person she should be? *No, thank you.*

But part of owning up to her mistakes would be confessing them to the people she loved. Otherwise, how could she start over with a clean conscience? It was part of her warped twelve-step program...if only she could find the courage.

Catherine sighed. "Maybe one of these days. I'm not ready yet."

"I'm here if you need me."

"Thanks."

"Oh, and Dad said he'd love to see you while you're in town."

Catherine hadn't worked up the courage to see him yet, either. She'd told herself she had too many other things going on—which she did—but the truth was, she wasn't sure she could put on a happy face for her father. Despite her agreement with the Caulfields that they wouldn't interfere with her father's life—that they'd forgive him for being involved in their son's death and not block his attempts at parole—his release had been denied again.

Doug Bailey, her father, still had several more years on his vehicular manslaughter sentence. When Mike Caulfield died in that wreck, it was as if Catherine's father had died, too. He lived through his daughters, had told Catherine he couldn't wait for her letters and phone calls, loved hearing about his successful girls.

But Catherine wasn't a success. If she visited him, he would see it written all over her face.

"I'll get out there to see him." It had been over a year since her last face-to-face visit. *Time to face the music.*

The prison was a half hour away—the same place where Tony Moreno was supposed to be locked up. The violent criminal was free, while her father, who was quietly serving his time and had turned his life around behind bars, was doomed to a life in captivity.

"Let me know when and we'll go together," Rachel said.

After a few minutes, they said goodnight and Catherine hung up. Still restless, she shot up from the bed, determined to search the dark, quiet house for a midnight snack or a shot of alcohol. Something, anything, to make her sleepy and relaxed.

She jerked open her door to find Max standing there, his hand raised as if he'd been about to knock. He was bare-chested and barefoot, sweatpants hanging low on his waist, the untied cords left dangling like a hypnotist's watch chain. Her gaze paused on a greenish-yellow bruise at his shoulder and then noted a couple old scars. The imperfections only heightened her awareness of his strength and resilience. She swallowed and searched her brain for a coherent thought.

He lowered his fist. "Thought I heard your voice. You can't sleep either?"

She stood there in a tank top and thin cotton sleep pants, feeling utterly exposed. "My mind seems to be wide awake." She'd probably never sleep again with the image of Max's washboard abs and broad chest burned into her brain. And that trail of hair that led from his navel and disappeared into his waistband made her mouth go dry.

He grinned. "Wanna raid the fridge?"

A few minutes later, Catherine found herself sitting opposite the man of her dreams, in a house she'd never imagined she'd set foot in, sharing a piece of leftover cheesecake in the romantic glow of the under-cabinet lighting. They sat side-by-side on the kitchen island's granite countertop—a behavior Lillian would probably lose her head over.

"Seriously, who has leftover dessert?" Catherine licked a graham cracker crust crumb from her fork.

Max's eyes followed the movement. "My mother always makes sure we have enough on hand for an army. In case company drops by."

"On a ranch, miles from town?"

"She used to have two growing boys, their friends and several stray cowboys who'd meander in and out at any time of day. That was before..."

Before his brother had died, Catherine guessed. "She changed?"

He nodded, looking off into the distance. "My brother died just before I turned eighteen. Car accident. After that, the whole family changed, though my father was always a hardass businessman."

"He's also a successful one."

"And Mike was supposed to follow in his very large footsteps."

Catherine swallowed hard. She knew the abyss that was created when a loved one made a mistake...or when a mistake cost someone his life. The pain was like no other.

His eyes took on a haunted look. "He was a few years older than me. Just about to graduate college. Had his whole life ahead of him. Unfortunately, it was the life my parents had mapped out for him." He shook his head and pushed off of the counter, then came to stand in front of her, nudging her knees apart so he could stand between them. "I don't know why I feel so comfortable talking to you."

"Maybe you needed someone to talk to," she said softly. *God knows you shouldn't talk to me. Your brother's death was my father's fault.*

She and her sister had gone by her mother's maiden name after the crash. Montgomery wasn't as notorious around these parts as Bailey. Her father's name had been plastered all over the papers at the time of the accident, but Hayworth had helped protect Catherine and Rachel, keeping them out of the news. For that, and for supporting Rachel's education, she owed him. He hadn't let her forget it.

"Being at the ranch has stirred up a lot of memories." He shook his head. "But it's more than that. How come I never noticed before?"

"Noticed what?"

"How incredible you are? What, was it like a superhero's secret identity or was I just oblivious?"

She sputtered out a laugh. "Both? Or maybe you were distracted by the pile of beautiful women at your feet."

"I was an idiot." He leaned forward and captured her mouth with his. His tongue flicked over her lips, encouraging her to open to him. Pleasurable sensations overwhelmed her as his hands moved from where they'd boxed her in on the counter to her knees, and then blazed a slow trail up her thighs to her hips. She restrained herself from hooking her legs around his waist and locking her ankles behind his back like she wanted to, settling for focusing on his mouth instead. Her hands stroked his wide shoulders, gently on his injured one, and then twined in the dark hair that brushed his collar. She liked that it was longer than the military allowed—slightly reckless, like his attitude.

Like this kiss. She couldn't afford to be reckless.

She pulled back to look at him. "You pushed me away on New Year's. What's changed?"

"You're too tempting to resist."

"Or you need a distraction from things you don't want to deal with. Your family. Your heritage and your inheritance."

He released her hips and stepped back. "Maybe I was wrong. You're not so different from the others. It always comes down to money and power."

Her jaw dropped.

He shoved a hand through his hair and muttered something under his breath. "I'm going to bed." He stalked out.

"LET HIM GO."

Startled, Catherine tripped in the living room on her way to follow Max. She'd wanted to stop him, to talk to him—to what end, she didn't know, but she couldn't let him think she only wanted money and power. She wanted *him*.

Before she fell, she caught herself on an end table and spun to face Lillian Caulfield. Max must not have seen his mother sitting in the darkened corner.

"Care for a drink?" Lillian gestured to a silver serving tray that held a couple of crystal-cut decanters. She did the honors and held two fingers of whiskey out to Catherine.

Catherine's shoulders slumped, the fight gone out of her, but the alcohol burned a trail to her belly, warming her cold insides. "How much did you hear?"

"Enough to know my son is hurt." Lillian stared into her drink. "Which means he cares about you. So this almost-engaged nonsense isn't entirely a ruse?"

"Of course it is. He's just away from his normal life. He doesn't trust the good things in his life. Can you blame him?"

Lillian sighed. "I'm afraid I...circumstances...helped make him that way." Her gaze moved to the hall where he'd disappeared toward his room.

"I swear I'm not trying to get the Caulfield money or name."

Lillian quietly assessed her, and then shocked her with a smile. "I know."

"You do?"

"You're a beautiful girl. And smart. If you'd tried, you could have had Max by now. Not that he would have stayed for long..."

Gee, thanks. But Catherine knew it was true. Max wasn't a one-woman type of man. He'd proven it with his string of brief, empty relationships. No, not relationships. Encounters.

"You're wise to keep your distance," Lillian continued. "When this is over, Hayworth and I can help you move on."

"Move on?" They were offering her *more* money? She'd refused it in the past, unless it helped Rachel or her dad. This time, it sounded like a severance package. Hush money. It made her feel even more dirty.

"You're an excellent personal assistant. I'm certain one of Hayworth's colleagues in another company, another state, could give you a fresh start."

Far away from her son. "Thank you for the offer, but I'm sure I'll figure things out on my own."

"Suit yourself, but not until your job here is done. I want Max to participate in that auction. It'll be the perfect place to see what options are available here."

"By options, you mean women?"

Lillian scowled. "And career or political opportunities."

"You really don't know him at all." Catherine shook her head and took another swallow of whiskey before setting down the glass. She turned to leave.

"Catherine."

At Lillian's regal tone, she turned back. "Yes?"

"You don't have a future with Max, but somebody out there does. You might as well help him find it—since you are his *friend*."

"That's right, I'm his friend. As a friend, I won't push him toward a life he doesn't want. And as a friend, I should tell him to get his ass back to Chicago as fast as possible." The liquor had lit a fire in her belly and she couldn't seem to stop the words coming out of her mouth, despite Lillian's shocked expression. "And as his friend, I'll make sure he gets what he deserves."

"You owe us."

"No, I don't. I wasn't driving that night." Angry tears burned in her eyes, but she caught Lillian's flinch. "I've repaid any debts my family incurred. I'll stick to our agreement. I'll even encourage the bachelor auction, mainly because, unlike you, I believe Max is man enough to make his own decisions and deal with the ramifications. But I'll also make sure he isn't railroaded."

"Isn't that what you've been doing to him for years?" Lillian smirked, knowing she'd hit on Catherine's weakness. Her damn conscience.

"I've been watching over him for you, yes. But I never forced him back to Texas. Whether he stays will be his choice."

"Choices can be shaped. We just have to make sure Max sees being back with his family, with a secure future, is the best choice."

"There is no *we* in this. I'll support Max until he makes his decision. In a month, I'll be gone. I'll *move on* without your help."

CHAPTER 13

Monday

Johnny's eyes locked on her the moment she walked into the club, but Catherine made a beeline for the office. He was certain to have more questions after how she'd left things—promising she might have information on how Dick was screwing him over—but it had been a lie. She'd deal with that later. Maybe he'd settle into his lunch special, admire the dancers and leave her alone.

A minute later, Johnny came in and closed the door. "So?"

Catherine tensed. "We can't talk here."

"Dick left on an errand thirty minutes ago. He looked nervous."

Well, that was an interesting tidbit, but the man had so many creditors breathing down his neck that he was bound to be anxious. "That doesn't mean he couldn't walk in again at any second."

Johnny shoved a hand through his hair and muttered something. "You didn't want to talk at my place, you don't want to talk here…I'm beginning to think you're lying to me. What I can't figure out is why. I'm getting really tired of people trying to play me."

"He's got some big money moving in and out." She tapped a finger on the ledger on the desk. "But I can't figure out who's on the other end. I just need some time."

"If he's stealing from—" Johnny stopped and shook his head. Had he been about to say *the Circle*? "This had better go some-where, or I'm screwed with my boss and with Dick."

"But if it's what I think it is, it's big." That should string Johnny along. "Be patient. I'm still digging."

He came close enough for her to smell the beer on his breath. Did the man drink all day? He grinned as he stalked toward her. "I think you do like me, or you wouldn't be doing this."

No, she'd only done this to cover up the real reason she'd been following him.

She resisted the urge to shove him out of her way and bolt from the office. "I told you, I'm not like that."

He stopped and his expression darkened. "You're not a tease, are you? I've got plenty of women who'd be down on their knees in a second if I ordered them to." He pointed to the two-way mirror, where they could see a dancer on stage.

Catherine swallowed and forced a shy smile. "I'm different, but I'm worth the wait."

Thankfully, they were interrupted by the ringing of Johnny's phone. "Walker here." There was a long pause as he listened. "I'm on it. Yeah, I know. I'll make it up to you. She'll be taken care of."

Catherine's heart climbed to her throat. Was he talking about her? But when he hung up, he didn't look ready to kill her. But who was the woman he spoke of, and how was he planning to take care of her?

Friday

CATHERINE SPENT THE NEXT SEVERAL DAYS WORKING AT LUCKY Dick's and avoiding Max. He was doing a fine job of ignoring her, too, even though they drove to and from all of his activities together. She'd often excused herself after dropping him off at the SSAM house, trying to separate herself from the group, though it hurt. Still, she could see the team members' mounting frustration as there were no new leads on Tony. But there were no new murders, either. Maybe the man had left town.

Max had yet to change the locks and clear her to move back into the guesthouse, but they barely talked as they shared space in the main house without seeing each other. Sure, she heard him in the shower in the mornings, which wreaked havoc on all of her senses, but she was a big girl. She could take it—for a little while longer, anyway.

"Ready to go?" she asked as she entered his office at CI. It was five o'clock and he should be ready to run out the door.

He looked up from his computer screen. "Yeah, just about. What time should we leave for the charity auction?"

"Shit." She'd forgotten.

At her curse, his eyebrows shot up. "You're not going to try to get out of it, are you?"

"I don't need to be there."

"You're my fiancée, remember?"

"You know very well that's not real."

His mouth tightened. "I need you at this event. As a friend."

"So you no longer think I'm after your money?"

He gave a short laugh. "Hell, you're not after me at all. You can't seem to stand being around me."

"It's not that—"

"No? What is it, then? Look, I'm sorry about what I said last weekend. If nothing else, I want our friendship back."

"They're going to auction you off to the highest bidder right in front of me." Her tone was sour and she turned away, disgusted with herself. These people continued to get under her skin.

"And he'll bring in a lot of money for a good cause." At the sound of Lillian's voice, both Max and Catherine turned to the doorway. Lillian's sharp gaze flicked over them. She held a fur coat in her arms. Diamonds dripped from her neck to merge with the sequins of her bodice. "That is, if he gets ready in time." She glanced pointedly at the clock on the wall. "I told Hayworth to let you go early today."

"I've been waiting for Catherine."

Sure, throw me under the bus. She rolled her eyes at him. "Don't let me hold you up."

Lillian's eyes assessed Max. "I'll expect you there by seven and you'd better be dressed to bring in the big bucks. I had Claudia rent a tux and hang it in your closet." She remained in the doorway until Max sighed and shuffled his papers around, piling them on the corner of his desk. Satisfied he was on his way to obeying her decree, she left.

Catherine's cell phone rang. Lucky Dick's. She felt Max's eyes on her as she answered.

"I know it's your night off, but I need you here," Dick said. His voice was tight, controlled.

"I can't. Not tonight."

Max stood and packed some paperwork into a leather satchel he'd adopted for work, then crossed his arms over his chest and narrowed his gaze on her. Max couldn't hear Dick's half of the conversation, but he was curious.

Dick sounded frazzled. He'd grown more and more anxious as the week went by. "I didn't get the liquor delivery and it's a Friday. Imagine how the weekend will play out without any alcohol."

"Will there be someone I can talk to this late?"

"Damn straight, or they'll lose my business. And they'll have a higher power to answer to. We all will."

A higher power? *The Circle?* "Okay, but it'll have to be late." She ended her call, mentally calculating when she'd be able to get to the club. The auction followed an elegant dinner, and if she stayed to watch Max be given to the highest bidder, she might not get to Lucky Dick's until ten or later.

"Who was that?" Max was still watching her with a scowl.

"Well, it wasn't Tony Moreno calling to turn himself in. Nobody else matters, right?"

He narrowed his eyes on her. "What are you hiding?"

If you only knew... "That was my boss. Don't worry about it."

He came close and tipped her chin up so he was looking directly into her eyes. "I can't help it, especially when you're agreeing to meet strange men late at night, God knows where. Why won't you tell me about your new job?"

"He's my boss, not some stranger." Maybe it was time to let someone else help, but under Max's glare, she couldn't bring herself to. Besides, he had too much on his plate already.

"And where is this new job?"

"You don't need to know."

His brows drew together. "Why are you so secretive about it?" He suddenly stepped back and retrieved his bag from his desk. "Never mind. Keep your secrets. We have to get to the ranch and dress."

"FIND OUT WHERE SHE WORKS." MAX GLANCED AT HIS APPEARANCE in the mirror while holding the cell phone in one hand. He could hear Catherine in the bathroom on the other side of his wall, getting ready for their evening. He hated the charade he'd forced them into, and he hated that she wouldn't talk to him.

"You're sure you want me to do this?" Einstein's doubts echoed loudly over the phone line. "Looking into a certain someone's past might be viewed as an invasion of privacy by that someone. And whatever you find can't be unfound. She wasn't too happy when I tracked her to her sister's clinic."

"I'm sure." The car ride from the office to the ranch had been quiet, except for the tension that seemed to pulse between them like a scream. "If she insists on finding employment outside of SSAM, I want to make sure she's dealing with the right people." Max said goodbye and hung up as he heard the bathroom door open, just outside his closed bedroom door.

He'd pick up his *date* to head back into town in a second, but he needed a moment to gather his thoughts. Catherine had his head spinning. One minute, she was pushing him away and hiding her thoughts and feelings. The next, she was open and vulnerable—and sexy as hell. In those unguarded moments, he could have sworn the emotions tangling in the depths of her eyes had included guilt, but over what?

What would she do tonight, while he was being auctioned like prime beef? He wasn't sure he could stand another four weeks of this pretense, giving his parents hope he would return to the ranch and the business when he had no intention to do so. But jumping through their hoops had kept the lines of communication between SSAM and the authorities open.

And after the auction, Catherine would move on to her other, secretive job, and who would protect her then? *That's* why he'd called Einstein. Because whether she liked it or not, Catherine was going to have a shadow protecting her tonight.

Determined to fight any objections she had to staying at his side like a normal near-fiancée, he marched to her bedroom door and knocked sharply. "Time to hit the road." As she pulled open the door, his final word drifted off and he stifled the urge to whistle in approval. He wasn't sure he even had the power to whistle, given that his lungs had ceased to function.

In a curve-hugging charcoal-gray gown, with her blond hair curled and piled up on her head in an elegant style that had the subtle orange-red strands catching the light, she was breathtaking.

She finished putting on an earring and frowned at him. "What? Is it okay? I had to borrow something from Rachel..."

He fumbled for words. "It's fine." *Fine?* He was an imbecile.

She ducked into her room to snatch a silk wrap from the bed and then sailed past him, bringing other senses to life as he caught a whiff of her perfume. Light, yet sultry, it socked him in the gut as he recalled the last time she'd worn it. He'd been nuzzling her neck at the New Year's party—right before he'd lost his senses and kissed her.

She'd always been pretty, but this was a whole new, seductive side of Catherine Montague. Had she made herself gorgeous to please him and fulfill her role of millionaire's son's fiancée—or had she dolled herself up for whomever she was meeting later tonight? A surge of powerful jealousy made him dizzy and he leaned against the doorjamb, which gave him a fine view of her backside.

She turned and arched a brow at him. "Coming?"

Well, hell. Who was this assertive woman who hid secrets behind her Caribbean-sea gaze? He continued to discover new sides of her. The more he learned, the more he wanted to strip her down and discover all of her secrets.

Catherine let the bluesy music of the jazz band that had been hired for the charity event flow over her. She wished her mind could drift to some beach somewhere, or maybe the French Quarter of New Orleans, eating a beignet or sipping a Ramos Gin Fizz.

A little escape therapy never hurt anyone, especially when the women seemed to be lining up to meet Max. She wondered how much of that was staged by his parents and how much was due to Max's innate charm. He could easily handle this crowd like a pro, a future politician or whatever he wanted to be. For a big, bad ex-SEAL, he certainly was sociable. Every laugh he coaxed from a flirtatious bachelorette cracked Catherine's heart open a little more. This was his element and these were the eligible women he should be pursuing.

In her mind, she was just settling onto a towel on a private beach with a good book when she felt a pinch at her elbow and looked up—right into Max's frustrated eyes.

"When I said I wanted you by my side, I meant mentally, too." His words were a low growl. "Where do you keep drifting off to?"

She hadn't realized he'd noticed, what with all the female attention. "What do you mean?"

"I can tell by that silly smile on your face that you're not here, at this party." His gaze moved around the room as if cataloging all of its faults. He looked like his imperial mother in that moment. And here, she'd thought her benign smile was an excellent cover. Apparently, he'd used his super-SEAL powers and seen right through it.

"Sorry," she said. "I'm here, I just don't want to be."

His anger softened and he blew out a breath. He opened his mouth to say something, then closed it abruptly and pulled her by the arm out of the crowd. The banquet room at the country club opened onto a golf course. Each hole was lit up like a beacon, but in between there was darkness. The perfume of moist grass and fresh blossoms filled the warm night air. Max tugged her along with him until they were on the edge of the green, in the shadows.

She pulled loose from his gentle but firm hold. "You wanted to talk?"

"Yes. No. *Shit.*" He tugged at the bowtie of his tux and she automatically lifted a hand to soothe him, then let it fall when she realized what she was doing. She couldn't be that for him. She couldn't be anything for him—just a friend and a pretend fiancée, for a short time longer.

So, take advantage of that time.

She reached up and cupped his cheek, rubbing a thumb against a sharp cheekbone. "What? Did you want to work on your swing?" She hoped teasing would ease his frustration.

He groaned and his hand moved to hold hers against his cheek. "I don't know what I want, but my swing sure seems to need some work lately. Why can't I seem to get things right with you? Everything I say is wrong. I don't know what I did to mess things up, Cat, but I want what we had." He shook his head as his fingers curled around hers. "No, I want more than what we had."

God, this was so much better than the fantasy beach in her head. And it was just as far from reality. "You're confused." He was simply overwhelmed and a fish out of water and any other excuse she could make up to explain why he would say this now. Being this close to everything she'd wanted for so long, right when it was all about to crash to the earth around her, was like some sadistic torture.

He tugged her closer until her breasts pressed against his chest. "I know what I want." His mouth descended on hers and every argument fled from her mind as she gave herself up to the abyss of pleasure, where want and desire and need swirled and swelled and burst into such amazing sensations, she never wanted it to end. Max's tongue slipped inside, beyond her barriers, and the heat built until she was the one demanding, coaxing, taking.

The buzzing of her purse yanked her back to reality and she pulled away with a start.

Max frowned as she glanced at the screen. The seductive mood burst like a bubble. "Your boss?" No, it was the local prison. As she pressed the button to answer, he narrowed his eyes. "You're going to take a call now?"

"I have to. Hello?" she said into the phone.

"Hey, darlin'." And with those two words, Catherine was a little girl again, sitting on her father's knee as he told stories and smelled of cigarettes and whiskey. As a child, she'd thought that was normal. Her childhood smelled like addiction and tasted like disappointment. But she still loved her father.

"Hey." Her voice went soft. She stepped away from Max, who blew out a frustrated breath.

"Sorry to bother you," her father said. "Rachel gave me your new cell number and I'd earned a call."

"No, no bother."

Max muttered a curse and turned on his heel. She watched his long strides carry him across the turf as if he couldn't get away fast enough. *It's for the best.*

Catherine stayed in the shadows and hugged herself. "I've been meaning to come by and see you."

"Prison's no place for my girls." There was a long pause. "I enjoyed your last letter."

"I guess it's been a while. Life's been busy, but that's no excuse. You've been on my mind."

"I guess Rachel told you my last parole hearing was a bust." He chuckled, but there was no humor.

"Don't give up."

"I gave up hope a while back, but it's sweet of you to try."

Catherine squeezed her eyes shut against a wave of emotions; anger, disappointment, fear and hope tangled like seaweed in the ebb and flow. "Please don't stop fighting. We want you to come back to us."

"I want that too, but..." His voice trailed off.

Annoyed with herself and him, she swiped at a stray tear. "I'll come by and see you sometime soon, okay?"

"I'd like that. I want to hear everything you've been up to." Not everything. She didn't want him to have a tarnished image of his little girl. They chatted for a few more minutes until his call time was over. "Take care of yourself and your sister, sweetie. You two are my life."

Afraid she'd start bawling like a baby, she tried to wrap up the conversation quickly. After saying goodbye, she hung up and stood for a long moment, hesitant to go back to the party. She felt torn in too many directions, like a much-used ragdoll ready to fall to pieces with one more indelicate yank.

You've been here before.

When her mother had died, leaving behind fourteen- and twelve-year-old daughters who needed her badly. When, four years later, their father's drinking had gotten so bad that he'd done the unthinkable and then gone to prison. When an eighteen-year-old Catherine had smothered her own dreams to take her sister in rather than see Rachel go into foster care. When she'd sold her soul to the Caulfields to protect what sense of family the Baileys had left, changed her and Rachel's last name to Montgomery—their mother's maiden name, and helped get Rachel through high school, college and then medical school.

She'd definitely been here, in this place of despair and frustration, before. Sometimes, she felt as if she'd never left. *You'll survive this, too. Suck it up, paste a smile on your face and put one foot in front of the other.*

She suited actions to words and found herself back in the party. The laughter and music were cacophonous after the soft night sounds out on the golf course. And the atmosphere seemed to build with excitement like an electrical charge waiting for release as the emcee stepped onto the small stage at one end of the room, farthest from where Catherine stood.

"You're just in time, honey." The woman beside her was a stranger but winked as if she knew Catherine. "Your man is about to go on the chopping block, but they'll start with the less meaty options first. You have time to get your checkbook out."

Max was certainly a *meaty* option. Catherine searched the side of the stage and spied him laughing with a woman who was retying his bowtie. It was Melissa, the physical therapist. Catherine stiffened her knees against a crippling jolt of jealousy. She'd had her chance and she'd blown it. Outside, Max had made his desires clear. She'd been a coward and taken a phone call rather than face the consequences.

But according to the Caulfields, her job was to present the bright prospects of Max's future. Let him choose the path he wanted to take. She wouldn't be like his parents and stand in his way.

She turned to the woman at her side. "He's well worth the money."

"So, you're going to bid?"

"That would defeat the purpose, wouldn't it?" The price tag would be beyond her means, and a date with Max would give her another night to fall deeper in love. "Besides, the money should come from one of these charitable people, right?"

"Oh, honey, I'm sure charitable thoughts will be furthest from the mind of whatever lucky woman wins a night with him."

Aching inside, Catherine ignored the throng gathering near the stage and skirted the periphery of the room until she reached the door. She'd go to Lucky Dick's, where she could do the most good right now. Max would be fine. He was surrounded by adoring females. If nothing else, tonight would remind him of the benefits of the single status he'd worked so hard to preserve. He'd soon see his desire to form a relationship with her had been a momentary lapse in sanity.

CHAPTER 14

Catherine walked into Lucky Dick's at nine o'clock. She didn't expect to see Dick himself in the office, but he was, looking even more frazzled than he'd let on. Was somebody higher up on the food chain coming down on him?

"Liquor guy still giving you trouble?" Catherine laid her purse and wrap on the arm of the couch.

"We've got more trouble than just the liquor guy." His tone was gruff, and he had a tumbler half full of amber liquid at his elbow on the desk. His eyes roved over her, taking in her attire. "I interrupted your evening."

"It's fine." She raised an eyebrow, trying to hide a fluttering of unease at his abrasiveness. He'd seemed on a downward spiral all week, but hadn't indicated what was wrong. "Tough night?"

"The police were here. Another woman was found dead, stabbed the same way Bea was and dumped in about the same place."

"She was from here?" Her gaze moved to the two-way mirror. A dancer was working the stage. Darla made her way through the crowd, delivering drinks. All seemed normal.

"They weren't sure at first, but no. I saw the pictures." He took a long swallow of his drink. "Not one of my girls."

"But they think the cases are related."

"They asked if they could hang out tonight, undercover, ask some questions of the regulars." Maybe that explained his fidgetiness.

"And you agreed?"

He shrugged. "I suppose it couldn't hurt business if they lie low. And if one of them out there is a killer and we can catch him..."

Catherine sat on the opposite side of the desk and turned the computer screen to face her. She pulled the keyboard over to her side. "Let's see if we can solve your other problem. I know I sent the liquor company a payment earlier this week."

He sighed. "Thank God. If my boss came down on me..."

"Boss?" Her senses went on full alert. *The* Boss, from the Circle?

He took another gulp of his drink. "I'm actually just a manager here. Someone else owns the place."

"Who?"

He cocked his head to the side. "You're asking a lot of questions tonight."

Catherine backed off, sensing he wouldn't talk about it. If she pressed, she'd show her hand. "No worries. I'll get to work."

After several phone calls, she'd settled things with the distributor by threatening to take their business elsewhere if they didn't fulfill the order by ten the next morning. She stood and arched her back. Dick had left a little while ago, after making the rounds within the club. It was near ten o'clock, and the work had provided a welcome distraction, but now she wondered what Max was up to. Who had won a night with him? Melissa? Was he with her now? What were they doing? Had he even noticed she'd left?

Angry with herself for caring, she went out to the bar and ordered a drink. Darla sidled up to her as she waited for the bartender to fill her tray with an order, too.

"How are you?" Catherine asked.

Darla shrugged. "Been okay. Making bank tonight with the convention staying at the hotel down the street. They're a pretty civilized bunch. Tip surprisingly well for accountants. I think they're relieved tax season is over."

Catherine surveyed the room, trying to pick out the under-cover cops who might be asking questions. "I heard about the new murder."

Darla frowned. "Yeah. Sad when someone targets women just trying to make a buck the best way they know how."

Catherine examined Darla. "And what about you? Is this the best way?"

"It works for me. I didn't have the staying power to stick it out through even one semester of college."

Would Rachel have ended up in a job like this if Catherine hadn't made a deal with the Caulfields? Or would Catherine have ended up somewhere like here to help pay for college expenses for Rachel and herself? Maybe she'd been too hard on herself. She'd done what she had to do to get by, much like these women were doing.

Her gaze moved to Kim as she approached the stage in her kimono. Yeah, life was hard sometimes, but separating what you did on the outside from what you thought of yourself on the inside was sometimes the difference between survival and the slow death of a soul.

"Whatever your dream is, go after it," Catherine said. "Don't let anyone stop you."

Darla nodded. "Always great advice."

JOHNNY LET THE DARKNESS AT LUCKY DICK'S ENVELOP HIM LIKE A cloak. The Boss wasn't so happy with him. They still hadn't found Tony after he'd escaped Johnny's apartment over a week ago. The asshole had stolen some things, too.

Still, if Johnny could find Tony—or if the Boss appreciated the new task he'd completed yesterday—he'd be golden again. And maybe he could ignore the bad taste in his mouth.

A fourteen-year-old girl...

As ordered, he'd snatched her as she'd walked home from school yesterday, branded her shoulder with the Circle symbol and driven her to the spot the Boss had specified, where he'd handed her over to the Boss' man. It wasn't like the usual exchange of human flesh. In the past, the women he'd driven to the border for a human trafficking op had either owed the Circle a debt or had given up on life already, the emptiness in their eyes indicating they'd halfway checked out of this world. A few of the Circle's Cattle Call prospects were runaways nobody would miss. But this girl...she'd looked well cared for.

"Your table's waiting," Darla said as she shuttled by with a tray filled with drinks. She looked back over her shoulder with a smile just for him. He sat down and Darla brought him his drink within a minute. "You weren't in on Wednesday."

"Didn't know you were my secretary."

For an instant, she looked wounded, but she quickly shrugged it off. "Just making conversation."

He took a deep swallow of his beer and felt his nerves steady. "I had an appointment. But it's nice to know someone noticed."

"I always watch for one of my best tippers." The sultry invitation returned to Darla's voice, but his gaze went to the stage, where Kim had just moved in front of his table and was dancing for him and him alone. Damn, it was good to be king.

Darla moved away to take an order and he sat back to enjoy. With the warm headiness of the alcohol lining his insides, he began to relax. Everything was going to be okay. He'd done what he'd been paid to do and that was that.

"You a regular?" One of the suits at the table beside him leaned forward when Johnny made the mistake of making eye contact. "Saw the way that waitress automatically brought you a drink."

Johnny hid his irritation. This wasn't a fucking church social. Did he look like he wanted to chat? He grunted in response.

But Chatty Cathy was persistent. "I heard one of the dancers ended up dead last week. And another one tonight, from a different joint."

What? His muscles bunched with tension, but he kept his laid-back pose and sipped his drink. "Really? Who?"

"Angelique. Danced in some feathered contraption over at Cabaret on Main."

No. No, no, no. He'd gone out with Angelique just a few days ago. He didn't often frequent Cabaret, but the Circle had asked him to report on a woman there and make a drug run while he was at it. Besides, the place had a killer midweek lunch special. He'd picked up Angelique after her set and woken up Wednesday morning, after a damn good time, to find her gone. He hadn't thought of it since.

The guy leaned closer, as if sharing a secret. "How about Bea? Was she hot?"

They didn't call her Busty Bea for nothing.

Before he could answer, Darla reappeared with a bowl of nuts and set it on his table, along with a napkin. He glanced at the small square when she tapped a fingertip against it, pointing out three letters that chilled his blood.

Cop.

Johnny looked the man in the eye. "No, man. I didn't know her."

"Did I mention he's an ex-SEAL?" Max's mother should have been a saleswoman, but she was also perceptive enough to know when she wasn't welcome. "Well, I'll give you two time to sort out the details of your date. Your father is probably talking the poor senator's ear off." As she left Max and Melissa at the table and headed for the senator, she shot Max a look that warned him to behave.

Melissa smiled seductively, but her determination faltered as he continued to brood. He couldn't help it, damn it. He was pissed. Catherine had ducked out on him again. And now she was God knows where with God knows who.

Melissa's look turned questioning. "Everything okay?" She'd just spent several thousand dollars on a few hours of his time but he couldn't seem to get into the charitable spirit.

What was it with Catherine lately? She'd been the steadfast nurturer at SSAM and then she'd left Chicago without a word of goodbye. It looked like she'd be taking a leave of absence from his life as well. Sure, *he'd* walked away from *her* when she'd received that phone call, but he couldn't stand the soft note that had crept into her voice when she spoke to whatever lucky man was on the other end. They'd been sharing a moment, and then she'd broken it. Had it been her new boss?

And shit, why should he care? He needed some perspective.

"Your mother told me you aren't really engaged," Melissa probed when he remained silent. "Is that true?"

"I'm not engaged." His statement was far from warm, and held a surprising amount of bitterness. He'd never wanted to be tied down in any way. What had changed?

"Perhaps we should save our date for another night, when I can have your *undivided* attention?" She placed a soothing hand on his arm, her manicured nails staking claim. She reached into her purse and removed a pen and business card, then wrote on the back. "Here's my number."

Great. He could look forward to going through this again at a later time.

What was wrong with him? The old Max Sawyer would have had her in his bed by midnight. This mixed-up man he'd become wasn't even viewing the smart, beautiful woman beside him as a sexual creature.

He blamed it all on Catherine, and he'd tell her so when he saw her.

His eyes scanned the room again for her, and then came back to Melissa as the woman rose. "I'll look forward to your call," she said.

Seeing Melissa's imminent departure, his mother headed their way again. "Thank you, dear, for supporting the hospital," his mother told Melissa as they passed each other. When Max and his mother were alone, she scowled at him. "What happened?"

"Have you seen Catherine?" Impatience sharpened his question.

"Not since you dragged her out of here to the golf course— which most of the town gossips saw, by the way."

"She's supposedly my fiancée, so I'm not sure what they'd be gossiping about." He couldn't give a flying fuck, anyway. Apprehension crawled up his spine. He wouldn't have pegged Catherine as the secret-liaison type, but his doubts were growing. As was the gut feeling that he was overlooking something important.

"You're being rather rude," his mother pointed out. "Melissa paid a lot of money to spend a few hours with you. The least you could do is thank her."

"I will during our date—which was your idea, by the way. Besides, who bids on a man who has a fiancée?"

"Near-fiancée. And no, I haven't seen Catherine." His mother gave him a smug look. "Maybe you should keep your options open."

His eyes narrowed on her. "Did you pay her off, too? The reason I moved away was to keep you and Dad from meddling in my life."

She froze. "I wouldn't do that. I wouldn't interfere in that way. I don't want you to leave again."

He was surprised at the way her voice softened, but steeled his heart against it. His parents had committed some despicable acts to manipulate his future, and he didn't doubt that appealing to his pity was in her wheelhouse. "You realize you would have had an eleven-year-old grandchild about now had you not *interfered* in my business?" Max's gut tightened at the thought of the son or daughter he would never know.

She paled and had the decency to look away. But when she looked back, there was a hardness in her gaze born of self-preservation. "I didn't tell Trish to have an abortion."

Her words sliced like a knife, reopening old wounds. Why had he gone there? "And yet you hinted she had no choice but to raise the baby alone, or not at all. We were barely eighteen, Mother."

"Exactly. And your judgment was clouded by grief for your brother and teenage immaturity. You didn't know what you wanted, and she sure as hell only wanted our money. She took off with it fast enough."

That much was true. His high school girlfriend had gotten pregnant in their senior year, soon after Mike's death. Max hadn't cared about what happened to himself, hadn't thought to be careful about anything. He'd barely noticed when Trish disappeared from his life, and hadn't known she was pregnant until she'd shown up six months later, telling him the whole sordid tale —including how she'd gone to his mother first with the news, and had been paid to quietly disappear. She'd asked him for more money. He'd signed up for the military the next day. Bile burned the back of his throat at the memory.

Already grieving his brother, Max had barely had the energy to grieve the loss of his child. Joining the SEALs had been his saving grace, though on occasion, he thought about what might have been. His dad had tried to null and void his contract with the military. Thank God he'd had no influence there. Failure to control Max's decision had eaten at Hayworth Caulfield's pride, even though he'd already lost one son because of the same type of manipulation.

His mother was right about one thing—Max hadn't loved Trish, not in a mature, lasting type of way. But he would have been there for their child. In some ways, his career path had been determined by that loss. He'd decided, if he couldn't save himself, he'd spend his life saving others.

Catherine refused to be saved. She was hiding something, something that brought pain and fear to her eyes, and he was damn well going to figure out what it was.

His mother was watching him carefully. "I don't want to discuss this now," he said.

As he turned to leave, his mother's hand shot out and she grabbed his arm. "I'll see you at the ranch? Don't forget our weekly dinner is tomorrow. Claudia's preparing another of your favorites."

"I'll be there. It's part of the deal." Only four more weeks until he was a free man again. Or, if he found Tony sooner, he'd no longer be beholden to his father. But first, he had to find Catherine.

Outside, as he waited for the valet to flag down a cab, he dialed Einstein on his cell phone.

"How much money did you bring in?" His friend sounded wide awake despite the late hour.

Max snorted. "More than you would. Lay off the Red Bulls, would you?"

"Hey, you gave me an assignment, right? Besides, I'm also looking into some leads regarding Circle activity in the area. A new murder victim was discovered this evening."

"Anything we can use?"

"She was a dancer at a club."

"Like Bea?" He wondered how Catherine would react to this news. If SSAM had let her go undercover at Lucky Dick's, could she have prevented this new murder?

"Same MO, different club. I'll let you know when I find out more. In the meantime, I did discover where Catherine is working."

"Where?"

"For someone with one foot out the door, our girl seems determined to help SSAM."

A chill ran down his spine. "Just give me the address."

CHAPTER 15

It was after midnight. Outside the office, the crowd had thinned, but many tables remained occupied, including Johnny's. She'd gone into the office to avoid his curious gaze and get some work done. She'd even done some searching for connections to the Circle, but Dick was careful. If there were connections to be found, she wasn't finding them.

Other than the mysteries of Dick and Johnny, the club and its occupants had become part of her life. Even the sight of all that skin had become normal. She knew Kim was hoping to go back to college in the fall. Darla was difficult to get to know, but Catherine sensed she had a big heart. Leeann had a young son in another state. And Bea…she'd been a sort of mentor to all the girls. They missed her and had created a makeshift vigil at her dressing room locker.

Catherine went out into the main room, but stood at the bar where she could watch everyone. Was one of these men a killer? The undercover cops had left sometime in the past half hour.

Darla sank onto a barstool next to her.

"Long night?" Catherine asked.

"The longest. But it paid off." She lifted a wad of cash from her pocket.

"I bet you make just as much as the dancers."

"Not really, but I don't have to take my clothes off." Her gaze shifted toward the front row. Kim was on stage, but seemed to be dancing only for Johnny.

"You never wanted to do anything else?"

"Maybe. But I wouldn't have been good at it." When she continued, Darla mimicked a deep, masculine voice. "You were meant to serve, so you might as well get used to it."

Clearly, someone had told her that long ago, some man whom Darla had believed. She wondered where this young woman's family was. "Did your father tell you that?"

"My father was practical. But he also liked to spend his nights in clubs like this. No wonder I ended up in one."

"And your mother? Did she agree?"

She shrugged. "I never had a mother worth speaking of. She wasn't around long enough for me to find out." And she certainly wasn't around when Darla needed a woman's influence to soften the hard edges. Darla was...prickly. But one did what one had to do in self-defense.

Catherine felt a pang of sympathy. "My mother died just when it seemed I needed her most. If you ever want to talk..."

"Thanks, but life sucks, end of story." The shields were up again. Darla moved over to a nearby table of three gentlemen and started taking their order. One of the men slid a hand up the back of Darla's thigh and she froze. Beside him, his cohort laughed and pulled Darla into his lap. She squirmed. The bouncer at the door, Robert, was busy speaking with a customer, so Catherine headed to the table.

"Hey, guys. The show's on the stage." She tried to keep her tone light. Unfortunately, they didn't take her seriously. At least it was enough to pull their attention from Darla, who sprang away when the man released her to reach for Catherine.

"Relax, hon," he said. "There's enough of us to go around. No need for jealousy."

"Jealousy?" Catherine laughed, which apparently was the wrong thing to do. The man tugged her sideways into his lap. His arms held her against him like a vice, pushing her breasts painfully against his chest. Darla stood there, shocked, but looking mad enough to smash a bottle over the man's head.

"Get Robert," Catherine told Darla, but the girl wasn't meeting her eyes. "Get him," she hissed again as the man's hand started climbing up Catherine's knee, his fingertips slipping under the hem of her silky evening dress.

"Stop," she warned, all lightness gone from her voice. "I'll shove that knee somewhere very tender and very vulnerable if you don't let me up."

"You're feisty." He grinned. "I like this look you've got going on. Sexy, yet bossy. If you have a whip, I'll pay extra."

"Let her go."

Catherine looked up sharply at the familiar voice. Her body went into full-alert mode as her eyes traveled upward over Max's tuxedo-clad body to meet his angry gaze. Still in his tuxedo from the auction, he looked like the hero in a spy movie, confident, determined and dressed to thrill. A muscle leapt in his jaw, and she knew he was silently furious. There was no hint of his good-ole-boy, laidback charm now.

"I'm fine." She tried to reassure him and avoid a scene. How had he found her, anyway? Did he put out a BOLO on her vehicle? Or had Einstein worked his magic again?

"*Fine?* You sure you don't want to amend that statement?"

Right. She was working in the club he'd told her to avoid, sitting in some stranger's lap, being pawed like a piece of meat, while women took off their clothes in the background.

Her heart sank.

"The lady says she's fine," the man holding her said.

"That doesn't mean I want to be in your lap." She drove her heel into his shin. His breath whooshed out against her ear like an alcohol-soaked emission from a humid distillery, but his arms dropped away. He cursed as his friends erupted in laughter.

She sprung to her feet and smoothed her dress, and then walked past Max to the bar. Out of the corner of her eye, she noticed Johnny had left. Feeling shaky, she ordered a vodka martini and slid onto a stool. She felt Max approach before she saw him lean against the bar beside her.

"Fancy meeting you here," she muttered. "How'd you find me?"

"I have my sources." He still sounded pissed.

Her eyes met his in the mirror over the bar. "Remind me to ream Einstein later for digging into innocent people's private information."

Max's gaze pinned her. "I'm not so sure you're innocent." Her heart stopped for a split second. What else had Einstein found?

Darla came to Catherine's other side and touched her arm. "Um, thanks for that, back there."

Catherine smiled. "We solo girls have to stick together, right?"

"Right." But Darla looked perplexed. "You okay?" Her question was directed at Catherine, but her attention went to Max, whose stormy scowl was imposing. He looked like a big, bad physical threat, but the biggest risk was to Catherine's heart. Part of her had always wanted him to notice her, to care about her, but not like this. She didn't want to be his damsel.

"Yeah, I'm fine," she said.

Darla nodded and went back to taking orders, giving a wide berth to the three accountants who were now being escorted to the door by Robert.

"*Fine?*" Max shook his head in disbelief. "You're still going with that?"

"I am fine."

"Your secret job is at Lucky Dick's—a strip club?"

"They prefer *gentlemen's club.*"

His brows went up. "Those men didn't seem like gentlemen. God, Catherine, is this where you've been working?"

She took a healthy swallow of her martini. "Maybe it's what I deserve."

He shifted closer, lowering this voice. "You deserve baring yourself to these men, for money? What the hell? Do you think so little of yourself?"

She nearly choked on her drink. "I don't dance here. I'm a bookkeeper."

Relief relaxed his features. "I still don't get it. Why won't you come back to SSAM? Or is this *for* SSAM? Hell, Cat, we're not even sure the Circle's connected to this club."

"I think it is."

He muttered an expletive. "Even more reason not to be here. Why would you do this?"

"It's a long story."

"I've got all night. And I'm not leaving without you."

MAX COULDN'T IMAGINE ANY EXPLANATION THAT WOULD MAKE A lick of sense, but he was willing to give Catherine a chance to explain. She looked ready to drop as her prior bravado wore off and was replaced by fatigue. "Talk to me."

The hairstyle she'd worn for the auction had come loose and waves cascaded down her back. He tucked a curl behind her ear and let his fingers linger against its silkiness. As his hand drifted further down, he couldn't resist brushing his fingertips across her neck, the vulnerable place where someone had almost ended her life a few weeks ago. She leaned into him. She sniffed, though she hadn't been crying. She was holding back again, but he sensed a crack in the walls.

He repeated his soft demand. "Talk to me." *Let me in, baby.*

"Not here." She downed the rest of her martini and set a bill on the bar, disappeared through a door to the left and returned a moment later with her wrap and purse. She walked to the front door without a backward glance. He followed, wondering what the hell was going through her beautiful mind.

Once in the parking lot, she stopped suddenly and turned to face him, looking lost. "What are we doing, Max?"

He reached for her keys. "We're finally going to talk. Let me drive."

She looked surprised. "Can you drive?"

"Actually, I was cleared to drive a few days ago. I took a cab to get here tonight, but my range of motion is practically normal. I'm even planning to hit the shooting range with Einstein soon."

"That's wonderful!" Her glee faded as rapidly as it appeared. "Why didn't you tell me?"

"I enjoy our drives together. It's the only time I see you lately." He opened the passenger side for her and then jogged around to the driver's side. "Where to?"

She seemed at a loss. "I don't know. Wait, you need to go to SSAM. Another body was discovered. It appears to be linked to Bea's murder."

"Einstein already knows about it."

She bit her lip. "You think it could be Tony?"

"It's hard to believe he would be hanging around here, committing crimes that might get him caught. He seemed smarter than that." Though Max hoped the guy wasn't that smart, or that connected. He wanted to throw his ass back in prison. Either way, it looked as if there was a killer in the area, possibly a serial killer. And Catherine had inserted herself in the middle of it all. This type of investigation that was right up SSAM's alley. "Let me text Einstein the info and we'll see how they want to handle it." He'd rather not give up this opportunity to break down Catherine's barriers. He typed a text and hit send.

Catherine suddenly sat up straight in her seat. "Aren't you supposed to be on a date or something?"

"Postponed. Even Melissa agreed tonight wasn't the right time."

"Melissa. I figured you might end up with her." Was that regret he heard in her voice? It gave him hope. "I bet she's disappointed."

That curl had fallen forward again, so he reached out to tuck it behind her ear, then let his hand stay at the back of her neck so she'd look at him. "I don't really care. I only thought about finding you and I'm glad I did." The memory of her in the dank club, trapped in another man's embrace, brought hot anger bubbling to the surface. She began to shake her head and fury and frustration welled up further still. To silence the rejection he sensed was coming, he quickly leaned forward and took her mouth with his—and took and took.

His chest filled with anticipation as she responded, tentatively at first, then with definite interest. Her hand slid up his chest to cup his cheek. She tipped her head and slanted her mouth over his, releasing a moan of pleasure as she deepened the contact. But it wasn't enough, because she slid her hand from his cheek into his hair and gripped the back of his head, holding him to her. The kiss turned hotter, more demanding as she nipped and sucked at his bottom lip, then consumed him again.

God, he could take her right here, in her Jeep, with the gearshift sticking into his side, and he had the feeling it would be the best sex of his life. His good-girl image of her had been shattered tonight, seeing her in Lucky Dick's. That she'd taken a job there to help SSAM showed she was a risk-taker beneath her efficient, composed exterior. Would she take a risk with him? He wanted to break through Catherine's calm façade and taste the bad girl beneath the surface.

Her tongue slid over his and the heat moved all the way through him. *A bed.* That would be the best place for this—and he would keep her there all night, where he could enjoy her properly.

He broke the kiss. "The guesthouse. I changed the locks yester-day, so it's secure."

She nodded, slightly breathless. "Drive fast."

Why had he wasted his time and energy resisting her all of

these months? *Because your head knew your heart wouldn't stay out of it.* Not with her. If he crossed a certain line, he wouldn't be able to walk away. He had no idea where that imaginary boundary was, but he was willing to push the limits.

As he pulled onto the street, his cell phone began to vibrate. "Could you get that?" His focus was on getting them back to the ranch as fast as possible.

Catherine took the phone from the console. "It's Damian. Maybe it's about the murder."

His hopes sank.

"Einstein just heard from someone at the police station. There's been another murder." Damian pulled pants on one-handed and searched the closet for a fresh shirt as he talked to Max and Catherine on the phone.

"Other than the exotic dancer?" Max asked. "Catherine said there was another body found this evening, a woman named Angelique, from a different gentlemen's club across town. But the body was found in the same location where Bea was dumped."

"This is different. This victim was young." Damian's hand started to shake and he sat on the bed. "She was Sam's age." Barely a teenager.

"*Jesus.* The Circle?"

"Sounds like it, based on what our contact reported." In addition to hunting for Tony, the SSAM team had been cultivating relationships among the local authorities, hoping it would lead to increased sharing of information.

"Could this be Tony, killing again? What does Lorena think?"

"His crimes involved sexual gratification, usually with women in their twenties." Damian looked toward his closed door. Lorena was in the bedroom across the hall, getting dressed. He could still envision the tousled black hair and dark, sleepy eyes that had greeted him when she'd answered his knock a few minutes ago. "I haven't had the chance to talk to her in detail yet. We're heading to the murder scene to see if we can get some more details."

"Catherine's with me. We'll meet you there."

Damian gave him the location, a rest area off Interstate 10 about twenty minutes away, and hung up. He finished dressing and found Lorena making a pot of coffee in the kitchen. The clock read two-thirty, but she looked ready for a day at the office, her hair now tamed into a twist at her nape. She lifted a mug in question.

"Yes, please. Where's Einstein?" He didn't know when it had become awkward to be alone with Lorena, but a tension was starting to grow between them, something he suspected was sexual and wasn't sure was two-sided. He was still her boss, however, so any thoughts he had of a relationship with her beyond those boundaries was shady territory.

"In the den, trying to contact the detective in charge."

"That would save us some hassle."

"If we can win the guy over." She passed him a filled mug and then nudged the creamer toward him.

"Catherine will be there. Maybe she can sweet-talk them, if necessary."

"Your wheels seem to be turning already. Got some ideas?"

He shook his head. "Just thinking about the victim." Thoughts of Lorena had only been a short diversion.

Her expression darkened. "So young."

"I'm not sure we should say anything to the SAPD about Samantha, or any possible links between the two murders. Not yet, anyway."

"Why not?"

"They might not let us help with the investigation." He had too much of a personal stake in the outcome to be shut out.

Her hand touched his and he stiffened, not because he didn't like her touch, but because he liked it entirely too much. Apparently sensing a rejection, she pulled away.

He reached out and stopped her hand as it slid across the counter. "I'm sorry," he said. "I'm just not sure where my head's at right now."

She searched his face, and then nodded. "I know the feeling." Her lips curved into a small smile and his heart quickened. Was she saying that the attraction was mutual?

Einstein rushed in and grabbed a travel mug, filling it with coffee and breaking the moment. "Ready to go?"

"Is the SAPD willing to cooperate?" Damian asked.

"I've got it on good authority that the detective who's been assigned to the case is sympathetic to our cause. I've spent a couple nights having beers with the men in a bar near the precinct, so I've gotten to know a couple of them."

Lorena's jaw dropped. "You stepped away from your computer long enough to make live, human connections?"

Einstein smirked. "Hey, I can do whatever's needed for a mission. I'm multitalented."

"I'm sure you are—and I bet you're the best at everything you try." She appeased Einstein with her words and sent a wink Damian's way. Just like that, they were back on even footing, easygoing coworkers, as if none of the tension between them had existed. Perhaps the attraction *was* all one-sided.

But why did that increase his frustration?

CHAPTER 16

Bright lights had been set up on the scene—a wooded area just off the walking path that ran along the rest area off Interstate 10. Definitely a different dumpsite than where the two exotic dancers had been left in a ravine behind a truck stop closer to town. Max parked Catherine's Jeep at the edge of the lot, closest to the scene where bright lights had been set up, and glanced at Catherine. "Ready?"

"You sure it's okay I'm here?" She pulled her wrap tighter around her. She'd wanted to come with him as a show of support.

"You're part of the team."

"I must seem like a yo-yo, but I really don't think I can come back to SSAM when this is all over. Still, you're my friends. And, *God*, if this is related to Sam's death, this is huge for Damian. I can't just walk away."

She was clearly miserable, wanting to be there for her friends but not feeling able to. Why was she torturing herself? Before Damian's call, Max had been so close to figuring out something about what made Catherine tick, but her emotional walls were up again.

"Come with me—unless you'd rather stay in the car where it's warm?" While the days had been warming up, the spring nights, especially the early morning hours, were chilly.

Damian emerged from the wooded area. Lorena and Einstein had to be nearby, too.

She reached for the door handle. "I'm coming."

As Max got closer to Damian, he examined him for cracks in his composure. The man was a rock, always steady, but underneath it all he had to be aching at the reminder of his daughter's death. If what Einstein had told him was true, this girl had been killed in a manner similar to Samantha Manchester.

They'd known there were others. Lorena's contacts at the FBI had connected Samantha's murder to almost a dozen other murders throughout the country over the past twenty years, but they'd never been on the scene of one so soon after the time of death.

Stress was evident in the whiteness around Damian's mouth and the pronounced lines around his eyes, but his lips curved as he spied them approaching.

Catherine's hand reached out to touch Damian's arm. Her body was stiff, as if she wanted to hug the man but was restraining herself. More walls. "How are you, sir?" she asked.

Damian's throat moved as he swallowed. "Holding up. The detective is keeping us back to preserve the scene as they process it."

"But he's not shutting us out?" Max asked. He'd hate to go to his father to request yet another favor.

"No. He seems willing to work with us. The girl hasn't been identified yet, but the coroner is here. Says she looks to be a young teen from a good home." That likely meant the victim wasn't malnourished, didn't appear to have a drug addiction, and was decently clothed. Someone had loved and cared for her. It also meant someone was missing her and would have to endure the depth of pain Damian still suffered.

"Does Lorena think this is Sam's killer at work again? Is it the Charmer?"

"Yes. He left his signature at the scene."

The CPD had kept certain details of Sam's murder from the public, but the serial killer who'd taken Sam had come to be known to the press as the Charmer, as he'd lured each of his victims away from relatively public places, seemingly without a struggle and without witnesses. But the other side of that nickname, the one that hadn't been leaked to the press, was that the killer had left a calling card—a charm, like the kind that dangled from bracelets—tucked into the palm of each girl's hand. Recently, they'd learned that the Charmer was also known as the Boss of the Circle organization. But nobody seemed to know the killer's real name.

"Why would he be in Texas and why would he claim another victim right under our noses?" Max asked, anger pushing any tiredness to the fringes. "Is he taunting us?"

Damian rubbed a hand along his jaw. "Probably. Lorena thinks he even arranged for the brick to be thrown through the clinic window to show us he is keeping tabs on all of us, telling us he even knows where our wayward receptionist has gone."

Catherine paled. Was she thinking about her work at Lucky Dick's? Was the Boss, or the Charmer, aware of her position there?

Damian released a tired sigh. "I had hoped he'd limit his obsession to me—and Tony. Since we learned he's linked to the upper level of the Circle, it's likely he was in Texas to kill Tony during the transfer. But it appears he stuck around to create more destruction." Damian looked toward the woods, his face etched with pain. "I'm the one who brought this upon that young woman by moving Tony down here."

Max would do anything to erase the pain in Damian's eyes. "But if we hadn't made that move, we would never have found out that Tony likely knows something he's been withholding from us."

"I suppose so." Damian swallowed and looked away. "But why did he have to kill again? The thought that another girl died..."

Catherine squeezed Damian's arm. "This isn't your fault."

"No, it's my fault," Max said.

Her gaze whipped to his. "What? No." The denial was heated, as if she were angry he would suggest out loud what he knew to be true.

He'd let Tony Moreno slip through his fingers, and led a monster to his hometown. He'd failed to apprehend the man, no matter how many neighborhoods he'd scoured, doors he'd knocked on and profiles he'd helped create and distribute. "If Tony is the killer, then yes, this is my fault. I didn't stop him."

"You tried." Catherine was insistent, her tone passionate. If only he deserved her conviction.

Damian wasn't meeting his gaze, instead looking off into the distance, toward the crime scene. Had Damian lost faith in him?

"None of this is anybody's fault," Catherine said. Her gaze shifted between the two men before she made a guttural sound of disgust and spun on her heel, marching toward where Lorena and Einstein had stepped from the woods onto the sidewalk and had their heads bent in conversation.

"I'm sorry." Max didn't know what else to say to the man, who was in obvious pain.

"Catherine's right. This isn't your fault." Damian scrubbed a hand down his face. "And it's not mine, either. It's the monster. The Charmer, or the Boss, or whatever the hell his name is, is driven by his compulsions. But we'll stop him. Each time he strikes, we learn more about him. Hopefully, this murder will be the last, providing the final piece we need to catch him. I can't bear to watch another parent go through this kind of pain."

CATHERINE WAITED ON THE SIDELINES, HUGGING HER WRAP AROUND herself to ward off the early morning chill as she watched the

SSAM agents intermingle with the crime scene technicians. This was her surrogate family. Could she leave them, especially with Damian going through so much right now? For five years, she'd watched him hunt his daughter's killer, and it seemed SSAM was finally getting close. Was she prepared to desert them now?

She went to stand next to Damian on the edge of the parking lot. He looked to the east, where the sunrise turned the tips of the trees red-orange like a blazing wildfire. Traffic on the interstate had picked up, but the rest area had been cordoned off by the police. She'd notified an officer at the entrance that a food truck should be arriving soon. She'd called and arranged for breakfast and coffee for everyone who'd been working hard for hours.

She dug her hands into her pockets because she wasn't sure he'd want to be touched. He looked so stiff, so stoic. So alone. "This had to have hit you particularly hard."

"Life goes on for most people, but for the parents of this girl? Their lives will never be the same. There's a gaping black hole inside that nobody can see. You try to fill it, try to pretend the things you do can make up for whatever you lost, whatever ways you failed her, but nothing works."

Sensing silence was what was required at that moment, but not wanting to leave him alone, Catherine stayed by Damian's side as the edges of the trees turned golden and then green in the lightening sky. In the distance, Max, Lorena and Einstein moved with calm efficiency, involved with all that went on while staying out of the way when necessary.

Her gaze continually strayed to Max. Confident. Capable. Content. Why couldn't his parents see this side of him? They should be proud of the man he'd become. Then again, maybe she was projecting her own emotions onto him. She'd observed him as a coworker for five years, and they'd slowly built a deep friendship. Should she have held more of herself back, and not let her feelings grow? No, she wasn't sure she could have avoided falling for him anyway.

"Come back to SSAM." Damian's words were so surprising after a long period of quiet that Catherine wasn't sure she'd heard him correctly. "You belong with us in Chicago," he continued. He'd been watching her watch the team. "Whatever you're dealing with, I promise you it can be overcome. Choose the life you want and go after it, Catherine. If you've learned anything from your time with SSAM, it should be that our time in this world is over in the blink of an eye."

Damian moved toward the scene, leaving her with her thoughts. Could she make things work at SSAM? Only if she could come clean and they forgave her. Damian was right. Time was short, and if you wanted a certain life, you had to go after it with gusto, no holds barred, running full steam ahead.

Her heart ached as the coroner and a couple of officers came out of the woods, hefting a gurney with a body bag on it. Life was also a gift some people would never get to fully explore.

JOHNNY WINCED AS SUNLIGHT HIT HIM SQUARE IN THE EYEBALLS. THE sun's overly cheerful rays were shooting through the windshield of his van, slicing right on through to the back, where he'd apparently fallen asleep on the mattress he stowed on the floor there for some of the Circle's *special projects.* Just because women had to be sold into slavery didn't mean he couldn't make the transition a bit more comfortable. But he hadn't been on an operation last night.

He was alone, his head ached like a motherfucker and his mouth was dry as the creeks around these parts—when they weren't flooded with spring rains. It was a bitch of a hangover, but he didn't recall drinking that much last night.

That's the problem, dickhead. That's why it's called a blackout.

Jesus, had he driven somewhere while intoxicated? Had he been alone? Why couldn't he remember?

He shifted into a sitting position, ignoring the stabbing pain in his head, and reached for the water bottle in the cup holder.

Maybe some liquid would reduce the swollen, furry feeling of his tongue.

He froze as he caught sight of his arm. The long sleeves of his shirt were coated in a slightly wet, sticky, dark substance. His nose came to awareness at the same time as his brain and his heart galloped to catch up. He patted down his chest and arm, checking for open wounds, but found nothing amiss—except all of the goddamn blood.

He looked back at the mattress and found more blood. Whose was it?

As he turned, his boot kicked something and a flash of light on metal caught his eye. A hunting knife. One of *his* knives, he realized as he spied the initials engraved in the handle, and there was blood on the blade. Shaking now, he stuffed the knife under the mattress.

Get yourself together.

But the shakes continued. Withdrawal or adrenaline? *Both*, mixed with a good bit of fear.

Survival instincts kicked in as he realized the sun would only continue to get higher, exposing whatever crime had been committed here. Peering out the window, he saw no bloody body, nothing unusual. In fact, he knew where he was—a gas station on a corner within walking distance of his apartment. He often stopped here for coffee and smokes. Shit. What had he done? Where had he been? And whose blood was this?

He drove to his apartment complex, hoping it was too early on a Saturday for his neighbors to be out and about. He parked in his assigned spot and grabbed his jacket. He shoved his shaking, bloodied arms into the sleeves and zipped up to cover all traces. Checking himself in the rearview mirror, he saw dilated pupils, pale cheeks and a sheen of perspiration on his forehead, but he would pass as normal if nobody looked too close. Thankfully, the blood was relegated to his sleeves and chest and hadn't touched the rest of his clothing.

He grabbed an old shopping bag from the floor behind his seat and stuffed in the sheets and the knife, careful to wipe off the handle before pitching it in. He tied the bag shut. After checking to be sure nobody was around, he left the van and started down a sidewalk but was stopped by a shout.

"Yo, Johnny, wait up!" Footfalls indicated his neighbor was jogging toward him.

Johnny turned. "Hey, Troy."

"You in tonight?"

Their monthly poker game. Attending would make the most sense based on his usual schedule, but his day had taken a definite detour. He had to clean up whatever mess he'd created first. And figure out how he'd created it. "Last night was a long one, so I'm not sure."

Troy chuckled and slapped him on the shoulder. "Yeah, man. I heard you in your apartment, real late. Sounded like a wild night. Who's Kim, by the way?"

"Kim?" Just like that, he had an image of Kim, the dancer from Lucky Dick's, bouncing on top of him, head thrown back, kimono wide open. Where was she now? He felt dizzy. Was it her blood all over him? *Fuck.* People were bound to connect the dots if three women he'd had sex with turned up dead. And if the police turned their attention his way, the Circle would cut him loose—or worse. Fuck, fuck, *fuck.*

And the gas station where he'd woken up…had that been where Bea and Angelique had been found? No. No, he was certain the reports he'd heard had mentioned the dumpsite was more like a truck stop, closer to the freeway. That had to be several miles away. But was Kim's body out there somewhere right now, waiting to be discovered? Was his DNA on her?

Maybe it wasn't as much blood as he'd thought. Maybe whoever had been in his van had been wounded, and he'd tried to help, and they'd left.

Right. Because he was such a Good Samaritan.

Troy's grin nearly split his face in half. "Yeah. Must have had to shout each other's names over the music you had thumping. Hey, if you come tonight, bring more of that primo weed."

"Yeah, sure." The shakes were intensifying. Johnny needed to get cleaned up and eat something. Maybe then he'd be able to think clearly. Thankfully, Troy moved along, heading to his car.

The bag handle seemed to burn his fingers. He had to get rid of it now. Keeping his head down and striding with purpose, Johnny went to the dumpster, pitched the bag and circled to the stairs that led up to his apartment. He changed shirts, wrapping up the bloody one in his jacket. He'd have to dispose of the bundle some-where. *Fuck.* Why hadn't he kept the bag until he could put it all together? Then again, he probably should have dumped everything somewhere far away from his apartment. *Think, man. Be smart.*

If something bad had happened, how would he cover his ass? Keeping to his routine. Sticking to what was normal and ordinary. Working hard for the Circle so they'd remember the reasons they kept him around.

The need for a drink to steady his nerves nearly overpowered him but he'd bide his time until the afternoon, when he usually showed up at Lucky Dick's. Routine. He'd stick to it and every-thing would be okay.

It will be okay.

DAMIAN SET A TRAY OF COFFEE MUGS ON THE DESK IN THE DEN. Nobody had much appetite this morning, though they'd been up all night and it had been hours since they'd been fed by the food truck vendor Catherine had called. Her thoughtfulness had kept them all going for a few hours more.

Now, however, fatigue was beginning to catch up to them. For Damian, sleep would bring nightmares about the new victim— whom the police had identified as Tiffany Allsup, a fourteen-year-old who'd been reported missing Thursday afternoon—merged with details from Sam's murder. Over the years, whenever another Charmer victim had been found, it had been the same thing—weeks of sleep loss and frustration.

Lorena accepted her mug with a grateful smile. Einstein barely looked up from his computer screen but gulped the coffee as if it were a lifeline.

They'd fallen into a routine at the house over the past couple weeks. Up early for a jog around the neighborhood, home for coffee. Damian would fix breakfast while his team dove into the work of finding Tony Moreno. Some days, Max and Catherine would join them. Today, Max had insisted on taking Catherine back to the ranch to change out of their evening attire from the previous night's events. But they'd be back soon. And now they were hunting two murderers, possibly three: the Charmer, also known as the Circle's Boss, Tony and whoever was killing local dancers.

"Ready to review Sam's file?" Lorena asked. The twist of her mouth showed her sympathy. Yeah, this wasn't going to be easy. It never was. But after two decades, Damian had every word in her file memorized.

Damian plucked his own mug of coffee from the tray. "It needs to be done."

They hoped a review of the old cases would lead to more about the Charmer, and a theory about why he'd targeted Samantha and now this new victim.

"Einstein, you have the transcripts of our interviews with Tony?" He was hoping there'd be a clue in there they'd missed. Something about the Boss's identity and how he and the Charmer were likely the same person. He'd paid Tony an enormous fee to kidnap Samantha all those years ago. Had he done the same thing with this new victim?

"Just emailed them to you," Einstein said. He didn't look up from his efforts to track Tony's whereabouts via the computer, looking into past cases, cross-referencing Tony's crimes against victimology against, well, whatever else the man thought to run his algorithms on. Damian trusted he'd crack the code eventually.

"Let's go in the other room," Lorena suggested to Damian.

They settled on the back porch. The golf course beyond was busy at nine in the morning on a beautiful spring weekend.

Lorena followed his gaze. "You should be out there." At his questioning look, she smiled. "Don't you ever want to take a break?"

"I don't know what that would look like."

"You really can't remember what a vacation feels like, can you?"

The last vacation he'd taken had been to a theme park with Priscilla and Samantha, back when their family had been happy, healthy and whole. A year after Sam's disappearance, when her body had been discovered and they'd had a tiny degree of closure, Priscilla had paid for a month at a house on Lake Michigan to retreat with her grief. Damian had thrown himself into his work. But numbers and money and financial reports had failed to excite him anymore. He'd begun an obsession with serial killers—finding them, connecting with the people who found them and creating SSAM.

The Society for the Study of the Aberrant Mind was his solace, his way of educating basic citizens to watch for signs of deviance, and training them to protect themselves and fight back. Nearly twenty years ago, Lorena had been his first mindhunter, hired away from the FBI's Behavioral Analysis Unit when she'd been a bright-eyed and fresh recruit, one of their best.

"Why have you stuck with me?"

Startled by his question, Lorena's soft smile faded. "What do you mean?"

"All this time, we've been hunting and not always finding who we're looking for…"

"Is this a performance review?" Her tone was lightly teasing, but the solemnity in her dark eyes told him she understood the emotions that haunted him.

One side of his mouth tipped up. "We both know you'd get a gold star and a healthy bonus. You're the best there is." Her olive skin turned pink. Blushing was so unlike her, Damian could only stare for a long moment.

She took a sip of coffee and cleared her throat. "Thank you for the compliment. I thought maybe, since we hadn't found Sam's killer yet, you were disappointed."

"In you? I wouldn't be half this close without your help. And we *are* close. I can feel it." All of his employees had gotten him through the horrible years, and the numb years, and the angry years. Every year, he'd had family around because he had SSAM.

"Any day now, we'll find him." Her eyes were warm with compassion and support, things he hadn't seen to that degree from Priscilla. He and his ex-wife had been pulled in different directions by the trauma they'd endured. She'd survived by relocating to New York City and creating a life for herself that reignited her other passions—art, music and drama. He was happy for her.

Damian's only passion had been finding his daughter's killer. It had consumed him. It still did, though he'd learned to reach out to other people again and reconnect with the world.

He felt the connection here, now.

As if she was thinking the same thing, Lorena reached out and squeezed his hand. She pulled it away as Max appeared in the doorway. "Thought I'd find you two with your heads together." Max walked over and leaned against the railing, the golf course at his back.

Damian looked toward the door. "Where's Catherine?"

"I told her to stay at the ranch and get some rest." He frowned. "I'm not sure we'll get her back."

Faith and hope had gotten him through a lot of tough times. He still had faith Catherine would come back into the fold, especially after she'd expressed so much concern for him and the other agents at the crime scene earlier this morning, but he had the feeling whatever was keeping her apart was big. He'd thought about hiring his private investigator to do more digging, but he'd made a promise to Catherine when she'd taken her leave of absence. He'd sworn to let her have her time and space. He trusted she'd find her way back to them.

"She's got a few weeks left on her personal leave," Damian said. "Give her time."

Max shook his head. "I get the feeling nothing's going to change her mind."

"I don't know about that. If she's working at Lucky Dick's, she's doing it for us." Damian had been surprised to hear the news from Catherine at the scene this morning, but he'd also been impressed with the connections she'd made. He'd insisted he help provide backup, but she'd refused, saying it would compromise her position there.

"But she's still talking about not coming back to Chicago."

"If anything or anyone can help change her mind, it's you."

Max looked up in surprise. "Me? I've tried."

Lorena laughed. "You don't have a clue, do you?" She shook her head. "Men." She went back inside as Max turned a confused gaze on Damian, but he wasn't about to enlighten Max. If Max couldn't see how much Catherine cared about him, he didn't deserve her.

But the great thing about faith was it permeated all areas of life. And Damian had faith that, given enough time, Max and Catherine would find their way to each other, maybe even permanently.

CHAPTER 17

A knock at the office door interrupted Catherine's thoughts—thoughts that were too often tuned to Max and the way they'd left things. For the past thirty-six hours, he'd been busy working with SSAM and the authorities and she'd spent Saturday recuperating and visiting with Rachel, so they hadn't had time to reconnect since learning of Tiffany Logan's murder. Catherine and Max had even canceled last night's dinner with Lillian and Hayworth—a decision Catherine was certain she'd have to pay for later.

"Come in," she called.

Darla poked her head in. "You busy?"

Catherine set down her pen and leaned back in Dick's chair, stretching her neck. There'd been no sign of Dick today, but he liked to take Sundays off. Catherine doubted it was for religious reasons. "Frankly, I'd welcome a distraction. My eyes are about to cross. What's up?"

"I'm worried about Kim. Some of the guys are asking for her. She had yesterday off, but was supposed to be back today."

"She was supposed to come in at three, wasn't she?" Catherine glanced at her phone to check the time. It was nearly five. And she had a text message from Max.

Dinner. Tonight. Guesthouse. Seven p.m. No more distractions.

She'd be off work by then, so she couldn't use that as an excuse. Rachel, apparently inspired by Catherine's so-called relationship with Max, had a dinner date, so Catherine couldn't use her as a reason to say no either. Not without lying to Max again.

Darla clasped her hands together. "Yes, she should have been here hours ago, and she hasn't even called. It isn't like her."

No, it wasn't. Kim had actually been asking for extra shifts, saying she needed the money. "Did you try contacting her?"

Darla slanted her a look as if to say, *I'm not stupid.* But Catherine was used to the attitude by now, and suspected it was a cover. The young woman genuinely seemed to care. "I tried a few times over the last hour. No answer. I'm worried. After what happened to Bea and that other woman..."

Catherine rose and went to her, but stopped short of hugging her, settling for putting her hands on Darla's shoulders. "Don't go there. I'm sure she's just not feeling well, or forgot her schedule."

Darla nodded and sniffed, then squared her shoulders. Clearly, she'd had enough compassion. Catherine's hands dropped away.

"We're also out of whiskey." Darla turned to go, but stopped at the door. "You're doing good. This place hasn't run smoothly in months. Maybe not ever." And then she was gone.

Catherine grinned. She suspected that was as big a compliment as Darla ever paid anyone. Her attention returned to the text from Max. Maybe it was time. Maybe she should face life head-on and see where the cards fell. She texted him back while her courage ran high.

I'll see you at seven.

THE GUESTHOUSE'S LIGHTS WERE ON, WELCOMING CATHERINE AS SHE pulled up to the ranch house. Two days ago, Max had installed new locks and Catherine had moved back in. The main house, however, was dark except for a light in a corner room—Hayworth's home office. Her phone rang as she turned off the ignition. It was Mr. Caulfield calling.

"Hello?" She glanced toward the office, but couldn't see the man. Had he been watching for her arrival?

"You've been avoiding Max, and us."

"Max had a legitimate reason for missing last night's dinner." Apparently, searching for the killer of a fourteen-year-old girl didn't trump dinner with the Caulfields.

"Do I need to sweeten the pot?"

God, no. She just wanted to be left alone. "Max is still working at CI this week. What's the problem?"

"He doesn't want to be there. His head and his heart aren't in it. He's distracted, spending more hours at night looking for a killer than studying up on the family business. His priorities are mixed up."

"You can't force an interest that isn't there."

"No, but I can close off some of those avenues of investigation so he stops this nonsense. He belongs at CI. You need to straighten him out."

"Me?"

"He listens to you." Clearly, Hayworth couldn't stomach that fact, but he'd still use it to his advantage.

"Have you tried connecting with him, one-on-one, as a father and son?" She'd thought, after they'd spent last Sunday riding around the ranch, looking for signs of the intruder who'd broken into the guesthouse, that maybe they'd have gotten somewhere. Their relationship wouldn't be repaired in one day, but she'd hoped they'd made progress.

"Hell, I'm bad at this."

"You don't have to be good. You just have to show him you're trying." Catherine thought of her own father, and her heart squeezed. Rachel was right. Catherine needed to go see him soon.

"You agreed to be the go-between until Max and I get on even footing. I expect you to start putting in more time and effort toward this. There may be a job in it for you, especially if Max wants to keep you around."

"I already have a job and a family who need me."

There was a pause. "I can help your father, too."

Catherine's breath caught. So, this is what he'd meant by sweetening the pot. What new carrot would this man dangle that would make her sell her soul again? And did she have any soul left to sell?

She squeezed her eyes shut as if, by doing so, she could block out her conscience. "What are you offering?"

"I can convince the governor to release your father from the rest of his sentence. A word from me, the father of the victim, would go a long way."

The hope that swelled in her chest pressed painfully against her ribcage. Hayworth had the power and influence to do everything he offered. "In exchange for?" Her words were a croak in her tight throat.

"Sticking to Max and making sure he starts to stick to the company."

"I have obligations."

"Whatever they are, rearrange them. We're running out of time."

She'd already made a bargain with the Caulfields. The only risk in this new offer was to her heart. She trusted Max would make whatever decision was right for him. Continuing the game just a little longer was a small price for her to pay if everyone else in her world got what they needed. "Okay."

"Smart girl. I'll start working on your father's case ASAP. I'll expect you to do the same with Max." Hayworth hung up.

Catherine took several moments to sit in her Jeep and breathe deeply before going inside and facing Max. She was tired of hiding the truth, yet she sensed telling him who and what she was now would only make things worse. At least her sister and father would get something good out of this deal, and wasn't that her life's purpose? To help those she loved? But Max was in that group of people she cared about, too.

Despite her indecision, she admired the view as she entered the guesthouse. Max stood at the stove, stirring a pot of something that smelled heavenly. There was nothing sexier than a man who cooked. Her mouth watered, both for the food and for Max.

He looked over his shoulder and grinned. "Hey, good-looking."

"What's cookin'?" she finished.

"Chili and cornbread."

"I've never seen you cook before. You must want something."

"Darlin', I *always* want something." It was true. He was never satisfied, at least not with women. *And you couldn't begin to fulfill his appetite.*

But she could play along. "And what is it you want tonight?"

He set the spoon aside and turned to face her, leaning back against the counter. His apron ordered her to *kiss the cook* and she had to force herself to stay on the other side of the small kitchen. His eyes burned with desire and doubt in equal measure. "Are you stalking me?"

Her pulse rate went from a canter to a gallop. "What?"

"It's a bit of a coincidence, don't you think? Your job in Chicago at SSAM. After growing up around here, you must have heard about me." His eyes pinned her to the wall like a bug under a fly swatter. She knew she should have turned down his dinner invitation.

Nobody expects the Spanish inquisition.

"What?" he asked. A smile now pulled at his lips and she realized she'd spoken her thoughts aloud.

"I didn't mean to say that out loud. I don't know why I can't seem to control myself around you."

"I like it when you don't have your walls up around me. Which is why I'm confused. It can't be fate that you come from the same area as me, which means..."

"That I'm stalking you."

"Stupid, isn't it?" He gave a one-shouldered shrug. "It was just a thought that crossed my tired brain last night."

Except it was one hundred percent correct. Sort of. Her heart sank to her toes. "I've never hurt you."

"No."

"Never asked anything of you."

"No. I'm a cynic, I suppose." He shook his head and smiled as if he'd dispelled the repugnant ideas running around there. He *wanted* to trust her, which made her feel even worse about deceiving him. His voice dropped and he stalked toward her, stopping with just a foot of space between them. "You said you couldn't control yourself around me. I feel the same way about you. You tempt me beyond all reason."

The impact of his statement tightened her belly and heated her skin. She licked her lips against their sudden dryness. "I still think it's a lack of options that has you suddenly noticing me."

With a finger, he tipped her chin up. His eyes were serious. "I've always noticed you."

"But you didn't want me? I thought, I mean, after..." Words failed her.

His finger drifted down her neck and she shivered. "After New Year's? Sweetheart, that kiss threw me into a tailspin. I've been wanting different things lately." He gave a wry grin. "I think it started with that kiss. But I don't know what to think about it all. I've never wanted...*more*." He dropped his hand and turned back to the stove, changing the tension in the room with such speed, she felt dizzy. Or maybe it had been his touch.

He's worried he's not going to be enough—or good enough—for me. The realization nearly made her laugh out loud. She needed a moment to reorient herself, so she took his lead and moved to safer territory. "Anything new with the investigations? Damian's got to be agonizing over it." She'd tried to keep her distance, but her heart was with them.

His smirk said he knew she was more curious than her tone indicated. "Still trying to take care of us all?"

She shrugged. "Old habits die hard."

"Good. I'm counting on that." He moved to the oven to remove the tin that held a dozen golden-brown cornbread muffins.

"I'm not coming back, Max." He wouldn't want her back, and neither would Damian, if only they knew.

He looked over his shoulder as he took two bowls down from the cupboard. "We'll discuss it after we've had dinner and a couple of beers. For now, let someone take care of you for a change."

She arched an eyebrow at that. "You need to liquor a girl up these days to get her to say yes?"

"Beer compliments the chili, but if you want to use it as an excuse to cut loose, I'm game." He turned toward her, and the light of challenge heated his gaze as it roved over the length of her body. He mirrored her arched eyebrow.

She was the first to break contact. They both knew she'd be saying yes to a lot more than dinner if he dedicated his efforts to persuading her. They'd nearly crossed that line two nights ago.

She took a bowl from him and busied herself by spooning chili into it. He moved to get two beers from the refrigerator. She hadn't bought them, so he must have, along with all the fixings for dinner. He was thinking of everything, almost as if he'd planned this...*seduction*. The word had her searching for safer, neutral ground.

"Where'd you learn to cook?"

He shrugged and followed her to the counter where they sat at barstools, side by side. His knee bumped hers and she shifted to break the contact. He didn't seem to notice.

"I picked up a few things, mostly from Claudia, but also from the cowboys on the ranch. I grill a mean steak, too." His grin was boyish and breathtaking. Catherine looked away and dug into her chili. "She always said a woman would appreciate that talent."

"Oh, we do." But he was a man of *many* talents.

"Back to my stalking question…"

She took a deep swallow of beer to give her time to think of a response. "We're both from the same area. It happens." Except her area, the trailer park several miles away, was actually a totally different world from the ranch and country club lifestyle he'd grown up with.

"But you had to have learned at some point over the last few years that I was from here, and yet you never spoke of it, never talked about your family, or anything deeply personal, for that matter." He had given up the pretense of eating and was watching her carefully.

"It's not like you talked a lot about your background," she pointed out. "Besides, I didn't think someone like you would want to hear about this particular coincidence."

His brows came together in a V. "Someone like me?"

Under the table, she rubbed a sweaty palm on her skirt. Her body sensed the coiled tension in him, waiting to be released. She tried to smile and shrug, but it came out awkward. "You mean to tell me if I'd come to you sooner about our shared roots, you wouldn't have suspected I was one of those women constantly trying to hit on you? Or, as you're insinuating, *stalk* you? It's no secret you enjoy the freedom of being the hunter rather than the prey."

"Maybe." He studied her thoughtfully. "But I'd like to think I care more about my friends, that I would have given you the benefit of the doubt."

"I've seen you care about friends plenty. But with women? There's an automatic suspicion in your eyes. Maybe I didn't want to be one of those women."

"And if I've changed? If I want a steady relationship now?"

Her heart leapt, but she clamped down fiercely on her gut reaction. "I can't afford the risk." He'd be gone one day soon—or she would—regardless of their good intentions. "I can't gamble that you'll be there for me when I need you."

Regret hardened his eyes. "Message received. I can't believe I'm saying this, but maybe my mother was right. Maybe I should explore my options."

Catherine resisted screaming at him. *She* was his best option. And his worst. She wanted to pull her hair out and she definitely didn't want to stick around while he *explored his other options.* "You still haven't honored your date from the auction, have you? You would make Melissa one happy woman." And make Catherine miserable.

"Great idea." Except his tone indicated he loathed the idea and resented her for bringing it up. But she'd taunted him to the point he couldn't back down. "I'm sure she'd appreciate me."

"And Max Sawyer loves to be appreciated by a beautiful woman."

"You really believe I'm that shallow?"

"You haven't done much to dispel that image." She shook her head and laid down her fork, no longer the least bit hungry. "I'm not sure what we're even arguing about. You and I would never work out. Sure, there's a physical attraction, but I want more than that from a man."

"And you don't think I can bring more to a relationship."

"Do you even know how to have a *relationship*? You've run from every one you've ever had. Maybe you should start by trying to rebuild things with your parents."

"I thought you, of all people, understood me." He stood and shucked the apron. A moment later, her front door closed behind him with a soft click. A slam would have been better, would have echoed the chaos slamming through her heart, which screamed at her to chase after him, to tell him there was so much more she wanted to say.

Why? So he can reject you again when the truth comes out?

Disgusted with herself, she turned with a strangled groan and looked for a way to take out her frustrations. She scooped up their bowls from the counter and ran hot water in the sink. The steam was soothing, shaping a new plan for the evening. She'd forget about Max and her problems and indulge in a luxurious bath in the bathroom's garden tub—after she tackled the cleanup.

Lost in the idea of a good, long soak as she scrubbed dishes, she was blindsided by the arm that suddenly wrapped around her throat. Submitting to panic, she struggled, but her wet fingers slipped as she clawed at a hairy brown forearm. A sharp pain at the base of her spine warned her the man had a weapon.

This wasn't Max. Besides, he wouldn't scare her like this. *The door.* In her anger, she'd forgotten to lock it after Max left. He'd gone to the trouble of installing a motion-sensor security light and new locks, but neither would help her now.

She tried to throw an elbow into her attacker, but he shifted to protect himself. His change in position further restricted her air and had her arching backward, off balance. Hot, rank breath, smelling of tobacco, fanned her ear. Her body screamed in warning, remembering another time she'd been caught unaware. That time, she'd been naive. This time, she should have known better and paid attention to her surroundings. She slowed her breathing and tried to think calmly.

A chuckle sounded against her neck. "I knew you'd be a spitfire." *Tony Moreno.* She recognized his voice from the interview tapes she'd overheard the SSAM team listening to.

"My boyfriend is in the other room." She was grasping at straws.

"Nice try. But our mutual friend Max is long gone. You're all mine now."

MAX REPLAYED CATHERINE'S WORDS, BOILING HER POINTS DOWN TO the basic problem. While he could be counted on as a friend, he wasn't good relationship material. He wasn't good for more than a good time, which was exactly what he'd always wanted—until now. It would have been funny if it had been anybody but

Catherine hitting him over the head with this newsflash. But the part that hurt, the essence of their argument, was that she didn't want him.

Full of restless energy, he wandered to the living room and poured a drink. But a drink wasn't what he needed. Fuck all if he knew what it was he *did* need, but he was spoiling for a fight and he knew just where to find one.

He headed for his father's office. He'd seen the light on. His mother was still in town, working with one of her charity groups, probably telling her friends her son had brought in the big bucks on Friday. Maybe she was even arranging to auction him off again.

He rapped on the office door.

"Come in," his father called.

He pushed the door open. "Got a minute?"

"For you? Always." That was a first.

Max stood in front of the desk, unsure of what he'd come to say, but at the tired lines on his father's face, the fight suddenly went out of him.

His father's eyebrows went up. "Want to take a seat, or are you in a hurry, as usual?"

Max sat, feeling the plush leather give with a creak. The couch had been there as long as he could remember, but he'd never sat on it. Even that small gesture had been forbidden when he was a kid, and when he'd entered a rebellious stage as a teenager, he'd refused to answer his father's infrequent summons. All of it seemed ridiculous now. Was he his own man or not? Did he know his own mind, or were all of his actions to this point simply reactions to perceived threats? Was he constantly running from relationships?

"You ever reach a point in your life when you start doubting everything that came before?" Max voiced the question, then immediately wished he could call it back. Of course his father had never felt that insecure. The man ran a multimillion-dollar corporation and a successful ranch.

"Many times." His father removed his reading glasses and

tossed them on the desk. Max was shocked to see empathy in his eyes. "But that's a good thing. It's important to reassess periodically, to discover what's working and what's not working."

"And if it's not working?"

"Fix it or accept it and move on. What's this about, Son, Caulfield Industries?"

"No." He'd never doubted that he didn't fit in at the company. It was life in general that had him confused. "I'm not sure I should be talking to you about this."

A grim smile contorted his lips. "You must really need to talk to someone if you came to me. I'm sure I'm the last person you feel safe confiding in." His gaze moved to the window. The guesthouse was beyond, and Max figured his father was considering Max's so-called fiancée.

"Catherine gets me." Though he'd just accused her of not understanding him, there'd been a kernel of truth in her statements. She got him like nobody else did, and she was strong enough to call him on his bullshit. His heart rolled over in his chest just thinking of all the times she'd been there for the SSAM team, and for him. "But I can't talk to her right now."

His father nodded. "Okay, then, what do you need?"

Christ, wasn't that the question? He shoved a hand through his hair. "I don't know. I thought I did, for so long, but... Forget it. Maybe I'm just crazy. I'm having a midlife crisis or something."

"You're barely thirty. But hell, Son, I'd worry about you if you *weren't* having thoughts like this."

"What do you mean?"

"You're back home after a long time away. It's bound to stir up memories—of all kinds." His gaze moved to the bookshelf behind Max, where Mike smiled down at them from his high school graduation picture. Young, innocent, unaware he only had a few more short years to live. "I know I failed you. I just don't know what to do to make things better." He cleared his throat and seemed to come out of a trance.

The jiggling of Max's phone against his hip grabbed his attention. He pulled it out to glance at the screen and froze.

"What is it?" His father must have read the stark fear on his face.

"A text from Catherine." Max stood and crossed the room in two long strides, but outside the window, the guesthouse was just as he'd left it, with light filtering through the living room curtains. But the new floodlight above the driveway was on, illuminating what was missing. Catherine's car.

He looked back to his dad. "Call the police. Her text says *9-1-1*."

CHAPTER 18

Catherine's attention was divided between the freeway, the man in the backseat of her car and the knife he held to her neck, but her mind was free to think up an escape.

Have a plan of action. That was chapter one, page one of the Catherine Montague Survival Guide. Her plan was to learn Tony's plan, while figuring out a way to throw a major wrench into the works by getting away.

"What's taking so long?" Tony asked.

"I'm searching my contact list for the number." She was quickly texting Max a 9-1-1 message. Luckily, his text from earlier had been cued up when she'd entered her phone's password, so she typed as fast as she could before Tony could see over her shoulder. She only hoped Max hadn't turned off his phone, or blocked her number entirely. As she hit send, she distracted Tony. "Why did you kill those girls?"

He snorted. "Which ones?"

"The recent ones, here in Texas. The dancers."

In her rearview mirror, he scowled. "Not my work. Is someone trying to pin it on me?"

"The timing is pretty convenient. You're out of prison just when a crime spree is beginning."

Please, God, let Max get my message and know how to find me. He had to. If anybody would come to her rescue, it would be Max, even if he was angry with her. Despite what she'd told him, she would bet on him with her last dollar.

The knife pressed harder into her skin and she felt a hot drop of blood slip beneath her shirt. "Stop stalling and make the call." Sweat beaded on Tony's upper lip and brow. He'd stumbled while pushing her from the guesthouse to her car, indicating he was injured. Demanding she call her sister to meet at the clinic confirmed it. How he knew about Rachel and her clinic, Catherine had no clue.

"What's wrong, by the way?" she asked.

Tony sneered. "You a doctor, sweetheart? Just call your fucking sister."

"How do you know *she's* a doctor?" He'd even known the name of the clinic, and that it had moved in recent weeks.

"You hear a lot if you pay attention. Or scan through someone's text messages when that someone leaves a phone in plain sight."

A chill crept across her skin. "You're the one who broke into my place last week." Had he been hiding out on the ranch, injured, the whole time? How bad off was he?

"Just call." His shout indicated he was done answering questions. "Put it on speaker. No warning her or I'll kill you and then hunt her down." His mouth pressed against her ear and she couldn't control a shudder. His lips curved. "You may be familiar with my previous body of work, but I learned a few new things in prison. I've been dying to try them out."

Catherine dialed and prayed her sister wouldn't answer. Would Tony let Catherine take him to the emergency room as a backup plan, or would he simply kill her if she were no longer useful?

Unfortunately, Rachel answered on the first ring. "What's up?"

"Are you still on your date?" Catherine fought to keep her voice steady as her mind raced to think of a way to warn Rachel.

"The guy was a dud. Want to grab some dessert?"

"Actually, I need your help. There's a man—" She stopped as the tip of the knife jabbed into her neck and had her hissing out a breath.

Rachel laughed. "A man? Maybe a man named Max Sawyer? Definitely a topic to discuss over something chocolate."

The exit for the clinic was coming up and Catherine had to make a quick decision. Risk her sister or her own life?

"Exit here," Tony whispered into her ear. He knew where the new clinic was located, which meant he could easily fulfill his threat to go after her sister. Aware of his record from her work at SSAM and recent discussions during the manhunt, Catherine suspected he wasn't likely to simply kill. He was a serial rapist in addition to a murderer. Plus, he was seriously injured and hiding from some extremely bad Circle men. He had nothing to lose by hurting Catherine and Rachel if they got in his way.

"I need to swing by the clinic," she told Rachel. "A friend needs help. Is David available, too? He could be useful."

She suppressed a moan of pain as the knife nicked her and the sticky heat on her neck increased. "David is a doctor," she whispered to Tony. "Keep that up and you'll make me pass out and run us off the road."

Tony positioned his mouth close to her ear and acid rose in the back of her throat. "No other people," he said. "Just your sister." But the pressure from the blade let up.

"David?" Rachel asked, confused.

"Wasn't that your doctor friend's name?" David was the police officer who'd responded when Lee had threatened them all, but Catherine wasn't sure Rachel would remember him. "Never mind. I'll be there in five minutes."

"See you then." Judging by Rachel's upbeat tone, her sister hadn't understood the warning, which left their fates in the hands of serial rapist Tony Moreno and stubborn bachelor Max Sawyer —neither of whom gave a flying flip about Catherine right now.

MAX HADN'T BEEN IN CHICAGO THE LAST TIME CATHERINE WAS IN danger, but he'd damn well be there for her now—if only he could figure out where *there* was. The guesthouse had held no answers. Catherine had obviously been washing dishes when she'd been interrupted, but by whom? There was no sign of struggle, yet drops of blood on the hardwood floor indicated someone had at least a slight injury. Could it be the same intruder who'd left a smear of blood near the back door last week?

Or was it Catherine's blood? But if that were the case, why wouldn't she come to the main house for help rather than take off in her car? His gut told him Catherine was in danger, and he'd better find her fast.

"Anything yet?" Max had Einstein on speaker as he entered the highway in the pickup truck he'd borrowed from his father.

"She may not be answering your calls, but she left her cell phone on. Tracking her now."

"Did you get her sister's number yet?" He was trying the next best alternative.

"Yeah, but she's not answering, either. And nobody's answering at the clinic—the old or the new one."

All they had to go on was gut instinct, but that was something to which he and Einstein were accustomed. A sense of urgency had Max pushing his speed beyond the legal limit as he merged with traffic. He was a good fifteen minutes from Rachel's clinic. If he hadn't walked out on Catherine earlier, hadn't let stupid pride drive him away...

"Any word from local authorities?" Max asked. "My dad said he'd call in a favor and have someone set up an APB on Cat's Jeep."

"Depending on how long it takes him to call his friend and get the favor taken care of, it should be happening anytime now.

Haven't heard it go out over the radio yet." Einstein was monitoring all the communication methods he could.

The calm assuredness in his friend's voice made Max feel a tiny bit better. "Thanks, man." There was a pause in which Max could only hear the steady hum of his tires racing across pavement and the throbbing of his pulse in his ears.

"You don't think this was some ploy to get your attention, do you?"

Max laughed shortly. "By Catherine?" He realized their argument had been for nothing. He trusted the woman implicitly. It wasn't her style to jerk him around.

"Yeah, it sounded stupid coming out of my mouth."

"I'm almost to town. I'll try her sister's place, but—"

"No, head to the new clinic. Her cell signal's coming from that area."

Max made a quick right and hit the gas. His hand moved to the gun he'd shoved under his seat. He felt some reassurance just touching it. He'd be there for Catherine this time, and he wouldn't let anybody stand in his way.

"IS THIS FROM A BULLET?" RACHEL'S GLOVED HANDS WERE STEADY AS she examined Tony's wound. His pants were torn clear up to his thigh, exposing a bloody gash. If only Catherine had known he was this injured when he'd taken her from the guesthouse, she would have targeted his thigh as an area of weakness. The angry, puffy edges and discharge indicated infection. But Tony was a large man, muscular and taller than them—and he had a knife. She and Rachel exchanged a glance.

To her credit, Rachel had taken one look at them as they'd entered the clinic, caught sight of the filthy man behind Catherine, his hand wrapped around her as he held the blade to her neck, and assessed the situation quickly and correctly. She'd probably recognized Tony from the news reports. Still, she'd led them past the empty waiting room and reception area and into an exam room without asking any questions.

Well, not out loud, anyway. Her eyes were filled with them.

Tony hissed as Rachel cleaned the wound. His arm, still wrapped around Catherine's neck as insurance, tightened and she tried not to wince. "Yeah. A guy shot at me."

Rachel didn't look up from her work. "That tends to happen when you're running from the law."

"Or from the Circle," Catherine added.

Tony's arm squeezed until he'd nearly pulled Catherine into his lap on the exam table. "You've both got smart mouths, you know that?"

"Comes with the smart brains, I guess." Rachel's words dripped with bravado, but she blew out a shaky breath as she straightened. "I'll have to sew the edges together. And you've got a raging infection." She moved to pick up a needle from the counter.

"You told me this happened about a week ago?" Catherine shuddered to think Tony had been on the ranch all that time. And where had he been those first few days?

But Tony wasn't listening. He shifted away from Rachel, tugging Catherine with him. "Whoa, wait. What's that?"

"Painkiller." Rachel's eyes shot to Catherine for a brief second.

"No."

She shrugged. "Suit yourself. But you need antibiotics, unless you want to lose your leg, and maybe your life. We have a few samples on hand, but you'll need a whole supply."

"I'll take what I can get and find the rest somewhere else. And I'll take the painkillers, to go. I'll need them more than you will."

"Because we'll be dead?" Rachel asked the question that weighed heavily in the air.

"Not if you do what I say. I don't need any more trouble, but I'm happy to bring it if necessary." The tip of his knife caressed Catherine's jaw and she fought a shudder.

"Then let's get you sewed up and on your way." As Rachel made the first stitch, he flinched and his blade flicked against Catherine's neck. Her sister looked up, anger flashing in her eyes. "You okay?"

"I'll be fine," Catherine assured her. "Especially when Tony makes good on his promise and leaves us in peace."

"You get me fixed up, I leave." Tony seemed sincere, his energy focused on getting out of there, but could Catherine trust him to leave them untouched? Should she try to use a self-defense move to break his hold? Could she and Rachel both get away safely if she did that? Which was the bigger gamble? "And you can tell your boyfriend he's not looking high enough for the Boss."

The statement shocked Catherine. "What do you mean, *high enough*? Are you talking physically or metaphorically?"

Tony grinned. "Both. But I'm saving the details as my bargaining chip. Since the Boss didn't want to take my deal, maybe SSAM will. If I get caught, that is."

A couple minutes went by, during which the only sounds in the room were the in and out of needle pulling through flesh, Tony's raspy breathing and Rachel removing and replacing instruments from the tray. Tony hadn't let her have anything sharp, only the needle and thread. He'd wielded his knife when it was necessary to cut.

Rachel straightened and stood, kicking her rolling stool out of the way. "All done. Let me grab some antibiotics for you, though."

"Be quick about it." As Rachel left the room, he called after her. "Bring all the painkillers you've got, too. If you're not back in twenty seconds, your sister dies."

Rachel was back in ten seconds with two handfuls of blister packs. She stuffed them into a bag and handed it to Tony. "The tiny round ones are painkillers. The larger ones are antibiotics. But these are just samples. You need a ten-day supply of the antibiotics, possibly something stronger and more immediate, like an IV. You'd have to go to the hospital for that."

"I'll make do." He dropped his hold on Catherine and backed

out of the room, then loped down the hall, leaning more heavily on his healthy leg.

"You'll pull the sti—" Rachel ended her warning abruptly as Tony exited via the emergency door in back. She shook her head. "I don't know why I care."

Catherine wrapped her arms around her sister and they embraced for a long moment. She released a shaky sigh and stepped away. "I'm so sorry to have dragged you into this."

"If this is the kind of criminal you had to deal with, you were right to leave SSAM."

"It's not like this happens every day." Just twice in a lifetime. Maybe everyone was right and karma *was* a bitch.

The sound of sirens had them rushing toward the front of the clinic in time to see two police cruisers pull up and the officers jump out.

"Tony went out the back," Catherine called out. "He's on foot and his leg is wounded."

As the officer coordinated a plan with the driver of the other cruiser, a pickup truck pulled up. *Max.*

He rushed over to her. "Are you okay? God, your neck." He brought a hand to her chin, gently turning her head to get a better look.

"I was just about to mention that," Rachel said.

"It's not that bad." Catherine pushed his hand away. "You need to go."

His eyes darkened. "You're hurt."

"It was Tony. He was the vagrant hiding out at the ranch. He was the one who broke into the guesthouse. The police went after him."

His attention remained on her. "You'll be okay?"

"She's in good hands," Rachel assured him.

"Just go," Catherine said.

He pulled her close for a hot, quick kiss before taking off on foot. Stunned by the sudden sensual assault, Catherine stood and watched as Max disappeared down the dark street beyond the clinic.

"Let's get you checked out," Rachel said.

"What?" Absently, she touched her lips.

Rachel gave her a bemused grin. "I suppose I'll have to check you for shock now, too."

CHAPTER 19

Max's hands tightened on the truck's steering wheel. He was driving Catherine home because the police had taken her Jeep to search it for evidence. Tony had escaped. *Again.* Max hadn't been there to stop him—not from escaping, and not from hurting Catherine.

Max examined her profile for a long moment, watching the dance of light and shadow as they sped beneath the streetlights. Uncertainty, anxiety and fatigue lined her face. He wanted his calm, self-assured Cat back. He wanted the woman who'd gone toe-to-toe with him in the guesthouse.

After nearly an hour of answering police questions, Catherine and Max escorted Rachel to a friend's house, where Rachel would be staying until they caught Tony, just in case he came after her. Their next stop had been the SSAM house to give Lorena, Einstein and Damian the full story, including Tony's cryptic comment about the team not looking *high enough* in their search for the Boss. Now, it was near midnight.

After a few more minutes of silence, he glanced over again.

218 ANNE MARIE BECKER

Catherine was looking out the window, watching the quiet streets, nibbling on her bottom lip.

"Are you thinking about what Tony did tonight...or what happened before?" he asked.

Her hand fluttered to her neck. "He did stir up some memories. But I survived."

"Yes, you did. Both times—because you're strong."

"Thank you for the compliment." Her hand dropped to her lap. "And for coming to my rescue tonight."

"Don't thank me." Fuck, he hadn't *done* anything. Catherine and Rachel had handled everything—expertly. Had things gone differently, Max might not have made it in time. The thought of his time with Catherine coming to an end helped him make a decision. Max bypassed their exit.

Catherine's head snapped toward him. "Where are we going?"

"You're not staying at the ranch." He couldn't stand the thought of taking her back to a place where her privacy had been invaded and her safety compromised. He was in lockdown mode, wanting nothing more than to protect, which meant securing her somewhere safe. Somewhere Tony wouldn't look for her.

She sighed. "I was kind of dreading going back there tonight. But where are we headed? I don't have any of my stuff."

"You've got everything you need." She was alive, whole and had him watching out for her. But she was looking worried. "Will you trust me to take care of you?"

"You're not the only one who has trust issues, you know. It's hard for me to let someone else be in control. I have trouble believing that someone would help me unless they're looking to get something in return."

"Cat, I—"

She waved her hand as if to erase her comments. "It's okay. We were both right and both wrong earlier. I could have stayed at the SSAM house tonight."

"Not enough room." Besides, he wanted her all to himself. He'd hold her all night if she'd let him, but even if she didn't, he'd at least be in the same room with her.

She went back to looking out the window. "We've passed quite a few hotels."

"I thought we could both use a break. Maybe catch some Fiesta activities tomorrow?" The annual April events were a huge celebration in San Antonio. "Or see if there are any pre-Cinco de Mayo things going on?"

"What about your deal with your dad? Tomorrow's a work day."

"Everyone needs a day off now and then, and I think he'll understand after the night we had. And if he doesn't, I'll make it up to him later." He exited into downtown and headed for the River-walk. Neither of them spoke again until he'd pulled into a parking garage at one of the hotels.

After parking, he turned in his seat to face her. "I'm going to be sharing a room with you. I'm tired of dancing around this—around *us*. And I'm damn well not going to leave you alone tonight, not even for a room across the hall. Tony's out there, somewhere, and he took you once." The thought of the rapist who'd violated and killed several women holding a knife to Catherine's throat made him ache for revenge. Her shudder seemed to echo the chill that shot through him. She nodded and he released the breath he'd been holding.

Max made quick work of obtaining a room. Inside the suite, Catherine stopped by the large window to look down at the river. He could see the twinkling of the lights in the trees that lined Paseo del Rio.

"It's beautiful," she said. "I haven't been here during Fiesta since I was a kid."

"I haven't been in years."

She glanced at the bed. "You only got a king."

He hid his disappointment. "Like I said, I'm not going to insist on sleeping in the same bed. I can sleep on the floor, or the fold-out couch if necessary." It wouldn't be the worst conditions he'd endured. Not by a long shot.

"No," she said. His breath stuck in his throat as he waited for her to complete her thought. "I'd like to share a bed. But..."

In two long strides, he was standing in front of her, pulling her into his arms. "I'd settle for holding you."

She clutched at him. "I know you said to stop thanking you, but *thank you* for finding me and Rachel. I knew you would, and it kept me strong."

He tunneled his fingers through the hair on either side of her head, careful of the gauze bandage Rachel had taped across the two-inch shallow wound Tony had made at her neck, and pulled her face close to his. "I can't believe he took you, right out from under my nose." The monster had been living on the ranch, observing them, watching Catherine. He closed his eyes to compose himself and breathed deeply of her scent.

She pressed closer and kissed each of his eyelids. "You can't be super-SEAL all the time." There was a hint of a smile in her voice.

"I should have been there with you. I shouldn't have walked away."

"You're here now. Be here for me, *with me*."

Catherine pressed her mouth to his jawline, tasting the salty tanginess of his skin and feeling the light scrape of his dark stubble against her lips. She breathed deep of his spicy scent, a combination of Max's unique musk, a hint of sweat and fresh Texas air. Her hands slid to his waist and slipped under his shirt. He groaned as her fingertips skimmed his abdomen. The muscles there contracted and her pulse quickened at his reaction to her. A rush of power and control—two things she'd sorely lacked in the last several hours—made her spirit soar.

"How would you feel about a shower first?" he asked against her ear.

Her skin heated at the thought of water sluicing over Max's taut, naked body. "As long as I'm invited." She punctuated each word with a kiss—cheekbone, earlobe, shoulder, collarbone—she wanted to pay homage to every part of him.

It took them a few minutes to get to the bathroom as they paused frequently to strip off an item of clothing and kiss and nip the newly bared skin. His mouth was hot, yet provoked shivers. His hands were everywhere, yet not where she needed them to be. Her ache for him was bone-deep.

Her heart skipped its way up her throat, strangling a little moan as she watched him strip off the last article of clothing. His lithe body entered the shower and he turned on the spray. She locked her knees against their sudden weakness.

"Join me." Max's heavy-lidded gaze skimmed over her bare breasts and continued downward, pausing on her lace-trimmed panties.

She slid the remaining clothing to the floor and stepped inside the shower. The warmth of the water was no match for the heat flaring in his eyes. His long brown lashes had turned spiky and dark, highlighting the flecks of gold in his hazel eyes. His hair was slicked back, accentuating the sharpness of his cheekbones.

She stepped closer, pressing her breasts against his chest and feeling a jolt of electricity move through her as his hair teased her nipples. She slid her palms from his elbows to his shoulders, and then wrapped her arms around his neck.

He leaned back to look into her face. "This is so much better than my dreams."

She grinned. "You've dreamed about this?"

He bit and sucked at her bottom lip, the shadow of his beard delicately scraping her chin, heightening her senses. "This, and so much more."

"Like what?"

"I'd be happy to show you. We can act out every one."

"I've had my own dreams about you, Mr. Sawyer. You and that great-smelling body wash you use at the ranch."

With a deep-throated growl, he bent his head and kissed her. Max didn't do tame. His kisses were fire and sparks, raw desire and want. She was surprised the water hitting them didn't sizzle and steam upon contact. His hands moved to cup her ass, hoisting her body against his length so she cradled his erection. She wanted to wrap her legs around his waist and let him sink into her. But he set her down to grab the body wash. They washed each other, the skim of hands over skin arousing both of them, until they were a little short of breath.

"Bed." He turned to lead her out of the shower.

"Wait," she reached for him, afraid losing physical contact would break the spell.

"I have condoms in my jeans."

"We don't need them."

His entire body froze. "I don't operate that way."

"I know. I wouldn't risk anything so serious, I just..." She blushed bright red. "Let me show you what I want." She couldn't put it into words, but she wanted to give him pleasure, to show him how much she cared about his happiness. She sent him a wicked grin. "One of those dreams I mentioned..."

She tugged him back to her, and then slid down his body until she was on her knees before him. Taking his length into her hands, she licked and sucked until his hands plunged into her hair.

"Christ, Catherine." His words ended with a hiss and a moan as she went to work pleasing him. Showing him with her body and her actions what she couldn't tell him in words.

MIND-BLOWING. THAT'S WHAT THIS WAS. AND HE DIDN'T THINK HE'D last much longer if she didn't stop now. Max gently tugged at her hair until she was looking up at him. The image of her on her knees, eager to please him, water droplets shimmering on her eyelashes and cheeks, shot hot desire to every nerve ending.

"Tell me what you want." She blinked as rivulets began to stream down her face.

Everything. "You, in bed. Now." Caveman speak seemed all he was capable of at the moment. He wanted to be inside her when they came together.

"Another dream?" She slowly slid up his body.

"I hope to hell this is reality." He reached behind her to turn off the water and then wrapped Catherine in a towel before donning one himself. Pulling her against him, he walked backward to the bedroom, kissing her as he tugged her with him. Somewhere along the way, they lost the towels, but their skin was warm. His back hit the bed as she pushed him down and crawled across him, her lips igniting fire along his skin as she kissed her way from his knee to his chin. Her hands roamed over him, stirring electricity in their wake. His body clenched against the urge to take her, to make her his. He flipped their bodies over. She gasped as her head hit the pillow.

He pulled back to look down at her. "Did I hurt you?"

She gave him a siren's grin. "Cool sheets. Just a shock."

"I can warm you up." He quickly retrieved a condom from the pocket of his pants, which lay on the floor, and put it on, then covered her body with his.

Her wet hair lay across the pillow, the light from the bedside lamp making it flame golden-red. She looked like a nymph, sent there to charm him, so different from the friend he'd gotten to know over the last couple years. And yet she still had that inner spark that had always drawn him in, that same soft smile. This time, he'd put that there. He leaned down to kiss her lips, then forced himself to pull back before taking it deeper.

She met his gaze, her eyes soft and filled with emotion. There was nothing false or hidden about her feelings now. It was *love* he saw there. The realization rushed through his chest like a spring thaw, melting the walls he'd erected long ago and releasing a lightness he'd never experienced before. A fierce need to hang onto this feeling, to capture it and be completely one with Catherine, had him stroking and kissing and nibbling until she writhed beneath him. He sank into her and she quivered, her thighs tightening around his flanks.

"*Max.*" His name on her lips was a gasp as he surged into her.

They were both so close to release. He shifted against her, reaching between them to find the spot that would detonate her climax. He stroked and thrust until they were both panting.

"Oh!" Her entire body pulsed, her muscles convulsing around him. Even her limbs tightened, clinging to him as if she would never let go. As he found his own release, he was surprised to discover he was okay with that. He could happily stay in Catherine's arms for as long as she'd let him.

CHAPTER 20

Catherine hurried to Dick's office, where he sat across from a detective. Dick's phone call had woken her in the Riverwalk hotel room late this morning, pulling her from a beautiful dream and Max's arms. Those arms that had held her all night and most of the morning were now crossed as Max stood by the door, looking big, bad and ready for a fight. She hadn't thought she could be more aware of the man, but every breath, every twitch of his lips, was on her radar.

Dick scowled at Max but, seeing the nod of recognition Max gave the detective, didn't object to his presence.

"Detective McCoy." The stranger introduced himself, rising to shake her hand before he sat again.

She looked at Dick. "You said there was another body. Whose?"

"Kim. They found her body late last night." Dick pressed the heels of his hands to his eyes. "Fuck. Who's doing this?"

"We'll find out soon, I'm sure." She looked to McCoy who nodded, but his expression was less than hopeful. "Taking two women from the same place. That has to be something to go on." Had it been Johnny? Or Dick? Tony? Or someone else entirely?

McCoy nodded. "We'll reinstate the plainclothes detectives and watch the club, but we're not one hundred percent sure this is the same killer."

"Why not?" Max asked.

"She was found at a different dumpsite. Same MO, but it could have been a copycat."

"Or the killer knows you've got cruisers paying extra attention to the ravine behind the truck stop where the other two dancers were found. What other similarities were there?"

The detective looked down at a pad of paper lying across his knee. "There was no sign of struggle at Kim's apartment, which is similar to the other victims. The killer either nabs them where there are no witnesses or they meet with him willingly."

"Like, on a date?" Catherine asked. Rachel had mentioned she thought Bea was starting to make money on the side by selling herself to the men at Lucky Dick's. Maybe someone who'd been here a while would know if Bea or Kim had actually taken that step. "Have you talked to Darla?" she asked McCoy.

Dick's scowl deepened. "Why would he need to talk to her?"

"Sometimes the dancers will earn a little extra cash by dating the customers after hours."

Dick gave her a dark look. "That's not sanctioned by me."

McCoy scribbled something in his notebook. "Is Darla here now?"

"I saw her when we came in," Catherine said.

"Could you ask her to come in here?"

"Sure." Catherine left the somber room and entered the parallel universe, where the lunchtime crowd was growing. For a Monday, it was a good showing. Most of them were enthralled by the dancer on stage. She spied Darla and made her way over to her. "You're needed in the office."

Darla's expression turned suspicious. "What for?"

"You know how you mentioned that some of the customers *date* the dancers?"

It was hard to tell in the dim lighting, but Catherine thought Darla had gone pale. "Yeah?"

"You were right to be worried when Kim didn't show up yesterday. She was murdered. The detective in charge of the investigation would like to talk to you."

"How could you?" The vehemence in Darla's tone shocked Catherine. "Why would you get me involved? You could have just signed my death warrant."

"No. I mean...how would anyone know you were involved?"

"By hearing I talked to a damn detective." Darla looked around, wetting her dry lips with one nervous swipe of her tongue. "He could be here now, watching."

"Darla, please. Think of Bea and Kim, and Angelique, and any other potential victims. Coming forward could save someone's life." She put a hand on Darla's arm—whether to prevent her from bolting or to reassure her, she wasn't sure. Probably both. Her gaze found Max's over by the bar. She sensed his concern, and his readiness to come to her aid. She gave him a quick gesture that she had it covered and he moved back into the office. Looking as if she were marching to the gallows, Darla let Catherine escort her to the office.

Darla warily eyed the three men waiting there. "There are customers waiting."

"This'll only take a minute," McCoy assured her. "We need to know if there's anybody who regularly dates the girls, maybe pays them extra for something on the side."

"No. Nobody I can think of." Darla's defensive posture told the truth. She'd practically curved in on herself as she hunched near the door, clearly eager to leave. She was protecting someone.

"What about Johnny?" Catherine asked.

"He wouldn't do this."

"But he does date the girls?"

She looked at the ground. "On occasion. But they've always come back raving about him the next day. He treats them well."

ANNE MARIE BECKER

"Who did he date?"

"Bea and…Kim." Her face fell. She clearly liked the man.

"You've done the right thing," Catherine said.

"Can I go now?" Without waiting for an answer, Darla turned and walked out.

MAX FOLLOWED DARLA OUT AND PERCHED ON A STOOL AT THE BAR, his gaze roving across the room. Catherine had given them a description of Johnny, but the man wasn't in the club. His usual table was empty.

Catherine took the stool next to him after she finished talking to Dick. "Enjoying the show?"

A dancer hung upside down from a pole, anchoring herself with her legs. "I'm more into private entertainment." Lately, there was only one woman he'd like to get naked. "I filled Einstein in on the latest."

"You all have your hands busy with Tony and the Boss. The police can focus on this for now." She nibbled on her bottom lip as her gaze moved to Darla, who was serving drinks to a table of men he'd ruled out as potential suspects.

"Bachelor party," he murmured. "What's worrying you?" She was going to chew her lip off, and that had to be a felony of some sort.

"I'm worried about Darla. She cares about Johnny."

"He sounds like a charmer, someone who keeps his admirers' attention on the surface to disguise the deeper issues."

"I had a run-in with Johnny."

Max swung to face her. "Run-in?"

"I followed him home one night. It was stupid, but I thought he seemed suspicious and I didn't think he'd see me. And I thought maybe he was connected to the Circle, or Tony, or…I don't know. He has a tattoo on his hand of the Circle's symbol."

"Jesus, Cat, why didn't you say anything?"

"He didn't seem to know anything of value. I talked myself out of the situation."

He stood. "We're getting out of here. I don't want you near this place when this goes down. Besides, my mother called a few minutes ago. She's insisting I join her for a late lunch. Says I owe her since I missed Saturdays' dinner and that she has something to tell me. Join me?"

Her eyes clouded with something like fear. She looked around the room again and sighed. "I'm not sure there's much I can do here, anyway."

"You can give McCoy Johnny's address."

She nodded. "That, I can do."

He took her hand. "And then let's get out of here. McCoy and the plainclothes police will watch out for Johnny. They'll call us the moment they find anything."

MAX PARKED AT THE RANCH HOUSE AND WALKED WITH CATHERINE to the front door. The long skirt they'd bought in the hotel shop that morning swished about her legs. He'd explored her body several times during the night and this morning, and now knew every curve, every tender spot beneath her clothes, including the one behind her knee that made her laugh and squirm. He wanted to investigate them all over again.

She raised her hand to knock, but he pulled her into his arms to kiss her soundly. Her body went soft in his arms as they took a moment to enjoy each other.

With regret, he broke the connection. "That's a little better."

"What?" She wore a bemused expression.

"You were too tense."

Her eyes heated, and he wondered if she was thinking of all the ways they'd loosened each other up last night. Judging by the wicked gleam in her eyes, she hadn't fully come back to reality when the door swung open.

His mother's sharp gaze moved between him and Catherine and she frowned as if sensing they'd grown closer without her permission. "Glad I could lure you away from wherever you've been hiding out." Censure colored her words.

Max's whole body tightened in defense. "You said you wanted to see me. Here I am—take it or leave it."

She led them to the dining room and lifted a glass of white wine to her lips. The half-empty bottle sat on the table. "I've had Claudia prepare King Ranch casserole. I'll have her add a salad." Her gaze ran over Catherine's curves as if they were less than ideal. Max wouldn't change a thing—they fit perfectly in his hands.

Catherine stiffened at the insult. "I'm sure it'll be delicious."

His mother switched to a softer tone that was deceptively sympathetic. "Lord knows you'll have to watch what you eat if you're dancing at Lucky Dick's."

Catherine's shocked gaze moved to Max. "You told them?"

"Not me." He should have suspected they'd find out. This time, however, their informant had left out a vital piece of information. "She's not a dancer."

"As if that matters," his mother snapped. "Simply being associated with that place, and then linked to you, is enough to sink your reputation." Catherine's cheeks colored.

Max braced himself as if he could physically defend her. "She did it for SSAM. For an investigation."

"Whatever you say, dear. Your dad is trying to get home from the office, but he might be late. Let's start before it gets cold."

A VISIT WITH THE CAULFIELDS WAS LIKE TAKING A HIKE THROUGH A field of rattlesnake nests. One wrong step and you'd get bitten. Catherine longed to return to the cozy hotel room on the Riverwalk.

Max sent her an apologetic look as he pulled out her chair at the dining room table. Inwardly, she braced herself for Lillian's next attack. She didn't have to wait long.

"You two certainly seem to have grown closer." Lillian's eyes bored into Catherine's. "I suppose you'll be making that engagement official soon? Of course, you might want to take it slow. People around here might not approve of a Caulfield living in sin with a girl from the trailer park. I believe that's two strikes against you now."

Catherine's cheeks flamed like the surface of the sun and she took a fortifying gulp of wine. The message was clear. She would never be good enough for Lillian's son or the Caulfield name, no matter how much she did to ingratiate herself with them.

Max scowled. "Then maybe we should return to Chicago, where our relationship would be more acceptable."

Lillian's wineglass halted halfway to her lips. "I'm simply protecting my only son."

"Because you couldn't protect your other one. Because you manipulated Mike *to death*, harping at him about a future he never wanted until he couldn't stand it any longer and turned to booze and drugs. If you don't stop attacking Catherine, you'll push me away, too. *Again.*"

Catherine heard a sharp intake of breath and realized it was hers. Rumors had surfaced at the time of the accident that had indicated Mike Caulfield was as much an alcoholic as her father. But stories of Mike's volunteer positions and athletic accomplishments had quickly surfaced, painting the picture of a well-rounded kid who'd had a bright future. Doug Bailey, on the other hand, had been slammed by the press until he looked like a washed out mechanic who neglected his daughters and could barely pay the bills.

Ultimately, it didn't matter. It had been her father who'd made the fateful decision to drink and drive that night, her father who'd given Mike a ride home from a bar and then crashed the car into a tree, killing Mike instantly and seriously injuring himself. A series of horrendous mistakes had led to the disastrous consequence—the loss of two lives: Mike's had physically ended, and her father's had come to a screeching halt.

"I'm sorry," Max said to Lillian. "That was uncalled for. Maybe we should leave."

The skin around Lillian's mouth was white, as if the pressure of holding in her words was almost too much. She put her hands under the table, but not before Catherine saw them tremble. Losing a child had to be even worse than losing a parent. Then again, pain was pain.

"No, you don't get to leave," Lillian said. "You've made a deal to attend one dinner a week. I'm calling in your debt now. As for your accusations, well, you'd be surprised how many people use manipulation to get what they want." Thankfully, Max missed the pointed look Lillian gave Catherine. Lillian smiled suddenly. "Let's change the topic, shall we? When is your date with Melissa?"

Max frowned. "I haven't set a date yet. I'm not sure it's a good idea, anyway…"

"She paid for you. You committed to doing this and Caulfields always keep their promises. Besides, Melissa's from a good family. No skeletons in her closet."

"Not like ours?"

"Not like many families I know." Over the rim of her wineglass, Lillian shot Catherine another loaded glance.

CONVERSATION HAD TURNED TO BUSINESS ONCE HAYWORTH arrived, but Catherine's mind was on Lillian's words. Somehow, she choked down lunch and made it back to the guesthouse.

Max followed, closing the door behind them. "If I could find Tony sooner, I'd be gone in a heartbeat." He looked at the dishes still in the sink and frowned. Was he thinking of the argument they'd had before he'd walked out, or of the way Tony had stolen her away? He entwined his fingers with hers. "And I'd take you with me."

"Back to Chicago." She tugged loose on the pretense of slipping off her sandals and light sweater. "I told you, I can't."

He followed and stopped so close to her that they shared a breath. He ran his hands from her elbows to her wrists. "I thought we'd made it past all the barriers between us."

God, how could any woman resist those eyes? Apparently, none could—or none she'd ever heard of. She wanted to tell him things about herself, to share herself. To *be* herself.

"My father's in prison," she heard herself say, as if from far away. "That phone call I took Friday night, on the golf course... that was him. He'd earned a call."

"What was he found guilty of?"

She took a moment to count to ten and find the strength to come out with it. "Vehicular manslaughter. He was an alcoholic and the addiction had taken over his life. He was making horrible decisions."

"Like Mike." There was a surprising amount of understanding in Max's tone, and none of the judgment she'd expected. His hands remained at her wrists, his thumbs brushing her pulse points. Maybe she could get through this after all. She released a shaky breath.

"Except my dad was responsible for someone else's death." *Mike's.*

But he didn't understand what she was hinting at. "And you thought I'd hold you responsible for that, for what your father had done?"

In surprise, her gaze shot to his. "No." *Had she?*

"Liar." The term was spoken without heat. She opened her mouth to respond, but he spoke first. "You're so good at telling me, at telling Damian, at reassuring anyone but yourself they're not to blame for others' actions. But you don't give yourself the same consideration. I understand that feeling of responsibility. Like you could have—*should* have—done something to prevent disaster. In the years before his death, I watched my brother binge drink and pick fights, overheard my father bailing him out of jail. These were Mike's subtle cries for help, and I did nothing."

She'd known what happened to Mike had hit the family like a meteorite, kicking up dust that never quite settled and decimating the bonds between Max and his family, but she hadn't known he'd blamed himself. "What could you have done?"

He turned the question back onto her. "What could *you* have done for your father?"

What she *had* done was go to Hayworth and negotiate a truce to keep the media from tearing the remains of her family apart—and she'd paid dearly for it.

What could she have done to avoid the horrible event from even happening, though? She'd given it a lot of thought. "I could have listened more. Paid attention to the signs my father was spiraling out of control after my mother died. Kept him from going to the bars, or dragged him home sooner."

His eyes turned fierce. "You were, what, a teenager?"

"I was fourteen when Mom died."

"See—"

"But I was eighteen when Dad hit bottom." She'd moved out on her own as soon as possible, hoping to escape the misery that seemed to fill every square inch of the tiny mobile home. Rachel had found her own escape through her schoolwork and after-school programs. They'd left their father alone.

"You weren't even old enough to be allowed in the bars."

"You were eighteen when you signed on for a career with the SEALs." They were the same age and would have gone to the same school if his parents hadn't sent him to a private school across town. Not that Max would have noticed Catherine if they had gone to the same school.

He grinned. "So stubborn. What I'm trying to say is your dad is his own person. Yes, we want to do everything we can to prevent a loved one from feeling pain, but we can't be there twenty-four-seven. It's time you forgave yourself. Stop trying to make up for it by being there for everyone else and be there for yourself."

Is that what she'd been doing? Beating herself up all these years, doing penance for her family's mistakes by selling her own soul?

"HOW CAN I MAKE YOU SEE YOU CAN LET THINGS GO, THAT YOU deserve happiness?" Max wanted Catherine to see herself as he saw her—beautiful in every way.

"Embrace the new, and the now?" There was a question in her tone.

She'd remembered his words from New Year's Eve. "Exactly like that."

It had been a novel, totally in-the-now event when he'd first kissed Catherine.

The winter night was cold on the Chicago rooftop where the party was being held, the warming effect of the alcohol just enough to cut the chill. While he never allowed himself to get completely drunk, Max was enjoying a nice buzz that numbed serious thought about the year to come.

It was, in short, perfect.

Except his date had left in a huff ten minutes ago. Max didn't miss the latest model to grace his arm. Her kind of drama was a buzzkill. But he didn't appreciate the way she'd left him high and dry just before midnight.

Max took a swallow of champagne and surveyed the Chicago skyline from the top of the SSAM office building. Damian rented the available space to some quiet companies, and kept the entire top floor, as well as a couple other levels, for his agency. That space included the glorious rooftop. Max's territory was the basement level, where Damian provided everything a weapons expert and trainer could want to keep the SSAM agents up to snuff. Shooting range, gym, anything they could need was at Max's disposal.

In the wake of his date's departure, the party had taken on a different vibe. Or maybe he'd had more attention to give to his friends, who were gathered in small groups on the outdoor couches and chairs set up in intimate clusters. There was much laughter as they recounted the escapades of the past year.

Only Catherine stood apart from the group, hanging out at the buffet table and dipping a strawberry into the chocolate fountain. Some unseen force propelled him in her direction. He snatched a glass from a side table where another fountain—this one flowing with champagne—was set up. He filled the fresh glass and topped off his own.

"Fancy meeting you here." He handed a glass to Catherine.

She rolled her eyes, but accepted the offering. "Does that line work for you?"

"It's not one of my best." But he often found himself unaccountably tongue-tied around Catherine Montague. He wasn't self-conscious about that, though, because Catherine was...comfortable. She represented SSAM, and therefore was a symbol of the only place Max had considered home. There was a time, before he'd joined the military and found his true calling, that he'd been self-conscious about everything and everyone. The pressures put on him to be perfect had been stifling.

But being around Catherine wasn't that kind of pressure. It was no pressure at all, in fact.

"Having fun?" She bit off the meat of the strawberry, then set aside the stem and licked her finger, completely oblivious to the answering tug in his groin.

"I am now." His gaze remained on her mouth.

Her lips curved and surprise widened her winter-blue eyes. "Are you flirting with me?"

He gave a casual shrug, though he felt coiled tight inside and... curious. Like he was anticipating something wonderful. With Catherine? No, that would be bad. He never hunted this close to home base. Still, the promise of something both forbidden and fulfilling hung in the air.

"Maybe. Is it working, Cat?" He reached out and brushed a fingertip along a long strand of hair. He loved how the waves seemed to hug her shoulders. Tonight, the moonlight caused the color luminesce like the crown of a fairy queen.

She narrowed her eyes on him. "Is this because the Model of the Year walked out on you?"

"Model of the week, maybe." He never dated anyone for long. It was part of his code. *So is avoiding complications in the workplace.*

"No, she really was named Model of the Year by a famous fashion magazine."

"Hmm."

"And you didn't know that?" Catherine snorted.

"She may have said something about it. I don't remember."

"You're so blasé about life."

"Maybe I have reason to be. The world is too serious. And the people who seem black and white often are many shades of gray on the inside."

She studied him a moment, thoughtful. "I know that. Probably better than anybody."

"Do you?" He took a step closer, his nose flaring, taking in the delicious scent of strawberries and champagne on the breath she exhaled. "You surprise me, Cat, and I should warn you. I love unraveling a good mystery."

She looked away, and then at the slim gold watch on her wrist. "Oh! It's almost midnight. I should start the countdown." The others had already clustered in small groups and were watching their phones or watches as they counted down the final thirty seconds. She didn't need to organize this event any more than she already had. The woman in front of him had planned most of this spectacular night.

Like riding his motorcycle on the roads outside of the city

limits, Catherine was familiar, yet full of possibilities. A spark of anticipation roared to life inside him.

"Ten, nine, eight..." A chorus of voices, their coworkers with their dates, began to shout the final seconds of the year.

Max took a step closer. "Help me ring in the new year in style, Cat?"

Her eyes widened as his gaze dropped to her mouth. She licked her lips nervously and then glanced around, still the prim and proper administrative assistant who didn't want to be seen with the office bad boy.

"Seven, six, five..."

Max tugged her behind a tall topiary at the end of the buffet table, where no one could see them.

"Four, three..."

He took their champagne glasses and set them on the waist-high ledge that lined the roof. He slid his hands through her silken hair and looked into eyes that mirrored his own desire.

"Two, one. Happy New Year!"

On the street below, car horns blared and people shouted. The notes of "Auld Lang Syne" played from a saxophone somewhere in the distance. Fireworks exploded in the sky around them. On the rooftop, friends were offering good wishes and hugging. Ethan and Maggie were engaged in a serious lip lock. Holt and Sara were hugging Holt's son Theo, forming a circular family unit and grinning from ear to ear. Becca, Lorena and Damian were exchanging hugs. Suddenly, Max was glad his date had walked out, because he only wanted to be with family—his SSAM family.

It took only a split second for Max to take this in. He shoved aside his conscience and his code and claimed Catherine's luscious mouth. The burst of ripe berries, the hint of champagne, the heat of sliding into a warm, familiar place—all of these sensations hit him at once, making him lightheaded. Max Sawyer was never unsteady, but at that moment, Catherine's hands, gripping at the front of his shirt as if she held on for dear life, and her mouth, so soft and giving beneath his, were the only things anchoring him to the ground. Or the rooftop. Fuck, he didn't care where he was right now, as long as he was doing *this*.

Catherine brushed her tongue along his and pulled a moan from deep within him. He slipped his hand behind her head to tilt it and take the kiss deeper. But this wasn't the only way he wanted to take her. He throbbed with need, and the shock of that had him jerking away. Her grip on his shirt prevented him from going far.

His grin was shaky and he fought for familiar ground. "Now that's the best thing I've had all year."

"The year just started thirty seconds ago." Her voice was breathy and he felt a flush of pride that he'd brought out that sensual rasp.

"Exactly. And I hope it continues this way for a little while longer."

"But...I'm not what you want."

"Maybe you are. Embrace the new, and the now. I think that'll be my motto this year."

The sound of laughter from beyond their secluded spot was like being doused in ice water, waking them from the dream world they'd created. Catherine's eyes went wide. She unclenched her fists and stepped away from him, smoothing her hands over her coat and skirt.

"Cat?" He reached out but dropped his hand when she took another step toward the group celebrating several yards away.

"What? You said you hope this continues a little while longer. What does that mean? A few minutes, a few days?" She laughed without humor. "The flavor of the week?"

"No." Hell. What, precisely, was he trying for here? She was right. He couldn't commit. They'd enjoy each other for a brief time and then they'd break things off. And they'd stop being friends. He couldn't bear that.

She gave him a bright smile. "Thanks for the kiss. At least it kept me warm." Parts of him were still *very* warm. Her next words had them going cold. "But can we just forget about it? I don't want to become one of your temp girls, and I really, really don't want to lose the respect of my coworkers or Damian. I can't lose this job."

Direct hit. Going out with him would be a move in the wrong direction for her. "Sure. Everyone is impulsive once in a while, right?"

"Like you said, *embrace the new, and the now.*"

Except he wanted her reaction to him to be more than impulse, more than a moment in time. The heat, the electricity... He'd sensed it building toward some special explosion he knew he'd regret missing. *Not as much as you'd regret losing her friendship.*

Max smiled at the memory as he came back to the present. "Kissing you on New Year's was the best idea I ever had."

Catherine snorted. "I find that hard to believe."

"Then I'll just have to convince you I'm a genius." He pulled her to him.

Her lips twitched. "That might take some time."

"Oh, I hope so. We're taking the rest of the day off." He bent to kiss her, intent on showing her how many great ideas he had to share.

CHAPTER 21

Johnny tried not to show fear, but as he entered his second hour in the SAPD interrogation room, it was getting more and more difficult. Fear was for pussies. But damn, the timing couldn't have been worse. He'd just returned to his apartment after an all-night project when the police showed up at his door. Thank God he'd taken the time to clean out his van yesterday.

He reminded himself he was strong and had connections. The police couldn't touch him.

He told himself that over and over, until the door opened and two men came in. One of them, Detective McCoy, had been in before, asking a bunch of questions about the dead dancers. The other was a stranger.

McCoy carried two coffees, a pack of cigarettes and a bag of Fritos. The breakfast of champions. He set the food between them and eyed him over it like it was the Berlin wall. Jesus, they were stuck in some lame cop movie. *Keep it up, fucker. I ain't talkin'.*

Not that Johnny would know what to say, anyway. The time-line of the past few days was a blur. After waking up covered in blood, he'd spent Saturday looking for a body back at the truck stop where Bea and Angelique had been found, but he hadn't found Kim. Johnny had gone to the poker game, gotten high and then gone on a bender until the shakes went away. By Monday, he'd sobered and had nearly convinced himself the weekend's events had been a nightmare he could forget.

He'd managed to convince himself Kim was still alive some-where when he heard the police found the bitch murdered and dumped in the woods not far from a different gas station—the one where he'd woken up covered in blood. Within walking distance of his apartment. But fuck all if he could remember doing the deed. Shit, for all he knew, his nosy neighbor Troy had killed Kim.

"This is a friend of the department." McCoy gestured to the man who'd entered with him. "Max Sawyer."

The guy didn't say a word. Didn't even nod. He had the muscles and stance of a bodyguard, and the eyes of someone who'd seen some hard shit. Johnny's eyes flicked back to McCoy, who was much easier to handle.

"Want something?" McCoy gestured to the wall of goodies.

"Don't smoke," Johnny lied. He'd be damned if he'd take a thing from them. His mouth watered at the thought of the coffee and Fritos, though. He hadn't eaten since… He couldn't remember the last good meal he'd had, though he must have had the munchies at some point.

With a knowing smile, McCoy slid a cup toward him. "I'm guessing you like it black. The crime scene unit found old cups under the seat of your van. And a mattress in back. I wonder what that was for."

Fuck, fuck, fuck. They'd already searched his van? He'd cleaned things carefully after each run to the border, as the Circle had trained him to do. But wasn't there some purple shit or something the police could spray and it would detect traces of blood you couldn't see with the naked eye? He was so fucked. Prickles of fear had his hairs standing on end.

No. He was smart. He had connections. What would an intelligent, connected person do in this situation? "I want a lawyer."

McCoy sat back in his chair, in no hurry to comply. "Do you *need* a lawyer, Johnny?"

It was the detective's lazy-ass, cocky attitude that finally had things falling into place. Johnny was a suspect, which was to be expected given his connection to the victims, but the cops didn't have anything concrete on him. Not yet, anyway. Nobody had read him his Miranda rights.

"Don't need one." Johnny leaned back and copied McCoy's posture. "*Want* one. Just playing it smart."

Irritation and impatience flashed across McCoy's face before he relaxed again. The man was faking it, hoping to trip Johnny up. Well, Johnny wouldn't comply. With a surge of confidence, he reached for the cigarette pack and shook one out, putting it to his lips.

"Thought you didn't smoke," McCoy said.

"I'm surprising myself these days."

McCoy tossed a lighter across the table. "You like hanging out at Lucky Dick's. A *lot*."

He shrugged. That kind of information was public knowledge. It didn't link him to the murders. The puff of nicotine went straight to his system, infusing him with more strength. He was fucking unstoppable. "I do. It's a nice, clean place compared to some clubs."

"Two girls from there have been murdered."

"You live the life those girls live, I suppose there are some consequences. Not all men are honorable."

"Is that what you are? Honorable?"

"I try."

"And you consider it honorable to pay women to have sex with you."

Johnny schooled his face into what he hoped was a neutral

expression, but his insides were roiling. "I don't know what you're talking about. And about that lawyer…"

"I'll look into that for you right now. But if you cooperate with us now, I'm sure we can make some suitable arrangement."

Like twenty to life without parole. No, thank you.

McCoy closed the door behind him, presumably to track down a lawyer, leaving Johnny alone with the guy named Max.

Max stared at him several long seconds before speaking. "I'm staying on a ranch not far from here."

Johnny grew uncomfortable at the long pause that followed that odd statement. "Well, good for you."

"A friend was kidnapped at knifepoint from that ranch by Tony Moreno."

"That's bad for her." So, that son of a bitch Tony had survived. Fucking great. One more thing to make the Boss angry, and that anger could potentially be directed at Johnny.

"It's also bad for you."

"How do you figure?"

"I've had the cowboys at that ranch searching all day. Know what they found?"

"Old, rusted horseshoes? Arrowheads? Bricks of gold? Come on man, don't keep me in suspense." He was throwing all the bravado he had at this man, but inside, Johnny's mind was racing. Had Tony said something? Had he thrown Johnny under the bus?

The man's jaw clenched. "Camping gear. What do you bet I can trace it back to you, especially since your initials were in the blade of the knife Tony used to abduct my friend?" Anger flashed in the man's eyes. He was seriously pissed, but controlling it, which was somehow scarier than if he'd unleashed it.

Johnny's heart thumped so hard he was sure the guy could hear it. "Oh, that. It was stolen a couple weeks ago."

"You report that?"

"No, man. I didn't figure the cops could do anything about a few hundred bucks in gear."

"Or maybe you don't want cops around because you work for the Circle."

His face suddenly felt numb. So, this was what it felt like when the blood drained from your head. "The Circle?"

Max reached out and grabbed Johnny's hand, slamming it down on the table and holding on. "The organization whose symbol you wear on your wrist."

Johnny swallowed hard. "I just liked the image."

"Right." Max stared until Johnny felt his skin prickle all over. "The only way Tony Moreno, an escaped convict, would have your gear is if he knew you. I think you helped him. If you don't want to be charged with aiding and abetting a known felon, I suggest you start talking." Max leaned forward and dropped his voice low. "You're going to help me find Tony or I'm going to make sure we pin every murder from the last several weeks on you. And there have been a *lot* of murders around here lately, Johnny."

"Have you seen Dad yet?" Rachel looked up from where she was lining up her cue stick with the eight ball.

Tuesday nights were ladies' nights at the Lone Star Bar. Half-price pool and brews. Catherine was glad Rachel had been available to keep her mind off Max and Melissa. When she'd last seen Max that morning, she'd convinced him to keep his commitments. Max had finally arranged for the date he'd auctioned off, though he'd seemed reluctant to go. What would Melissa demand of him, and would Max be able to resist temptation?

"Planning to visit him tomorrow." Catherine's stomach churned at the thought. Seeing her father behind bars was always difficult. And Hayworth hadn't said anything more about obtaining the governor's pardon. Since she hadn't exactly come through with her part of the bargain and convinced Max to stay on at CI, she'd been afraid to ask. And she didn't mention the possibility to Rachel. She hadn't wanted to get her hopes up.

At Catherine's expression, Rachel's brow furrowed. "Want me to come with?"

"Thanks, but I think I should see him alone."

"You may want to prepare yourself."

"What's wrong? Is he sick or something?"

"No, but it was a shock to me, seeing him months ago, after the years in Chicago when I didn't see him. He looks much older and he's lost weight."

"Why didn't you tell me?"

Rachel cocked an eyebrow at her. "He insisted he's fine, and then told me under no circumstances was I to tell you."

"Why not?" How could they keep this from her?

Rachel laughed. "Because you would have come running back here. And wielding axes, bows and arrows, or whatever it took to make things right."

Catherine stiffened. "What's wrong with that?"

Rachel took her shot, sunk the eight ball, did a little fist pump in the air, and then came over to hug Catherine. "Nothing's wrong with the way you love. It's fierce and beautiful. You fight for us. But there's nothing you can do for Dad. I wish you'd use a little of that fight to get you what *you* need."

What she needed was a new start. A sparkling clean conscience. The closer she and Max became, the more the pressure mounted— and the higher the cost would be when she eventually lost him.

"Besides," Rachel said, "it's not like you're not keeping things from me."

Catherine's stomach sank. "What do you mean?"

"Max Sawyer. Maxwell Sawyer Caulfield. I saw the Caulfield ranch brand on the side of the truck when he rode to the rescue at the clinic the other night."

She knew who Max really was? Catherine opened her mouth to explain but Rachel raised her hand.

"It's okay." Rachel's brow furrowed. "I know you'll tell me the whole story when you're ready. I just hope you know what you're doing with him. Does he know?"

"That Dad is responsible for his brother's death?" Catherine shook her head. "No. And I owe it to Max to tell him the truth first."

"No time like the present..." Rachel gestured to Catherine to turn around.

Max. Across the crowded bar, just inside the front door, he stood below the rows of neon signs proclaiming various kinds of beer. His gaze connected with hers but his fierce expression didn't relax.

"Want me to give you some time?" Like a sentry, Rachel stood at her side, the end of her cue stick resting against the floor between her feet as she gripped it with both hands. They watched Max move through the ladies' night crowd, dodging interested looks from several women as he headed toward Catherine.

"That might be best." Catherine had practically shoved Max toward another woman, encouraging him to enjoy his date with Melissa. Yet, here he was.

"He looks serious. Is there trouble in paradise?"

"What?"

"Oh, come on. Like I haven't figured out that it had to be a hottie like him that has you all tied in knots lately. Hmmm...knots. That's an interesting idea."

Catherine rolled her eyes. "Well, he doesn't have to intrude on our sister time tonight."

"Oh, no. Don't use me as an excuse."

"But—"

"Hello," Max said to Rachel. "Sorry to interrupt, but I need to talk to Catherine." The look on his face was intent.

Had his parents told him the truth? That she was a fraud and their spy, and had been deceiving him for years? She pressed a hand to her stomach, where a wild fluttering had begun. "How did you find me? Never mind. I can guess." She'd have to have a long talk with Einstein about privacy.

"I'll be at the bar," Rachel said, and hurried away.

"What's wrong?" Catherine asked, secretly hoping he'd say he'd had a horrible date with Melissa.

"I didn't know where you'd gone. I guess I assumed you'd stick close to the ranch this evening."

"And wait for you to return from your date? No, thank you. Besides, the police called to say my Jeep was ready to be returned to me. Rachel was kind enough to come pick me up and drive me into town to get it." As she spoke, his gaze carefully surveyed the bar's occupants. "What's going on?"

"I didn't make it to my date. Something came up. When you weren't at the ranch, I got worried." He shook his head, his expression turning businesslike. "I'm working on a hunch and I could use your help."

"What do you need?"

"Johnny told me about some of his drug connections—"

Catherine held up a hand. "Wait, what? Johnny is helping with the investigation? I thought he was a suspect. Besides, he doesn't strike me as the generous type."

"More like the type to be concerned with self-preservation. I made it clear he didn't have a choice or he was going down for all the murders."

"But he really might have murdered Bea, Angelique and Kim."

"And we'll be keeping an eye on him. For now, I needed a lead to find Tony."

"And you got one?"

"He wouldn't admit he'd hidden Tony at his place, but he did say Tony *could* have been in the neighborhood, and that Tony *might* have witnessed a drug deal go down. Johnny also revealed that when Tony took off, he *might* have taken a stash of drugs, including pain pills, that *someone* might have been holding for a customer."

"I knew Johnny was into some bad stuff."

"Yeah, well, we'll let the cops sort that part out. For now, I want Tony behind bars before he can hurt anyone else. With his injuries and lack of resources, I figure he has to be in that neighborhood near Lucky Dick's. The only thing he had to barter were the pain pills Rachel gave him. Johnny mentioned the name of the guy that Tony might have seen during a drug exchange—Lee. Wasn't that the name of the guy who held a gun on you and Rachel at the clinic?"

"Yes." She shivered as she recalled Lee's wild eyes. "And he'd been after painkillers that day." She didn't doubt Tony could talk his way into getting Lee to help him hide out, especially if Tony had any drugs to pay him with.

"The address on Lee's arrest record is invalid. I need to find him." Max's gaze slid to the bar, where her sister was chatting with the bartender.

"You think Rachel might have a different address in her patient records? I suppose that's possible."

"Would you mind asking her to cooperate?"

"Of course. But if this pans out, I'm coming with you." When he scowled at her, she held her ground. "That bastard put a knife to my throat and threatened to rape and kill my sister and me. I'll get the address from Rachel, but I'm not giving it to you. I need to be a part of this." She'd been a victim too many times. This time, she was going to make sure Tony went back to prison, where he belonged.

Max pulled up to the curb a few houses down from the address Rachel had given them. "Stay here."

Catherine itched to go with him, but he was the one with the skills—and the gun. This was meant to be a reconnaissance mission, to find out if Tony was hiding out at Lee's—if this was even a valid address for Lee—and then she was going to be the one to call the cops. She'd take charge of finding her own justice.

Max leaned over and gave her a quick kiss, then was out of the car and jogging across the dark, quiet street in a flash. She watched as he merged with the shadows on the side of the rundown, postage-stamp sized house Rachel's files had indicated was Lee's home. Catherine gripped her phone tightly, ready to hit send on her 9-1-1 call as she watched for Max. The nerves got to her as the seconds crept by and nothing happened—or maybe something was happening but she couldn't see it.

A car slowed down in front of the house. The vehicle turned into the driveway and the garage door went up. A moment later, Lee walked around the back of the car and removed a couple of grocery bags from the trunk.

Shit. Where was Max? Did he hear Lee arrive?

Screw it. Better safe than sorry. She pressed *Dial* on her phone and reported her suspicions to the 9-1-1 operator. As she hung up, the silence of the night was cracked open by a gunshot.

MAX HAD JUST ENTERED THE UNLOCKED BACK DOOR OF THE HOUSE when he heard a door to his right open. There was no time to find cover as Lee walked in. Spying Max, Lee dropped two bags of groceries and went for the gun tucked into his waistband. Max went for his own weapon.

"Did you get the smokes and the medicine? If not, you don't get the painkill—" Tony's eyes went wide as he emerged from the hallway to Max's left and saw Lee and Max in a standoff, guns drawn.

"Put the gun down," Max warned Lee. He didn't take his eyes off the gun as he addressed Tony. "Tony, put your hands up and kneel on the floor. Now!"

Lee sneered. "I don't think you're in a position to give orders. I believe I have the right to shoot intruders on my private property."

"I believe you do," Tony added, his two gold teeth winking as he grinned and moved to stand beside Lee. "Go ahead and shoot him."

Max hoped Lee didn't have the stomach to take him down in cold blood. After all, Lee's thing was drugs and vandalism, not murder. Of course, there was a first time for everything.

Lee eyed Max's gun. "Toss it aside."

"You first." No way was Max giving up his only defense. But his heart climbed up his throat as he spied his secret weapon inching open the door from the garage, just behind Lee. *Catherine.* His heart froze as icy fear crept in, but he kept his mind focused on the threat at hand. Now he had even more reason to disarm Lee quickly—and then he'd give Catherine hell for leaving the truck.

She held two fists up behind Lee. She was going to attack the man while he held a gun? He wanted to yell at her to run, but Lee would turn the weapon on her next. Max realized she had something in her clenched hands. In a quick series of movements, she reached around Lee's head and clapped her hands over his eyes as if she were playing a twisted game of Guess Who. She opened her fingers as she did so, releasing some kind of dirt or dust into Lee's eyes.

Lee howled and his gun went sliding to the floor as his hands went to defend himself. "What the fuck!" He lunged for the kitchen and the sink.

Catherine knelt to retrieve Lee's gun at the same time Tony did. Max rushed forward. Unlike Lee, Tony wouldn't hesitate to kill a person in cold blood.

Catherine pushed the gun across the linoleum, away from Tony, toward Max, then let out a grunt of pain as Tony tried to grab her and ended up pulling her hair, yanking her head back sharply. As Max grabbed the gun, Catherine launched her elbow into Tony's injured thigh, connecting with precision and sending him backward. He howled in pain, clutching his leg and rolling on the ground as she got to her feet.

"The police should be here any minute," she said. She ran her hands down Max's chest, and then hugged his waist while he pointed one gun at Tony and the other at Lee. "I'm sorry. I would have stayed out there like you ordered, but I saw Lee come home and I thought it was two against one."

She'd put herself at risk for him, and it had taken several years off his life, but he understood her motivation. He would do anything for her, too. He placed a quick kiss on the top of her head and took a deep breath, inhaling her calming scent. They were both safe. The siren and screeching of tires outside told him the worst was over. Tony would be taken back to prison.

Lee, on the other hand, was still at the sink, obsessed with trying to wash something out of his eyes.

"What was that you used on him?" he asked.

She smiled. "Kitty litter. There was a tub of it in the garage, right by the door." She shrugged at his stunned look. "You always told us to use whatever was on hand in a crisis. What? You didn't think I was paying attention when you gave the team training seminars?"

His lips twitched. "I'm just glad you're on my side."

CHAPTER 22

T he smell of the prison was familiar. Over the years, Catherine had associated the scents with the loss of hopes and dreams, but it could be crystallized into more tangible odors. Near the wall where the guards took their smoke breaks, just outside the main doors, was the scent of nicotine and juniper bushes. Inside was the chlorine scent of industrial-strength floor cleaner, leather from the guards' gear and the leftover scent of whatever food they'd had in their break room. Today, it was pizza, honoring someone's birthday, if the lonely Mylar balloon was any indication.

Would her father ever celebrate milestones like that again? And how many birthdays did he have left? How many more family events would he miss? She needed to talk to Hayworth about the status of her father's pardon.

She'd dissuaded Max from coming with her to visit her father, knowing Max would likely recognize her father's face or name as linked to his brother's death. Besides, he was meeting with the SSAM team to consider how to proceed with Tony. The convict was under guard in the prison infirmary, receiving treatment for his injury before they transferred him to a regular cell—in this same prison. Lee had been taken to jail and was being arraigned later this morning.

After clearing security, Catherine was escorted to an area where the public could meet with prisoners during visiting hours. Doug Bailey rose from a table as she approached. As Rachel had mentioned, he seemed thinner, but there was still a glow of life to his eyes. Though he was only in his mid-fifties, he looked at least ten years older. He studied her a long moment before gathering her up for a hug. When he pulled back, his eyes, so similar to hers, were filled with tears.

"It's been a while," he said.

"I'm sorry, I—"

He held up a hand. "No, don't apologize. It wasn't meant as a criticism. Fill me in. Rachel says you're moving back to Texas?"

As they took their seats, she shrugged as if leaving SSAM wasn't tearing her up inside. "Thought I might move closer to home for a while."

"But you love it in Chicago. In your letters, it sounded like that place had become home." She couldn't explain that the reason she loved Chicago was because it was where Max was, and what they had would soon be over.

"Sweetie, don't move back for me or Rachel, if that's what this is about. You deserve a life of your own."

"I'm working on it. A new life." *Embrace the new, and the now.*

"What was wrong with your old one?" He squeezed her hand as her eyes filled. "Tell me." The tender note in her father's voice shot her right back to the days when they'd been a happy family. "You've always taken care of us, now let me..." He cursed and released her hand.

"What?"

"How can I do anything from in here?" He swiped at his eyes, quick to compose himself while guards and other prisoners were within listening distance. "And why should you let me? I ruined your life."

"No, that's not it—"

"I never should have taken that deal. I thought it would help, but I should have known you couldn't trust Hayworth."

Her gaze flew to his face. "Hayworth Caulfield?" A chill of foreboding raised gooseflesh as her father's expression twisted with pain. "What does this have to do with him?"

"He made me a deal. I should never have taken it, but at the time I was a no-good drunk, a widower and a terrible father. He convinced me you two were better off without me. I thought, if I agreed to take the blame, it might shield you girls from worse— maybe even provide you a better life."

"*Take the blame?* What does that mean?" But she had a sick feeling she knew.

"I wasn't driving that night, but I made a deal in exchange for saying I was responsible."

Her heart lurched in her chest. All this time, she'd worked for Hayworth and Lillian, thinking *she* was the lucky one, capitalizing on some moment of generosity to help her family. She'd been a fool. "And what was the deal?"

"Hayworth was a legend in this town, even back then. His family had money and a golden reputation. That one summer, his son Mike spent almost every night drinking at the same bar as me, except he was a novice at knowing his limits and holding his alcohol. One night—*that* night—Mike became belligerent and was kicked out of the bar. I saw that nobody had called for a ride, as they usually did for him, and I worried, so I followed. He was already in his car, and I tried to tell him to stop, that I hadn't drunk as much as him, so I could drive." The distant look in her father's eyes was painful to see. He was reliving a horrible night. "He started the car and I made an instant choice. A bad one, maybe. Or maybe us getting in that wreck kept him from plowing into someone else."

Her father swallowed hard. "I *had* been drinking and shouldn't have been behind the wheel either. But my thought was to help. He was only a bitter, angry kid..."

"Why didn't you say anything sooner? Tell at least Rachel and me the truth?" She'd thought everything was her fault, that God was punishing her for something she'd done by taking her mother, and then her father.

"You wouldn't have understood the choices I made. You were too young. And it was part of the deal with the Caulfields. They'd watch out for you two, see you had everything you needed, which was more than I'd been doing anyway. I thought it was the one good thing I could do as a father. His shoulders lifted a fraction in a small shrug. "It was a small price to pay."

"But why?" She shook her head. "Never mind. I can guess. They wanted to keep their son's name untarnished, their family reputation intact."

"I couldn't blame them. Just as I had daughters, they had another son to protect."

"Max." Her chest hurt. God, what had she done? Yes, she'd lied to Max, but her whole adult life had been a lie. She'd thought she'd been doing the right thing, helping the Caulfields, who'd helped her father and her sister. But she'd been so very wrong. She'd trusted the wrong people. Was Hayworth even speaking to the governor on her father's behalf, as he'd said he would?

"Don't beat yourself up." Her father must have read her thoughts in her face. "If you hadn't taken that job at CI, how would you have supported yourself and your sister all those years? I figured the Caulfields could watch out for you better than I could, from in here—or from out there, still a drunk." He gave a harsh laugh. "The one good thing that came from prison was sobriety. And that brought me closer to my daughters, in a way." He glanced around. "I'm glad to have helped a lot of the men in here gain that new perspective, too." He'd served as a mentor in the Alcoholics Anonymous meetings and set up a library. He'd even helped a few prisoners learn to read.

"You're a good man, Daddy."

"Maybe. I just wish I could take back that one night. That one mistake changed all our paths."

"We can't change the past." They could only take control of the present and hope for the future.

MAX SOUGHT OUT EINSTEIN IN THE OFFICE AT THE FRONT CORNER of the SSAM house. Outside, the spring day promised to be a gorgeous one, but his friend noticed none of that. Max crossed the room and opened the blinds, releasing the midday light into the room.

"Hey!" Einstein looked up from his computer screen and blinked several times. "I like it dark."

"It's like a cave in here." Max plopped into an armchair opposite the desk. "How goes it?"

Einstein tapped away at the keyboard. "I'm revisiting commonalities between Sam's murder and the others, especially the new one. Hoping I can get a hit on who the Boss might be, or what city he calls home. Each murder was in a different city, which has made it difficult to pin him down." With Tony in a holding place while he received treatment for a raging infection and the police focusing on the exotic dancer murders, SSAM's attention was primarily on finding the Boss and solving the murder of the young woman named Tiffany Allsup.

"If anyone can solve this mystery, you can."

"Thanks for the vote of confidence, but this case is a twisted mess. And how about you and your woman of mystery?"

"Catherine? She's no mystery." Not anymore, anyway. She'd told him about her father's past.

Einstein arched a brow. "Whatever you say."

"What? Do you know something I don't?" The hairs on his arms stood at attention.

"No. It's nothing."

"Then why bring it up?"

"Because that's just it. I *don't* know anything about her other than she's a good girl, good at her job, a good friend...so much goodness it can't be real, you know? Nobody can be that good at being good." Einstein rocked back in his chair and gave Max his full attention. "Look, man, I like her. A lot. But you're my best friend." They'd been through hell together. They were practically brothers and Max understood it was that bond that had Einstein voicing his doubts now. "You care about her, which means I had to peek into her background."

Anger on Catherine's behalf warred with curiosity. The latter won when he realized maybe Einstein had found a clue as to why Catherine wouldn't even consider returning to SSAM, and wouldn't confide in him about her reasons. It had to be more than having a convict for a father. "And?"

"She changed her name."

Max grunted. "We already knew that. And, hell, I changed mine too. So do a lot of people."

"Yeah, people who want to distance themselves from their pasts. I used her sister's last name—Montgomery—and found a Catherine from this area who might be our Catherine."

"So? They're sisters, of course they shared the same last name at some point."

"But that's just it. When Damian did a background check before hiring Catherine *Montague*, all the usual records were in place for that name and everything looked legit. However, there's no background to be found on Catherine *Montgomery*. Not even high school records or college transcripts. Her sister, though, graduated from a local high school before going to college in town, then attending medical school in Chicago."

"Well, there you go. Whatever her legal name is, wanting to be near her sister is what brought Catherine to Chicago, and to SSAM." He felt better knowing there was an explanation behind what had seemed too coincidental.

"I searched for a Catherine who graduated from the same high school as Rachel a couple years before and found her picture in the high school yearbook."

Max shrugged. "So? Did she torch her high school or something?"

"No."

"Then why the red flags?"

"Just a gut instinct. Feel free to tell me to shut up any time."

But the cat—or *Cat*—was out of the bag now. "None of that sounds bad. Besides, Damian would have vetted her before he hired her, right?"

"Right. She had impeccable references—"

"See. Nothing to worry about."

"—from companies here in Texas." Max's scalp prickled. There was more coming. "One of those companies is a subsidiary of Caulfield Industries, and she never received a paycheck from them."

"Which means?"

Einstein shrugged. "You tell me."

His heart sank to his stomach, and then rose up to his throat with alarming speed. Catherine had received an endorsement from his father when she'd gone to work for SSAM? She'd *known* Hayworth Caulfield before coming to Chicago? She'd been pulling one over on him this whole time.

"What was her last name before she changed it?" he asked, not sure he wanted to know any more but unable to stop this freight train.

"Bailey."

"Bailey." The name was merely an exhalation of air across his lips, but sounded like a shout inside his head.

"Ring a bell?"

"That's the same last name as the guy who killed my brother."

"That's what I was afraid of."

CATHERINE WENT DIRECTLY FROM THE PRISON TO THE RANCH. Hayworth's days of manipulating her family were over. She was going to quit and walk away...and tell Max the whole sordid story.

She found Hayworth in the horse barn, brushing a beautiful chestnut. His head was bent to the horse's head, and he murmured words she was certain were soothing and sweet—and probably entirely false.

He straightened, wiped sweat from his brow, and then froze as he spied her in the doorway. "You need something?"

"Yes, as a matter of fact, I do." She stepped forward. The tangy scents of hay, manure and horseflesh tickled her nose.

Hayworth snorted. "What else is new?"

Her chin shot up a notch at the insult. "Everybody needs something. Finding out what that something is and exploiting it is your...*talent*. And then you use those needs, those desires, to get what you need. You wouldn't be the local icon you are if nobody needed your money and power, would you?"

He went back to brushing his horse, and she thought he might be dismissing her. Then he spoke. "What is it that you need this time?"

"The truth."

He glanced at her sideways. "About?"

"My father. Your son. That night."

He snorted. "So Bailey talked, did he?" He straightened and came over to her. "What will it take for you to keep this a secret? I'll rush that governor's pardon for your father. Is that enough?"

Her stomach clenched. Everything seemed so much clearer. The man before her was scared of losing everything, while she had nothing left to lose—not even Max, since he'd be gone when he learned the truth of what she'd done. "This is about Max."

"Has he told you if he's staying yet?"

Her chest pinched at the need that flashed across Hayworth's face. It made him look older, and weaker. He would have hated that she saw it, had he been aware. "He hasn't said, though you shouldn't get your hopes up."

Hayworth turned his back. "My instructions were clear. You had years to convince him while you were in Chicago. You failed."

"Max is his own man."

"He's *my* son." His words were so quiet, she almost thought she'd misheard the misery in his voice. He patted the horse on the nose. "There's still time. I'll ask again, what do you need?"

She doubted there was enough time in a hundred lifetimes to convince Max his place was on this ranch or his future in Texas politics, or for Hayworth to convince her she'd done the right thing by lying to Max all these years. But she had to salvage what she could. "I need that pardon for my father. And I need you to make sure the SSAM team continues getting the cooperation of the local authorities."

"*SSAM*. Damn that place, always pulling him away—"

"I *chose* to stay away." Max's voice reverberated through the barn, shaking Catherine to her very core and sending her heart plummeting through her stomach. It seemed to land with a thud at her feet.

She spun to face him. His disgusted gaze flicked over her, dismissing her immediately as he stalked toward his father. She'd had so many chances to tell the truth and now it was coming out in the worst way possible, looking as if she were using his family to get what she wanted, going behind his back, lying, breaking their trust. How much had he heard?

Scanning the granite hardness of his face, her gaze landed on the one part of him that showed any emotion, the twitching muscle along his clenched jaw, and she knew the answer.

All of it.

. . .

"SON." MAX'S FATHER SAID THIS AS IF IT WERE A SOOTHING WORD. He used a tone he might use to gentle an upset horse.

Max kept his fists at his sides, afraid he might take a swing at his dad, or at the wall. Definitely not at Catherine, though he was mad enough to walk away and never look back. She wanted to leave Chicago? Fine. Let her go. His chest swelled with words he couldn't put a voice to—and pain, so much pain.

"Max, we can explain," Catherine said.

"*We?*"

She winced and he hardened his heart against any sympathy. She was well aware of how he felt about his father, and she'd joined forces with him. How? Why? *When?*

"Explain, then," he said.

"He only wanted to make sure you were okay. When you returned from Afghanistan, wounded, but didn't come home to recuperate..."

Max held up a hand to stop her, then put it down and closed his fingers again as he realized they were shaking with the effort to control his emotions. "Afghanistan? I think this goes back farther than that." Catherine swayed, but he resisted the urge to reach out and steady her. He wouldn't be taken advantage of any longer.

His father put down the brush in slow motion, as if he were afraid he'd startle an animal. Max damn well felt like an animal at the moment, and he was more likely to charge than run away. His dad came forward to stand at Catherine's side.

Max gave a harsh laugh. "A united front. How sweet. Maybe we should get Mom in on this."

"Catherine was only doing what I hired her to do," his father said.

"How much did you have to pay, Dad? Did she come cheap?"

Catherine pressed her lips together and shook her head once in denial.

Max arched a brow. "Good. At least you hit him where it hurts. I wouldn't have thought you the type, though."

"He hired me to..." She stopped and seemed to search for the words she wanted. But there were no words that would make this right.

Bile rose in his throat and he choked it down. "No, don't tell me. He hired you to take a job away from your family, leaving everything you loved, to follow me around like a puppy dog in a strange city. And you accepted because the price was right." He refused to be affected by the moisture filling her eyes. "You'd think I'd have learned the first time. Mom paying off Trish..." How could he have developed such deep feelings for any woman? He'd thought he'd learned his lesson. Yet, he'd let himself be manipulated again. "This is my fault. I should have known better, although you were a great actress. I wouldn't have believed you capable of this. Fabulous performance. *Brava.*"

"It wasn't a performance. I mean, it was, at first. *Shit.*" Even the sound of good-girl Catherine cursing didn't lighten his mood. She stepped forward and held a hand out to him. "Please, can we just go somewhere and talk?"

He took a step backward before she could touch him. She was his kryptonite, and he wouldn't be crippled any longer. "Just tell me, what does this have to do with Mike?"

She pressed a hand to her stomach. "What?"

"I found out your real name. The one before you changed it —*twice.* Your last name was Bailey. That's the guy who killed my brother."

"No, it wasn't like that. My father was involved, but he didn't kill Mike—"

Max turned away. He was done here. Done with the lies. "Don't try to contact me again. Either of you."

Ignoring Catherine's pleas for him to hear her out, he kept walking until he got to the truck. Talk was cheap. He'd always done better when he took action, when he moved—moved out of the country, moved to a new job, moved on.

It was time to wrap things up with Tony and head home to

Chicago, where his parents and Catherine couldn't touch him anymore.

CHAPTER 23

Damian found Max and Einstein in the office of the SSAM house, surrounded by papers and photos.

"Can I talk to Max alone for a moment?" Damian asked.

Einstein stood and stretched. "I was going to make a run for lunch anyway. Want anything?"

"No, thanks," Max said. He wouldn't meet anyone's gaze, but a current of anger simmered in the air around him.

Catherine had called Damian a short while ago, explained what had gone down this morning at the ranch and asked if someone could check on Max. She'd also said she'd stop by with her resignation soon. Damian wasn't about to let that happen. In fact, he'd told her he wouldn't accept it at this time, that she had a couple weeks left on her personal leave and she was to use the time to reconsider her options.

Damian and Einstein exchanged worried glances as Einstein headed to the door.

"Burying yourself in paperwork?" Damian asked Max. He relocated a stack of folders so he could sit down.

"I find it calming."

It didn't appear that way, but Damian didn't comment on that. "I hear you're bunking here."

"I'd like to, if that's okay. I'll take the couch. I'm sure we'll be back in Chicago within a few days, once Lorena gets what you need out of Tony." Tony was due to be transferred from the prison infirmary to a regular cell tomorrow and they'd be able to question him further.

"You're that angry with your parents that you'd leave early?"

Max gave up all pretense of studying the files and shoved his hands through his hair. "Is it so hard to understand why I'm angry? I don't think I'm being unreasonable."

"No, I understand. And I'm sure you're especially upset because it was Catherine who betrayed you this time."

Max huffed out a humorless laugh. "She called you? The woman's got moxie, that's for sure. Did she tell you the whole story or spin it so she looks good?"

"She told me the truth because she cares about us." He'd heard the fear in her voice. She was afraid to lose Max, and to lose SSAM, though she hadn't admitted it.

"You're not angry? Hell, she pulled this secretive shit on you, too."

"I knew there were some holes in her past, but she earned her place as my assistant, earned my trust in the little things she did everyday that showed her talents and her heart. I'd hire her back in an instant."

"*Hire her back?* Did she quit?" The flash of emotion in Max's eyes was telling.

"Not officially. Not yet, anyway. But she mentioned a resignation."

Max let out a harsh laugh. "She did her job for my dad and now she's moving on. The well is dry."

"I don't think that's it."

"No? Then what is it?"

"I think she's ashamed of what she's done." Catherine wasn't the devious type. She wasn't glorying in her success. In fact, he doubted her bank accounts would show any large deposits. The more he'd thought about it, and her family's circumstances, the more he understood what she'd done. But he didn't have as large an emotional stake in this as Max did. "I trust her," he added. And that was all that mattered.

"How can you?" Max was genuinely perplexed. What's more, he seemed to want to understand how someone could come to trust another person in the first place, and that gave Damian hope. The man wanted a relationship.

"I'd bet most people have some big, bad mistake haunting them. It's how a person behaves after, how he or she moves on—or doesn't move on—that is his or her true measure. Trust is in the little things, in our daily actions and how we treat people."

Max remained quiet as he absorbed this. Frustration and pain were written on his features.

"Why don't you give her a chance to explain?" Damian suggested. "That's all she's asking for."

"I don't see how that could help. She's leaving, anyway."

"Only because she thinks we're not big enough men to under-stand and forgive her."

"She doesn't trust *us*."

"Can you blame her? Has there ever been anyone in her life she could totally count on?"

Max looked up as understanding dawned. "Other people in her life let her down. They left her to fend for herself."

Damian clapped him on his good shoulder. "Lorena would be proud. You're thinking like a profiler would. Catherine's mother died. Her father fell apart, and then went to prison, leaving her to pick up the pieces. It sounds like she set her own dreams aside to take a job with your father so she could raise her sister."

"Christ. You make her sound like a saint."

Damian chuckled. "There was a time we would easily have

nominated her for sainthood—several times over the years, in fact. I don't think, in her heart, she wants to hurt us, and I think you recognize that. You've been hurt enough in the past to be cautious. You don't trust easily."

"True."

"Give her another chance." Damian took a gamble, but Max needed to understand what he stood to lose. "Don't let the woman you love walk away."

Max went completely still, and then blew out a breath. "I do. I love her." He shoved a hand through his hair. "Shit, what a mess."

MAX TOOK A LONG RUN AROUND THE NEIGHBORHOOD TO THINK, showered and then drove back to the ranch.

His chest clenched as he noticed Catherine's Jeep was gone. Had she packed up and moved on already? Had she had so little faith he'd come around? *Believe in me just a little longer, baby.*

In the guesthouse bedroom, he found her clothing and suitcase and breathed a sigh of relief. His reaction reaffirmed what he'd decided during his run.

He sought out his dad in the main house, listening to a Johnny Cash record on the old turntable in his office. He had a drink in his hand and was standing by the window, gazing out at the ranch. Catching Max's reflection, he turned in surprise. "Son."

"You like to call me that." Max moved a little further into the office.

"I hope I still have the right." The uncertainty and fear in Hayworth Caulfield's voice would have stunned any one of his employees or business colleagues. It certainly shocked the hell out of Max.

"That depends."

"On?"

"You being honest with me now. I need the whole story. No

more family secrets. Tell me everything that happened years ago, and how Catherine is involved."

"Your mother should be here for this."

Max arched a brow. "Safety in numbers? I'd rather hear it from you."

His father released a heavy sigh and slumped into his chair. "I suppose it's time." He gestured to the couch and Max took a seat. "Your mother and I may seem like we love business and politics more than you, but that's not the case. Otherwise, I never would have hired Catherine to keep tabs on you. She was supposed to lure you back here, you know."

During his run, Max had catalogued his memories of Catherine over the past five years. He couldn't recall one instance where she'd tried to steer him in a particular direction, or one time when she'd suggested a course of action that wasn't in his best interests. She'd been a sounding board at times, and had offered helpful suggestions, but all decisions had been his own. And she'd been that for the entire SSAM team, not just for him.

"She didn't want to accept the assignment at first," his father continued, "but I knew she'd be the type to win her way into your world. And she was a damn good assistant."

"She was your assistant?"

"For several years, while you served tour after tour in that godforsaken place." He huffed out a short laugh. "I hired her for selfish reasons—to watch her and make sure her father would keep his end of the bargain."

"Bargain?"

Hayworth took a large swallow of his drink and met Max's gaze evenly. "Doug Bailey, Catherine's father, didn't kill Mike."

Max's abdomen tightened as if he'd been gut-punched. Everything he thought he knew about that horrible time was a lie. "Who did?"

"I suppose, if what you say is true, *I* did. I killed your brother."

"What?"

"I pushed Mike hard, but I meant to prepare him for the world. Once he was away in college, though, he got into alcohol and drugs. When he came home on breaks, the habits continued, and our arguments got worse. The night of the accident, Mike was driving and Doug Bailey was in the car. Don't get me wrong. They were both to blame. Neither should have been behind the wheel."

Max filled in the rest of the blanks. "You took advantage of Cat's dad, and made a deal."

His father nodded. "I was an elected official at the time. I couldn't afford the bad press. Bailey took the fall, and our name— your inheritance—remained untarnished. In exchange, I agreed to watch out for his daughters."

"And instead, you took advantage of Cat's youth and innocence and used her guilt to manipulate her." She'd been just as much a pawn in this as Max had. "She didn't know the truth about that night, about Mike's part in it?"

"She must have spoken to her father earlier today, because she knows everything now."

Her world had been blown apart just as much as Max's had. She'd been confronting his father when Max had seen them together earlier. And then, he'd turned his back on her, not giving her the chance to explain.

"She was at SSAM only to bring me home?" he asked. For the life of him, he couldn't remember one thing she'd said that had been an effort to drag him back here. Instead, she'd become his friend. Had that all been a ruse?

His father frowned. "That was the plan. Unfortunately, she doesn't have the heart for that kind of deception. She reported to us monthly, usually just a few lines about how you were doing. It frustrated me and your mother to no end, not having more details, but that's all Catherine would give. She was our only link to you, so we were at her mercy." He chuckled. "Son, I think she was protecting you. She must have thought we didn't have access to newspapers and the internet. It's not like you didn't end up with some actress or model in the society section now and then."

Max grinned. Catherine had insulated him from his parents' interference in many ways. But there were certain things he couldn't forgive.

His father spoke up again before Max could ask. "I understand your concerns, Son, but Catherine wasn't in it for the money."

"You expect me to believe you didn't pay her?"

"She only wanted her salary to live on, which she earned by working hard at Caulfield Industries, and tuition for Rachel."

"How did you fool Damian?"

"I have just as many connections as he does. I had some friends write letters of recommendation and serve as references when I insisted Catherine apply to SSAM. Helped her change her last name."

"She must have leapt at the chance to leave Texas." And get out from under his father's thumb.

"Truth is, I think we all talked you up so much she was eager to meet you. I'm sure she thought you were a hero." And Max had stomped all over that image by rejecting her. His father sighed. "As much as I hate to admit it, she has a good heart. I took advantage of that and your mother and I will have to make amends, if you two will let us. Catherine cares about you. Hell, I think she loves you. It takes a strong woman to love a stubborn Caulfield man." He held up a hand when Max opened his mouth. "No, I know you don't have the Caulfield name anymore, and don't want it, but you have our blood. And that's not so bad, if you'd really think about it. Our bloodline is strong, determined and noble. Hell, we had two ancestors who fought at the Alamo."

"So there's military in our blood, too."

"Damn right. And though I never told you, I *am* proud of your service. I just resented that it took you away from us, especially so soon after losing Michael." His father cleared his throat. "But you had to find yourself. We just couldn't go on not knowing how you were doing. So yes, we used Catherine."

So had Max, on occasion, he realized. Assuming he could kiss her on New Year's without consequences. Presuming she'd pretend to be his fiancée while he stayed at the ranch. She'd been there for him in so many ways.

Little daily acts.

CATHERINE TRIED TO IGNORE THE CONSTANT ACHE IN HER CHEST BY keeping busy at Lucky Dick's. At least this horrible day was almost over.

She'd thought about calling Max, but he'd told her—emphatically—not to contact him again. He didn't want to talk to her, wasn't going to hear her out. Like the turning of invisible screws, her chest tightened more with every remembered word and expression.

It's your own damn fault. If she'd taken the time to sit him down and tell him her version of things he'd have...what? Did she truly believe he'd hear her out calmly and she'd be able to at least keep their friendship?

She muttered a curse and Darla looked over from where she was ringing up tickets behind the bar. "You don't look so good."

"Tough day." The worst day of her life, except for when she'd lost her mother, or the day she'd watched her father go to prison.

"Guy problems?" Darla's gaze moved across the darkened room to Johnny, who was sitting at his usual table near the stage, his eyes riveted on a new dancer as if she were his next meal. The police hadn't found anything concrete that showed Johnny had murdered those dancers or hidden away Tony, and they'd let him go. Maybe he hadn't done any of those things. At least he'd left Catherine alone lately, no longer bugging her about Dick's ledgers.

"You deserve better," Catherine said.

Darla shrugged. "The heart wants what it wants." And wasn't that the unfortunate truth?

Johnny looked their way and Darla gave him a little wave, but his gaze was on Catherine. She couldn't read the emotion across the dim room, but she was certain he hadn't appreciated Catherine talking to Detective McCoy about him.

She tried to refocus on the bills Dick had left for her to go through, but her thoughts kept winding back to the look of disappointment and betrayal on Max's face. Worried about him, she'd called Damian and told him the truth over the phone. Perhaps that was the cowardly thing to do, but she hadn't wanted to face any more disillusionment today. Damian had seemed forgiving, and had even encouraged her to consider coming back to SSAM, but she wasn't sure she could forgive herself. She'd mangled this situation badly.

Disgusted with herself, she scooped up her papers and went into the office. Dick wasn't around tonight and she had the place to herself. Suddenly feeling fatigued all the way to her bones, she decided to lie down on the couch and rest.

Catherine came awake with a start when the door was thrown open and Johnny entered. The hard, eager look on his face was one from her nightmares. She scrambled to sit up but he crossed the room in a few quick strides and pinned her horizontally against the cushions. His hips wiggled suggestively against hers.

His harsh laughter echoed in the room. "You've been trying to get my attention for weeks, but turning me over to the police was the wrong way to go about it."

"I didn't—"

He pressed harder against her, keeping her arms pinned at her sides with his body. "Don't lie, bitch. Darla told me you're the one who brought my name up to the police. That got me in a lot of trouble, and not just with the cops."

She opened her mouth to scream but he clamped his hand over it. Panic flowed through her, flooding her mind and limbs with adrenaline and fear, and she struggled to remember her self-defense training. If she could have opened her mouth, she would have bitten Johnny, but his fingers were pressed firmly there. Her nostrils flared, picking up the smell of beer and peanuts as he huffed out a laugh. She couldn't even lift her knee to slam it into his groin.

Signs of his arousal pushed into her pelvis. Her struggles were turning him on. She remembered the mindhunters at SSAM talking about how some serial killers received sexual gratification from their victims' fear, but she wasn't sure she could force herself to go utterly still and calm.

"You're a feisty one." His humid words blew across her cheek. "What a nice surprise."

"GET OFF OF HER!" THE ROAR CAME OUT OF MAX THE MOMENT HE stepped through into the office and saw Johnny's body covering Catherine's. The police had let him go, but Max wouldn't make the same mistake.

He didn't wait for the sleazebag to comply. Taking two fistfuls of Johnny's shirt, he lifted him off Catherine and threw him to the ground. Darla dropped a tray as she skidded to a stop in the doorway. Her hand flew to her mouth.

"Call the police," Max told her.

"Like hell," Johnny said. "Don't listen to them, Darla. The bitch wanted me. Ask her. She'll probably lie, though. Those goody-goody types always do."

Always do? How many women had this monster gone after? Bea? Angelique? Kim? Was he like Tony, a serial rapist and killer?

Max took a threatening step toward Johnny, but Catherine's hand on his arm stopped him. She'd reached a sitting position, but her eyes were wide with shock. A pink-and-white pattern across her lips and cheeks marked where Johnny had held his hand over them. Another wave of anger washed over Max. He crouched in front of her, which was when Johnny bolted, pushing Darla aside so he could get by.

"Stay with her," Max ordered Darla, pointing to Catherine. "And call the cops."

"But—" Darla's objection was cut off as Max darted by her. Several yards ahead of him, Johnny dodged through the crowd toward the front door, where the bouncer watched with bewilderment as Johnny, and then Max, sped past.

In the twilight, the parking lot was already dark and a light rain had misted the cars. As Max jogged by each vehicle, he peered inside, but he didn't see Johnny. At the street, he stopped to glance both ways. Nothing but normal street traffic.

Behind him, an engine roared to life. Max spun. A truck came barreling toward him. He jumped out of the way just before it clipped him, but his rapid movement caused him to tumble to the pavement. He rolled and pulled his gun from his ankle holster, but the truck was already speeding away.

Max cursed and took out his phone to call Einstein, filling him in as he made his way back to the office. Darla hadn't stayed with Catherine. In fact, she was nowhere in sight. But Catherine wasn't the pale, faint woman he'd seen a few minutes ago. She was a woman on a mission, railing at someone on the office phone, probably a police officer, as she ordered him to find Johnny Walker now, before Johnny hurt someone else.

And for Johnny's sake, they'd better find him before Max did.

Catherine hung up, feeling a bit stronger for having taken some action. But seeing Max standing in the middle of the office gave her a sinking feeling. "He got away?"

"Yeah." Max's hand ran through his hair, and that's when she saw the blood.

She gasped. "You were hurt."

He seemed surprised when his hand came away bloody. He

gingerly pressed his fingertips to an abrasion on his forehead. "He tried to run me down. I had to make a choice—the truck hitting me or me hitting the pavement."

"Sit down. How's your shoulder?"

"It'll be a little sore, but it's okay."

"Stay put." She went out to the bar, cupped a clean bar towel in one hand, shoveled ice into it, and then bundled it up. She went back into the office and sat next to Max on the couch. She wanted to hold the cold towel to his head for him, but she wasn't sure how he was feeling about her just now. In fact, she was pretty sure he hated her. "I'm glad you came when you did, but why are you here? Is it about one of the investigations?"

"I'm giving you that chance to explain. That is, if you still want to." He held the ice to his head with one hand, and reached for her with the other.

She interlaced her fingers with his, trying to rein in the hope that soared through her. He was giving her a shot at redemption? "You don't seem angry. Shouldn't you still be angry?"

He laughed and then winced. "Giving me more orders?"

"Not a chance. I'm not interfering anymore."

His gaze softened and she dared to let one small ray of hope warm her soul. "You never did. Not really. I had a long talk with Damian. And then I talked to my dad."

"You did?" If he could sit down for a talk with his father, maybe he really was willing to listen to her.

"I did, like a big boy."

She grimaced. "It's not that you aren't a grownup."

"No, it's just that I don't always act like one."

"With your parents, there are so many other things going on. A lot of past pain gets into the mix."

He narrowed his eyes at her. "I don't get you. You really don't think about yourself, do you?"

"What do you mean? I took money to spy on you. For *years*."

"And you didn't use a bit of it for yourself."

"No, but—"

He leaned forward suddenly and cut her off, using his lips to prevent her objection. Just when she was breathless, her mind filling with physical ways she wanted to make things up to him, he broke the kiss.

He grinned. "That's how I like you. Panting and slightly bewildered."

"Well, that's how you've got me now. And I definitely don't understand." Was he saying everything was okay? That he forgave her? Or that he only wanted a sexual relationship?

A uniformed police officer arrived before she could figure it out. Rain droplets gleamed on his coat like glitter. "Are you Miss Montague?" Catherine nodded. "I understand there was an assault?" The man's eyes shifted to Max and narrowed with suspicion.

"Not by this man," she said.

Max stood and removed the ice pack. "A man named Johnny Walker had her pinned down on the couch when I walked in. Ask Detective McCoy for more details on the ongoing investigation in which Johnny is a prime suspect."

The officer removed a notepad and pen from his pocket, and then gestured to Max's forehead. "He do that to you?"

"He tried to run me down with a truck."

The officer's radio squawked to life on his shoulder, and he moved to turn the volume down as a report came through.

Catherine lurched forward. "Wait, was that something about a riot at a prison?"

The officer turned up the radio so they could hear the operator. "Officers down. Fatalities reported, number uncertain. All available units..."

Max shot Catherine a look, but she was already moving toward the door. "I have to go. My father's in that prison." Her eyes widened. "And Tony's there, too. Is the Circle responsible?"

"Stay here," Max said. "They won't let you near there, anyway.

Give your report to the officer and then call your sister to come get you. Stay with her until I can get back, okay?"

"But, my dad…"

"I promise I'll find out everything I can and report to you ASAP."

Catherine nodded. Max was her best shot at helping her dad.

"You'll have patrol cars out there looking for Johnny?" Max asked the officer. "I only got a partial plate." He gave the officer the first three letters on the Texas plate.

The officer nodded. "I'll put out an APB once I get a description from Miss Montague. I'll make sure she gets to her sister's safely, too."

"Thanks." Max framed Catherine's face with his palms. "You'll be okay?"

"I will," she assured him. "Please just make sure my dad's okay. And you stay safe, too."

He gave her a hard kiss that left her body burning for more. She was still reeling when he disappeared out the door.

An hour later, safely ensconced in Rachel's tiny bungalow, Catherine and her sister settled on the couch with two pints of ice cream and dug in. There was no word yet from Max about their father, and they were doing their best to distract themselves.

Rachel leaned back and sighed. "I've missed this."

"Which one? Ben or Jerry?"

Rachel rolled her eyes. "You. Having a sister within driving distance to lean on." She popped another spoonful of ice cream into her mouth. "So, are you okay?"

"I don't know yet." She didn't know a lot of things, and wouldn't until she and Max could sit down and talk.

"Your personal leave ends soon, doesn't it? Are you leaving town?"

Catherine set the carton on the table and sighed. "I have a

couple weeks left to decide."

"You love being at SSAM. I always knew that. So why not go back?"

Max and Damian knew everything now. There was nothing keeping her from sharing it with her sister, except she wasn't sure how Rachel would take the news that Catherine had done some underhanded things to support her. "I wasn't sure I'd be welcome at SSAM after they knew the truth."

"What truth are you talking about?"

"The ugly one."

Rachel took one look at Catherine's face and raised her brows. "Maybe I should get out a bottle of wine instead?"

"No. This is long overdue already. I've wanted to talk to you about it so many times." She'd felt so alone keeping it to herself, but she couldn't share the burden, couldn't risk her sister walking away from a medical career because she didn't like that Catherine had done some underhanded things to secure Rachel's education.

"What is it? You can tell me anything." Rachel set the ice cream aside and took Catherine's hand in her own, the tender gesture bringing tears to Catherine's eyes. "You're scaring me. Am I adopted?" she teased.

Catherine released a strangled laugh. "I love you."

"I love you, too. And nothing you could tell me would make me feel any differently."

"I paid for your schooling by working undercover for the Caulfields, reporting on Max's activities."

Rachel blinked twice. "Like a superspy."

"Like a babysitter," Catherine bit out, still angry with herself. "And he deserved better than that."

"He couldn't get anyone better than you." Rachel's proclamation was fierce.

"I deceived him. He didn't know why I was there, why I was befriending him or spending time with him." Catherine couldn't let her sister forgive her so easily.

"Would you have spent less time with him, or done anything differently had you not been paid to do so?"

"No."

"I thought so."

"You're not mad?"

"Because my sister loves me enough to put her life on hold and find a way to help me pursue my dream? Hell, no. I'm confident enough to know I earned my own way into medical school—and I'm *confident* because you pulled me through a tough time in both our lives and gave me a firm foundation. It couldn't have been easy for you to take me in, to love me like a sister *and* a mother would, but you did it. Our family's story could so easily have ended another, more tragic way. Because of you, we're still going strong."

Catherine blinked back tears. "I didn't think about it like that."

"Yeah, you wouldn't. Because you're too busy trying to be Miss Perfect, thinking you have to be responsible for everyone. I always thought you took that job years ago at CI because you felt guilty for what Dad did to the Caulfields' son. And the other night, when I realized who Max really was...well, I kind of figured something was going on."

"Speaking of which...I have some other news. I saw Dad earlier. He told me today that he wasn't responsible for Mike's death. Mike was."

Rachel paled. "*What?*"

"One of the reasons I took a job with the Caulfields was because they promised to stop the media from slamming our family. They offered to protect us and I thought it was generous of them." She pressed her lips together to stifle the surge of anger. "Instead, they were using Dad to keep the dirt away from their family name."

Rachel cocked her head. "How did southern-and-sultry take the news?"

"Not well, at first, but he's adjusting. We haven't had a chance to talk about it." But the kiss had spoken volumes. Could he really have forgiven her?

"And if things work out with him? Will you be going back to Chicago?"

"I haven't thought that far ahead."

"Sure you have. You've probably dreamed of the best possible scenario, even if you're always prepared for the worst. I know you, sis."

She'd pictured herself with Max in Chicago only on those rare occasions when she'd allowed herself to dream. She'd work at SSAM, supporting her coworker-family and encouraging Max to follow his heart's desire.

But then there was her other family, bound by blood.

"I'm torn," she admitted.

"Because of me and Dad. We'll be fine. I'm all grown up now. I even know how to put bandages on my own boo-boos." Rachel grinned. "And I know how to get to Chicago."

"I don't know." Catherine bit her lip.

"Now you're insulting me. Don't you think I can survive without you? Sure, I'll miss you like hell, but you've helped make me the strong woman I am today. Trust that."

"But I'd miss you, too."

Rachel squeezed Catherine's hands. "You don't know how to pursue your own dreams, do you? You've put them aside for so long. This time is for you, Cat. Embrace it. Even if there's no Max in your future, go where you want to be. Do what you want to do. You gave me my turn, now it's yours."

Tears filled her eyes and Catherine pulled her fingers from Rachel's to wrap her in a tight hug. "Thank you." It was like a baptism. A new start.

"Just be happy." Rachel pulled away to wag a finger in her face. "And if Max hurts you, I'll break his legs." She sighed. "And then I'll probably fix them up for him. You know, since I took that oath and all."

CHAPTER 24

Johnny sank back into the shadows behind Lucky Dick's. If Darla was a creature of habit, she'd be taking a smoke break any minute now. It had been two hours since he'd barreled out of the parking lot in the truck she'd let him borrow after picking him up at the police station. Too bad he hadn't taken half of Max with him. The guy was probably getting a sweet reward from Kitty Cat as Johnny waited in the cold drizzle wondering what the fuck he was going to do next. And to think he'd warmed Catherine up for the asshole. Life wasn't fair.

But Darla wasn't a bad consolation prize. And he owed her for more than the truck. Yesterday, while Max had been figuratively twisting Johnny's arm until he'd been forced to cooperate, Darla had thrown some names of other potential suspects at the police and taken the heat off of Johnny. In addition, she had an apartment where he could crash. She'd given him green-light signals for months, so it wasn't like anybody was going to get hurt if he asked for a favor.

Unless you kill her, too.

He pressed his hands hard against his ears. The voices of doubt were getting louder lately. Was he going crazy? He certainly didn't remember murdering three women and disposing of their bodies, but all signs pointed to him. And he couldn't forget waking up with the bloody sleeves.

The back door swung open and he pressed closer against the wall. *Darla. Finally.* He stepped forward as she was putting a cigarette to her lips.

"Jesus!" The cigarette fell into a puddle as she jumped back in fright. She pressed a hand to her chest. "You scared me."

"Sorry about that."

She looked left and right. Was she nervous or simply checking that nobody was after him? "Were you waiting for me?" Hallelujah. That was definitely a hopeful tone in her voice.

"Yeah. I figured you'd be out here soon."

"You know my habits." Her expression went soft. The girl was desperate to be noticed, to be needed. Those were all the weapons he needed.

"I wanted to see you."

"You took a chance, just to see me?" She was totally eating this shit up.

"Uh-huh." And to score a place to crash for the evening, and maybe something to eat and drink. The cops would be all over his place. The fuckers still had his van, so that wasn't an option. Darla was his last option. He'd make her see that she had no choice but to help him.

He stepped closer, taking the pack of cigarettes from her apron pocket and shaking out one for each of them. Mesmerized, she watched his hands as he put one to her lips, and then one to his. He reached back into her pocket, his thumb grazing her abdomen as he found the lighter and withdrew it.

"The police were here after you took off." She blew a puff of smoke out of the side of her mouth.

His insides clenched, but he was careful not to let his nerves show on his face. "*Were?*"

"The officer left about an hour ago with Catherine. She told him you attacked her in her office. We're supposed to call him if you come back."

"*She* came on to *me*. She's been teasing me for weeks. I was just trying to teach her a lesson. I wouldn't have gone any further with her."

She gave a hesitant smile. "It looked like the cop was eating her story up."

Johnny cocked his head to the side and looped a finger into the dip in her blouse that exposed a generous amount of her cleavage. Using his finger like a hook, he tugged her closer. "Who do you believe?"

Her breath came out in a whoosh against his lips. "You. I've always believed in you."

And she had. She'd even called the cops on his behalf when they'd been questioning him. She'd led them in a different direction when he'd been their primary suspect. "I'm finally seeing that."

"I'm glad." Her smile bloomed. "Because I've always thought we were meant to be together."

"You got that right, darlin'." They'd be together. At least for a few nights, until the heat died down or the Circle found him other accommodations. Maybe he'd get a transfer to a new town with a new start.

She took another drag and blew it out. "You know, I'm the most senior employee here at the moment. No cops inside now. Come in and have a drink."

He dipped his lips to her ear. "How about we do that at your place?"

She shuddered and leaned against him, but tipped her head back to look into his face. "I can't leave yet. My shift doesn't end for another couple of hours. But you can wait in Dick's office. I'll give you a heads-up if the cops or Catherine show up again."

Free alcohol and a warm place to wait right under the stupid cops' noses? Sweet irony. "Sounds good to me, babe. And then?"

"My place." She pressed her lips to his. Her kiss was hot, going from zero to sixty in two seconds flat. Her hand slipped down between them to cup his hard-on. He caught her hand with his, holding it against him for a long moment.

She pulled away and licked her lips. "I can't wait."

Inside, Darla ushered him into the office before the bouncer could see him. He had a great view of the place through the two-way mirror.

Darla left, but returned quickly and set a beer down. "I got your usual."

"I'm limiting it to one, though." He couldn't afford any more blackouts. "I want to be able to enjoy our time together later."

"I get off in an hour."

"Yeah, you will." He palmed Darla's ass and she grinned before sashaying back to work. Life was good. He'd figure out a solution to his problem. Maybe even with Darla's help. Perhaps she could sit up with him all night and see if he blacked out. He'd conquer his weakness. Overcome it. The blackouts weren't going to rule, or ruin, his life.

A POLICE CAMP HAD BEEN HASTILY ERECTED ON THE PRISON grounds. Above, smoke mingled with the black rainclouds and tried to block out the moon. At least the authorities were keeping SSAM in the loop—not that Max could do much to help. The prisoners had taken control and set several fires, if the smoke billowing out of broken windows was any indication. Judging by the shouts and chants coming from beyond prison walls, their blood was running hot.

Max wondered how Tony was faring. Not well, he'd guess, if the Circle had anything to do with this, but the convict could take care of himself. Max's concern was mainly for Catherine's dad and the guards who'd been overtaken inside. Yes, Doug Bailey had been with Mike that fateful night, but apparently he hadn't killed Max's brother. In fact, it sounded as if the man had been trying to help. And, from the warden's comments, Bailey had been a model prisoner for the past twelve years. When this was over, Max would make sure his father set the record straight and Bailey was pardoned.

"We've made contact," someone shouted from the other side of the tent. The tarp that formed the cornerstone of their makeshift camp gave shelter from the cold drizzle that made the building in the distance, lit by bright, portable lights, seem to glow.

Max shifted closer as the police chief took the phone. That was when Max spied Damian, Lorena and Einstein hustling toward him from the parking area. He waved them over.

"What's the status?" Damian's gaze went to the chief.

"They just established contact with someone inside," Max said.

"Where's Catherine?"

"I asked her to stay with her sister. Their dad's in this prison, you know."

"Hopefully he's keeping his head down," Lorena said.

The police chief ended his call and called for silence. They turned toward him with the group of waiting officers. "That was the appointed spokesperson for the prisoners. He claims there are three casualties and several injuries. He says one rogue prisoner, who has now been locked away, instigated the riot. The rest of them want leniency in exchange for letting us in."

"That's it?" The words were out of Max's mouth before he could stop them, but this was entirely too easy.

The chief's gaze narrowed on him. "Maybe you missed the number of dead people, but I think that's enough for tonight."

"Are we sure this isn't a trap?"

"He reported the instigator's target is dead."

"Target?" Max's gaze found Damian's. "Tony Moreno?" He was supposed to be released from the infirmary into a regular cell by tomorrow, and SSAM had made plans to talk to him. Had someone silenced him before he could reveal what he'd meant by saying they weren't looking *high enough* for Sam's killer?

The SSAM team brought up the rear as officials led them into the prison. Inside, firefighters hurried forward to extinguish the flames, and the prison guards who were uninjured herded the prisoners to their cells.

They found Tony Moreno's body in a bathroom, laid out on the floor of the community shower, trussed up like a turkey. But the blood drained from Damian's face as he leaned forward to look at the body. "Now we'll never know what key piece Tony was keeping from us," he murmured. Lorena put a steadying hand on his shoulder.

"There's something in his hand," Einstein said, motioning for a guard to examine further.

Carefully, the guard used a gloved hand to open Tony's fingers. A circular charm rolled out and onto the floor.

"It's a butterfly charm." The guard looked up in question.

"That's a message to me." Damian's face turned to stone. "When Samantha died, most of her jewelry was gone—a necklace and an earring with butterflies on them. One earring was still with her, along with a charm depicting a butterfly. The bastard wants me to know he was one step ahead of us yet again."

Lorena squeezed his shoulder. "Then we'll chase him until we get him."

"Any sign of an inmate named Doug Bailey?" Max asked the guard.

Einstein's brow furrowed. "I overheard someone saying there was a group of prisoners still barricaded in the library. The police are about to bust in."

Max looked to Damian, who seemed lost in his thoughts, then back to Einstein. "I can stay if you need me."

"Go," Einstein said. "Lorena and I will take care of Damian."

Max raced to the wing where the education room was located, just off the library. Several guards and policemen were preparing a battering ram to knock the door down. Others had drawn their guns and were prepared to shoot.

"Wait!" Max shouted. "I think I know someone in there. He can end this peacefully. Give me a chance to talk to him."

"We've tried that. Nobody's answering the phone."

He tamped down on the adrenaline raging through his system. He felt the need to protect Catherine's father—the man was important to her, but he'd also taken the fall for the Caulfields. Max owed Doug Bailey a second chance at life.

"Do you have a bullhorn?" he asked one of the guards.

"I think there's one in the warden's office."

"Go get it." He turned to the others. "I'm going to try to go around the outside. There's a window up high on that wall." He pulled two guards into service with him, leaving another at the library's door with two sheriff's deputies. "Do not fire unless they fire at you," he ordered, hoping they would listen, though he didn't have authority. "Give me five minutes."

Outside, Max had the guards give him a boost up the wall. He pressed his body flat against the wet surface, his head slowly reaching window height. He saw about a dozen inmates within, and a couple of wounded were on the tables. The wounded wore guard uniforms. *Shit.*

Max knocked on the window to get the occupants' attention, and then held his hands up to show he was unarmed. One of the inmates aimed a gun at him, but a tall, thin, silver-haired man pushed it down and said something to the man. They seemed to respect him, to listen to him. *Bailey.* Max recognized him from the news reports all those years ago.

Max gestured to the door and yelled through the closed window. "It's safe. Let us in."

Bailey nodded and moved toward the door. There was some arguing from the other inmates, but Max couldn't hear the discussion.

Hurrying back inside, Max maneuvered himself to the frontlines. If the police or the prisoners were going to open fire, he'd take the hit. After all, he'd talked everyone into trying this more peaceable method. From behind the door came the sound of heavy furniture scraping across the floor.

Bailey's worry-lined face appeared in the doorway. "Is the riot over?"

"All clear," Max said.

Bailey opened the door wider. "You must be Max Caulfield. I'd recognize you anywhere." The guards and police rushed past them and took control of the room's occupants.

"Max Sawyer," he corrected. "And you're Doug Bailey, Catherine's dad."

The man's smile widened. "I am." Bailey moved out of the way of two paramedics pulling a gurney. "Two guards were hurt, so we brought them in here and barred the door. We didn't want any part of the violence."

Max nodded. "I'm sure the authorities will appreciate that when this all gets sorted out. Catherine will be relieved you're alive and well."

Bailey winced as a guard attempted to escort him into the hall.

"You're hurt?" Not waiting for the man's answer, Max crouched and gently tugged up the leg of Bailey's pants. Blood was pooling into his sock from a gash at his ankle. Max looked up at him. "What happened?"

"Got between an inmate out for blood and one of them." He gestured with his head toward the injured guards. "The guard was unconscious, so it wasn't exactly a fair fight."

"You probably saved his life." Bailey would be a hero. And once the facts of Mike's death were sorted out, he would be a free man.

"HE'S REALLY OKAY?" CATHERINE BREATHED A SIGH OF RELIEF AND nodded to Rachel, who was watching while she took Max's call.

"He's back in his cell," Max reported, "but he's in one piece."

But Max had hesitated just a moment too long. "What are you not telling me?"

"He was wounded, but it'll be fine."

"They took care of it?"

"Right away. But Tony Moreno is dead."

"The Circle got to him? Damian must be upset."

"He'll be okay. He's got Lorena helping him. But the good news is your dad's a hero, Cat. He helped save a couple prison guards. They were unconscious and defenseless. He herded the injured and a bunch of fellow prisoners into the library and they barricaded themselves inside. I'm sure his brave actions will look good to the governor."

"Thank you. Thank you for being there, for helping him, for...*everything*." For forgiving me.

"I'm wrapping some things up here, and then I'll come get you—unless it's too late? If you want to stay at your sister's tonight and talk tomorrow, I'd understand."

"I'd like to see you."

"Okay. I'll be by, but it'll be at least an hour."

She realized how much he'd been through today, too. "If *you'll* be too tired—"

"I won't." The determination and other things—heat, promise, desire—in his voice made her shudder with need.

She hung up and faced her sister. "I'll probably go back to the ranch with Max so we can talk."

Rachel grabbed her sister up in a hug. "It's so nice to see you in love."

"In love?" Catherine's heart thudded madly against her chest. It was that evident? Could Max see it, and if so, how would he react? He was afraid of long term attachments. Would her feelings have him running the other way?

Rachel pulled away, laughing. "Of course you're in love. Max was the guy you talked about most in Chicago, even if you did only call him a friend. Love looks good on you."

ACCEPTABLE RISK 291

Catherine's cheeks burned. "What do I do?"

"Be honest. Max deserves all of you, and you deserve to be happy."

A grin split her face. "I *am* happy, or at least I have the feeling I'm going to be." Her phone rang and she groaned. It was Lucky Dick's again. She'd be quitting her job there, too, as soon as she could meet with Dick. She hadn't unearthed any big Circle scam and she was ready to resume her place at SSAM. Maybe this was Dick calling now. "Hello?"

"Catherine? It's Jade."

Catherine recognized the name of one of the new exotic dancers from the club. "Hi, Jade. What's up?" Rachel hummed happily in the kitchen as she returned their ice cream containers to the freezer.

"I was the last set tonight and then I took a call from my boyfriend while I was changing. Guess it took longer than I thought because when I came out front, the place was cleared out. I can leave, but I don't have a key to lock up."

"Darla's not there?" The longtime waitress was the only other person Dick had trusted with a key. "Or Robert?" Usually, the bouncer walked the girls out after lockup.

"Nobody's here, that I can tell. I checked the office and everywhere. I have to get home. My sitter's going to flip if I'm any later."

"Go ahead. I'll be right over." She could be there and back to Rachel's within ten minutes.

Catherine hung up and stared at her phone a moment. Where had Darla gone? Something didn't feel right. The young woman might be socially awkward at times, but she had always been dependable, on time and honest. "Rachel, I've got to go out. Can I borrow your car?" She'd left hers at the club when the officer gave her a ride to Rachel's.

Rachel peeked out from the kitchen. "Sure." Her brow creased. "Want me to come with?"

"No, just something I need to do at the club real quick. I'll have an officer meet me there before I get out of the car." Just in case Johnny had returned to the scene. She was hoping he would be that stupid and then the police could arrest him.

"Lucky Dick's? Why do you have to go back there? It's after two in the morning."

"Dick's out of town, and there's nobody else who can lock up. I'll be fine." She moved forward to hug her sister. "Thanks for the talk tonight. I love you."

Rachel squeezed her back and pulled away. "Love you, too."

Ten minutes later, Catherine sat in her locked car in the parking lot at Lucky Dick's, waiting for Robert. The bouncer had agreed to meet her here, since the police had said it might be a half hour before they could get a patrol car to her location. The parking lot was empty except for her Jeep and Rachel's car. Jade had left. But Robert pulled up a minute later and walked her to the door.

"Thank you for doing this," she said. "I know you must have just gotten home."

He shrugged. "I appreciate the offer of overtime pay." He flashed a grin that lit up his dark face. "And I'm always happy to help a beautiful woman." He obliged her by checking out the place. "All clear."

"Thanks. Go home and get some sleep."

He frowned. "What about you?"

"I need a few minutes to finish something." She wanted to look for Darla's number and check on her, make sure she was okay, and find out why the woman hadn't stayed to lock up as Catherine had asked her to do.

With a shrug, Robert left and she locked the door behind him, then walked through the building to double-check everything was in order. The club was empty and nearly dark, quiet and still, as if the life had gone out of it. Shaking her head at her melodramatic thoughts, Catherine went to the office and searched through the employee records until she found Darla's number. It took several rings before someone picked up.

"Hello?" Darla's voice sounded different.

"Are you okay?"

"Who is this?"

"Catherine. You didn't stay to lock up."

Darla giggled. "Had a better offer."

"Are you drunk?" Catherine couldn't hide her incredulity. It seemed so unlike the cautious, cynical Darla to drink to the point of irresponsibility.

"No. Are you?" She giggled again, and then cleared her throat. "I just had a drink with Johnny. We're experimenting."

Johnny? "Is he with you now?"

"Not really."

"What does that mean? Darla, listen to me. You have to get out of there. Did you not see what Johnny tried to do to me?"

"I saw what you wanted everyone to see. I just didn't believe it like the rest of them." In her blind adoration of the man, Darla must have let Johnny spin the situation to his advantage.

"Meet me at the club." No. Darla was too drunk. "No, wait, don't drive. I'll be right there."

"No, don't. I can get to you. I'm not drunk, just happy."

Happy? How could she be happy when the man she cared about could possibly be a rapist and a murderer and obviously didn't care about anyone but himself? She had to talk some sense into her. "I need to see you."

"Yes, boss." There was sarcasm in her voice.

"This is serious, Darla. So is the issue with Johnny. Are you okay enough to call a cab?"

"Of course—"

"Please come now." She felt an urgency she couldn't express. In her condition, Darla wouldn't listen over the phone, anyway. "There's something wrong, and I really do need to talk to you. If you're not here soon, I'm calling the police to go over to your place." She'd call them anyway, in case Johnny was there.

"Fine. Party pooper. But it's just you and me at the club, right? No tall, dark and broody there?" *Max.*

"Right. It's just me here."

"I'll be there in five. Make it ten, I'm not dressed yet." She sounded sober now.

Catherine stared at the receiver and hoped to God Darla meant she was in her jammies, and hadn't just been naked with the sleazebag Johnny Walker.

CHAPTER 25

D arla hung up and smiled, dismissing Catherine's concerns. Everything was finally falling into place. She wanted only one thing in life—to love and be loved. Technically, she supposed that was two things. But she'd had to settle for having only the first one too many times. It was time for the latter.

It was her *turn*, damn it.

And she'd chosen the lucky candidate months ago. Not that Johnny Walker realized how deep her feelings went—not until recently, anyway. No, he'd been stubborn and played hard to get. He'd tested her. Made her jealous by going out with other women. He'd almost ruined things by going after Catherine tonight, but now...now, he'd understand he was hers and would be forever.

"Who was that?" Johnny asked, slurring his *S*. "Damn. That must have been a strong drink." He held the glass up to his face and peered at it, as if he expected to see the drug she'd put in it—the one that mimicked a blackout. The one that made him forget the other women. The one that had him doubting himself so he'd lean on her.

He tried to set the glass down but missed the coffee table, and it went crashing to the wood floor where it shattered. "Damn," he said again, looking at the shards, confused.

"I'll take care of it. I'll take care of everything. Do you want something else? Something harder?"

"I'll show you something harder." A light glowed in Johnny's semi-glassy eyes. She'd made his one drink extra strong.

"Do you know when I first noticed you?" she asked, curious what his response would be—or if he could change her mind about what she had planned for him tonight. She'd come to realize that there was only one way Johnny could be hers permanently.

He grinned. "A few weeks ago?" She stifled her anger. He didn't even know when she'd started paying special attention to him. She'd catered to his every need for *months*.

She quickly smoothed out her frown. "It was that night last fall when you gave me a huge tip and told me I deserved it, that I worked too hard." He'd said all the right things, and she'd fallen for him.

"I said that?"

He didn't remember. Did he recall the blowjob she'd given him in the back of his van a couple weeks later?

She shoved her irritation aside. She didn't have much longer before Catherine was expecting her at the club. Darla had no doubt she would call the cops if she didn't show. Catherine was always getting in the way. She wasn't worried about Darla. She was fucking worried about Johnny and who he was slipping his dick into. The bitch had paraded her goods around the club for weeks, acting holier-than-thou and then crying wolf when a man responded. Catherine was just as bad as Johnny. When Darla was done here, she'd teach Catherine a lesson, too.

She smiled sweetly at Johnny, kneeling in front of him. He sat slouched on the couch. His grin spread as she put her hands on his thighs. His eyes glittered—with the drug or in response to the sexual advances, she wasn't sure.

"You treated me like a goddess that night, but then you started dating those other women." Darla was tired, so tired, of trying to show him that *she* was the woman for him. She reached for his zipper and licked her lips as if she were eager to please. "How about we take this into my bedroom?" She brushed her hand across his erection and he nearly jumped from his seat.

"How about we finish what you started right here?" He grabbed her hair and tugged her toward his lap.

"No." She pushed him away and stood. "My bed is bigger." It had more room for what she had planned.

For weeks now, she'd eliminated the competition, all the while quietly framing Johnny for the murders of Bea, Angelique and Kim, in case he didn't fall in line. He hadn't fallen in line—until tonight. He'd come crawling, but it was too late. He only wanted her for her apartment and her cigarettes and her food. And whatever else he could use her for. When she'd seen him on top of Catherine tonight, she'd realized the truth. He would never put Darla first.

And if she couldn't have him, nobody would.

The Rohypnol she'd purchased from one of the Circle's drug dealers hadn't failed her yet. It was damn convenient that she was Johnny's favorite waitress. When she'd seen him making arrangements with Bea, or Angelique—that night, she'd followed him to the other club—or Kim, she'd slipped a roofie into his last drink of the night. Johnny had been oblivious to her following him.

She'd wait until he'd finished the deed and then she'd approach them and remove the problem in whatever way was necessary. With Bea, Darla had used tears in the parking lot of Johnny's apartment complex. Bea had invited her for a drink at her place, but Darla had asked to go for a drive instead. Darla felt a surge of power as she remembered her first kill. Bea had driven her right to the truck stop, thinking she was driving Darla home. She'd even followed her into the dense foliage of the ravine beyond the parking lot when Darla had pretended she was going to be sick. She'd made Darla's job easy. Stupid woman.

With Angelique, Johnny had fucked her right there in the back of his van. Idiot. There had to be DNA everywhere. Darla had simply waited until he passed out, approached Angelique, and offered to give the woman a ride home. They'd ended up at the truck stop.

With Kim, Darla had taken her time and enjoyed it. The slut had been all over Johnny at his apartment, even though she'd known he was Darla's man. Darla had shown up and proposed a threesome. Kim had laughed at her.

That kill had been fun, because Johnny had been passed out in his apartment. When she'd shaken him awake, wanting him to be with her during the body dump, he'd kissed her. Then he'd come with her meekly, the powerful drug making her mere suggestions seem like commands. He'd even helped carry Kim's bloody body to the van, and then from the van to the woods behind the gas station near his apartment. After making sure he'd passed out in his van, Darla had walked back to the apartment complex, got into her car, and drove away.

After each kill, Johnny didn't remember a thing. The last time, Darla had left him to wake up at the gas station, figuring it would serve him right to experience a bit of panic after continually throwing his affairs in her face. Nobody treated her that way. Not anymore.

Unfortunately, the downside of the roofies was he didn't remember Darla's part in it, and couldn't learn his lesson. He was doomed to repeat his mistakes.

She'd done all of this for nothing. Well, not exactly *nothing*. She had found a wonderful new stress reliever. Who knew murder was so therapeutic?

She giggled and Johnny's eyes narrowed.

"What's so funny?" he asked.

"Nothing. I'm just excited." Her knives were in the bedroom, in the top drawer of the bedside table. Beside the handcuffs she'd bought to secure him to the wrought iron headboard. Oh yes, he'd finally learn his lesson and there would be no more mistakes.

His lips curved. "You want me." His hand still gripped her hair and he tried to tug her back toward his erection.

She resisted. "In my bed." Before he passed out and she wasn't able to move him at all. She had to support him, slinging his arm around her shoulder and letting him lean against her. But people were always underestimating her strength. Hefting all of those trays of food and drinks had paid off.

Johnny flopped back on the bed. "You take such good care of me."

She appreciated the compliment, but it was too little too late. There was no *I love you* in his words. She helped him out of his clothes and climbed on top of him. He hissed out a breath.

"You're overdressed." He laughed, but his eyes widened as she pulled a set of fuzzy handcuffs from the drawer. "Man, I should have noticed you sooner."

"Yeah, you should have." She clicked one wrist into the cuffs, looped them through a post on the headboard, and then locked the other wrist.

She leaned over and reached into the bedside drawer. When she pulled out the first knife, a nine-inch blade with a bone handle —one of her stepfather's favorite weapons when he'd been in a threatening mood—Johnny's eyes widened.

She grinned. "I bet you're noticing me now, Johnny."

"OH, THANK GOD," CATHERINE SAID AS SHE UNLOCKED THE FRONT door of Lucky Dick's. Darla limped past her. "Are you okay?"

"Been better." Upon closer inspection, Darla's breathing sounded labored and her face was pinched. She winced and hissed out a breath.

"What's wrong?" Catherine closed the door and helped her to a barstool.

Darla shoved back her hood, scattering waterdrops across the floor and bar. Catherine gasped as the dim lighting hit Darla's face —or, rather, lit up her face. Her cheek was swollen and there were dark red spatters. *Blood?*

"Oh, my God. What did he do?" She hurried around the bar to fill a towel with ice, remembering how Johnny's attempt to run down Max a few hours ago had her doing this very same thing for his wound. How many more people would Johnny hurt? "Where's Johnny now?"

"Gone." Darla bit her bottom lip so hard it turned white as her eyes filled with tears. "When he heard I was leaving, he got really angry. But I got away."

"Does he know you came here?" She gently pressed the ice-filled towel to Darla's cheek.

Fear and doubt chased each other through Darla's doe-like eyes, their brown color accentuated by the purple and blue bruise. "No. I don't think so. I don't think he'd expect me to come here."

"I'm calling the police." But as Catherine started to move away, Darla's fingers gripped her arm like claws. Desperation was written in every rigid line of the young woman's body.

"No! You can't."

"But the bruises, the blood…"

"It's his blood."

That stole the breath from Catherine. "What?" She set the ice down on the counter and sank onto the barstool facing Darla. "Tell me everything."

"It was self-defense."

"Wait." A chill skipped across Catherine's scalp. "Did you kill him?" Is that what she'd meant when she'd said he was *gone*?

Tears slipped unchecked down Darla's cheeks. "I don't know. I think I might have…" She began sobbing and leaned heavily against Catherine.

She stroked a hand down Darla's hair and over her back. "Shhh. It'll be okay."

Darla's whole body shook with the force of her emotion. "Will it?"

"That report I filed with the police earlier tonight will help your case. He attacked me and nearly ran down Max. Even if they can't pin the three dancers' murders on him, we've illustrated a pattern of violent behavior."

Darla sat up and considered this. She sniffed. "You think so?"

Catherine took a strand of hair that had stuck to Darla's wet cheeks and tucked it back behind her ear. "I really think he killed Bea, Angelique, and Kim." And he'd probably been after Darla next. "We'll let the police see you, document the evidence of his violence, and get your statement on record." Catherine rose and moved toward the office. Darla followed.

"So you think we should call the cops?" Darla sounded less hesitant and more confident.

"I do." Catherine moved behind the desk, but was surprised when Darla put a hand on the phone to stop her from picking up the receiver.

"We can't make that call. Not yet. I'll do it after I get done here." Her hand disappeared beneath her jacket and she withdrew a knife. The six-inch blade caught the light and pulsed with the same cold, dark fire as Darla's eyes.

Catherine's limbs weakened, but she steeled herself against the urge to collapse. This time, she'd fight like hell to get the future that was finally within her grasp. She wasn't going down without a fight.

"Is Catherine there?" Max hated waking up Rachel with his call, but he had an odd tingling at the back of his neck. Actually, it wasn't so much odd as terrifying, since it was the same sensation he sometimes got while out in the field, working with the SEAL team, right before everything went FUBAR.

"Let me check." The sound of rustling and creaking told him he had, indeed, woken Rachel. At nearly three in the morning, that wasn't a surprise. "She's not on the couch."

The tingles intensified. "Where is she?"

"I'm sure she's fine. I just thought she'd be back by now."

"Back? Where would she go at this hour?" Maybe she'd returned to the ranch to wait for him? But he'd hoped she'd stay at her sister's.

"She said she had to go lock up at the club, but that was about an hour ago. She's not answering her phone?"

"No."

Rachel paused. "Okay, I'm officially worried now."

So was Max. "I'll swing by Lucky Dick's first. Anywhere else she could be?"

"Maybe she decided to wait for you at the ranch?"

"Thought about that, but she gets reception there. Why isn't she answering my calls?"

"Maybe she's sleeping, or has her phone off?"

"I'll see if she's still at the club first. I'm sure she just fell asleep on the couch in the office or something."

"Yeah, maybe." Rachel sounded more hopeful. "She did have a long day."

Clinging to that thought, he sped across the miles between the prison, where order had been restored and Tony's murder scene was being processed, to Lucky Dick's. His heart sank as he pulled into the club parking lot and found Rachel's car. Parked next to it was Catherine's Jeep and a familiar truck. Max would recognize it anywhere. The thing had tried to end his life earlier that evening.

"DARLA, WHAT ARE YOU DOING?" THE QUESTION SOUNDED CRAZY even to Catherine's ears, but there was nothing sane about the woman threatening her with a knife. Words were Catherine's best defense.

"Sit down." Darla jabbed the blade in the direction of the couch. "And shut up."

"I'm not your enemy." Catherine held her hands up in what she hoped was a nonthreatening manner as she did as she was told. The gesture also gave her more room to move her hands, to fight back if Darla came close.

"I believe I said *shut up*. If you're not my enemy, I don't know who is. You tried to steal Johnny."

"This is about Johnny?" Well, hell, she'd always known Darla liked the man, but this was ridiculous. She eyed the bruise. It looked real. "You said he attacked you."

"It was pretty much the opposite, actually." Her lips curved. "He barely noticed me until tonight." She stalked toward the couch where Catherine was perched and waved the knife in her face.

Catherine tried not to cringe, though fear was pumping through her at a rapid rate. "Where is this coming from? We were friends before tonight."

Darla laughed. "I don't have friends. Not female ones. Don't trust them. Come to think of it, I don't have male friends. Can't trust them, either."

"Not all men are like the ones who've hurt you."

"Nobody's hurt me!" she shouted, and the knife slashed. Catherine leaned back, just avoiding the tip. "I take care of myself and *nobody* hurts me." Darla was in serious denial. She'd obviously been hurt by Johnny.

"You can still find the right man, one who respects and takes care of you. One who loves you."

"In prison? I don't think so."

Catherine felt her skin go clammy. If Darla believed she had nothing left to live for, she was a much more dangerous and unpredictable threat. "I told you, the police will understand you killed Johnny in self-defense."

Darla grinned again. "But how would I explain the others?"

"Others?" As comprehension dawned, Catherine wished she could withdraw the question. Darla didn't like women, especially women like Catherine, who appeared to tread on Darla's territory. "You killed those three dancers, didn't you?" Her stomach churned.

Darla shrugged as if it were nothing. "They knew the risk when they teased and screwed men for money. They never knew who they were making themselves vulnerable to, and yet they took a chance because they wanted to steal Johnny from me. Besides, you told me to follow my dream, remember?"

This was more like a nightmare. "And Johnny? Did he know what you'd done?"

"Not until tonight. He thought he'd murdered those women. Technically, he didn't, though they wouldn't have died if he hadn't chosen them. I drugged Johnny. Rohypnol. You know, the date rape drug? He thought he was having blackouts from drinking too much, just like his dear old dad. He'd told me about his family months ago. Stupid me, I thought he was being open with me because he cared, because he trusted me. Apparently, he was only drunk. But the joke's on him, because in the end, he trusted me too much."

Think, Catherine. She had to get out of this. Get back to her sister, to her father—to Max.

Thinking about Max gave her an idea. Darla wanted that all-encompassing, unconditional love Catherine had with Max. If Max could forgive Catherine's transgressions, as he'd indicated he could, then what they had was a bond like no other.

She forced herself to ignore the knife and look at Darla. "Not all men are like Johnny. There's someone out there for you."

"Like there's someone for you? Hah! You're alone."

"I'm not. I love a man with all my heart. No, not Johnny," she added when Darla's scowl deepened. "Never Johnny. Max. I've loved him for years, probably since before I met him. His reputation as an honorable, decent man preceded him."

The tip of the knife dipped a bit as Darla's arms relaxed slightly. She was listening.

"He can be stubborn and oblivious sometimes," Catherine continued, "but he's got a good heart and a passion for making the world better. I know he's made my world better just by being in it. You can find that too, someday."

"Not in prison."

"You won't go to prison if you disappear." Catherine eyed the knife, thinking how she could disarm Darla before she could use the thing. Her muscles bunched at the thought.

Darla looked hesitant. "You're going to let me walk out of here?"

"I don't have a choice."

Darla seemed to consider this, and then her gaze shifted to the side, toward the two-way mirror. "I knew I couldn't trust you." At the anger contorting Darla's face, Catherine didn't have time to question what the woman had seen. If she wanted to claim her new life, it was time to act.

MAX HAD BEEN FOLLOWING THE VOICES TOWARD THE OFFICE WHEN A shout of surprise had him running the last few steps, entering in time to see Catherine gripping Darla's wrist. And—*God*—in that hand was a knife with a blade nearly as long as Darla's forearm. It hovered dangerously close to Catherine's face.

He ran forward to grasp Darla's hand, squeezing hard so she'd drop the knife.

"No!" Darla shouted as his pressure, combined with Catherine's grip on her wrist, forced her fingers open. The knife fell with a thud to the carpet. He spun Darla away from it, pushed her to her knees, then further until she was face down on the floor. He put his knee into her back to keep her there as he searched her for other weapons.

"Don't hurt her," Catherine said from behind him. With shaky hands, she picked up the knife and placed it on the desk, well away from Darla. "She's been hurt enough."

He shot Catherine an incredulous look. "Didn't this woman just try to skewer you?"

"She needs psychological help." Catherine was still campaigning for the underdog, still letting love and trust color her view of the world. But he loved that about her. In fact, he loved everything about her.

"That'll be her lawyer's problem. Are you okay?" His gaze swept over her, inch by inch.

She nodded. "I'm okay. Nothing's going to keep us from having that talk."

"You're damn right. The police should be here any second and then I'm taking you back to the ranch." He might not let her out of the guesthouse for a week. He'd been patient enough and they had a lot to sort out.

It was time to take Catherine far away from here, somewhere safe, and make her his forever. He was tired of being afraid to let someone love him, tired of distrusting the world around him. The future was whatever he wanted it to be and he knew exactly what —or who—he wanted.

CHAPTER 26

A few hours later, at six that same morning, after settling things with the police and making sure Darla was locked away, Max finally returned to the ranch. He'd insisted on sending Catherine home a few hours ago, hoping she could catch some rest while he'd stayed to see the investigations wrapped up. The final piece had fallen into place when Johnny's body was discovered cuffed to Darla's bed, naked and stabbed in the chest multiple times. There had also been significant damage to certain parts of his anatomy. Max could only hope, for Johnny's sake, that particular mutilation had been done postmortem.

Physically exhausted but exhilarated to finally have Catherine to himself with no barriers between them, he was disappointed when he didn't find her in the guesthouse bed. Her Jeep was here, so she had to be around.

He quietly let himself into the main house. Surprised to hear sounds coming from the kitchen, he followed them and found Catherine in the least likely place, with the least likely person comforting her.

Looking disheveled, her hair mussed as if she'd been startled from sleep and her robe askew, his mother darted about the kitchen, clanging pots and pans loudly enough to wake the dead. Catherine sat at the island, looking tired but relaxed in yoga pants and a soft cotton shirt, sipping on something from a steaming mug. Her hair was damp as if she'd showered, and a clip held it up off of her long, slender neck. Her eyebrows raised as she watched Lillian Caulfield shove slices of bread into a toaster and crack eggs in a pan like some sort of deranged short order cook.

Catherine caught him in the doorway and smiled. It was the most beautiful thing he'd seen in days. "Good morning," she said.

He walked straight to her and kissed her on the lips. Across the room, his mother froze, but he didn't care. He'd waited too long to lay an honest, open, no-holds-barred kiss on his woman. *His.*

"Well, I can see you two have some things to catch up on," his mother said as Max came up for air. "I'll leave you alone."

But as she turned the burner off and headed toward the door, she stopped beside him. "I'm so glad you're okay. I don't know what I would have done..." Her uneasy gaze darted about the room, as if she would find something written on the cupboards that would help her express her feelings. "Your Dad told me you know everything. We're not perfect, but I hope you'll give us a chance to make up for our mistakes." Her gaze moved to Catherine. "I hope both of you will forgive us and find a way to include us in your lives."

Max had thought he'd run the gamut of emotions tonight, but his chest ached again. This was a huge step for his mother. What's more, he believed she was sincere. And, she'd admitted Catherine had a future next to him. He arched a brow at Catherine and his heart swelled with love as she met his gaze and nodded.

"We can certainly try," Catherine said. Happiness shone in her eyes and Max realized that there were truly no more barriers. Gone was the shield she usually wore. She'd finally let him all the way in. "Especially since they're trying, too. Your dad's in the den, talking to the governor."

"At this hour?"

"He insisted." She wrapped her arms around his waist and squeezed. "He's determined to tell the truth and get my dad out of prison."

"Is that enough for you to forgive him? He lied to you all these years, and it cost your family everything." After all they'd put her through, this generous woman was giving them another chance. Her capacity to love, trust and forgive was inspiring.

"My dad made his own choices, too. It'll take some time for us all to put the pieces back together, but I'm hopeful for the first time in months." Her grin was like a beacon and he bent to kiss her again. He'd never get enough of her.

But his mother was still waiting for his response, so he ended the kiss too soon.

"Consider this a probationary period," he told his mother. "One attempt to manipulate me or come between me and Catherine and I'm gone." His tone softened as he saw the relief in his mother's face. She really wanted to make this work. "I'm willing to try. That's all I can promise."

If he'd learned anything from his time in the SEALs, and from observing Damian's grief, it was that life was too short. What time they had should be treasured, what wounds were inflicted should be given a chance to heal. He had room in his life for more than his own restricted world and could be open to relationships that lasted more than a night or two. After all, it was immensely more rewarding...when he was with the *right* woman.

His mother sniffed. "Yes, well, I suppose you could start by calling me, at least once a month. Otherwise, I'll have to resort to asking Catherine to submit reports again."

Catherine sputtered out a laugh. "I'm retired from the secret spy world."

"And be forewarned, I plan to visit in the fall. See that you have a hotel recommendation for me." His mother turned to leave, but stopped and looked back. "And I'd like to see you, too, Catherine."

She left and Max turned to Catherine, tucking a wayward strand of hair behind her ear.

Catherine sighed and reached up to press his palm to her cheek. "I can't believe this nightmare is over. And I can't believe your parents might accept me in your life."

"From now on, we're a package deal." His fingers slipped into his jacket pocket where the printout was tucked away. Einstein had done a quick search for him, but Max was eager for his new life to begin. *Embrace the new, and the now.*

If only he could convince the practical, passionate woman beside him to join him on this adventure. He *had* to convince her, because it wouldn't work without her. He was counting on her love for him to sway her toward accepting his argument.

Catherine moved toward the skillet his mother had abandoned. "Can I get you breakfast? You must be exhausted."

As she passed, he snaked out an arm and pulled her close again. "I don't need food. I just need you." She snuggled into his chest and he buried his nose in the crook of her neck, breathing deeply of her scent.

"I missed you." Her words were muffled against his shoulder.

He pulled back just enough to look at her. He wanted to see her eyes when he told her everything he'd been hiding in his heart. Everything he'd been too scared to acknowledge was building there. Now, it was too big to be contained.

"Come back with me to Chicago. Come back to SSAM. Damian will need you. All of SSAM will be focused on finding the Boss, and you should be there, too."

He reached between them to pull the printout from his pocket. "I've got a list of apartments for rent. We'll find something you love. Einstein is already looking for a new roommate."

She skimmed the listings. "You think you've won me over, huh?" He could tell by the humor in her voice that he had.

"I'm a self-confident guy."

"Gee, I hadn't noticed. Am I going to have to step over a mound of girls to get to you each night?"

He grinned. "The only woman I want at my feet is you."

Her eyes heated as they both recalled their time in the shower. "I suppose, once in a while, that could be arranged..."

He groaned. "You're going to be the death of me, woman. Just say yes. You know you want to."

She grinned. "Yes. I want to."

He swooped down to claim her lips in a long, slow kiss, sealing the deal.

"I love you," she said when he finally released her mouth.

"Oh, I know." He enjoyed the way her mouth dropped open. "I believe you said something about being in love with me for years?"

Her eyes widened. "You overheard what I said to Darla."

Just the end of it, but it had cracked his heart open like a chisel to a rock. "I heard it and I want to hear it again every day for the rest of my life." He kissed her mouth fast and hard. "Twice on Sundays."

She smiled. "Did you also hear the part about you being stubborn and oblivious?" He grinned and she laughed. "You're incorrigible."

"Self-confident," he corrected and she laughed again. He wanted to make her laugh for the rest of their lives. "I did hear that, but I figured you were talking about another man during that part."

"Yep, definitely oblivious." She turned serious. "I love you."

"I love *you*." She'd taught him there was such a thing as true, unconditional love—the kind people make sacrifices for. The kind worth taking a risk for.

A SPECIAL SNEAK PEEK...

~

The Mindhunters Series continues (and concludes!)...

END GAME
(The Mindhunters, Book 6)

"Are you going to do it, or should I?" He gestured to the pill in Rocky's hand. He was being generous, giving the man control over his destiny—the final chapter, anyway.

As the boss of an international crime ring, he wore many hats —including one few people knew about: the serial killer known as the Charmer. Each hat he wore had its own specific responsibilities and challenges, but he could handle it all—as long as his hired help did what they were paid to do. Unfortunately, the idiot on his knees in front of him had failed.

Rocky's lip quivered and he pressed his mouth into a thin line, as if he could prevent the inevitable.

The Charmer's nostrils flared. "I've got things to do." He

glanced at his watch. "The outcome is the same, no matter what. But if you choose the easy way, it's less mess for me to clean up." Not that he'd actually have to do much. Rocky was kneeling on a plastic tarp in the warehouse on one of Chicago's piers. He'd have the Circle's cleaner collect the garbage and toss him into Lake Michigan. It would give him a chance to try the new guy out. Maybe *he* could manage to complete a simple order.

"The easy way?" Rocky's voice cracked. "I can't commit suicide. I have a wife and two young daughters. The shame would..." His Adam's apple bobbed as hope battled reality.

The Charmer grinned. "I've seen your girls. They're going to be beauties in about ten years."

Panic widened Rocky's eyes. "You stay away from them. You and your...perversions."

"Perversions?" He laughed. "You don't have a clue what I do with my girls. It's not about that at all. I tell you what... I'll keep a close eye on your girls for you." They'd never know their dad was an incompetent ass.

"Don't." Rocky's eyes flicked to the gun as the Charmer raised it.

"You should have thought of them before you fucked up." He hadn't led the biggest, most respected organized crime syndicate in the world for decades by going easy on employees. "All you had to do was take the girl."

"I'll get her next time. I promise, I..." Sweat mingled with snot and tears as Rocky finally saw the writing on the wall. Saw that his boss didn't forgive. Forgiveness was for the weak. The Charmer was far from weak. He was in control, having learned early and often that those in power got what they wanted. That was the way the world worked. But Rocky's fuckup would delay his plans for Damian Manchester and the agents at SSAM.

He pulled the trigger, and the gun, its silencer in place, made a soft *thwump* before Rocky fell on his side. The sequence was so quick that the sound of the plastic crumpling beneath him was louder than Rocky's death moan. *See?* He could be merciful when the occasion allowed.

But not with Damian and his crew. They would see no mercy. And they would acknowledge the Charmer's power—right before he killed them.

END GAME, the thrilling conclusion to the Mindhunters series, is available now!

ACKNOWLEDGMENTS

My heartfelt gratitude goes to Andrea Edwards, Kim Law, and Ann Briggs for volunteering to be beta readers and to Rita Henuber and Autumn Jordon for the last minute brainstorming and support. Also, thank you to Toni Anderson, whose advice was so helpful.

As always, this series wouldn't be what it is without the invaluable input of Deborah Nemeth. And to Leah and Victoria, many thanks for their assistance during the editing process.

Thank you to Beth and Crista for the medical advice and terminology (any mistakes made are mine).

Last, but never least, thank you to Tim and our kids. You are my world.

ABOUT THE AUTHOR

Anne Marie has always been fasci-
nated by people—inside and out—
which led to degrees in Biology,
Chemistry, Psychology, and Counseling. Her passion for understanding the human race is now
satisfied by her roles as mother,
wife, daughter, sister, and award-
winning author of romantic
suspense.

She writes to reclaim her sanity.

Find ways to connect with Anne
Marie at AnneMarieBecker.com.
There, sign up for her newsletter to receive the latest information
regarding books, appearances, and giveaways.